HARLEQUIN

HARLEQUIN

BERNARD CORNWELL

HarperCollins*Publishers*

HarperCollins*Publishers*
77–85 Fulham Palace Road,
Hammersmith, London W6 8JB

www.harpercollins.co.uk

This paperback edition 2001

1

First published in Great Britain by
HarperCollins*Publishers* 2000

ISBN 978 0 00 787760 7

Set in PostScript Linotype Meridien with Photina display by
Rowland Phototypesetting Limited,
Bury St Edmunds, Suffolk

Printed and bound in Great Britain by
Clays Ltd, St Ives plc

HARLEQUIN

is for
Richard and Julie Rutherford-Moore

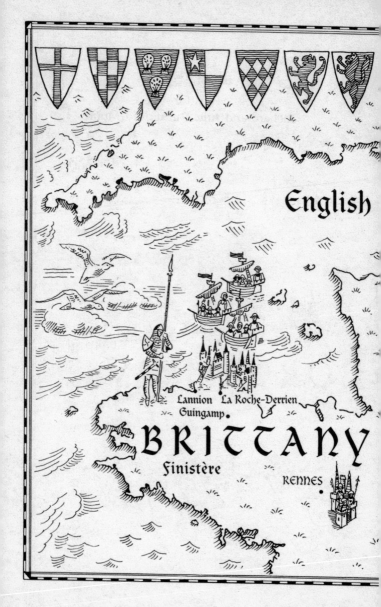

English

Lannion   La Roche-Derrien

Guingamp.

BRITTANY

Finistère

RENNES

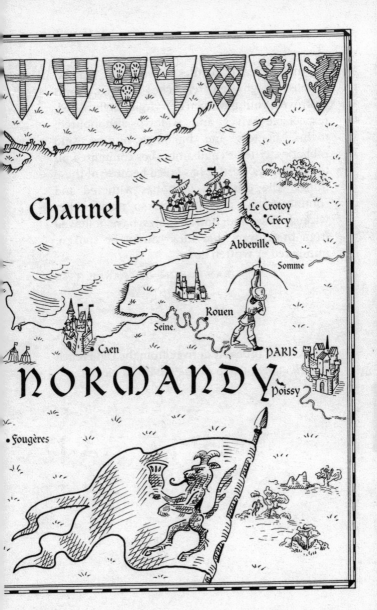

Channel

Le Crotoy
Crécy

Abbeville

Somme

Rouen

Seine

Caen

PARIS

NORMANDY

Poissy

Fougères

'. . . many deadly battles have been fought, people slaughtered, churches robbed, souls destroyed, young women and virgins deflowered, respectable wives and widows dishonoured; towns, manors and buildings burned, and robberies, cruelties and ambushes committed on the highways. Justice has failed because of these things. The Christian faith has withered and commerce has perished and so many other wickednesses and horrid things have followed from these wars that they cannot be spoken, numbered or written down.'

JEAN II, KING OF FRANCE, 1360

Harlequin, probably derived from the Old French *hellequin:* a troop of the devil's horsemen.

CONTENTS

Prologue

The treasure of Hookton was stolen on Easter morning 1342.

It was a holy thing, a relic that hung from the church rafters, and it was extraordinary that so precious an object should have been kept in such an obscure village. Some folk said it had no business being there, that it should have been enshrined in a cathedral or some great abbey, while others, many others, said it was not genuine. Only fools denied that relics were faked. Glib men roamed the byways of England selling yellowed bones that were said to be from the fingers or toes or ribs of the blessed saints, and sometimes the bones were human, though more often they were from pigs or even deer, but still folk bought and prayed to the bones. 'A man might as well pray to St Guinefort,' Father Ralph said, then snorted with mocking laughter. 'They're praying to ham bones, ham bones! The blessed pig!'

It had been Father Ralph who had brought the treasure to Hookton and he would not hear of it being taken away to a cathedral or abbey, and so for eight years it hung in the small church, gathering dust and growing spider webs that shone silver when the sunlight slanted through the high window of the western tower. Sparrows perched on the treasure and some mornings there were bats hanging from its shaft. It was rarely cleaned and hardly ever brought down, though once in a while Father Ralph would demand that ladders be fetched and the treasure unhooked from its chains and he would pray over it and stroke it. He never boasted of it. Other churches or monasteries, possessing such a prize, would have used it to attract pilgrims, but Father Ralph turned visitors away. 'It is nothing,' he would say if a stranger enquired after the relic, 'a bauble. Nothing.' He became angry if the visitors persisted. 'It is nothing, nothing, nothing!' Father Ralph was a frightening man even when he was not angry, but in his temper he was a wild-haired fiend, and his flaring anger protected the treasure, though Father Ralph himself believed that ignorance was its best protection for if men did not know of it then God would guard it. And so He did, for a time.

Hookton's obscurity was the treasure's best protection. The tiny village lay on England's south coast where the Lipp, a stream that was almost a river, flowed to the sea across a shingle beach. A half-dozen fishing boats worked from the village, protected at night by the Hook itself, which was a tongue of shingle that curved around the Lipp's last reach, though in the famous storm of 1322 the sea had roared across the Hook and pounded the boats to splinters on the upper beach. The village had never really recovered from that tragedy. Nineteen boats had sailed from the Hook before the storm, but twenty years later only six small craft worked the waves beyond the Lipp's treacherous bar. The rest of the villagers worked in the saltpans, or else herded sheep and cattle on the hills behind the huddle of thatched huts which clustered about the small stone church where the treasure hung from the blackened beams. That was Hookton, a place of boats, fish, salt and livestock, with green hills behind, ignorance within and the wide sea beyond.

Hookton, like every place in Christendom, held a vigil on the eve of Easter, and in 1342 that solemn duty was performed by five men who watched as Father Ralph consecrated the Easter Sacraments and then laid the bread and wine on the white-draped altar. The wafers were in a simple clay bowl covered with a piece of bleached linen, while the wine was in a silver cup that belonged to Father Ralph. The silver cup was a part of his mystery. He was very tall, pious and much too learned to be a village priest. It was rumoured that he could have been a bishop, but that the devil had persecuted him with bad dreams and it was certain that in the years before he came to Hookton he had been locked in a monastery's cell because he was possessed by demons. Then, in 1334, the demons had left him and he was sent to Hookton where he terrified the villagers by preaching to the gulls, or pacing the beach weeping for his sins and striking his breast with sharp-edged stones. He howled like a dog when his wickedness weighed too heavily on his conscience, but he also found a kind of peace in the remote village. He built a large house of timber, which he shared with his house-keeper, and he made friends with Sir Giles Marriott, who was the lord of Hookton and lived in a stone hall three miles to the north.

Sir Giles, of course, was a gentleman, and so it seemed was Father Ralph, despite his wild hair and angry voice. He collected books which, after the treasure he had brought to the church, were the greatest marvels in

Hookton. Sometimes, when he left his door open, people would just gape at the seventeen books that were bound in leather and piled on a table. Most were in Latin, but a handful were in French, which was Father Ralph's native tongue. Not the French of France, but Norman French, the language of England's rulers, and the villagers reckoned their priest must be nobly born, though none dared ask him to his face. They were all too scared of him, but he did his duty by them; he christened them, churched them, married them, heard their confessions, absolved them, scolded them and buried them, but he did not pass the time with them. He walked alone, grim-faced, hair awry and eyes glowering, but the villagers were still proud of him. Most country churches suffered ignorant, pudding-faced priests who were scarce more educated than their parishioners, but, Hookton, in Father Ralph had a proper scholar, too clever to be sociable, perhaps a saint, maybe of noble birth, a self-confessed sinner, probably mad, but undeniably a real priest.

Father Ralph blessed the Sacraments, then warned the five men that Lucifer was abroad on the night before Easter and that the devil wanted nothing so much as to snatch the Holy Sacraments from the altar and so the five men must guard the bread and wine diligently and, for a short time after the priest had left, they dutifully stayed on their knees, gazing at the chalice, which had an armorial badge engraved in its silver flank. The badge showed a mythical beast, a yale, holding a grail, and it was that noble device which suggested to the villagers that Father Ralph was indeed a high-born man who had fallen low through being possessed of devils. The silver chalice seemed to shimmer in the light of two immensely tall candles which would burn through the whole long night. Most villages could not afford proper Easter candles, but Father Ralph purchased two from the monks at Shaftesbury every year and the villagers would sidle into the church to stare at them. But that night, after dark, only the five men saw the tall unwavering flames.

Then John, a fisherman, farted. 'Reckon that's ripe enough to keep the old devil away,' he said, and the other four laughed. Then they all abandoned the chancel steps and sat with their backs against the nave wall. John's wife had provided a basket of bread, cheese and smoked fish, while Edward, who owned a saltworks on the beach, had brought ale.

In the bigger churches of Christendom knights kept this annual vigil. They knelt in full armour, their surcoats embroidered with prancing lions and stooping hawks and axe heads and spread-wing eagles, and their helmets mounted with feathered crests, but there were no knights in Hookton and only the youngest man, who was called Thomas and who sat slightly apart from the other four, had a weapon. It was an ancient, blunt and slightly rusted sword.

'You reckon that old blade will scare the devil, Thomas?' John asked him.

'My father said I had to bring it,' Thomas said.

'What does your father want with a sword?'

'He throws nothing away, you know that,' Thomas said, hefting the old weapon. It was heavy, but he lifted it easily; at eighteen, he was tall and immensely strong. He was well liked in Hookton for, despite being the son of the village's richest man, he was a hard-working boy. He loved nothing better than a day at sea hauling tarred nets that left his hands raw and bleeding. He knew how to sail a boat, had the strength to pull a good oar when the wind failed; he could lay snares, shoot a bow, dig a grave, geld a calf, lay thatch or cut hay all day long. He was a big, bony, black-haired country boy, but God had given him a father who wanted Thomas to rise above common things. He wanted the boy to be a priest, which was why Thomas had just finished his first term at Oxford.

'What do you do at Oxford, Thomas?' Edward asked him.

'Everything I shouldn't,' Thomas said. He pushed black hair away from his face that was bony like his father's. He had very blue eyes, a long jaw, slightly hooded eyes and a swift smile. The girls in the village reckoned him handsome.

'Do they have girls at Oxford?' John asked slyly.

'More than enough,' Thomas said.

'Don't tell your father that,' Edward said, 'or he'll be whipping you again. A good man with a whip, your father.'

'There's none better,' Thomas agreed.

'He only wants the best for you,' John said. 'Can't blame a man for that.'

Thomas did blame his father. He had always blamed his father. He had fought his father for years, and nothing so raised the anger between them as Thomas's obsession with bows. His mother's father had been a bowyer in the Weald, and Thomas had lived with his grandfather until he was nearly ten. Then his father had brought him to Hookton, where he had met Sir Giles Marriott's huntsman, another man skilled in archery, and the huntsman had become his new tutor.

8

Thomas had made his first bow at eleven, but when his father found the elmwood weapon he had broken it across his knee and used the remnants to thrash his son. 'You are not a common man,' his father had shouted, beating the splintered staves on Thomas's back and head and legs, but neither the words nor the thrashing did any good. And as Thomas's father was usually preoccupied with other things, Thomas had plenty of time to pursue his obsession.

By fifteen he was as good a bowyer as his grandfather, knowing instinctively how to shape a stave of yew so that the inner belly came from the dense heartwood while the front was made of the springier sapwood, and when the bow was bent the heartwood was always trying to return to the straight and the sapwood was the muscle that made it possible. To Thomas's quick mind there was something elegant, simple and beautiful about a good bow. Smooth and strong, a good bow was like a girl's flat belly, and that night, keeping the Easter vigil in Hookton church, Thomas was reminded of Jane, who served in the village's small alehouse.

John, Edward and the other two men had been speaking of village things: the price of lambs at Dorchester fair, the old fox up on Lipp Hill that had taken a whole flock of geese in one night and the angel who had been seen over the rooftops at Lyme.

'I reckon they's been drinking too much,' Edward said.

'I sees angels when I drink,' John said.

'That be Jane,' Edward said. 'Looks like an angel, she does.'

'Don't behave like one,' John said. 'Lass is pregnant,' and all four men looked at Thomas, who stared innocently up at the treasure hanging from the rafters. In truth Thomas was frightened that the child was indeed his and terrified of what his father would say when he found out, but he pretended ignorance of Jane's pregnancy that night. He just looked at the treasure that was half obscured by a fishing net hung up to dry, while the four older men gradually fell asleep. A cold draught flickered the twin candle flames. A dog howled somewhere in the village, and always, never ending, Thomas could hear the sea's heartbeat as the waves thumped on the shingle then scraped back, paused and thumped again. He listened to the four men snoring and he prayed that his father would never find out about Jane, though that was unlikely for she was pressing Thomas to marry her and he did not know what to do. Maybe, he thought, he should just run away, take Jane and his bow and run, but he felt no certainty and so he just gazed at the relic in the church roof and prayed to its saint for help.

The treasure was a lance. It was a huge thing, with a shaft as thick as a man's forearm and twice the length of a man's height and probably made of ash though it was so old no one could really say, and age had bent the blackened shaft out of true, though not by much, and its tip was not an iron or steel blade, but a wedge of tarnished silver which tapered to a bodkin's point. The shaft did not swell to protect the handgrip, but was smooth like a spear or a goad; indeed the relic looked very like an oversized ox-goad, but no farmer would ever tip an ox-goad with silver. This was a weapon, a lance.

But it was not any old lance. This was the very lance which St George had used to kill the dragon. It was

England's lance, for St George was England's saint and that made it a very great treasure, even if it did hang in Hookton's spidery church roof. There were plenty of folk who said it could not have been St George's lance, but Thomas believed it was and he liked to imagine the dust churned by the hooves of St George's horse, and the dragon's breath streaming in hellish flame as the horse reared and the saint drew back the lance. The sunlight, bright as an angel's wing, would have been flaring about St George's helmet, and Thomas imagined the dragon's roar, the thrash of its scale-hooked tail, the horse screaming in terror, and he saw the saint stand in his stirrups before plunging the lance's silver tip down through the monster's armoured hide. Straight to the heart the lance went, and the dragon's squeals would have rung to heaven as it writhed and bled and died. Then the dust would have settled and the dragon's blood would have crusted on the desert sand, and St George must have hauled the lance free and somehow it ended up in Father Ralph's possession. But how? The priest would not say. But there it hung, a great dark lance, heavy enough to shatter a dragon's scales.

So that night Thomas prayed to St George while Jane, the black-haired beauty whose belly was just rounding with her unborn child, slept in the taproom of the ale-house, and Father Ralph cried aloud in his nightmare for fear of the demons that circled in the dark, and the vixens screamed on the hill as the endless waves clawed and sucked at the shingle on the Hook. It was the night before Easter.

Thomas woke to the sound of the village cockerels and saw that the expensive candles had burned down almost to their pewter holders. A grey light filled the

11

window above the white-fronted altar. One day, Father Ralph had promised the village, that window would be a blaze of coloured glass showing St George skewering the dragon with the silver-headed lance, but for now the stone frame was filled with horn panes that turned the air within the church as yellow as urine.

Thomas stood, needing to piss, and the first awful screams sounded from the village.

For Easter had come, Christ was risen and the French were ashore.

The raiders came from Normandy in four boats that had sailed the night's west wind. Their leader, Sir Guillaume d'Evecque, the Sieur d'Evecque, was a seasoned warrior who had fought the English in Gascony and Flanders, and had twice led raids on England's southern coast. Both times he had brought his boats safe home with cargoes of wool, silver, livestock and women. He lived in a fine stone house on Caen's Île St Jean, where he was known as the knight of the sea and of the land. He was thirty years old, broad in the chest, wind-burned and fair-haired, a cheerful, unreflective man who made his living by piracy at sea and knight-service on shore, and now he had come to Hookton.

It was an insignificant place, hardly likely to yield any great reward, but Sir Guillaume had been hired for the task and if he failed at Hookton, if he did not snatch so much as one single poor coin from a villager, he would still make his profit for he had been promised one thousand livres for this expedition. The contract was signed and sealed, and it promised Sir Guillaume the one thousand livres together with any other plunder he could find in Hookton. One hundred livres had already been paid and the rest was in the keeping of Brother Martin in Caen's Abbaye aux Hommes, and all Sir Guillaume had to do to earn the remaining nine hundred livres was bring his boats to Hookton, take what he wanted, but leave the church's contents to the man who had offered him such a generous contract. That man now stood beside Sir Guillaume in the leading boat.

He was a young man, not yet thirty, tall and black-haired, who spoke rarely and smiled less. He wore an expensive coat of mail that fell to his knees and over it a surcoat of deep black linen that bore no badge, though Sir Guillaume guessed the man was nobly born for he had the arrogance of rank and the confidence of privilege. He was certainly not a Norman noble, for Sir Guillaume knew all those men, and Sir Guillaume doubted the young man came from nearby Alençon or Maine, for he had ridden with those forces often enough, but the sallow cast of the stranger's skin suggested he came from one of the Mediterranean provinces, from Languedoc perhaps, or Dauphine, and they were all mad down there. Mad as dogs. Sir Guillaume did not even know the man's name.

'Some men call me the Harlequin,' the stranger had answered when Sir Guillaume had asked.

'Harlequin?' Sir Guillaume had repeated the name, then made the sign of the cross for such a name was hardly a boast. 'You mean like the hellequin?'

'Hellequin in France,' the man had allowed, 'but in Italy they say harlequin. It is all the same.' The man had smiled, and something about that smile had suggested Sir Guillaume had best curb his curiosity

13

if he wanted to receive the remaining nine hundred livres.

The man who called himself the Harlequin now stared at the misty shore where a stumpy church tower, a huddle of vague roofs and a smear of smoke from the smouldering fires of the saltpans just showed. 'Is that Hookton?' he asked.

'So he says,' Sir Guillaume answered, jerking his head at the shipmaster.

'Then God have mercy on it,' the man said. He drew his sword, even though the four boats were still a half-mile from shore. The Genoese crossbowmen, hired for the voyage, made the sign of the cross, then began winding their cords as Sir Guillaume ordered his banner raised to the masthead. It was a blue flag decorated with three stooping yellow hawks that had outspread wings and claws hooked ready to savage their prey. Sir Guillaume could smell the salt fires and hear the cockerels crowing ashore.

The cockerels were still crowing as the bows of his four ships ran onto the shingle.

Sir Guillaume and the Harlequin were the first ashore, but after them came a score of Genoese crossbowmen, who were professional soldiers and knew their business. Their leader took them up the beach and through the village to block the valley beyond, where they would stop any of the villagers escaping with their valuables. Sir Guillaume's remaining men would ransack the houses while the sailors stayed on the beach to guard their ships.

It had been a long, cold and anxious night at sea, but now came the reward. Forty men-at-arms invaded Hookton. They wore close-fitting helmets and had mail shirts over leather-backed hacquetons, they carried swords, axes or spears, and they were released to plunder. Most were veterans of Sir Guillaume's other raids and knew just what to do. Kick in the flimsy doors and start killing the men. Let the women scream, but kill the men, for it was the men who would fight back hardest. Some women ran, but the Genoese crossbowmen were there to stop them. Once the men were dead the plundering could begin, and that took time for peasants everywhere hid whatever was valuable and the hiding places had to be ferreted out. Thatch had to be pulled down, wells explored, floors probed, but plenty of things were not hidden. There were hams waiting for the first meal after Lent, racks of smoked or dried fish, piles of nets, good cooking pots, distaffs and spindles, eggs, butter churns, casks of salt – all humble enough things, but sufficiently valuable to take back to Normandy. Some houses yielded small hoards of coins, and one house, the priest's, was a treasure-trove of silver plate, candlesticks and jugs. There were even some good bolts of woollen cloth in the priest's house, and a great carved bed, and a decent horse in the stable. Sir Guillaume looked at the seventeen books, but decided they were worthless and so, having wrenched the bronze locks from the leather covers, he left them to burn when the houses were fired.

He had to kill the priest's housekeeper. He regretted that death. Sir Guillaume was not squeamish about killing women, but their deaths brought no honour and so he discouraged such slaughter unless the woman caused trouble, and the priest's housekeeper wanted to fight. She slashed at Sir Guillaume's men-at-arms with a roasting spit, called them sons of whores and devils' grubs, and in the end Sir Guillaume cut her down with his sword because she would not accept her fate.

'Stupid bitch,' Sir Guillaume said, stepping over her body to peer into the hearth. Two fine hams were being smoked in the chimney. 'Pull them down,' he ordered one of his men, then left them to search the house while he went to the church.

Father Ralph, woken by the screams of his parishioners, had pulled on a cassock and run to the church. Sir Guillaume's men had left him alone out of respect, but once inside the little church the priest had begun to hit the invaders until the Harlequin arrived and snarled at the men-at-arms to hold the priest. They seized his arms and held him in front of the altar with its white Easter frontal.

The Harlequin, his sword in his hand, bowed to Father Ralph. 'My lord Count,' he said.

Father Ralph closed his eyes, perhaps in prayer, though it looked more like exasperation. He opened them and gazed into the Harlequin's handsome face. 'You are my brother's son,' he said, and did not sound mad at all, merely full of regret.

'True.'

'How is your father?'

'Dead,' the Harlequin said, 'as is his father and yours.'

'God rest their souls,' Father Ralph said piously.

'And when you are dead, old man, I shall be the Count and our family will rise again.'

Father Ralph half smiled, then just shook his head and looked up at the lance. 'It will do you no good,' he said, 'for its power is reserved for virtuous men. It will not work for evil filth like you.' Then Father Ralph gave a curious mewing noise as the breath rushed from him and he stared down to where his nephew had run the sword into his belly. He struggled to speak, but no words came, then he collapsed as the men-at-arms released him and he slumped by the altar with blood puddling in his lap.

The Harlequin wiped his sword on the wine-stained altar cloth, then ordered one of Sir Guillaume's men to find a ladder.

'A ladder?' the man-at-arms asked in confusion.

'They thatch their roofs, don't they? So they have a ladder. Find it.' The Harlequin sheathed his sword, then stared up at the lance of St George.

'I have put a curse on it.' Father Ralph spoke faintly. He was pale-faced, dying, but sounded oddly calm.

'Your curse, my lord, worries me as much as a tavern maid's fart.' The Harlequin tossed the pewter candle-sticks to a man-at-arms, then scooped the wafers from the clay bowl and crammed them into his mouth. He picked up the bowl, peered at its darkened surface and reckoned it was a thing of no value so left it on the altar. 'Where's the wine?' he asked Father Ralph.

Father Ralph shook his head. '*Calix meus inebrians*,' he said, and the Harlequin just laughed. Father Ralph closed his eyes as the pain griped his belly. 'Oh God,' he moaned.

The Harlequin crouched by his uncle's side. 'Does it hurt?'

'Like fire,' Father Ralph said.

'You will burn in hell, my lord,' the Harlequin said, and he saw how Father Ralph was clutching his wounded belly to staunch the flow of blood and so he pulled the priest's hands away and then, standing, kicked him hard in the stomach. Father Ralph gasped with pain and curled his body. 'A gift from your family,' the Harlequin said, then turned away as a ladder was brought into the church.

The village was filled with screams, for most of the women and children were still alive and their ordeal had scarcely begun. All the younger women were briskly raped by Sir Guillaume's men and the prettiest of them, including Jane from the alehouse, were taken to the boats so they could be carried back to Normandy to become the whores or wives of Sir Guillaume's soldiers. One of the women screamed because her baby was still in her house, but the soldiers did not understand her and they struck her to silence then pushed her into the hands of the sailors, who lay her on the shingle and lifted her skirts. She wept inconsolably as her house burned. Geese, pigs, goats, six cows and the priest's good horse were herded towards the boats while the white gulls rode the sky, crying.

The sun had scarcely risen above the eastern hills and the village had already yielded more than Sir Guillaume had dared hope for.

'We could go inland,' the captain of his Genoese crossbowmen suggested.

'We have what we came for,' the black-dressed Harlequin intervened. He had placed the unwieldy lance of St George on the graveyard grass, and now stared at the ancient weapon as though he was trying to understand its power.

'What is it?' the Genoese crossbowman asked.

'Nothing that is of use to you.'

Sir Guillaume grinned. 'Strike a blow with that,' he said, 'and it'll shatter like ivory.'

The Harlequin shrugged. He had found what he

18

wanted, and Sir Guillaume's opinion was of no interest.

'Go inland,' the Genoese captain suggested again.

'A few miles, maybe,' Sir Guillaume said. He knew that the dreaded English archers would eventually come to Hookton, but probably not till midday, and he wondered if there was another village close by that would be worth plundering. He watched a terrified girl, maybe eleven years old, being carried towards the beach by a soldier. 'How many dead?' he asked.

'Ours?' The Genoese captain seemed surprised by the question. 'None.'

'Not ours, theirs.'

'Thirty men? Forty? A few women?'

'And we haven't taken a scratch!' Sir Guillaume exulted. 'Pity to stop now.' He looked at his employer, but the man in black did not seem to care what they did, while the Genoese captain just grunted, which surprised Sir Guillaume for he thought the man was eager to extend the raid, but then he saw that the man's sullen grunt was not caused by any lack of enthusiasm, but by a white-feathered arrow that had buried itself in his breast. The arrow had slit through the mail shirt and padded hacqueton like a bodkin sliding through linen, killing the crossbowman almost instantly.

Sir Guillaume dropped flat and a heartbeat later another arrow whipped above him to thump into the turf. The Harlequin snatched up the lance and was running towards the beach while Sir Guillaume scrambled into the shelter of the church porch. 'Crossbows!' he shouted. 'Crossbows!'

Because someone was fighting back.

* * *

19

Thomas had heard the screams and, like the other four men in the church, he had gone to the door to see what they meant, but no sooner had they reached the porch than a band of armed men, their mail and helmets dark grey in the dawn, appeared in the graveyard.

Edward slammed the church door, dropped the bar into its brackets, then crossed himself. 'Sweet Jesus,' he said in astonishment, then flinched as an axe thumped into the door. 'Give me that!' He seized the sword from Thomas.

Thomas let him take it. The church door was shaking now as two or three axes attacked the old wood. The villagers had always reckoned that Hookton was much too small to be raided, but the church door was splintering in front of Thomas's eyes, and he knew it must be the French. Tales were told up and down the coast of such landings, and prayers were said to keep folk from the raids, but the enemy was here and the church echoed with the crash of their axe blows.

Thomas was in panic, but did not know it. He just knew he had to escape from the church and so he ran and jumped onto the altar. He crushed the silver chalice with his right foot and kicked it off the altar as he climbed onto the sill of the great east window where he beat at the yellow panes, shattering the horn down into the churchyard. He saw men in red and green jackets running past the alehouse, but none looked his way as he jumped down into the churchyard and ran to the ditch where he ripped his clothes as he wriggled through the thorn hedge on the other side. He crossed the lane, jumped the fence of his father's garden, and hammered on the kitchen door, but no one responded and a crossbow bolt smacked into the lintel just inches from his face. Thomas ducked and ran through the bean plants to the cattle shed where his father stabled a horse. There was no time to rescue the beast, so instead Thomas climbed into the hay loft where he hid his bow and arrows. A woman screamed close by. Dogs were howling. The French were shouting as they kicked down doors. Thomas seized his bow and arrow bag, ripped the thatch away from the rafters, squeezed through the gap and dropped into the neighbour's orchard.

He ran then as though the devil was on his heels. A crossbow bolt thumped into the turf as he came to Lipp Hill and two of the Genoese archers started to follow him, but Thomas was young and tall and strong and fast. He ran uphill through a pasture bright with cowslips and daisies, leaped a hurdle that blocked a gap in a hedge, then twisted right towards the hill's crest. He went as far as the wood on the hill's far side and there he dropped to catch his breath amidst a slope drifted with a haze of bluebells. He lay there, listening to the lambs in a nearby field. He waited, hearing nothing untoward. The cross-bowmen had abandoned their pursuit.

Thomas lay in the bluebells for a long time, but at last he crept cautiously back to the hilltop from where he could see a straggle of old women and children scattering on the further hill. Those folk had somehow evaded the crossbowmen and would doubtless flee north to warn Sir Giles Marriott, but Thomas did not join them. Instead he worked his way down to a hazel copse where dog's mercury bloomed and from where he could see his village dying.

Men were carrying plunder to the four strange boats that were grounded on the Hook's shingle. The first thatch was being fired. Two dogs lay dead in the street beside a woman, quite naked, who was being held down while Frenchmen hitched up their mail shirts to take their turns with her. Thomas remembered how, not long ago, she had married a fisherman whose first wife had died in childbirth. She had been so coy and happy, but now, when she tried to crawl off the road, a Frenchman kicked her in the head, then bent with laughter. Thomas saw Jane, the girl he feared he had made pregnant, being dragged towards the boats and was ashamed that he felt a sense of relief that he would not have to confront his father with her news. More cottages were fired as Frenchmen hurled burning straw onto their thatch, and Thomas watched the smoke curl and thicken, then worked his way through the hazel saplings to a place where hawthorn blossom was thick, white and concealing. It was there he strung his bow.

It was the best bow he had ever made. It had been cut from a stave that had washed ashore from a ship that had foundered in the channel. A dozen staves had come to Hookton's shingle on the south wind and Sir Giles Marriott's huntsman reckoned they must have been Italian yew, for it was the most beautiful wood he had ever seen. Thomas had sold eleven of the tight-grained staves in Dorchester, but kept the best one. He'd carved it, steamed the ends to give them a slight bend against the wood's grain, then painted the bow with a mix of soot and flax-seed oil. He had boiled the mix in his mother's kitchen on days when his father was away, and Thomas's father had never known what he was doing, though sometimes he would complain of the smell and Thomas's mother would say she had been making a potion to poison the rats. The bow had had to be painted to stop it from drying out, for then the wood would become brittle and shatter under the stress of the taut string. The paint had dried a deep golden colour, just like the bows Thomas's grandfather used to make in the Weald, but Thomas had wanted it to be darker and so he had rubbed more soot into the wood and smeared it with beeswax, and he'd gone on doing it for a fortnight until the bow was as black as the shaft of St George's lance. He'd tipped the bow with two pieces of nocked horn to hold a cord that was made from woven hemp strands that had been soaked in hoof-glue, then he'd whipped the cord where the arrow would rest with still more hemp. He'd stolen coins from his father to buy arrow heads in Dorchester, then made the shafts from ash and goose feathers and on that Easter morning he had twenty-three of those good arrows in his bag.

Thomas strung the bow, took a white-fledged arrow from the bag, then looked at the three men beside the church. They were a long way off, but the black bow was as big a weapon as any ever made and the power in its yew belly was awesome. One of the men had a simple mail coat, another a plain black surcoat while the third had a red and green jacket over his mail shirt, and Thomas decided that the most gaudily dressed man must be the raid's leader and so he should die.

Thomas's left hand shook as he drew the bow. He was dry-mouthed, frightened. He knew he would shoot wild so he lowered his arm and released the cord's tension. Remember, he told himself, remember everything you have ever been taught. An archer does not aim, he kills. It is all in the head, in the arms, in the eyes, and killing a man is no different from shooting a hind. Draw

23

and loose, that was all, and that was why he had practised for over ten years so that the act of drawing and loosing was as natural as breathing and as fluent as water flowing from a spring. Look and loose, do not think. Draw the string and let God guide the arrow.

Smoke thickened above Hookton, and Thomas felt an immense anger surge like a black humour and he pushed his left hand forward and drew back with the right and he never took his eyes off the red and green coat. He drew till the cord was beside his right ear and then he loosed.

That was the first time Thomas of Hookton ever shot an arrow at a man and he knew it was good as soon as it leaped from the string, for the bow did not quiver. The arrow flew true and he watched it curve down, sinking from the hill to strike the green and red coat hard and deep. He let a second arrow fly, but the man in the mail coat dropped and scurried to the church porch while the third man picked up the lance and ran towards the beach where he was hidden by the smoke.

Thomas had twenty-one arrows left. One each for the holy trinity, he thought, and another for every year of his life, and that life was threatened, for a dozen crossbowmen were running towards the hill. He loosed a third arrow, then ran back through the hazels. He was suddenly exultant, filled with a sense of power and satisfaction. In that one instant, as the first arrow slid into the sky, he knew he wanted nothing more from life. He was an archer. Oxford could go to hell for all he cared, for Thomas had found his joy. He whooped with delight as he ran uphill. Crossbow bolts ripped through the hazel leaves and he noted that they made a deep, almost humming noise as they flew. Then he

24

was over the hill's crest where he ran west for a few yards before doubling back to the summit. He paused long enough to loose another arrow, then turned and ran again.

Thomas led the Genoese crossbowmen a dance of death – from hill to hedgerow, along paths he had known since childhood – and like fools they followed him because their pride would not let them admit that they were beaten. But beaten they were, and two died before a trumpet sounded from the beach, summoning the raiders to their boats. The Genoese turned away then, stopping only to fetch the weapon, pouches, mail and coat of one of their dead, but Thomas killed another of them as they stooped over the body and this time the survivors just ran from him.

Thomas followed them down to the smoke-palled village. He ran past the alehouse, which was an inferno, and so to the shingle where the four boats were being shoved into the sea-reach. The sailors pushed off with long oars, then pulled out to sea. They towed the best three Hookton boats and left the others burning. The village was also burning, its thatch whirling into the sky in sparks and smoke and flaming scraps. Thomas shot one last useless arrow from the beach and watched it plunge into the sea short of the escaping raiders, then he turned away and went back through the stinking, burning, bloody village to the church, which was the only building the raiders had not set alight. The four companions of his vigil were dead, but Father Ralph still lived. He was sitting with his back against the altar. The bottom of his gown was dark with fresh blood and his long face was unnaturally white.

Thomas kneeled beside the priest. 'Father?'

25

Father Ralph opened his eyes and saw the bow. He grimaced, though whether in pain or disapproval, Thomas could not tell.

'Did you kill any of them, Thomas?' the priest asked.

'Yes,' Thomas said, 'a lot.'

Father Ralph grimaced and shuddered. Thomas reckoned the priest was one of the strongest men he had ever known, flawed perhaps, yet tough as a yew stave, but he was dying now and there was a whimper in his voice. 'You don't want to be a priest, do you, Thomas?' He asked the question in French, his mother tongue.

'No,' Thomas answered in the same language.

'You're going to be a soldier,' the priest said, 'like your grandfather.' He paused and whimpered as another bolt of pain ripped up from his belly. Thomas wanted to help him, but in truth there was nothing to be done. The Harlequin had run his sword into Father Ralph's belly and only God could save the priest now. 'I argued with my father,' the dying man said, 'and he disowned me. He disinherited me and I have refused to acknowledge him from that day to this. But you, Thomas, you are like him. Very like him. And you have always argued with me.'

'Yes, Father,' Thomas said. He took his father's hand and the priest did not resist.

'I loved your mother,' Father Ralph said, 'and that was my sin, and you are the fruit of that sin. I thought if you became a priest you could rise above sin. It floods us, Thomas, it floods us. It is everywhere. I have seen the devil, Thomas, seen him with my own eyes and we must fight him. Only the Church can do that. Only the Church.' The tears flowed down his hollow unshaven

26

cheeks. He looked past Thomas into the roof of the nave. 'They stole the lance,' he said sadly.

'I know.'

'My great-grandfather brought it from the Holy Land,' Father Ralph said, 'and I stole it from my father and my brother's son stole it from us today.' He spoke softly. 'He will do evil with it. Bring it home, Thomas. Bring it home.'

'I will,' Thomas promised him. Smoke began to thicken in the church. The raiders had not fired it, but the thatch was catching the flames from the burning scraps that filled the air. 'You say your brother's son stole it?' Thomas asked.

'Your cousin,' Father Ralph whispered, his eyes closed. 'The one dressed in black. He came and stole it.'

'Who is he?' Thomas asked.

'Evil,' Father Ralph said, 'evil.' He moaned and shook his head.

'Who is he?' Thomas insisted.

'*Calix meus inebrians.*' Father Ralph said in a voice scarce above a whisper. Thomas knew it was a line from a psalm and meant 'my cup makes me drunk' and he reckoned his father's mind was slipping as his soul hovered close to his body's end.

'Tell me who your father was!' Thomas demanded. Tell me who I am, he wanted to say. Tell me who you are, Father. But Father Ralph's eyes were closed though he still gripped Thomas's hand hard. 'Father?' Thomas asked. The smoke dipped in the church and sifted out through the window Thomas had broken to make his escape. 'Father?'

But his father never spoke again. He died, and Thomas, who had fought against him all his life, wept like a child. At times he had been ashamed of his father, but in that smoky Easter morning he learned that he loved him. Most priests disowned their children, but Father Ralph had never hidden Thomas. He had let the world think what it wanted and he had freely confessed to being a man as well as a priest and if he sinned in loving his housekeeper then it was a sweet sin that he never denied even if he did say acts of contrition for it and feared that in the life hereafter he would be punished for it.

Thomas pulled his father away from the altar. He did not want the body to be burned when the roof collapsed. The silver chalice that Thomas had accidentally crushed was under the dead man's blood-soaked robe and Thomas pocketed it before dragging the corpse out into the graveyard. He lay his father beside the body of the man in the red and green coat and Thomas crouched there, weeping, knowing that he had failed in his first Easter vigil. The devil had stolen the Sacraments and St George's lance was gone and Hookton was dead.

At midday Sir Giles Marriott came to the village with a score of men armed with bows and billhooks. Sir Giles himself wore mail and carried a sword, but there was no enemy left to fight and Thomas was the only person left in the village.

'Three yellow hawks on a blue field,' Thomas told Sir Giles.

'Thomas?' Sir Giles asked, puzzled. He was the lord of the manor and an old man now, though in his time he had carried a lance against both the Scots and the French. He had been a good friend to Thomas's father, but he did not understand Thomas, whom he reckoned had grown wild as a wolf.

'Three yellow hawks on a blue field,' Thomas said vengefully, 'are the arms of the man who did this.' Were they the arms of his cousin? He did not know. There were so many questions left by his father.

'I don't know whose badge that is,' Sir Giles said, 'but I shall pray by God's bowels he screams in hell for this work.'

There was nothing to be done until the fires had burned themselves out, and only then could the bodies be dragged from the ashes. The burned dead had been blackened and grotesquely shrunk by the heat so that even the tallest men looked like children. The dead villagers were taken to the graveyard for a proper burial, but the bodies of the four crossbowmen were dragged down to the beach and there stripped naked.

'Did you do this?' Sir Giles asked Thomas.

'Yes, sir.'

'Then I thank you.'

'My first dead Frenchmen,' Thomas said angrily.

'No,' Sir Giles said, and he lifted one of the men's tunics to show Thomas the badge of a green chalice embroidered on its sleeve. 'They're from Genoa,' Sir Giles said. 'The French hire them as crossbowmen. I've killed a few in my time, but there are always more where they come from. You know what the badge is?'

'A cup?'

Sir Giles shook his head. 'The Holy Grail. They reckon they have it in their cathedral. I'm told it's a great green thing, carved from an emerald and brought back from the crusades. I should like to see it one day.'

'Then I shall bring it to you,' Thomas said bitterly, 'just as I shall bring back our lance.'

Sir Giles stared to sea. The raiders' boats were long

gone and there was nothing out there but the sun on the waves. 'Why would they come here?' he asked.

'For the lance.'

'I doubt it was even real,' Sir Giles said. He was red-faced, white-haired and heavy now. 'It was just an old spear, nothing more.'

'It's real,' Thomas insisted, 'and that's why they came.'

Sir Giles did not argue. 'Your father,' he said instead, 'would have wanted you to finish your studies.'

'My studies are done,' Thomas said flatly. 'I'm going to France.'

Sir Giles nodded. He reckoned the boy was far better suited to be a soldier than a priest. 'Will you go as an archer?' he asked, looking at the great bow on Thomas's shoulder, 'or do you want to join my house and train to be a man-at-arms?' He half smiled. 'You're gently born, you know?'

'I'm bastard born,' Thomas insisted.

'Your father was of good birth.'

'You know what family?' Thomas asked.

Sir Giles shrugged. 'He would never tell me, and if I pressed him he would just say that God was his father and his mother was the Church.'

'And my mother,' Thomas said, 'was a priest's house-keeper and the daughter of a bowyer. I shall go to France as an archer.'

'There's more honour as a man-at-arms,' Sir Giles observed, but Thomas did not want honour. He wanted revenge.

Sir Giles let him choose what he wanted from the enemy's dead and Thomas picked a mail coat, a pair of long boots, a knife, a sword, a belt and a helmet. It was all plain gear, but serviceable, and only the mail coat needed mending, for he had driven an arrow clean through its rings. Sir Giles said he owed Thomas's father money, which may or may not have been true, but he paid it to Thomas with the gift of a four-year-old gelding. 'You'll need a horse,' he said, 'for nowadays all archers are mounted. Go to Dorchester,' he advised Thomas, 'and like as not you'll find someone recruiting bowmen.'

The Genoese corpses were beheaded and their bodies left to rot while their four heads were impaled on stakes and planted along the Hook's shingle ridge. The gulls fed on the dead men's eyes and pecked at their flesh until the heads were flensed down to bare bones that stared vacantly to the sea.

But Thomas did not see the skulls. He had gone across the water, taken his black bow and joined the wars.

PART ONE

Brittany

It was winter. A cold morning wind blew from the sea bringing a sour salt smell and a spitting rain that would inevitably sap the power of the bowstrings if it did not let up.

'What it is,' Jake said, 'is a waste of goddamn time.'

No one took any notice of him.

'Could have stayed in Brest,' Jake grumbled, 'been sitting by a fire. Drinking ale.'

Again he was ignored.

'Funny name for a town,' Sam said after a long while. 'Brest. I like it, though.' He looked at the archers. 'Maybe we'll see the Blackbird again?' he suggested.

'Maybe she'll put a bolt through your tongue,' Will Skeat growled, 'and do us all a favour.'

The Blackbird was a woman who fought from the town walls every time the army made an assault. She was young, had black hair, wore a black cloak and shot a crossbow. In the first assault, when Will Skeat's archers had been in the vanguard of the attack and had lost four men, they had been close enough to see the Blackbird clearly and they had all thought her beautiful, though after a winter campaign of failure, cold, mud and hunger, almost any woman looked beautiful. Still, there was something special about the Blackbird.

'She doesn't load that crossbow herself,' Sam said, unmoved by Skeat's surliness.

'Of course she bloody doesn't,' Jake said. 'There ain't a woman born that can crank a crossbow.'

'Dozy Mary could,' another man said. 'Got muscles like a bullock, she has.'

'And she closes her eyes when she shoots,' Sam said, still talking of the Blackbird. 'I noticed.'

'That's because you weren't doing your goddamn job,' Will Skeat snarled, 'so shut your mouth, Sam.'

Sam was the youngest of Skeat's men. He claimed to be eighteen, though he was really not sure because he had lost count. He was a draper's son, had a cherubic face, brown curls and a heart as dark as sin. He was a good archer though; no one could serve Will Skeat without being good.

'Right, lads,' Skeat said, 'make ready.'

He had seen the stir in the encampment behind them. The enemy would notice it soon and the church bells would ring the alarm and the town walls would fill with defenders armed with crossbows. The crossbows would rip their bolts into the attackers and Skeat's job today was to try to clear those crossbowmen off the wall with his arrows. Some chance, he thought sourly. The defenders would crouch behind their crenellations and so deny his men an opportunity to aim, and doubtless this assault would end as the five other attacks had finished, in failure.

It had been a whole campaign of failure. William Bohun, the Earl of Northampton, who led this small English army, had launched the winter expedition in hope of capturing a stronghold in northern Brittany, but the assault on Carhaix had been a humiliating failure, the defenders of Guingamp had laughed at the English, and the walls of Lannion had repulsed every attack. They had captured Tréguier, but as that town had no walls it was not much of an achievement and no place to make a fortress. Now, at the bitter end of the year, with nothing better to do, the Earl's army had fetched up outside this small town, which was scarcely more than a walled village, but even this miserable place had defied the army. The Earl had launched attack after attack and all had been beaten back. The English had been met by a storm of crossbow bolts, the scaling ladders had been thrust from the ramparts and the defenders had exulted in each failure.

'What is this goddamn place called?' Skeat asked.

'La Roche-Derrien,' a tall archer answered.

'You would know, Tom,' Skeat said, 'you know everything.'

'That is true, Will,' Thomas said gravely, 'quite literally true.' The other archers laughed.

'So if you know so bloody much,' Skeat said, 'tell me what this goddamn town is called again.'

'La Roche-Derrien.'

'Daft bloody name,' Skeat said. He was grey-haired, thin-faced and had known nearly thirty years of fighting. He came from Yorkshire and had begun his career as an archer fighting against the Scots. He had been as lucky as he was skilled, and so he had taken plunder, survived battles and risen in the ranks until he was wealthy enough to raise his own band of soldiers. He now led seventy men-at-arms and as many archers, whom he had contracted to the Earl of Northampton's service which was why he was crouching behind a wet hedge a hundred and fifty paces from the walls of a town whose name he still could not remember. His men-at-arms were in the camp, given a day's rest after leading the last failed assault. Will Skeat hated failure.

'La Roche what?' he asked Thomas.

'Derrien.'

'What does that goddamn mean?'

'That, I confess, I do not know.'

'Sweet Christ,' Skeat said in mock wonder, 'he doesn't know everything.'

'It is, however, close to *derrière*, which means arse,' Thomas added. 'The rock of the arse is my best translation.'

Skeat opened his mouth to say something, but just then the first of La Roche-Derrien's church bells sounded the alarm. It was the cracked bell, the one that sounded so harsh, and within seconds the other churches added their tolling so that the wet wind was filled with their clangour. The noise was greeted by a subdued English cheer as the assault troops came from the camp and pounded up the road towards the town's southern gate. The leading men carried ladders, the rest had swords and axes. The Earl of Northampton led the assault, as he had led all the others, conspicuous in his plate armour half covered by a surcoat showing his badge of the lions and stars.

'You know what to do!' Skeat bellowed.

The archers stood, drew their bows and loosed. There were no targets on the walls, for the defenders were staying low, but the rattle of the steel-tipped arrows on the stones should keep them crouching. The white-feathered arrows hissed as they flew. Two other archer bands were adding their own shafts, many of them firing high into the sky so that their missiles dropped vertically onto the wall's top, and to Skeat it seemed impossible that anyone could live under that hail of feather-tipped steel, yet as soon as the Earl's attacking column came within a hundred paces the crossbow bolts began to spit from the walls.

There was a breach close to the gate. It had been made by a catapult, the only siege machine left in decent repair, and it was a poor breach, for only the top third of the wall had been dismantled by the big stones and the townsfolk had crammed timber and bundles of cloth into the gap, but it was still a weakness in the wall and the ladder men ran towards it, shouting, as the crossbow bolts whipped into them. Men stumbled, fell, crawled and died, but enough lived to throw two ladders against the breach and the first men-at-arms began to climb. The archers were loosing as fast as they could, overwhelming the top of the breach with arrows, but then a shield appeared there, a shield that was immediately stuck by a score of shafts, and from behind the shield a crossbowman shot straight down one of the ladders, killing the leading man. Another shield appeared, another crossbow was loosed. A pot was shoved onto the breach's top, then toppled over, and a gush of steaming liquid spilled down to make a man scream in agony. Defenders were hurling boulders over the breach and their crossbows were snapping.

'Closer!' Skeat shouted, and his archers pushed through the hedge and ran to within a hundred paces of the town ditch, where they again loosed their long war bows and slashed their arrows into the embrasures. Some defenders were dying now, for they had to show themselves to shoot their crossbows down into the crowd of men who jostled at the foot of the four ladders that had been laid against the breach or walls. Men-at-arms climbed, a forked pole shoved one ladder back and Thomas twitched his left hand to change his aim and released his fingers to drive an arrow into the breast of a man pushing on the pole. The man had been covered by a shield held by a companion, but the shield shifted for an instant and Thomas's arrow was the first through the small gap, though two more followed before the dying man's last heartbeat ended. Other men succeeded in toppling the ladder. 'St George!' the English shouted, but the saint must have been sleeping for he gave the attackers no help.

More stones were hurled from the ramparts, then a great mass of flaming straw was heaved into the crowded attackers. A man succeeded in reaching the top of the breach, but was immediately killed by an axe that split his helmet and skull in two. He slumped on the rungs, blocking the ascent, and the Earl tried to haul him free, but was struck on the head by one of the boulders and collapsed at the ladder's foot. Two of his men-at-arms carried the stunned Earl back to the camp and his departure took the spirit from the attackers. They no longer shouted. The arrows still flew, and men still tried to climb the wall, but the defenders sensed they had repelled this sixth attack and their crossbow bolts spat relentlessly. It was then Thomas saw the Blackbird on the tower above the gate. He laid the steel arrow tip on her breast, raised the bow a fraction and then jerked his bow hand so that the arrow flew wild. Too pretty to kill, he told himself and knew he was a fool for thinking it. She shot her bolt and vanished. A half-dozen arrows clattered onto the tower where she had been standing, but Thomas reckoned all six archers had let her shoot before they loosed.

'Jesus wept,' Skeat said. The attack had failed and the men-at-arms were running from the crossbow bolts. One ladder still rested against the breach with the dead man entangled in its upper rungs. 'Back,' Skeat shouted, 'back.'

The archers ran, pursued by quarrels, until they could push through the hedge and drop into the ditch. The defenders were cheering and two men bared their backsides on the gate tower and briefly shoved their arses towards the defeated English.

'Bastards,' Skeat said, 'bastards.' He was not used to failure. 'There has to be a bloody way in,' he growled.

Thomas unlooped the string from his bow and placed it under his helmet. 'I told you how to get in,' he told Skeat, 'told you at dawn.'

Skeat looked at Thomas for a long time. 'We tried it, lad.'

'I got to the stakes, Will. I promise I did. I got through them.'

'So tell me again,' Skeat said, and Thomas did. He crouched in the ditch under the jeers of La Roche-Derrien's defenders and he told Will Skeat how to unlock the town, and Skeat listened because the York-shireman had learned to trust Thomas of Hookton.

Thomas had been in Brittany for three years now, and though Brittany was not France its usurping Duke brought a constant succession of Frenchman to be killed and Thomas had discovered he had a skill for killing. It was not just that he was a good archer – the army was full of men who were as good as he and there was a handful who were better – but he had discovered he

41

could sense what the enemy was doing. He would watch them, watch their eyes, see where they were looking, and as often as not he anticipated an enemy move and was ready to greet it with an arrow. It was like a game, but one where he knew the rules and they did not.

It helped that William Skeat trusted him. Skeat had been unwilling to recruit Thomas when they first met by the gaol in Dorchester where Skeat was testing a score of thieves and murderers to see how well they could shoot a bow. He needed recruits and the King needed archers, so men who would otherwise have faced the gallows were being pardoned if they would serve abroad, and fully half of Skeat's men were such felons. Thomas, Skeat had reckoned, would never fit in with such rogues. He had taken Thomas's right hand, seen the callouses on the two bow fingers which said he was an archer, but then had tapped the boy's soft palm.

'What have you been doing?' Skeat had asked.

'My father wanted me to be a priest.'

'A priest, eh?' Skeat had been scornful. 'Well, you can pray for us, I suppose.'

'I can kill for you too.'

Skeat had eventually let Thomas join the band, not least because the boy brought his own horse. At first Skeat thought Thomas of Hookton was little more than another wild fool looking for adventure – a clever fool, to be sure – but Thomas had taken to the life of an archer in Brittany with alacrity. The real business of the civil war was plunder and, day after day, Skeat's men rode into land that gave fealty to the supporters of Duke Charles and they burned the farms, stole the harvest and took the livestock. A lord whose peasants cannot pay rent is a lord who cannot afford to hire soldiers, so Skeat's men-at-arms and mounted archers were loosed on the enemy's land like a plague, and Thomas loved the life. He was young and his task was not just to fight the enemy, but to ruin him. He burned farms, poisoned wells, stole seed-grain, broke ploughs, fired the mills, ring-barked the orchards and lived off his plunder. Skeat's men were the lords of Brittany, a scourge from hell, and the French-speaking villagers in the east of the Duchy called them the *hellequin*, which meant the devil's horsemen. Once in a while an enemy war band would seek to trap them and Thomas had learned that the English archer, with his great long war bow, was the king of those skirmishes. The enemy hated the archers. If they captured an English bowman they killed him. A man-at-arms might be imprisoned, a lord would be ransomed, but an archer was always murdered. Tortured first, then murdered.

Thomas thrived on the life, and Skeat had learned the lad was clever, certainly clever enough to know better than to fall asleep one night when he should have been standing guard and, for that offence Skeat had thumped the daylights out of him. 'You were goddamn drunk!' he had accused Thomas, then beat him thoroughly, using his fists like blacksmith's hammers. He had broken Thomas's nose, cracked a rib and called him a stinking piece of Satan's shit, but at the end of it Will Skeat saw that the boy was still grinning, and six months later he made Thomas into a vintenar, which meant he was in charge of twenty other archers.

Those twenty were nearly all older than Thomas, but none seemed to mind his promotion for they reckoned he was different. Most archers wore their hair cropped short, but Thomas's hair was flamboyantly long and wrapped with bowcords so it fell in a long black plait to his waist. He was clean-shaven and dressed only in black. Such affectations could have made him unpopular, but he worked hard, had a quick wit and was generous. He was still odd, though. All archers wore talismans, maybe a cheap metal pendant showing a saint, or a dried hare's foot, but Thomas had a desiccated dog's paw hanging round his neck which he claimed was the hand of St Guinefort, and no one dared dispute him because he was the most learned man in Skeat's band. He spoke French like a nobleman and Latin like a priest, and Skeat's archers were perversely proud of him because of those accomplishments. Now, three years after joining Will Skeat's band, Thomas was one of his chief archers. Skeat even asked his advice sometimes; he rarely took it, but he asked, and Thomas still had the dog's paw, a crooked nose and an impudent grin.

And now he had an idea how to get into La Roche-Derrien.

That afternoon, when the dead man-at-arms with the split skull was still tangled in the abandoned ladder, Sir Simon Jekyll rode towards the town and there trotted his horse back and forth beside the small, dark-feathered crossbow bolts that marked the furthest range of the defenders' weapons. His squire, a daft boy with a slack jaw and puzzled eyes, watched from a distance. The squire held Sir Simon's lance, and should any warrior in the town accept the implicit challenge of Sir Simon's mocking presence, the squire would give his master the lance and the two horsemen would fight on the pasture until one or the other yielded. And it would not be Sir Simon for he was as skilled a knight as any in the Earl of Northampton's army.

And the poorest.

His destrier was ten years old, hard-mouthed and sway-backed. His saddle, which was high in pommel and cantle so that it held him firm in its grip, had belonged to his father, while his hauberk, a tunic of mail that covered him from neck to knees, had belonged to his grandfather. His sword was over a hundred years old, heavy, and would not keep its edge. His lance had warped in the wet winter weather, while his helmet, which hung from his pommel, was an old steel pot with a worn leather lining. His shield, with its escutcheon of a mailed fist clutching a war-hammer, was battered and faded. His mail gauntlets, like the rest of his armour, were rusting, which was why his squire had a thick, reddened ear and a frightened face, though the real reason for the rust was not that the squire did not try to clean the mail, but that Sir Simon could not afford the vinegar and fine sand that was used to scour the steel. He was poor.

Poor and bitter and ambitious.

And good.

No one denied he was good. He had won the tournament at Tewkesbury and received a purse of forty pounds. At Gloucester his victory had been rewarded by a fine suit of armour. At Chelmsford it had been fifteen pounds and a fine saddle, and at Canterbury he had half hacked a Frenchman to death before being given a gilded cup filled with coins, and where were all those trophies now? In the hands of the bankers and lawyers and merchants who had a lien on the Berkshire estate that Sir Simon had inherited two years before, though in truth his inheritance had been nothing but debt, and the moment his father was buried the moneylenders had closed on Sir Simon like hounds on a wounded deer.

'Marry an heiress,' his mother had advised, and she had paraded a dozen women for her son's inspection, but Sir Simon was determined his wife should be as beautiful as he was handsome. And he was handsome. He knew that. He would stare into his mother's mirror and admire his reflection. He had thick fair hair, a broad face and a short beard. At Chester, where he had unhorsed three knights inside four minutes, men had mistaken him for the King, who was reputed to fight anonymously in tournaments, and Sir Simon was not going to throw away his good royal looks on some wrinkled hag just because she had money. He would marry a woman worthy of himself, but that ambition would not pay the estate's debts and so Sir Simon, to defend himself against his creditors, had sought a letter of protection from King Edward III. That letter shielded Sir Simon from all legal proceedings so long as he served the King in a foreign war, and when Sir Simon had crossed the Channel, taking six men-at-arms, a dozen archers and a slack-jawed squire from his encumbered estate, he had left his creditors helpless in England. Sir Simon had also brought with him a certainty that he would soon capture some French or Breton nobleman whose ransom would be sufficient to pay all he owed, but so far the winter campaign had not yielded a single prisoner of rank and so little plunder that the army was now on half rations. And how many well-born prisoners

46

could he expect to take in a miserable town like La Roche-Derrien? It was a shit hole.

Yet he rode up and down beneath its walls, hoping some knight would take the challenge and ride from the town's southern gate that had so far resisted six English assaults, but instead the defenders jeered him and called him a coward for staying out of their crossbows' range and the insults piqued Sir Simon's pride so that he rode closer to the walls, his horse's hoofs sometimes clattering on one of the fallen quarrels. Men shot at him, but the bolts fell well short and it was Sir Simon's turn to jeer.

'He's just a bloody fool,' Jake said, watching from the English camp. Jake was one of William Skeat's felons, a murderer who had been saved from the gallows at Exeter. He was cross-eyed, yet still managed to shoot straighter than most men. 'Now what's he doing?'

Sir Simon had stopped his horse and was facing the gate so that the men who watched thought that perhaps a Frenchman was coming to challenge the English knight who taunted them. Instead they saw that a lone crossbowman was standing on the gate turret and beckoning Sir Simon forward, daring him to come within range.

Only a fool would respond to such a dare, and Sir Simon dutifully responded. He was twenty-five years old, bitter and brave, and he reckoned a display of careless arrogance would dishearten the besieged garrison and encourage the dispirited English and so he spurred the destrier deep into the killing ground where the French bolts had torn the heart out of the English attacks. No crossbowman fired now; there was just the lone figure standing on the gate tower, and Sir Simon, riding to within a hundred yards, saw it was the Blackbird.

This was the first time Sir Simon had seen the woman every archer called the Blackbird and he was close enough to perceive that she was indeed a beauty. She stood straight, slender and tall, cloaked against the winter wind, but with her long black hair loose like a young girl's. She offered him a mocking bow and Sir Simon responded, bending awkwardly in the tight saddle, then he watched as she picked up her crossbow and put it to her shoulder.

And when we're inside the town, Sir Simon thought, I'll make you pay for this. You'll be flat on your arse, Blackbird, and I'll be on top. He stood his horse quite still, a lone horseman in the French slaughter ground, daring her to aim straight and knowing she would not. And when she missed he would give her a mocking salute and the French would take it as a bad omen.

But what if she did aim straight?

Sir Simon was tempted to lift the awkward helmet from his saddle's pommel, but resisted the impulse. He had dared the Blackbird to do her worst and he could show no nerves in front of a woman and so he waited as she levelled the bow. The town's defenders were watching her and doubtless praying. Or perhaps making wagers.

Come on, you bitch, he said under his breath. It was cold, but there was sweat on his forehead.

She paused, pushed the black hair from her face, then rested the bow on a crenellation and aimed again. Sir Simon kept his head up and his gaze straight. Just a woman, he told himself. Probably could not hit a wagon at five paces. His horse shivered and he reached out to pat its neck. 'Be going soon, boy,' he told it.

The Blackbird, watched by a score of defenders, closed her eyes and shot.

Sir Simon saw the quarrel as a small black blur against the grey sky and the grey stones of the church towers showing above La Roche-Derrien's walls.

He knew the quarrel would go wide. Knew it with an absolute certainty. She was a woman, for God's sake! And that was why he did not move as he saw the blur coming straight for him. He could not believe it. He was waiting for the quarrel to slide to left or right, or to plough into the frost-hardened ground, but instead it was coming unerringly towards his breast and, at the very last instant, he jerked up the heavy shield and ducked his head and felt a huge thump on his left arm as the bolt slammed home to throw him hard against the saddle's cantle. The bolt hit the shield so hard that it split through the willow boards and its point gouged a deep cut through the mail sleeve and into his forearm. The French were cheering and Sir Simon, knowing that other crossbowmen might now try to finish what the Blackbird had begun, pressed his knee into his destrier's flank and the beast obediently turned and then responded to the spurs.

'I'm alive,' he said aloud, as if that would silence the French jubilation. Goddamn bitch, he thought. He would pay her right enough, pay her till she squealed, and he curbed his horse, not wanting to look as though he fled.

An hour later, after his squire had put a bandage over the slashed forearm, Sir Simon had convinced himself that he had scored a victory. He had dared, he had survived. It had been a demonstration of courage, and he lived, and for that he reckoned he was a hero and he expected a hero's welcome as he walked toward the tent that housed the army's commander, the Earl of Northampton. The tent was made from two sails, their linen yellow and patched and threadbare after years of service at sea. They made a shabby shelter, but that was typical of William Bohun, Earl of Northampton who, though cousin to the King and as rich a man as any in England, despised gaudiness.

The Earl, indeed, looked as patched and threadbare as the sails that made his tent. He was a short and squat man with a face, men said, like the backside of a bull, but the face mirrored the Earl's soul, which was blunt, brave and straightforward. The army liked William Bohun, Earl of Northampton, because he was as tough as they were themselves. Now, as Sir Simon ducked into the tent, the Earl's curly brown hair was half covered with a bandage where the boulder thrown from La Roche-Derrien's wall had split his helmet and driven a ragged edge of steel into his scalp. He greeted Sir Simon sourly. 'Tired of life?'

'The silly bitch shut her eyes when she pulled the trigger!' Sir Simon said, oblivious to the Earl's tone.

'She still aimed well,' the Earl said angrily, 'and that will put heart into the bastards. God knows, they need no encouragement.'

'I'm alive, my lord,' Sir Simon said cheerfully. 'She wanted to kill me. She failed. The bear lives and the dogs go hungry.' He waited for the Earl's companions to congratulate him, but they avoided his eyes and he interpreted their sullen silence as jealousy.

Sir Simon was a bloody fool, the Earl thought, and

shivered. He might not have minded the cold so much had the army been enjoying success, but for two months the English and their Breton allies had stumbled from failure to farce, and the six assaults on La Roche-Derrien had plumbed the depths of misery. So now the Earl had called a council of war to suggest one final assault, this one to be made that same evening. Every other attack had been in the forenoon, but perhaps a surprise escalade in the dying winter light would take the defenders by surprise. Only what small advantages that surprise might bring had been spoiled because Sir Simon's foolhardiness must have given the townsfolk a new confidence and there was little confidence among the Earl's war captains who had gathered under the yellow sailcloth.

Four of those captains were knights who, like Sir Simon, led their own men to war, but the others were mercenary soldiers who had contracted their men to the Earl's service. Three were Bretons who wore the white ermine badge of the Duke of Brittany and led men loyal to the de Montfort Duke, while the others were English captains, all of them commoners who had grown hard in war. William Skeat was there, and next to him was Richard Totesham, who had begun his service as a man-at-arms and now led a hundred and forty knights and ninety archers in the Earl's service. Neither man had ever fought in a tournament, nor would they ever be invited, yet both were wealthier than Sir Simon, and that rankled. My hounds of war, the Earl of Northampton called the independent captains, and the Earl liked them, but then the Earl had a curious taste for vulgar company. He might be cousin to England's King, but William Bohun happily drank with men like Skeat and Totesham, ate with them, spoke English with them, hunted with them and trusted them, and Sir Simon felt excluded from that friendship. If any man in this army should have been an intimate of the Earl it was Sir Simon, a noted champion of tournaments, but Northampton would rather roll in the gutter with men like Skeat.

'How's the rain?' the Earl asked.

'Starting again,' Sir Simon answered, jerking his head at the tent's roof, against which the rain pattered fitfully.

'It'll clear,' Skeat said dourly. He rarely called the Earl 'my lord', addressing him instead as an equal which, to Sir Simon's amazement, the Earl seemed to like.

'And it's only spitting,' the Earl said, peering out from the tent and letting in a swirl of damp, cold air. 'Bowstrings will pluck in this.'

'So will crossbow cords,' Richard Totesham interjected. 'Bastards,' he added. What made the English failure so galling was that La Roche-Derrien's defenders were not soldiers but townsfolk: fishermen and boatbuilders, carpenters and masons, and even the Blackbird, a woman! 'And the rain might stop,' Totesham went on, 'but the ground will be slick. It'll be bad footing under the walls.'

'Don't go tonight,' Will Skeat advised. 'Let my boys go in by the river tomorrow morning.'

The Earl rubbed the wound on his scalp. For a week now he had assaulted La Roche-Derrien's southern wall and he still believed his men could take those ramparts, yet he also sensed the pessimism among his hounds of war. One more repulse with another twenty or thirty dead would leave his army dispirited and with the prospect of trailing back to Finisterre with nothing accomplished. 'Tell me again,' he said.

Skeat wiped his nose on his leather sleeve. 'At low tide,' he said, 'there's a way round the north wall. One of my lads was down there last night.'

'We tried it three days ago,' one of the knights objected.

'You tried the down-river side,' Skeat said. 'I want to go up-river.'

'That side has stakes just like the other,' the Earl said.

'Loose,' Skeat responded. One of the Breton captains translated the exchange for his companions. 'My boy pulled a stake clean out,' Skeat went on, 'and he reckons half a dozen others will lift or break. They're old oak trunks, he says, instead of elm, and they're rotted through.'

'How deep is the mud?' the Earl asked.

'Up to his knees.'

La Roche-Derrien's wall encompassed the west, south and east of the town, while the northern side was defended by the River Jaudy, and where the semi-circular wall met the river the townsfolk had planted huge stakes in the mud to block access at low tide. Skeat was now suggesting there was a way through those rotted stakes, but when the Earl's men had tried to do the same thing at the eastern side of the town the attackers had got bogged down in the mud and the townsfolk had picked them off with bolts. It had been a worse slaughter than the repulses in front of the southern gate.

'But there's still a wall on the riverbank,' the Earl pointed out.

'Aye,' Skeat allowed, 'but the silly bastards have

broken it down in places. They've built quays there, and there's one right close to the loose stakes.'

'So your men will have to remove the stakes and climb the quays, all under the gaze of men on the wall?' the Earl asked sceptically.

'They can do it,' Skeat said firmly.

The Earl still reckoned his best chance of success was to close his archers on the south gate and pray that their arrows would keep the defenders cowering while his men-at-arms assaulted the breach, yet that, he conceded, was the plan that had failed earlier in the day and on the day before that. And he had, he knew, only a day or two left. He possessed fewer than three thousand men, and a third of those were sick, and if he could not find them shelter he would have to march back west with his tail between his legs. He needed a town, any town, even La Roche-Derrien.

Will Skeat saw the worries on the Earl's broad face. 'My lad was within fifteen paces of the quay last night,' he asserted. 'He could have been inside the town and opened the gate.'

'So why didn't he?' Sir Simon could not resist asking. 'Christ's bones!' he went on. 'But I'd have been inside!'

'You're not an archer,' Skeat said sourly, then made the sign of the cross. At Guingamp one of Skeat's archers had been captured by the defenders, who had stripped the hated bowman naked then cut him to pieces on the rampart where the besiegers could see his long death. His two bow fingers had been severed first, then his manhood, and the man had screamed like a pig being gelded as he bled to death on the battlements.

The Earl gestured for a servant to replenish the cups

of mulled wine. 'Would you lead this attack, Will?' he asked.

'Not me,' Skeat said. 'I'm too old to wade through boggy mud. I'll let the lad who went past the stakes last night lead them in. He's a good boy, so he is. He's a clever bastard, but an odd one. He was going to be a priest, he was, only he met me and came to his senses.'

The Earl was plainly tempted by the idea. He toyed with the hilt of his sword, then nodded. 'I think we should meet your clever bastard. Is he near?'

'Left him outside,' Skeat said, then twisted on his stool. 'Tom, you savage! Come in here!'

Thomas stooped into the Earl's tent, where the gathered captains saw a tall, long-legged young man dressed entirely in black, all but for his mail coat and the red cross sewn onto his tunic. All the English troops wore that cross of St George so that in a mêlée they would know who was a friend and who an enemy. The young man bowed to the Earl, who realized he had noticed this archer before, which was hardly surprising for Thomas was a striking-looking man. He wore his black hair in a pigtail, tied with bowcord, he had a long bony nose that was crooked, a clean-shaven chin and watchful, clever eyes, though perhaps the most noticeable thing about him was that he was clean. That and, on his shoulder, the great bow that was one of the longest the Earl had seen, and not only long, but painted black, while mounted on the outer belly of the bow was a curious silver plate which seemed to have a coat of arms engraved on it. There was vanity here, the Earl thought, vanity and pride, and he approved of both things.

'For a man who was up to his knees in river mud last

night,' the Earl said with a smile, 'you're remarkably clean.'

'I washed, my lord.'

'You'll catch cold!' the Earl warned him. 'What's your name?'

'Thomas of Hookton, my lord.'

'So tell me what you found last night, Thomas of Hookton.'

Thomas told the same tale as Will Skeat. How, after dark, and as the tide fell, he had waded out into the Jaudy's mud. He had found the fence of stakes ill-maintained, rotting and loose, and he had lifted one out of its socket, wriggled through the gap and gone a few paces towards the nearest quay. 'I was close enough, my lord, to hear a woman singing,' he said. The woman had been singing a song that his own mother had crooned to him when he was small and he had been struck by that oddity.

The Earl frowned when Thomas finished, not because he disapproved of anything the archer had said, but because the scalp wound that had left him unconscious for an hour was throbbing. 'What were you doing at the river last night?' he asked, mainly to give himself more time to think about the idea.

Thomas said nothing.

'Another man's woman,' Skeat eventually answered for Thomas, 'that's what he was doing, my lord, another man's woman.'

The assembled men laughed, all but Sir Simon Jekyll, who looked sourly at the blushing Thomas. The bastard was a mere archer yet he was wearing a better coat of mail than Sir Simon could afford! And he had a confidence that stank of impudence. Sir Simon shuddered.

There was an unfairness to life which he did not understand. Archers from the shires were capturing horses and weapons and armour while he, a champion of tournaments, had not managed anything more valuable than a pair of goddamned boots. He felt an irresistible urge to deflate this tall, composed archer.

'One alert sentinel, my lord,' Sir Simon spoke to the Earl in Norman French so that only the handful of well-born men in the tent would understand him, 'and this boy will be dead and our attack will be floundering in river mud.'

Thomas gave Sir Simon a very level look, insolent in its lack of expression, then answered in fluent French. 'We should attack in the dark,' he said, then turned back to the Earl. 'The tide will be low just before dawn tomorrow, my lord.'

The Earl looked at him with surprise. 'How did you learn French?'

'From my father, my lord.'

'Do we know him?'

'I doubt it, my lord.'

The Earl did not pursue the subject. He bit his lip and rubbed the pommel of his sword, a habit when he was thinking.

'All well and good if you get inside,' Richard Totesham, seated on a milking stool next to Will Skeat, growled at Thomas. Totesham led the largest of the independent bands and had, on that account, a greater authority than the rest of the captains. 'But what do you do when you're inside?'

Thomas nodded, as though he had expected the question. 'I doubt we can reach a gate,' he said, 'but if I can put a score of archers onto the wall beside the river then they can protect it while ladders are placed.'

'And I've got two ladders,' Skeat added. 'They'll do.'

The Earl still rubbed the pommel of his sword. 'When we tried to attack by the river before,' he said, 'we got trapped in the mud. It'll be just as deep where you want to go.'

'Hurdles, my lord,' Thomas said. 'I found some in a farm.' Hurdles were fence sections made of woven willow that could make a quick pen for sheep or could be laid flat on mud to provide men with footing.

'I told you he was clever,' Will Skeat said proudly. 'Went to Oxford, didn't you, Tom?'

'When I was too young to know better,' Thomas said drily.

The Earl laughed. He liked this boy and he could see why Skeat had such faith in him. 'Tomorrow morning, Thomas?' he asked.

'Better than dusk tonight, my lord. They'll still be lively at dusk.' Thomas gave Sir Simon an expressionless glance, intimating that the knight's display of stupid bravery would have quickened the defenders' spirits.

'Then tomorrow morning it is,' the Earl said. He turned to Totesham. 'But keep your boys closed on the south gate today. I want them to think we're coming there again.' He looked back to Thomas. 'What's the badge on your bow, boy?'

'Just something I found, my lord,' Thomas lied, handing the bow to the Earl, who had held out his hand. In truth he had cut the silver badge out of the crushed chalice that he had found under his father's robes, then pinned the metal to the front of the bow where his left hand had worn the silver almost smooth.

The Earl peered at the device. 'A yale?'

'I think that's what the beast is called, my lord,' Thomas said, pretending ignorance.

'Not the badge of anyone I know,' the Earl said, then tried to flex the bow and raised his eyebrows in surprise at its strength. He gave the black shaft back to Thomas then dismissed him. 'I wish you Godspeed in the morning, Thomas of Hookton.'

'My lord,' Thomas said, and bowed.

'I'll go with him, with your permission,' Skeat said, and the Earl nodded, then watched the two men leave. 'If we do get inside,' he told his remaining captains, 'then for God's sake don't let your men cry havoc. Hold their leashes tight. I intend to keep this town and I don't want the townsfolk hating us. Kill when you must, but I don't want an orgy of blood.' He looked at their sceptical faces. 'I'll be putting one of you in charge of the garrison here, so make it easy for yourselves. Hold them tight.'

The captains grunted, knowing how hard it would be to keep their men from a full sack of the town, but before any of them could respond to the Earl's hopeful wishes, Sir Simon stood.

'My lord? A request?'

The Earl shrugged. 'Try me.'

'Would you let me and my men lead the ladder party?'

The Earl seemed surprised at the request. 'You think Skeat cannot manage on his own?'

'I am sure he can, my lord,' Sir Simon said humbly, 'but I still beg the honour.'

Better Sir Simon Jekyll dead than Will Skeat, the Earl thought. He nodded. 'Of course, of course.'

The captains said nothing. What honour was there

in being first onto a wall that another man had captured? No, the bastard did not want honour, he wanted to be well placed to find the richest plunder in town, but none of them voiced his thought. They were captains, but Sir Simon was a knight, even if a penniless one.

The Earl's army threatened an attack for the rest of that short winter's day, but it never came and the citizens of La Roche-Derrien dared to hope that the worst of their ordeal was over, but made preparations in case the English did try again the next day. They counted their crossbow bolts, stacked more boulders on the ramparts and fed the fires which boiled the pots of water that were poured onto the English. Heat the wretches up, the town's priests had said, and the townsfolk liked that jest. They were winning, they knew, and they reckoned their ordeal must finish soon, for the English would surely be running out of food. All La Roche-Derrien had to do was endure and then receive the praise and thanks of Duke Charles.

The small rain stopped at nightfall. The townsfolk went to their beds, but kept their weapons ready. The sentries lit watch fires behind the walls and gazed into the dark.

It was night, it was winter, it was cold and the besiegers had one last chance.

The Blackbird had been christened Jeanette Marie Halevy, and when she was fifteen her parents had taken her to Guingamp for the annual tournament of the apples. Her father was not an aristocrat so the family could not sit in the enclosure beneath St Laurent's tower, but they found a place nearby, and Louis Halevy made certain his daughter was visible by placing their chairs on the farm wagon which had carried them from La Roche-Derrien. Jeanette's father was a prosperous shipmaster and wine merchant, though his fortune in business had not been mirrored in life. One son had died when a cut finger turned septic and his second son had drowned on a voyage to Corunna. Jeanette was now his only child.

There was calculation in the visit to Guingamp. The nobility of Brittany, at least those who favoured an alliance with France, assembled at the tournament where, for four days, in front of a crowd that came as much for the fair as for the fighting, they displayed their talents with sword and lance. Jeanette found much of it tedious, for the preambles to each fight were long and often out of earshot. Knights paraded endlessly, their extravagant plumes nodding, but after a while there would be a brief thunder of hoofs, a clash of metal, a cheer, and one knight would be tumbled in the grass. It was customary for every victorious knight to prick an apple with his lance and present it to whichever woman in the crowd attracted him, and that was why her father had taken the farm wagon to Guingamp. After four days Jeanette had eighteen apples and the enmity of a score of better-born girls.

Her parents took her back to La Roche-Derrien and waited. They had displayed their wares and now the buyers could find their way to the lavish house beside the River Jaudy. From the front the house seemed small, but go through the archway and a visitor found himself in a wide courtyard reaching down to a stone quay where Monsieur Halevy's smaller boats could be

61

moored at the top of the tide. The courtyard shared a wall with the church of St Renan and, because Monsieur Halevy had donated the tower to the church, he had been permitted to drive an archway through the wall so that his family did not need to step into the street when they went to Mass. The house told any suitor that this was a wealthy family, and the presence of the parish priest at the supper table told him it was a devout family. Jeanette was to be no aristocrat's plaything, she was to be a wife.

A dozen men condescended to visit the Halevy house, but it was Henri Chenier, Comte d'Armorique, who won the apple. He was a prime catch, for he was nephew to Charles of Blois, who was himself a nephew to King Philip of France, and it was Charles whom the French recognized as Duke and ruler of Brittany. The Duke allowed Henri Chenier to present his fiancée, but afterwards advised his nephew to discard her. The girl was a merchant's daughter, scarce more than a peasant, though even the Duke admitted she was a beauty. Her hair was shining black, her face was unflawed by the pox and she had all her teeth. She was graceful, so that a Dominican friar in the Duke's court clasped his hands and exclaimed that Jeanette was the living image of the Madonna. The Duke agreed she was beautiful, but so what? Many women were beautiful. Any tavern in Guingamp, he said, could throw up a two-livre whore who could make most wives look like hogs. It was not the job of a wife to be beautiful, but to be rich. 'Make the girl your mistress,' he advised his nephew, and virtually ordered Henri to marry an heiress from Picardy, but the heiress was a pox-faced slattern and the Count of Armorica was besotted by Jeanette's beauty and so he defied his uncle.

He married the merchant's daughter in the chapel of his castle at Plabennec, which lay in Finisterre, the world's end. The Duke reckoned his nephew had listened to too many troubadours, but the Count and his new wife were happy and a year after their wedding, when Jeanette was sixteen, their son was born. They named him Charles, after the Duke, but if the Duke was complimented, he said nothing. He refused to receive Jeanette again and treated his nephew coldly.

Later that same year the English came in force to support Jean de Montfort, whom they recognized as the Duke of Brittany, and the King of France sent reinforcements to his nephew Charles, whom he recognized as the real Duke, and so the civil war began in earnest. The Count of Armorica insisted that his wife and baby son went back to her father's house in La Roche-Derrien because the castle at Plabennec was small, in ill repair and too close to the invader's forces.

That summer the castle fell to the English just as Jeanette's husband had feared, and the following year the King of England spent the campaigning season in Brittany, and his army pushed back the forces of Charles, Duke of Brittany. There was no one great battle, but a series of bloody skirmishes, and in one of them, a ragged affair fought between the hedgerows of a steep valley, Jeanette's husband was wounded. He had lifted the face-piece of his helmet to shout encouragement to his men and an arrow had gone clean through his mouth. His servants brought the Count to the house beside the River Jaudy where he took five days to die; five days of constant pain during which he was unable to eat and scarce able to breathe as the wound festered and the blood congealed in his gullet.

He was twenty-eight years old, a champion of tournaments, and he wept like a child at the end. He choked to death and Jeanette screamed in frustrated anger and grief.

Then began Jeanette's time of sorrow. She was a widow, *la veuve Chenier*, and not six months after her husband's death she became an orphan when both her parents died of the bloody flux. She was just eighteen and her son, the Count of Armorica, was two, but Jeanette had inherited her father's wealth and she determined to use it to strike back at the hated English who had killed her husband, and so she began outfitting two ships that could prey on English shipping.

Monsieur Belas, who had been her father's lawyer, advised against spending money on the ships. Jeanette's fortune would not last for ever, the lawyer said, and nothing soaked up cash like outfitting warships that rarely made money, unless by luck. Better, he said, to use the ships for trade. 'The merchants in Lannion are making a fine profit on Spanish wine,' he suggested. He had a cold, for it was winter, and he sneezed. 'A very fine profit,' he said wistfully. He spoke in Breton, though both he and Jeanette could, if needs be, speak French.

'I do not want Spanish wine,' Jeanette said coldly, 'but English souls.'

'No profit in those, my lady,' Belas said. He found it strange to call Jeanette 'my lady'. He had known her since she was a child, and she had always been little Jeanette to him, but she had married and become an aristocratic widow, and a widow, moreover, with a temper. 'You cannot sell English souls,' Belas pointed out mildly.

'Except to the devil,' Jeanette said, crossing herself. 'But I don't need Spanish wine, Belas. We have the rents.'

'The rents!' Belas said mockingly. He was tall, thin, scanty-haired and clever. He had served Jeanette's father well and long, and was resentful that the merchant had left him nothing in his will. Everything had gone to Jeanette except for a small bequest to the monks at Pontrieux so they would say Masses for the dead man's soul. Belas hid his resentment. 'Nothing comes from Plabennec,' he told Jeanette. 'The English are there, and how long do you think the rents will come from your father's farms? The English will take them soon.' An English army had occupied unwalled Tréguier, which was only an hour's walk northwards, and they had pulled down the cathedral tower there because some crossbowmen had shot at them from its summit. Belas hoped the English would retreat soon, for it was deep in the winter and their supplies must be running low, but he feared they might ravage the countryside about La Roche-Derrien before they left. And if they did, Jeanette's farms would be left worthless. 'How much rent can you get from a burned farm?' he asked her.

'I don't care!' she snapped. 'I shall sell everything if I have to, everything!' Except for her husband's armour and weapons. They were precious and would go to her son one day.

Belas sighed for her foolishness, then huddled in his black cloak and leaned close to the small fire which spat in the hearth. A cold wind came from the nearby sea, making the chimney smoke. 'You will permit me, madame, to offer you advice? First, the business.' Belas paused to wipe his nose on his long black sleeve. 'It ails, but I can find you a good man to run it as your father did, and I would draw up a contract which would ensure the man would pay you well from the profits. Second, madame, you should think of marriage.' He paused, half expecting a protest, but Jeanette said nothing. Belas sighed. She was so lovely! There were a dozen men in town who would marry her, but marriage to an aristocrat had turned her head and she would settle for nothing less than another titled man. 'You are, madame,' the lawyer continued carefully, 'a widow who possesses, at the moment, a considerable fortune, but I have seen such fortunes drain away like snow in April. Find a man who can look after you, your possessions and your son.'

Jeanette turned and stared at him. 'I married the finest man in Christendom,' she said, 'and where do you think I will find another like him?'

Men like the Count of Armorica, the lawyer thought, were found everywhere, more was the pity, for what were they but brute fools in armour who believed war was a sport? Jeanette, he thought, should marry a prudent merchant, perhaps a widower who had a fortune, but he suspected such advice would be wasted. 'Remember the old saying, my lady,' he said slyly. 'Put a cat to watch a flock and the wolves eat well.'

Jeanette shuddered with anger at the words. 'You go beyond yourself, Monsieur Belas.' She spoke icily, then dismissed him, and the next day the English came to La Roche-Derrien and Jeanette took her dead husband's crossbow from the place where she hid her wealth and she joined the defenders on the walls. Damn Belas's advice! She would fight like a man and Duke Charles, who despised her, would learn to admire her, to support her and restore her dead husband's estates to her son.

So Jeanette had become the Blackbird and the English had died in front of her walls and Belas's advice was forgotten, and now, Jeanette reckoned, the town's defenders had so rattled the English that the siege would surely be lifted. All would be well, in which belief, for the first time in a week, the Blackbird slept well.

Thomas crouched beside the river. He had broken through a stand of alders to reach the bank where he now pulled off his boots and hose. Best to go barelegged, he reckoned, so the boots did not get stuck in the river mud. It was going to be cold, freezing cold, but he could not remember a time when he had been happier. He liked this life, and his memories of Hookton, Oxford and his father had almost faded.

'Take your boots off,' he told the twenty archers who would accompany him, 'and hang your arrow bags round your necks.'

'Why?' someone challenged him from the dark.

'So it bloody throttles you,' Thomas growled.

'So your arrows don't get wet,' another man explained helpfully.

Thomas tied his own bag round his neck. Archers did not carry the quivers that hunters used, for quivers were open at the top and their arrows could fall out when a man ran or stumbled or clambered through a hedge. Arrows in quivers got wet when it rained, and wet feathers made arrows fly crooked, so real archers used linen bags that were water-proofed with wax and sealed by laces. The bags were bolstered by withy frames that spread the linen so the feathers were not crushed.

Will Skeat edged down the bank where a dozen men were stacking the hurdles. He shivered in the cold wind that came from the water. The sky to the east was still dark, but some light came from the watch fires that burned within La Roche-Derrien.

'They're nice and quiet in there,' Skeat said, nodding towards the town.

'Pray they're sleeping,' Thomas said.

'In beds too. I've forgotten what a bed's like,' Skeat said, then edged aside to let another man through to the riverbank. Thomas was surprised to see it was Sir Simon Jekyll, who had been so scornful of him in the Earl's tent. 'Sir Simon,' Will Skeat said, barely bothering to disguise his own scorn, 'wants a word with thee.'

Sir Simon wrinkled his nose at the stench of the river mud. Much of it, he supposed, was the town's sewage and he was glad he was not wading barelegged through the muck.

'You are confident of passing the stakes?' he asked Thomas.

'I wouldn't be going otherwise,' Thomas said, not bothering to sound respectful.

Thomas's tone made Sir Simon bridle, but he controlled his temper. 'The Earl,' he said distantly, 'has given me the honour of leading the attack on the walls.' He stopped abruptly and Thomas waited, expecting more, but Sir Simon merely looked at him with an irritated face.

'So Thomas takes the walls,' Skeat finally spoke, 'to make it safe for your ladders?'

'What I do not want,' Sir Simon ignored Skeat and spoke to Thomas, 'is for you to take your men ahead

69

of mine into the town itself. We see armed men, we're likely to kill them, you understand?'

Thomas almost spat in derision. His men would be armed with bows and no enemy carried a long-stave bow like the English so there was hardly any chance of being mistaken for the town's defenders, but he held his tongue. He just nodded.

'You and your archers can join our attack,' Sir Simon went on, 'but you will be under my command.'

Thomas nodded again and Sir Simon, irritated by the implied insolence, turned on his heel and walked away.

'Goddamn bastard,' Thomas said.

'He just wants to get his nose into the trough ahead of the rest of us,' Skeat said.

'You're letting the bastard use our ladders?' Thomas asked.

'If he wants to be first up, let him. Ladders are green wood, Tom, and if they break I'd rather it was him tumbling than me. Besides, I reckon we'll be better off following you through the river, but I ain't telling Sir Simon that.' Skeat grinned, then swore as a crash sounded from the darkness south of the river. 'Those bloody white rats,' Skeat said, and vanished into the shadows.

The white rats were the Bretons loyal to Duke John, men who wore his badge of a white ermine, and some sixty Breton crossbowmen had been attached to Skeat's soldiers, their job to rattle the walls with their bolts as the ladders were placed against the ramparts. It was those men who had startled the night with their noise and now the noise grew even louder. Some fool had tripped in the dark and thumped a crossbowman with a pavise, the huge shield behind which the crossbows

70

were laboriously reloaded, and the crossbowman struck back, and suddenly the white rats were having a brawl in the dark. The defenders, naturally, heard them and started to hurl burning bales of straw over the ramparts and then a church bell began to toll, then another, and all this long before Thomas had even started across the mud.

Sir Simon Jekyll, alarmed by the bells and the burning straw, shouted that the attack must go in now. 'Carry the ladders forward!' he bellowed. Defenders were running onto La Roche-Derrien's walls and the first crossbow bolts were spitting off the ramparts that were lit bright by the burning bales.

'Hold those goddamn ladders!' Will Skeat snarled at his men, then looked at Thomas. 'What do you reckon?'

'I think the bastards are distracted,' Thomas said.

'So you'll go?'

'Got nothing better to do, Will.'

'Bloody white rats!'

Thomas led his men onto the mud. The hurdles were some help, but not as much as he had hoped, so that they still slipped and struggled their way towards the great stakes and Thomas reckoned the noise they made was enough to wake King Arthur and his knights. But the defenders were making even more noise. Every church bell was clanging, a trumpet was screaming, men were shouting, dogs barking, cockerels were crowing, and the crossbows were creaking and banging as their cords were inched back and released.

The walls loomed to Thomas's right. He wondered if the Blackbird was up there. He had seen her twice now and been captivated by the fierceness of her face and her wild black hair. A score of other archers had seen her too, and all of them men who could thread an arrow through a bracelet at a hundred paces, yet the woman still lived. Amazing, Thomas thought, what a pretty face could do.

He threw down the last hurdle and so reached the wooden stakes, each one a whole tree trunk sunk into the mud. His men joined him and they heaved against the timber until the rotted wood split like straw. The stakes made a terrible noise as they fell, but it was drowned by the uproar in the town. Jake, the cross-eyed murderer from Exeter gaol, pulled himself alongside Thomas. To their right now was a wooden quay with a rough ladder at one end. Dawn was coming and a feeble, thin, grey light was seeping from the east to outline the bridge across the Jaudy. It was a handsome stone bridge with a barbican at its further end, and Thomas feared the garrison of that tower might see them, but no one called an alarm and no crossbow bolts thumped across the river.

Thomas and Jake were first up the quay ladder, then came Sam, the youngest of Skeat's archers. The wooden landing stage served a timberyard and a dog began barking frantically among the stacked trunks, but Sam slipped into the blackness with his knife and the barking suddenly stopped. 'Good doggy,' Sam said as he came back.

'String your bows,' Thomas said. He had looped the hemp cord onto his own black weapon and now untied the laces of his arrow bag.

'I hate bloody dogs,' Sam said. 'One bit my mother when she was pregnant with me.'

'That's why you're daft,' Jake said.

'Shut your goddamn faces,' Thomas ordered. More archers were climbing the quay, which was swaying alarmingly, but he could see that the walls he was supposed to capture were thick with defenders now. English arrows, their white goose feathers bright in the flamelight of the defenders' fires, flickered over the wall and thumped into the town's thatched roofs. 'Maybe we should open the south gate,' Thomas suggested.

'Go through the town?' Jake asked in alarm.

'It's a small town,' Thomas said.

'You're mad,' Jake said, but he was grinning and he meant the words as a compliment.

'I'm going anyway,' Thomas said. It would be dark in the streets and their long bows would be hidden. He reckoned it would be safe enough.

A dozen men followed Thomas while the rest started plundering the nearer buildings. More and more men were coming through the broken stakes now as Will Skeat sent them down the riverbank rather than wait for the wall to be captured. The defenders had seen the men in the mud and were shooting down from the end of the town wall, but the first attackers were already loose in the streets.

Thomas blundered through the town. It was pitch-black in the alleys and hard to tell where he was going, though by climbing the hill on which the town was built he reckoned he must eventually go over the summit and so down to the southern gate. Men ran past him, but no one could see that he and his companions were English. The church bells were deafening. Children were crying, dogs howling, gulls screaming, and the noise was making Thomas terrified. This was a daft idea, he thought. Maybe Sir Simon had already climbed the walls? Maybe he was wasting his time? Yet white-feathered arrows still thumped into the town roofs, suggesting the walls were untaken, and so he forced himself to keep going. Twice he found himself in a blind alley and the second time, doubling back into a wider street, he almost ran into a priest who had come from his church to fix a flaming torch in a wall bracket.

'Go to the ramparts!' the priest said sternly, then saw the long bows in the men's hands and opened his mouth to shout the alarm.

He never had time to shout for Thomas's bow stave slammed point-first into his belly. He bent over, gasping, and Jake casually slit his throat. The priest gurgled as he sank to the cobbles and Jake frowned when the noise stopped.

'I'll go to hell for that,' he said.

'You're going to hell anyway,' Sam said, 'we all are.'

'We're all going to heaven,' Thomas said, 'but not if we dawdle.' He suddenly felt much less frightened, as though the priest's death had taken his fear. An arrow struck the church tower and dropped into the alley as Thomas led his men past the church and found himself on La Roche-Derrien's main street, which dropped down to where a watch fire burned by the southern gate. Thomas shrank back into the alley beside the church, for the street was thick with men, but they were all running to the threatened side of the town, and when Thomas next looked the hill was empty. He could only see two sentinels on the ramparts above the gate arch. He told his men about the two sentries.

'They're going to be scared as hell,' he said. 'We kill the bastards and open the gate.'

'There might be others,' Sam said. 'There'll be a guard house.'

'Then kill them too,' Thomas said. 'Now, come on!'

They stepped into the street, ran down a few yards and there drew their bows. The arrows flew and the two guards on the arch fell. A man stepped out of the guard house built into the gate turret and gawped at the archers, but before any could draw their bows he stepped back inside and barred the door.

'It's ours!' Thomas shouted, and led his men in a wild rush to the arch.

The guard house stayed locked so there was no one to stop the archers from lifting the bar and pushing open the two great gates. The Earl's men saw the gates open, saw the English archers outlined against the watch fire and gave a great roar from the darkness that told Thomas a torrent of vengeful troops was coming towards him.

Which meant La Roche-Derrien's time of weeping could begin. For the English had taken the town.

Jeanette woke to a church bell ringing as though it was the world's doom when the dead were rising from their graves and the gates of hell were yawning wide for sinners. Her first instinct was to cross to her son's bed, but little Charles was safe. She could just see his eyes in the dark that was scarcely alleviated by the glowing embers of the fire.

'Mama?' he cried, reaching up to her.

'Quiet,' she hushed the boy, then ran to throw open the shutters. A faint grey light showed above the eastern roofs, then steps sounded in the street and she leaned from the window to see men running from their houses with swords, crossbows and spears. A trumpet was calling from the town centre, then more church bells began tolling the alarm into a dying night. The bell of the church of the Virgin was cracked and made a harsh, anvil-like noise that was all the more terrifying.

'Madame!' a servant cried as she ran into the room.

'The English must be attacking.' Jeanette forced herself to speak calmly. She was wearing nothing but a linen shift and was suddenly cold. She snatched up a cloak, tied it about her neck, then took her son into her arms. 'You will be all right, Charles,' she tried to console him. 'The English are attacking again, that is all.'

Except she was not sure. The bells were sounding so wild. It was not the measured tolling that was the usual signal of attack, but a panicked clangour as though the men hauling the ropes were trying to repel an attack by their own efforts. She looked from the window again and saw the English arrows flitting across the roofs. She could hear them thumping into the thatch. The children of the town thought it was a fine sport to retrieve the enemy arrows and two had injured themselves sliding from the roofs. Jeanette thought about getting dressed, but decided she must find out what was happening first so she gave Charles to the servant, then ran downstairs.

One of the kitchen servants met her at the back door. 'What's happening, madame?'

'Another attack, that is all.'

She unbarred the door to the yard, then ran to the private entrance to Renan's church just as an arrow struck the church tower and clattered down into the yard. She pulled open the tower door, then groped up the steep ladders that her father had built. It had not been mere piety that had inspired Louis Halevy to construct the tower, but also the opportunity to look down-river to see if his boats were approaching, and the high stone parapet offered one of the best views in La Roche-Derrien. Jeanette was deafened by the church bell that swung in the gloom, each clapper stroke thumping her ears like a physical blow. She climbed past the bell, pushed open the trapdoor at the top of the ladders and clambered onto the leads.

The English had come. She could see a torrent of men flowing about the river edge of the wall. They waded through the mud and swarmed over the broken stakes like a torrent of rats. Sweet Mother of Christ, she thought, sweet Mother of Christ, but they were in the town! She hurried down the ladders. 'They're here!' she called to the priest who hauled the bell rope. 'They're in the town!'

'Havoc! Havoc!' the English shouted, the call that encouraged them to plunder.

Jeanette ran across the yard and up the stairs. She pulled her clothes from the cupboard, then turned when the voices shouted havoc beneath her window. She forgot her clothes and took Charles back into her arms. 'Mother of God,' she prayed, 'look after us now, look after us. Sweet Mother of God, keep us safe.' She wept, not knowing what to do. Charles cried because she was holding him too tight and she tried to soothe him. Cheers sounded in the street and she ran back to the window and saw what looked like a dark river studded with steel flowing towards the town centre. She collapsed by the window, sobbing. Charles was screaming. Two more servants were in the room, somehow think-ing that Jeanette could shelter them, but there was no shelter now. The English had come. One of the servants shot the bolt on the bedroom door, but what good would that do?

Jeanette thought of her husband's hidden weapons and of the Spanish sword's sharp edge, and wondered if she would have the courage to place the point against her breast and heave her body onto the blade. It would be better to die than be dishonoured, she thought, but then what would happen to her son? She wept helplessly, then heard someone beating on the big gate which led to her courtyard. An axe, she supposed, and she listened to its crunching blows that seemed to shake the whole house. A woman screamed in the town, then another, and the English voices cheered rampantly. One by one the church bells fell silent until only the cracked bell hammered its fear across the roofs. The axe still bit at the door. Would they recognize her, she wondered. She had exulted in standing on the ramparts, shooting her husband's crossbow at the besiegers, and her right shoulder was bruised because of it, but she had welcomed the pain, believing that every bolt fired made it less likely that the English would break into the town.

No one had thought they could. And why besiege La Roche-Derrien anyway? It had nothing to offer. As a port it was almost useless, for the largest ships could not make it up the river even at the top of the tide. The English, the townspeople had believed, were making a petulant demonstration and would soon give up and slink away.

But now they were here, and Jeanette screamed as the sound of the axe blows changed. They had broken through, and doubtless were trying to lift the bar. She closed her eyes, shaking as she heard the gate scrape on the cobbles. It was open. It was open. Oh, Mother of God, she prayed, be with us now.

The screams sounded downstairs. Feet thumped on the stairs. Men's voices shouted in a strange tongue.

Be with us now and at the hour of our death for the English had come.

Sir Simon Jekyll was annoyed. He had been prepared to climb the ladders if Skeat's archers ever gained the walls, which he doubted, but if the ramparts were captured then he intended to be first into the town. He foresaw cutting down a few panicked defenders then finding some great house to plunder.

But nothing happened as he had imagined it. The town was awake, the wall manned, and the ladders never went forward, but Skeat's men still got inside by simply wading through the mud at the river's edge. Then a cheer at the southern side of the town suggested that gate was open, which meant that the whole damned army was getting into La Roche-Derrien ahead of Sir Simon. He swore. There would be nothing left!

'My lord?' One of his men-at-arms prompted Sir Simon, wanting a decision as to how they were to reach the women and valuables beyond the walls, which were emptying of their defenders as men ran to protect their homes and families. It would have been quicker, far quicker, to have waded through the mud, but Sir Simon did not want to dirty his new boots and so he ordered the ladders forward.

The ladders were made of green wood and the rungs bent alarmingly as Sir Simon climbed, but there were no defenders to oppose him and the ladder held. He clambered into an embrasure and drew his sword. A half-dozen defenders lay spitted with arrows on the rampart. Two were still alive and Sir Simon stabbed the nearest one. The man had been roused from his bed and had no mail, not even a leather coat, yet still the old sword made hard work of the killing stroke. It was not designed for stabbing, but for cutting. The new swords, made from the finest southern European steel, were renowned for their ability to pierce mail and leather, but this ancient blade required all Sir Simon's brute force to penetrate a rib cage. And what chance, he wondered sourly, would there be of finding a better weapon in this sorry excuse for a town?

There was a flight of stone steps down into a street that was thronged by English archers and men-at-arms smeared with mud to their thighs. They were breaking into houses. One man was carrying a dead goose, another had a bolt of cloth. The plundering had begun and Sir Simon was still on the ramparts. He shouted at his men to hurry and when enough of them had gathered on the wall's top, he led them down into the street. An archer was rolling a barrel from a cellar door, another dragged a girl by an arm. Where to go? That was Sir Simon's problem. The nearest houses were all being sacked, and the cheers from the south suggested the Earl's main army was descending on that part of the town. Some townsfolk, realizing all was lost, were fleeing in front of the archers to cross the bridge and escape into the countryside.

Sir Simon decided to strike east. The Earl's men were to the south, Skeat's were staying close to the west wall so the eastern quarter offered the best hope of plunder. He pushed past Skeat's muddy archers and led his men towards the bridge. Frightened people ran past him, ignoring him and hoping he would ignore them. He crossed the main street, which led to the bridge, and saw a roadway running alongside the big houses that fronted the river. Merchants, Sir Simon thought, fat merchants with fat profits, and then, in the growing light, he saw an archway that was surmounted by a coat of arms. A noble's house.

'Who has an axe?' he asked his men.

One of the men-at-arms stepped forward and Sir Simon indicated the heavy gate. The house had windows on the ground floor, but they were covered by heavy iron bars, which seemed a good sign. Sir Simon stepped back to let his man start work on the gate.

The axeman knew his business. He chopped a hole where he guessed the locking bar was, and when he had broken through he put a hand inside and pushed the bar up and out of its brackets so that Sir Simon and his archers could heave the gates open. Sir Simon left two men to guard the gate, ordering them to keep every other plunderer out of the property, then led the rest into the yard. The first things he saw were two boats tied at the river's quay. They were not large ships, but all hulls were valuable and he ordered four of his archers to go aboard.

'Tell anyone who comes that they're mine, you understand? Mine!'

He had a choice now: storerooms or house? And a stable? He told two men-at-arms to find the stable and stand guard on whatever horses were there, then he kicked in the house door and led his six remaining men into the kitchen. Two women screamed. He ignored them; they were old, ugly servants and he was after richer things. A door led from the back of the kitchen and he pointed one of his archers towards it, then, holding his sword ahead of him, he went through a small dark hall into a front room. A tapestry showing Bacchus, the god of wine, hung on one wall and Sir Simon had an idea that valuables were sometimes hidden behind such wall-coverings so he hacked at it with his blade, then hauled it down from its hooks, but there was only a plaster wall behind. He kicked the chairs, then saw a chest that had a huge dark padlock.

'Get it open,' he ordered two of his archers, 'and whatever's inside is mine.' Then, ignoring two books which were of no use to man or beast, he went back into the hall and ran up a flight of dark wooden stairs.

Sir Simon found a door leading to a room at the front of the house. It was bolted and a woman screamed from the other side when he tried to force the door. He stood back and used the heel of his boot, smashing the bolt on the far side and slamming the door back on its hinges. Then he stalked inside, his old sword glittering in the dawn's wan light, and he saw a black-haired woman.

Sir Simon considered himself a practical man. His father, quite sensibly, had not wanted his son to waste time on education, though Sir Simon had learned to read and could, at a pinch, write a letter. He liked useful things – hounds and weapons, horses and armour – and he despised the fashionable cult of gentility. His mother was a great one for troubadours, and was forever listening to songs of knights so gentle that Sir Simon reckoned they would not have lasted two minutes in a tourney's mêlée. The songs and poems celebrated love as though it was some rare thing that gave a life enchantment, but Sir Simon did not need poets to define love, which to him was tumbling a peasant girl in a harvest field or thrusting at some ale-reeking whore in a tavern, but when he saw the black-haired woman he suddenly understood what the troubadours had been celebrating.

It did not matter that the woman was shaking with fear or that her hair was wildly awry or that her face was streaked with tears. Sir Simon recognized beauty and it struck him like an arrow. It took his breath away. So this, then, was love! It was the realization that he could never be happy until this woman was his – and that was convenient, for she was an enemy, the town was being sacked and Sir Simon, clad in mail and fury, had found her first.

'Get out!' he snarled at the servants in the room. 'Get out!'

The servants fled in tears and Sir Simon booted the broken door shut, then advanced on the woman, who crouched beside her son's bed with the boy in her arms.

'Who are you?' Sir Simon asked in French.

The woman tried to sound brave. 'I am the Countess of Armorica,' she said. 'And you, monsieur?'

Sir Simon was tempted to award himself a peerage to impress Jeanette, but he was too slow-witted and so heard himself uttering his proper name. He was slowly becoming aware that the room betrayed wealth. The bed hangings were thickly embroidered, the candlesticks were of heavy silver and the walls either side of the stone hearth were expensively panelled in beautifully carved wood. He pushed the smaller bed against the door, reckoning that should ensure some privacy, then went to warm himself at the fire. He tipped more sea-coal onto the small flames and held his chilled gloves close to the heat.

'This is your house, madame?'

'It is.'

'Not your husband's?'

'I am a widow,' Jeanette said.

A wealthy widow! Sir Simon almost crossed himself out of gratitude. The widows he had met in England had been rouged hags, but this one . . . ! This one was different. This one was a woman worthy of a tournament's champion and seemed rich enough to save him from the ignominy of losing his estate and knightly rank. She might even have enough cash to buy a baronage. Maybe an earldom?

He turned from the fire and smiled at her. 'Are those your boats at the quay?'

'Yes, monsieur.'

'By the rules of war, madame, they are now mine. Everything here is mine.'

Jeanette frowned at that. 'What rules?'

'The law of the sword, madame, but I think you are fortunate. I shall offer you my protection.'

Jeanette sat on the edge of her curtained bed, clutching Charles. 'The rules of chivalry, my lord,' she said, 'ensure my protection.' She flinched as a woman screamed in a nearby house.

'Chivalry?' Sir Simon asked. 'Chivalry? I have heard it mentioned in songs, madame, but this is a war. Our task is to punish the followers of Charles of Blois for rebelling against their lawful lord. Punishment and chivalry do not mix.' He frowned at her. 'You're the Blackbird!' he said, suddenly recognizing her in the light of the revived fire.

'The blackbird?' Jeanette did not understand.

'You fought us from the walls! You scratched my

arm!' Sir Simon did not sound angry, but astonished. He had expected to be furious when he met the Blackbird, but her reality was too overpowering for rage. He grinned. 'You closed your eyes when you shot the crossbow, that's why you missed.'

'I did not miss!' Jeanette said indignantly.

'A scratch,' Sir Simon said, showing her the rent in his mail sleeve. 'But why, madame, do you fight for the false duke?'

'My husband,' she said stiffly, 'was nephew to Duke Charles.'

Sweet God, Sir Simon thought, sweet God! A prize indeed. He bowed to her. 'So your son,' he said, nodding at Charles, who was peering anxiously from his mother's arms, 'is the present Count?'

'He is,' Jeanette confirmed,

'A fine boy.' Sir Simon forced himself to the flattery. In truth he thought Charles was a pudding-faced nuisance whose presence inhibited him from a natural urge to thrust the Blackbird onto her back and thus show her the realities of war, but he was acutely aware that this widow was an aristocrat, a beauty, and related to Charles of Blois, who was nephew to the King of France. This woman meant riches and Sir Simon's present necessity was to make her see that her best interest lay in sharing his ambitions. 'A fine boy, madame,' he went on, 'who needs a father.'

Jeanette just stared at him. Sir Simon had a blunt face. It was bulbous-nosed, firm-chinned, and showed not the slightest sign of intelligence or wit. He had confidence, though, enough to have persuaded himself that she would marry him. Did he really mean that? She gaped, then gave a startled cry as angry shouting erupted beneath her window. Some archers were trying to get past the men guarding the gate. Sir Simon pushed open the window. 'This place is mine,' he snarled in English. 'Go find your own chickens to pluck.' He turned back to Jeanette. 'You see, madame, how I protect you?'

'So there is chivalry in war?'

'There is opportunity in war, madame. You are wealthy, you are a widow, you need a man.'

She gazed at him with disturbingly large eyes, hardly daring to believe his temerity. 'Why?' she asked simply.

'Why?' Sir Simon was astonished by the question. He gestured at the window. 'Listen to the screams, woman! What do you think happens to women when a town falls?'

'But you said you would protect me,' she pointed out.

'So I will.' He was getting lost in this conversation. The woman, he thought, though beautiful, was remarkably stupid. 'I will protect you,' he said, 'and you will look after me.'

'How?'

Sir Simon sighed. 'You have money?'

Jeanette shrugged. 'There is a little downstairs, my lord, hidden in the kitchen.'

Sir Simon frowned angrily. Did she think he was a fool? That he would take that bait and go downstairs, leaving her to climb out of the window? 'I know one thing about money, madame,' he said, 'and that is that you never hide it where the servants can find it. You hide it in the private rooms. In a bedchamber.' He pulled open a chest and emptied its linens onto the floor, but there was nothing hidden there, and then, on an inspiration, he began rapping the wooden panelling. He had heard that such panels often concealed a hiding place and he was rewarded almost instantly by a satisfyingly hollow sound.

'No, monsieur!' Jeanette said.

Sir Simon ignored her, drawing his sword and hacking at the limewood panels that splintered and pulled away from their beams. He sheathed the blade and tugged with his gloved hands at the shattered wood.

'No!' Jeanette wailed.

Sir Simon stared. Money was concealed behind the panelling, a whole barrel of coins, but that was not the prize. The prize was a suit of armour and a set of weapons such as Sir Simon had only ever dreamed of. A shining suit of plate armour, each piece chased with subtle engravings and inlaid with gold. Italian work? And the sword! When he drew it from the scabbard it was like holding Excalibur itself. There was a blue sheen to the blade, which was not nearly as heavy as his own sword but felt miraculously balanced. A blade from the famous swordsmiths of Poitiers, perhaps, or, even better, Spanish?

'They belonged to my husband,' Jeanette appealed to him, 'and it is all I have of his. They must go to Charles.'

Sir Simon ignored her. He traced his gloved finger down the gold inlay on the breastplate. That piece alone was worth an estate!

'They are all he has of his father's,' Jeanette pleaded.

Sir Simon unbuckled his sword belt and let the old weapon drop to the floor, then fastened the Count of Armorica's sword about his waist. He turned and stared at Jeanette, marvelling at her smooth unscarred face. These were the spoils of war that he had dreamed about and had begun to fear would never come his way: a barrel of cash, a suit of armour fit for a king, a blade made for a champion and a woman that would be the envy of England. 'The armour is mine,' he said, 'as is the sword.'

'No, monsieur, please.'

'What will you do? Buy them from me?'

'If I must,' Jeanette said, nodding at the barrel.

'That too is mine, madame,' Sir Simon said, and to prove it he strode to the door, unblocked it and shouted for two of his archers to come up the stairs. He gestured at the barrel and the suit of armour. 'Take them down,' he said, 'and keep them safe. And don't think I haven't counted the cash, because I have. Now go!'

Jeanette watched the theft. She wanted to weep for pity, but forced herself to stay calm. 'If you steal everything I own,' she said to Sir Simon, 'how can I buy the armour back?'

Sir Simon shoved the boy's bed against the door again, then favoured her with a smile. 'There is something you can use to buy the armour, my dear,' he said winningly. 'You have what all women have. You can use that.'

Jeanette closed her eyes for a few heartbeats. 'Are all the gentlemen of England like you?' she asked.

'Few are so skilled in arms,' Sir Simon said proudly.

He was about to tell her of his tournament triumphs, sure that she would be impressed, but she interrupted him. 'I meant,' she said icily, 'to discover whether the knights of England are all thieves, poltroons and bullies.'

Sir Simon was genuinely puzzled by the insult. The woman simply did not seem to appreciate her good fortune, a failing he could only ascribe to innate stupidity. 'You forget, madame,' he explained, 'that the winners of war get the prizes.'

'I am your prize?'

She was worse than stupid. Sir Simon thought, but who wanted cleverness in a woman? 'Madame,' he said, 'I am your protector. If I leave you, if I take away my protection, then there will be a line of men on the stairs waiting to plough you. Now do you understand?'

'I think,' she said coldly, 'that the Earl of Northampton will offer me better protection.'

Sweet Christ, Sir Simon thought, but the bitch was obtuse. It was pointless trying to reason with her for she was too dull to understand, so he must force the breach. He crossed the room fast, snatched Charles from her arms and threw the boy onto the smaller bed. Jeanette cried out and tried to hit him, but Sir Simon caught her arm and slapped her face with his gloved hand and, when she went immobile with pain and astonishment, he tore her cloak's cords apart and then, with his big hands, ripped the shift down the front of her body. She screamed and tried to clutch her hands over her nakedness, but Sir Simon forced her arms apart and stared in astonishment. Flawless!

'No!' Jeanette wept.

Sir Simon shoved her hard back onto the bed. 'You want your son to inherit your traitorous husband's armour?' he asked. 'Or his sword? Then, madame, you had better be kind to their new owner. I am prepared to be kind to you.' He unbuckled the sword, dropped it on the floor, then hitched up his mail coat and fumbled with the strings of his hose.

'No!' Jeanette wailed, and tried to scramble off the

bed, but Sir Simon caught hold of her shift and yanked the linen so that it came down to her waist. The boy was screaming and Sir Simon was fumbling with his rusted gauntlets and Jeanette felt the devil had come into her house. She tried to cover her nakedness, but the Englishman slapped her face again, then once more hauled up his mail coat. Outside the window the cracked bell of the Virgin's church was at last silent, for the English had come, Jeanette had a suitor and the town wept.

Thomas's first thought after opening the gate was not plunder, but somewhere to wash the river muck off his legs, which he did with a barrel of ale in the first tavern he encountered. The tavern-keeper was a big bald man who stupidly attacked the English archers with a club, so Jake tripped him with his bowstave, then slit his belly.

'Silly bastard,' Jake said. 'I wasn't going to hurt him. Much.'

The dead man's boots fitted Thomas, which was a welcome surprise, for very few did, and once they had found his cache of coins they went in search of other amusement. The Earl of Northampton was spurring his horse up and down the main street, shouting at wild-eyed men not to set the town alight. He wanted to keep La Roche-Derrien as a fortress, and it was less useful to him as a heap of ashes.

Not everyone plundered. Some of the older men, even a few of the younger, were disgusted by the whole business and attempted to curb the wilder excesses, but they were wildly outnumbered by men who saw nothing but opportunity in the fallen town. Father Hobbe, an English priest who had a fondness for Will Skeat's men, tried to persuade Thomas and his group to guard a church, but they had other pleasures in mind. 'Don't spoil your soul, Tom,' Father Hobbe said in a reminder that Thomas, like all the men, had said Mass the day before, but Thomas reckoned his soul was going to be spoiled anyway so it might as well happen sooner than later. He was looking for a girl, any girl really, for most of Will's men had a woman in camp. Thomas had been living with a sweet little Breton, but she had caught a fever just before the beginning of the winter campaign and Father Hobbe had said a funeral Mass for her. Thomas had watched as the girl's unshrouded body had thumped into the shallow grave and he had thought of the graves at Hookton and of the promise he had made to his dying father, but then he had pushed the promise away. He was young and had no appetite for burdens on his conscience.

La Roche-Derrien now crouched under the English fury. Men tore down thatch and wrecked furniture in their search for money. Any townsman who tried to protect his women was killed, while any woman who tried to protect herself was beaten into submission. Some folk had escaped the sack by crossing the bridge, but the small garrison of the barbican fled from the inevitable attack and now the Earl's men-at-arms manned the small tower and that meant La Roche-Derrien was sealed to its fate. Some women took refuge in the churches and the lucky ones found protectors there, but most were not lucky.

Thomas, Jake and Sam finally discovered an unplundered house that belonged to a tanner, a stinking fellow with an ugly wife and three small children. Sam, whose innocent face made strangers trust him on sight, held his knife at the throat of the youngest child and the tanner suddenly remembered where he had hidden his cash. Thomas had watched Sam, fearing he really would slit the boy's throat, for Sam, despite his ruddy cheeks and cheerful eyes, was as evil as any man in Will Skeat's band. Jake was not much better, though Thomas counted both as friends.

'The man's as poor as we are,' Jake said in wonderment as he raked through the tanner's coins. He pushed a third of the pile towards Thomas. 'You want his wife?' Jake offered generously.

'Christ, no! She's cross-eyed like you.'

'Is she?'

Thomas left Jake and Sam to their games and went to find a tavern where there would be food, drink and warmth. He reckoned any girl worth pursuing had been caught already, so he unstrung his bow, pushed past a group of men tearing the contents from a parked wagon and found an inn where a motherly widow had sensibly protected both her property and her daughters by welcoming the first men-at-arms, showering them with free food and ale, then scolding them for dirtying her floor with their muddy feet. She was shouting at them now, though few understood what she said, and one of the men growled at Thomas that she and her daughters were to be left alone.

Thomas held up his hands to show he meant no harm, then took a plate of bread, eggs and cheese. 'Now pay her,' one of the men-at-arms growled, and Thomas dutifully put the tanner's few coins on the counter.

'He's a good-looking one,' the widow said to her daughters, who giggled.

Thomas turned and pretended to inspect the daughters. 'They are the most beautiful girls in Brittany,' he said to the widow in French, 'because they take after you, madame.'

That compliment, though patently untrue, raised squeals of laughter. Beyond the tavern were screams and tears, but inside it was warm and friendly. Thomas ate the food hungrily, then tried to hide himself in a window bay when Father Hobbe came bustling in from the street. The priest saw Thomas anyway.

'I'm still looking for men to guard the churches, Thomas.'

'I'm going to get drunk, father,' Thomas said happily. 'So goddamn drunk that one of those two girls will look attractive.' He jerked his head at the widow's daughters.

Father Hobbe inspected them critically, then sighed. 'You'll kill yourself if you drink that much, Thomas.' He sat at the table, waved at the girls and pointed at Thomas's pot. 'I'll have a drink with you,' the priest said.

'What about the churches?'

'Everyone will be drunk soon enough,' Father Hobbe said, 'and the horror will end. It always does. Ale and wine, God knows, are great causes of sin but they make it short-lived. God's bones, but it's cold out there.' He smiled at Thomas. 'So how's your black soul, Tom?'

Thomas contemplated the priest. He liked Father Hobbe, who was small and wiry, with a mass of untamed black hair about a cheerful face that was thick-scarred from a childhood pox. He was low born, the son of a Sussex wheelwright, and like any country lad he could draw a bow with the best of them. He sometimes accompanied Skeat's men on their forays into Duke Charles's country and he willingly joined the archers when they dismounted to form a battleline. Church law forbade a priest from wielding an edged weapon, but Father Hobbe always claimed he used blunt arrows, though they seemed to pierce enemy mail as efficiently as any other. Father Hobbe, in short, was a good man whose only fault was an excessive interest in Thomas's soul.

'My soul,' Thomas said, 'is soluble in ale.'

'Now there's a good word,' Father Hobbe said. 'Soluble, eh?' He picked up the big black bow and prodded the silver badge with a dirty finger. 'You've discovered anything about that?'

'No.'

'Or who stole the lance?'

'No.'

'Do you not care any more?'

Thomas leaned back in the chair and stretched his long legs. 'I'm doing a good job of work, father. We're winning this war, and this time next year? Who knows? We might be giving the King of France a bloody nose.'

Father Hobbe nodded agreement, though his face suggested Thomas's words were irrelevant. He traced his finger through a puddle of ale on the table top. 'You made a promise to your father, Thomas, and you made it in a church. Isn't that what you told me? A solemn promise, Thomas? That you would retrieve the lance? God listens to such vows.'

Thomas smiled. 'Outside this tavern, father, there's so much rape and murder and theft going on that all the quills in heaven can't keep up with the list of sins. And you worry about me?'

'Yes, Thomas, I do. Some souls are better than others. I must look after them all, but if you have a prize ram in the flock then you do well to guard it.'

Thomas sighed. 'One day, father, I'll find the man who stole that goddamn lance and I'll ram it up his arse until it tickles the hollow of his skull. One day. Will that do?'

Father Hobbe smiled beatifically. 'It'll do, Thomas, but for now there's a small church that could do with an extra man by the door. It's full of women! Some of them are so beautiful that your heart will break just to gaze at them. You can get drunk afterwards.'

'Are the women really beautiful?'

'What do you think, Thomas? Most of them look like bats and smell like goats, but they still need protection.'

So Thomas helped guard a church, and afterwards, when the army was so drunk it could do no more damage, he went back to the widow's tavern where he drank himself into oblivion. He had taken a town, he had served his lord well and he was content.

Thomas was woken by a kick. A pause, then a second kick and a cup of cold water in his face. 'Jesus!'

'That's me,' Will Skeat said. 'Father Hobbe told me you'd be here.'

'Oh, Jesus,' Thomas said again. His head was sore, his belly sour and he felt sick. He blinked feebly at the daylight, then frowned at Skeat. 'It's you.'

'It must be grand to be so clever,' Skeat said. He grinned at Thomas, who was naked in the straw of the tavern stables that he was sharing with one of the widow's daughters. 'You must have been drunk as a lord to sheathe your sword in that,' Skeat added, looking at the girl who was pulling a blanket over herself.

'I was drunk,' Thomas groaned. 'Still am.' He staggered to his feet and put on his shirt.

'The Earl wants to see you,' Skeat said with amusement.

'Me?' Thomas looked alarmed. 'Why?'

'Perhaps he wants you to marry his daughter,' Skeat said. 'Christ's bones, Tom, but look at the state of you!'

Thomas pulled on his boots and mail coat, then retrieved his hose from the baggage camp and donned a cloth jacket over his mail. The jacket bore the Earl of Northampton's badge of three green and red stars being

96

pounced on by a trio of lions. He splashed water on his face, then scraped at his stubble with a sharp knife.

'Grow a beard, lad,' Skeat said, 'it saves trouble.'

'Why does Billy want to see me?' Thomas asked, using the Earl's nickname.

'After what happened in the town yesterday?' Skeat suggested thoughtfully. 'He reckons he's got to hang someone as an example, so he asked me if I had any useless bastards I wanted to be rid of and I thought of you.'

'The way I feel,' Thomas said, 'he might as well hang me.' He retched drily, then gulped down some water.

He and Will Skeat went back into the town to find the Earl of Northampton sitting in state. The building where his banner hung was supposed to be a guildhall, though it was probably smaller than the guardroom in the Earl's own castle, but the Earl was sitting at one end as a succession of petitioners pleaded for justice. They were complaining about being robbed, which was pointless considering they had refused to surrender the town, but the Earl listened politely enough. Then a lawyer, a weasel-snouted fellow called Belas, bowed to the Earl and declaimed a long moan about the treatment offered to the Countess of Armorica. Thomas had been letting the words slide past him, but the insistence in Belas's voice made him take notice.

'If your lordship,' Belas said, smirking at the Earl, 'had not intervened, then the Countess would have been raped by Sir Simon Jekyll.'

Sir Simon stood to one side of the hall. 'That is a lie!' he protested in French.

The Earl sighed. 'So why were your breeches round your ankles when I came into the house?'

Sir Simon reddened as the men in the hall laughed. Thomas had to translate for Will Skeat, who nodded, for he had already heard the tale.

'The bastard was about to roger some titled widow,' he explained to Thomas, 'when the Earl came in. Heard her scream, see? And he'd seen a coat of arms on the house. The aristocracy look after each other.'

The lawyer now laid a long list of charges against Sir Simon. It seemed he was claiming the widow and her son as prisoners who must be held for ransom. He had also stolen the widow's two ships, her husband's armour, his sword and all the Countess's money. Belas made the complaints indignantly, then bowed to the Earl. 'You have a reputation as a just man, my lord,' he said obsequiously, 'and I place the widow's fate in your hands.'

The Earl of Northampton looked surprised to be told his reputation for fairness. 'What is it you want?' he asked.

Belas preened. 'The return of the stolen items, my lord, and the protection of the King of England for a widow and her noble son.'

The Earl drummed his fingers on the arm of the chair, then frowned at Sir Simon. 'You can't ransom a three-year-old,' he said.

'He's a count!' Sir Simon protested. 'A boy of rank!'

The Earl sighed. Sir Simon, he had come to realize, had a mind as simple as a bullock seeking food. He could see no point of view but his own and was single-minded about pursuing his appetites. That, perhaps, was why he was such a formidable soldier, but he was still a fool. 'We do not hold three-year-old children to ransom,' the Earl said firmly, 'and we don't hold women as prisoners, not unless there is an advantage which outweighs the courtesy, and I see no advantage here.' The Earl turned to the clerks behind his chair. 'Who did Armorica support?'

'Charles of Blois, my lord,' one of the clerks, a tall Breton cleric, answered.

'Is it a rich fief?'

'Very small, my lord,' the clerk, whose nose was running, spoke from memory. 'There is a holding in Finisterre which is already in our hands, some houses in Guingamp, I believe, but nothing else.'

'There,' the Earl said, turning back to Sir Simon. 'What advantages will we make from a penniless three-year-old?'

'Not penniless,' Sir Simon protested. 'I took a rich armour there.'

'Which the boy's father doubtless took in battle!'

'And the house is wealthy.' Sir Simon was getting angry. 'There are ships, storehouses, stables.'

'The house,' the clerk sounded bored, 'belonged to the Count's father-in-law. A dealer in wine, I believe.'

The Earl raised a quizzical eyebrow at Sir Simon, who was shaking his head at the clerk's obstinacy. 'The boy, my lord,' Sir Simon responded with an elaborate courtesy which bordered on insolence, 'is kin to Charles of Blois.'

'But being penniless,' the Earl said, 'I doubt he provokes fondness. More of a burden, wouldn't you think? Besides, what would you have me do? Make the child give fealty to the real Duke of Brittany? The real Duke, Sir Simon, is a five-year-old child in London. It'll be a nursery farce! A three-year-old bobbing down to a five-year-old! Do their wet nurses attend them? Shall we feast on milk and penny-cakes after? Or maybe we can enjoy a game of hunt the slipper when the ceremony is over?'

'The Countess fought us from the walls!' Sir Simon attempted a last protest.

'Do not dispute me!' the Earl shouted, thumping the arm of his chair. 'You forget that I am the King's deputy and have his powers.' The Earl leaned back, taut with anger, and Sir Simon swallowed his own fury, but could not resist muttering that the Countess had used a crossbow against the English.

'Is she the Blackbird?' Thomas asked Skeat.

'The Countess? Aye, that's what they say.'

'She's a beauty.'

'After what I found you prodding this morning,' Skeat said, 'how can you tell?'

The Earl gave an irritated glance at Skeat and Thomas, then looked back to Sir Simon. 'If the Countess did fight us from the walls,' he said, 'then I admire her spirit. As for the other matters . . .' He paused and sighed. Belas looked expectant and Sir Simon wary. 'The two ships,' the Earl decreed, 'are prizes and they will be sold in England or else taken into royal service, and you, Sir Simon, will be awarded one-third of their value.' That ruling was according to the law. The King would take a third, the Earl another and the last portion went to the man who had captured the prize. 'As to the sword and armour . . .' The Earl paused again. He had rescued Jeanette from rape and he had liked her, and he had seen the anguish on her face and listened to her impassioned plea that she owned nothing that had belonged to her husband except the precious armour and the beautiful sword, but such things, by their very nature, were the legitimate plunder of war. 'The armour and weapons and horses are yours, Sir Simon,' the Earl said, regretting the judgement but knowing it was fair. 'As to the child, I decree he is under the protection of the Crown of England and when he is of age he can decide his own fealty.' He glanced at the clerks to make sure they were noting down his decisions. 'You tell me you wish to billet yourself in the widow's house?' he asked Sir Simon.

'I took it,' Sir Simon said curtly.

'And stripped it bare, I hear,' the Earl observed icily. 'The Countess claims you stole money from her.'

'She lies.' Sir Simon looked indignant. 'Lies, my lord, lies!'

The Earl doubted it, but he could hardly accuse a gentleman of perjury without provoking a duel and, though William Bohun feared no man except his king, he did not want to fight over so petty a matter. He let it drop. 'However,' he went on, 'I did promise the lady protection against harassment.' He stared at Sir Simon as he spoke, then looked at Will Skeat, and changed to English. 'You'd like to keep your men together, Will?'

'I would, my lord.'

'Then you'll have the widow's house. And she is to be treated honourably, you hear me? Honourably! Tell your men that, Will!'

Skeat nodded. 'I'll cut their ears off if they touch her, my lord.'

'Not their ears, Will. Slice something more suitable away. Sir Simon will show you the house and you, Sir Simon,' the Earl spoke French again, 'will find a bed elsewhere.'

Sir Simon opened his mouth to protest, but one look

from the Earl quietened him. Another petitioner came forward, wanting redress for a cellar full of wine that had been stolen, but the Earl diverted him to a clerk who would record the man's complaints on a parchment which the Earl doubted he would ever find time to read.

Then he beckoned to Thomas. 'I have to thank you, Thomas of Hookton.'

'Thank me, my lord?'

The Earl smiled. 'You found a way into the town when everything else we'd tried had failed.'

Thomas reddened. 'It was a pleasure, my lord.'

'You can claim a reward of me,' the Earl said. 'It's customary.'

Thomas shrugged. 'I'm happy, my lord.'

'Then you're a lucky man, Thomas. But I shall remember the debt. And thank you, Will.'

Will Skeat grinned. 'If this lump of a daft fool don't want a reward, my lord, I'll take it.'

The Earl liked that. 'My reward to you, Will, is to leave you here. I'm giving you a whole new stretch of countryside to lay waste. God's teeth, you'll soon be richer than me.' He stood. 'Sir Simon will guide you to your quarters.'

Sir Simon might have bridled at the curt order to be a mere guide, but surprisingly he obeyed without showing any resentment, perhaps because he wanted another chance to meet Jeanette. And so, at midday, he led Will Skeat and his men through the streets to the big house beside the river. Sir Simon had put on his new armour and wore it without any surcoat so that the polished plate and gold embossment shone bright in the feeble winter sun. He ducked his helmeted head under the yard's archway and immediately Jeanette came running from the kitchen door, which lay just to the gate's left.

'Get out!' she shouted in French, 'get out!'

Thomas, riding close behind Sir Simon, stared at her. She was indeed the Blackbird and she was as beautiful at close range as she had been when he had glimpsed her on the walls.

'Get out, all of you!' She stood, hands on her hips, bareheaded, shouting.

Sir Simon pushed up the pig-snout visor of the helmet. 'This house is commandeered, my lady,' he said happily. 'The Earl ordered it.'

'The Earl promised I would be left alone!' Jeanette protested hotly.

'Then his lordship has changed his mind,' Sir Simon said.

She spat at him. 'You have already stolen everything else of mine, now you would take the house too?'

'Yes, madame,' Sir Simon said, and he spurred the horse forward so that it crowded her. 'Yes, madame,' he said again, then wrenched the reins so that the horse twisted and thumped into Jeanette, throwing her onto the ground. 'I'll take your house,' Sir Simon said, 'and anything else I want, madame.' The watching archers cheered at the sight of Jeanette's long bare legs. She snatched her skirts down and tried to stand, but Sir Simon edged his horse forward to force her into an undignified scramble across the yard.

'Let the lass up!' Will Skeat shouted angrily.

'She and I are old friends, Master Skeat,' Sir Simon answered, still threatening Jeanette with the horse's heavy hoofs.

'I said let her up and leave her be!' Will snarled.

Sir Simon, offended at being ordered by a commoner and in front of archers, turned angrily, but there was a competence about Will Skeat that gave the knight pause. Skeat was twice Sir Simon's age and all those years had been spent in fighting, and Sir Simon retained just enough sense not to make a confrontation. 'The house is yours, Master Skeat,' he said condescendingly, 'but look after its mistress. I have plans for her.' He backed the horse from Jeanette, who was in tears of shame, then spurred out of the yard.

Jeanette did not understand English, but she recognized that Will Skeat had intervened on her behalf and so she stood and appealed to him. 'He has stolen everything from me!' she said, pointing at the retreating horseman. 'Everything!'

'You know what the lass is saying, Tom?' Skeat asked.

'She doesn't like Sir Simon,' Thomas said laconically. He was leaning on his saddle pommel, watching Jeanette.

'Calm the girl down, for Christ's sake,' Skeat pleaded, then turned in his saddle. 'Jake? Make sure there's water and hay for horses. Peter, kill two of them heifers so we can sup before the light goes. Rest of you? Stop gawping at the lass and get yourselves settled!'

'Thief!' Jeanette called after Sir Simon, then turned on Thomas. 'Who are you?'

'My name is Thomas, madame.' He slid out of the saddle and threw his reins to Sam. 'The Earl has ordered us to live here,' Thomas went on, 'and to protect you.'

'Protect me!' Jeanette blazed at him. 'You are all thieves! How can you protect me? There is a place in hell for thieves like you and it is just like England. You are thieves, every one of you! Now, go! Go!'

'We're not going,' Thomas said flatly.

'How can you stay here?' Jeanette demanded. 'I am a widow! It is not proper to have you here.'

'We're here, madame,' Thomas said, 'and you and us will have to make the best of it. We'll not encroach. Just show me where your private rooms are and I'll make sure no man trespasses.'

'You? Make sure? Ha!' Jeanette turned away, then immediately turned back. 'You want me to show you my rooms, yes? So you know where my valuable properties are? Is that it? You want me to show you where you can thieve from me? Why don't I just give you everything?'

Thomas smiled. 'I thought you said Sir Simon had already stolen everything?'

'He has taken everything, everything! He is no gentleman. He is a pig. He is,' Jeanette paused, wanting to contrive a crushing insult, 'he is English!' Jeanette spat at Thomas's feet and pulled open the kitchen door. 'You see this door, Englishman? Everything beyond this door is private. Everything!' She went inside, slammed the door, then immediately opened it again. 'And the Duke is coming. The proper Duke, not your snivelling puppet child, so you will all die. Good!' The door slammed again.

Will Skeat chuckled. 'She don't like you either, Tom. What was the lass saying?'

'That we're all going to die.'

'Aye, that's true enough. But in our beds, by God's grace.'

'And she says we're not to go past that door.'

'Plenty of room out here,' Skeat said placidly,

watching as one of his men swung an axe to kill a heifer. The blood flowed over the yard, attracting a rush of dogs to lap at it while two archers began butchering the still twitching animal.

'Listen!' Skeat had climbed a mounting block beside the stables and now shouted at all his men. 'The Earl has given orders that the lass who was spitting at Tom is not to be molested. You understand that, you whoresons? You keep your britches laced up when she's around, and if you don't, I'll geld you! You treat her proper, and you don't go through that door. You've had your frolic, so now you can knuckle down to a proper bit of soldiering.'

The Earl of Northampton left after a week, taking most of his army back to the fortresses in Finisterre, which was the heartland of Duke John's supporters. He left Richard Totesham as commander of the new garrison, but he also left Sir Simon Jekyll as Totesham's deputy.

'The Earl doesn't want the bastard,' Will Skeat told Thomas, 'so he's foisted him on us.'

As Skeat and Totesham were both independent captains, there could have been jealousy between them, but the two men respected each other and, while Totesham and his men stayed in La Roche-Derrien and strengthened its defences, Skeat rode out into the country to punish the folk who paid their rents and owed their allegiance to Duke Charles. The hellequin were thus released to be a curse on northern Brittany.

It was a simple business to ruin a land. The houses and barns might be made of stone, but their roofs would burn. The livestock was captured and, if there were too many beasts to herd home, then the animals were slaughtered and their carcasses tipped down wells to poison the water. Skeat's men burned what would burn, broke what would break and stole what could be sold. They killed, raped and plundered. Fear of them drove men away from their farms, leaving the land desolate. They were the devil's horsemen, and they did King Edward's will by harrowing his enemy's land.

They wrecked village after village – Kervec and Lanvellec, St Laurent and Les Sept Saints, Tonquedec and Berhet, and a score of other places whose names they never learned. It was Christmas time, and back home the yule logs were being dragged across frost-hardened fields to high-beamed halls where troubadours sang of Arthur and his knights, of chivalrous warriors who allied pity to strength, but in Brittany the hellequin fought the real war. Soldiers were not paragons; they were scarred, vicious men who took delight in destruction. They hurled burning torches onto thatch and tore down what had taken generations to build. Places too small to have names died, and only the farms in the wide peninsula between the two rivers north of La Roche-Derrien were spared because they were needed to feed the garrison. Some of the serfs who were torn from their land were put to work heightening La Roche-Derrien's walls, clearing a wider killing ground in front of the ramparts and making new barriers at the river's edge. It was a winter of utter misery for the Bretons. Cold rains whipped from the wild Atlantic and the English scoured the farmlands.

Once in a while there would be some resistance. A brave man would shoot a crossbow from a wood's edge, but Skeat's men were experts in trapping and killing such enemies. A dozen archers would dismount and stalk the enemy from the front while a score of others galloped about his rear, and in a short while there would be a scream and another crossbow was added to the plunder. The crossbow's owner would be stripped, mutilated and hanged from a tree as a warning to other men to leave the hellequin alone, and the lessons worked, for such ambushes became fewer. It was the wrecking time and Skeat's men became rich. There were days of misery, days of slogging through cold rain with chapped hands and wet clothes, and Thomas always hated it when his men fetched the duty of leading the spare horses and then driving the captured livestock home. Geese were easy – their necks were wrung and the dead birds hung from the saddles – but cows were slow, goats wayward, sheep stupid and pigs obstinate. There were, however, enough farm-bred boys in the ranks to ensure that the animals reached La Roche-Derrien safely. Once there they were taken to a small square that had become a slaughteryard and stank of blood. Will Skeat also sent cartloads of plunder back to the town and most of that was shipped home to England. It was usually humble stuff: pots, knives, plough-blades, harrow-spikes, stools, pails, spindles, anything that could be sold, until it was said that there was not a house in southern England which did not possess at least one object plundered from Brittany.

In England they sang of Arthur and Lancelot, of Gawain and Perceval, but in Brittany the hellequin were loose.

And Thomas was a happy man.

*   *   *

Jeanette was loath to admit it, but the presence of Will Skeat's men was an advantage to her. So long as they were in the courtyard she felt safe in the house and she began to dread the long periods they spent away from the town, for it was then that Sir Simon Jekyll would haunt her. She had begun to think of him as the devil, a stupid devil to be sure, but still a remorseless, unfeeling lout who had convinced himself Jeanette must wish nothing so much as to be his wife. At times he would force himself to a clumsy courtesy, though usually he was bumptious and crude and always he stared at her like a dog gazing at a haunch of beef. He took Mass in the church of St Renan so he could woo her, and it seemed to Jeanette she could not walk in the town without meeting him. Once, encountering Jeanette in the alley beside the church of the Virgin, he crowded her against the wall and slid his strong fingers up to her breasts.

'I think, madame, you and I are suited,' he told her in all earnestness.

'You need a wife with money,' she told him, for she had learned from others in the town the state of Sir Simon's finances.

'I have your money,' he pointed out, 'and that has settled half my debts, and the prize money from the ships will pay much of the rest. But it is not your money I want, sweet one, but you.' Jeanette tried to wrench away, but he had her trapped against the wall. 'You need a protector, my dear,' he said, and kissed her tenderly on the forehead. He had a curiously full mouth, big-lipped and always wet as though his tongue was too large, and the kiss was wet and stank of stale wine. He pushed a hand down her belly and she struggled harder, but he just pressed his body against hers and took hold of her hair beneath her cap. 'You would like Berkshire, my dear.'

'I would rather live in hell.'

He fumbled at the laces of her bodice and Jeanette vainly tried to push him away, but she was only saved when a troop of men rode into the alley and their leader called a greeting to Sir Simon, who had to turn away to respond and that allowed Jeanette to wrench herself free. She left her cap in his grasp as she ran home, where she barred the doors, then sat weeping and angry and helpless. She hated him.

She hated all the English, yet as the weeks passed she watched the townsfolk come to approve of their occupiers, who spent good money in La Roche-Derrien. English silver was dependable, unlike the French, which was debased with lead or tin. The presence of the English had cut the town off from its usual trade with Rennes and Guingamp, but the shipowners were now free to trade with both Gascony and England and so their profits rose. Local ships were chartered to import arrows for the English troops, and some of the shipmasters brought back bales of English wool that they resold in other Breton ports that were still loyal to Duke Charles. Few folk were willing to travel far from La Roche-Derrien by land, for they needed to secure a pass from Richard Totesham, the commander of the garrison, and though the scrap of parchment protected them from the hellequin it was no defence against the outlaws who lived in the farms emptied by Skeat's men. But boats from La Roche-Derrien and Tréguier could still sail east to Paimpol or west to Lannion and so trade with England's enemies. That was how letters were sent out of

La Roche-Derrien, and Jeanette wrote almost weekly to Duke Charles with news of the changes the English were making to the town's defences. She never received a reply, but she persuaded herself that her letters were useful.

La Roche-Derrien prospered, but Jeanette suffered. Her father's business still existed, but the profits mysteriously vanished. The larger ships had always sailed from the quays of Tréguier, which lay an hour upriver, and though Jeanette sent them to Gascony to fetch wine for the English market, they never returned. They had either been taken by French ships or, more likely, their captains had gone into business for themselves. The family farms lay south of La Roche-Derrien, in the countryside laid waste by Will Skeat's men, and so those rents disappeared. Plabennec, her husband's estate, was in English-held Finisterre and Jeanette had not seen a penny from that land in three years, so by the early weeks of 1346 she was desperate and thus summoned the lawyer Belas to the house.

Belas took a perverse pleasure in telling her how she had ignored his advice, and how she should never have equipped the two boats for war. Jeanette suffered his pomposity, then asked him to draw up a petition of redress which she could send to the English court. The petition begged for the rents of Plabennec, which the invaders had been taking for themselves. It irked Jeanette that she must plead for money from King Edward III of England, but what choice did she have? Sir Simon Jekyll had impoverished her.

Belas sat at her table and made notes on a scrap of parchment. 'How many mills at Plabennec?' he asked.

'There were two.'

'Two,' he said, noting the figure. 'You do know,' he added cautiously, 'that the Duke has made a claim for those rents?'

'The Duke?' Jeanette asked in astonishment. 'For Plabennec?'

'Duke Charles claims it is his fief,' Belas said.

'It might be, but my son is the Count.'

'The Duke considers himself the boy's guardian,' Belas observed.

'How do you know these things?' Jeanette asked.

Belas shrugged. 'I have had correspondence from the Duke's men of business in Paris.'

'What correspondence?' Jeanette demanded sharply.

'About another matter,' Belas said dismissively, 'another matter entirely. Plabennec's rents were collected quarterly, I assume?'

Jeanette watched the lawyer suspiciously. 'Why would the Duke's men of business mention Plabennec to you?'

'They asked if I knew the family. Naturally I revealed nothing.'

He was lying, Jeanette thought. She owed Belas money, indeed she was in debt to half of La Roche-Derrien's tradesmen. Doubtless Belas thought his bill was unlikely to be paid by her and so he was looking to Duke Charles for eventual settlement. 'Monsieur Belas,' she said coldly, 'you will tell me exactly what you have been telling the Duke, and why.'

Belas shrugged. 'I have nothing to tell!'

'How is your wife?' Jeanette asked sweetly.

'Her aches are passing as winter ends, thank God. She is well, madame.'

'Then she will not be well,' Jeanette said tartly, 'when

she learns what you do with your clerk's daughter? How old is she, Belas? Twelve?'

'Madame!'

'Don't madame me!' Jeanette thumped the table, almost upsetting the flask of ink. 'So what has passed between you and the Duke's men of business?'

Belas sighed. He put the cap on the ink flask, laid down the quill and rubbed his thin cheeks. 'I have always,' he said, 'looked after the legal matters of this family. It is my duty, madame, and sometimes I must do things that I would rather not, but such things are also a part of my duty.' He half smiled. 'You are in debt, madame. You could rescue your finances easily enough by marrying a man of substance, but you seem reluctant to follow that course and so I see nothing but ruin in your future. Ruin. You wish some advice? Sell this house and you will have money enough to live for two or three years, and in that time the Duke will surely drive the English from Brittany and you and your son will be restored to Plabennec.'

Jeanette flinched. 'You think the devils will be defeated that easily?' She heard hoofs in the street and saw that Skeat's men were returning to her courtyard. They were laughing as they rode. They did not look like men who would be defeated soon; indeed, she feared they were unbeatable for they had a blithe confidence that galled her.

'I think, madame,' Belas said, 'that you must make up your mind what you are. Are you Louis Halevy's daughter? Or Henri Chenier's widow? Are you a merchant or an aristocrat? If you are a merchant, madame, then marry here and be content. If you are an aristocrat then raise what money you can and go to

113

the Duke and find yourself a new husband with a title.'

Jeanette considered the advice impertinent, but did not bridle. 'How much would we make on this house?' she asked instead.

'I shall enquire, madame,' Belas said. He knew the answer already, and knew that Jeanette would hate it, for a house in a town occupied by an enemy would fetch only a fraction of its proper value. So now was not the time to give Jeanette that news. Better, the lawyer thought, to wait until she was truly desperate, then he could buy the house and its ruined farms for a pittance.

'Is there a bridge across the stream at Plabennec?' he asked, drawing the parchment towards him.

'Forget the petition,' Jeanette said.

'If you wish, madame.'

'I shall think about your advice, Belas.'

'You will not regret it,' he said earnestly. She was lost, he thought, lost and defeated. He would take her house and farms, the Duke would claim Plabennec and she would be left with nothing. Which was what she deserved, for she was a stubborn and proud creature who had risen far above her proper station. 'I am always,' Belas said humbly, 'at your ladyship's service.' From adversity, he thought, a clever man could always profit, and Jeanette was ripe for plucking. Put a cat to guard the sheep and the wolves would eat well.

Jeanette did not know what to do. She was loath to sell the house for she feared it would fetch a low price, but nor did she know how else she could raise money. Would Duke Charles welcome her? He had never shown any sign of it, not since he had opposed her marriage to his nephew, but perhaps he had softened since then? Perhaps he would protect her? She decided she would pray for guidance; so she wrapped a shawl around her shoulders, crossed the yard, ignoring the newly returned soldiers, and went into St Renan's church. There was a statue of the virgin there, sadly shorn of her gilded halo, which had been ripped away by the English, and Jeanette often prayed to the image of Christ's mother, whom she believed had a special care for all women in trouble.

She thought at first that the dimly lit church was empty. Then she saw an English bow propped against a pillar and an archer kneeling at the altar. It was the good-looking man, the one who wore his hair in a long pigtail bound with bowcord. It was, she thought, an irritating sign of vanity. Most of the English wore their hair cropped, but a few grew it extravagantly long and they were the ones who seemed most flamboyantly confident. She wished he would leave the church; then she was intrigued by his abandoned bow and so she picked it up and was astonished by its weight. The string hung loose and she wondered how much strength would be needed to bend the bow and hook the string's free loop on the empty horn tip. She pressed one end of the bow on the stone floor, trying to bend it, and just then an arrow span across the flagstones to lodge against her foot.

'If you can string the bow,' Thomas said, still on his knees at the altar, 'you can have a free shot.'

Jeanette was too proud to be seen to fail and too angry not to try, though she attempted to disguise her effort which barely flexed the black yew stave. She kicked the arrow away. 'My husband was killed by one of these bows,' she said bitterly.

115

'I've often wondered,' Thomas said, 'why you Bretons or the French don't learn to shoot them. Start your son at seven or eight years, madame, and in ten years he'll be lethal.'

'He'll fight as a knight, like his father.'

Thomas laughed. 'We kill knights. They haven't made an armour strong enough to resist an English arrow.'

Jeanette shuddered. 'What are you praying for, Englishman?' she asked. 'Forgiveness?'

Thomas smiled. 'I am giving thanks, madame, for the fact that we rode six days in enemy country and did not lose one man.' He climbed from his knees and pointed to a pretty silver box that sat on the altar. It was a reliquary and had a small crystal window that was rimmed with drops of coloured glass. Thomas had peered through the window and seen nothing more than a small black lump about the size of a man's thumb. 'What is it?' he asked.

'The tongue of St Renan,' Jeanette said defiantly. 'It was stolen when you came to our town, but God was good and the thief died next day and the relic was recovered.'

'God is indeed good,' Thomas said drily. 'And who was St Renan?'

'He was a great preacher,' she said, 'who banished the *nains* and *gorics* from our farmlands. They still live in the wild places, but a prayer to St Renan will scare them away.'

'*Nains* and *gorics*?' Thomas asked.

'They are spirits,' she said, 'evil ones. They once haunted the whole land, and I pray daily to the saint that he will banish the hellequin as he drove out the *nains*. You know what the hellequin are?'

116

'We are,' Thomas said proudly.

She grimaced at his tone. 'The hellequin,' she said icily, 'are the dead who have no souls. The dead who were so wicked in life that the devil loves them too much to punish them in hell and so he gives them his horses and releases them on the living.' She hefted his black bow and pointed to the silver plate tacked to its belly. 'You even have the devil's picture on your bow.'

'It's a yale,' Thomas said.

'It is a devil,' she insisted, and threw the bow at him. Thomas caught it and, because he was too young to resist showing off, casually strung it. He made it appear effortless. 'You pray to St Renan,' he said, 'and I shall pray to St Guinefort. We shall see which saint is the stronger.'

'Guinefort? I've not heard of her.'

'Him,' Thomas corrected her, 'and he lived in the Lyonnaise.'

'You pray to a French saint?' Jeanette asked, intrigued.

'All the time,' Thomas said, touching the desiccated dog's paw that hung about his neck. He did not tell Jeanette anything more about the saint, who had been a favourite of his father's – who, in his better moments, would laugh at the story. Guinefort had been a dog and, so far as Thomas's father knew, the only animal ever to be canonized. The beast had saved a baby from a wolf, then been martyred by his owner, who thought the dog had eaten the baby when in truth he had hidden it beneath the cot. 'Pray to the blessed Guinefort!' had been Father Ralph's reaction to every domestic crisis, and Thomas had adopted the saint as his own. He sometimes wondered whether the saint was an

117

efficient intercessor in heaven, though perhaps Guinefort's whining and barking were as effective as the pleas of any other saint, but Thomas was sure that few other folk used the dog as their representative to God and perhaps that meant he received special protection. Father Hobbe had been shocked to hear of a holy dog, but Thomas, though he shared his father's amusement, now genuinely thought of the animal as his guardian.

Jeanette wanted to know more about the blessed St Guinefort, but she did not want to encourage an intimacy with any of Skeat's men and so she forgot her curiosity and made her voice cold again. 'I have been wanting to see you,' she said, 'to tell you that your men and their women must not use the yard as a latrine. I see them from the window. It is disgusting! Maybe you behave like that in England, but this is Brittany. You can use the river.'

Thomas nodded, but said nothing. Instead he carried his bow down the nave, which had one of its long sides obscured by fishing nets hung up for mending. He went to the church's western end, which was gloomily decorated by a painting of the doom. The righteous were vanishing into the rafters, while the condemned sinners were tumbling to a fiery hell cheered on by angels and saints. Thomas stopped in front of the painting.

'Have you ever noticed,' he said, 'how the prettiest women are always falling down to hell and the ugly ones are going up to heaven?'

Jeanette almost smiled for she had often wondered about that same question, but she bit her tongue and said nothing as Thomas walked back up the nave beside a painting of Christ walking on a sea that was grey and white-crested like the ocean off Brittany. A shoal of mackerel were poking their heads from the water to watch the miracle.

'What you must understand, madame,' Thomas said, gazing up at the curious mackerel, 'is that our men do not like being unwelcome. You won't even let them use the kitchen. Why not? It's big enough, and they'd be glad of a place to dry their boots after a wet night's riding.'

'Why should I have you English in my kitchen? So you can use that as a latrine as well?'

Thomas turned and looked at her. 'You have no respect for us, madame, so why should we have respect for your house?'

'Respect!' She mocked the word. 'How can I respect you? Everything that is precious to me was stolen. Stolen by you!'

'By Sir Simon Jekyll,' Thomas said.

'You or Sir Simon,' Jeanette asked, 'what is the difference?'

Thomas picked up the arrow and dropped it into his bag. 'The difference, madame, is that once in a while I talk to God, while Sir Simon thinks he is God. I shall ask the lads to piss in the river, but I doubt they'll want to please you much.' He smiled at her, then was gone.

Spring was greening the land, giving a haze to the trees and filling the twisting laneways with bright flowers. New green moss grew on thatch, there was white stitchwort in the hedgerows, and kingfishers whipped between the new yellow leaves of the riverside sallows.

Skeat's men were having to go further from La Roche-Derrien to find new plunder and their long rides took them dangerously close to Guingamp, which was Duke Charles's headquarters, though the town's garrison rarely came out to challenge the raiders. Guingamp lay to the south, while to the west was Lannion, a much smaller town with a far more belligerent garrison that was inspired by Sir Geoffrey de Pont Blanc, a knight who had sworn an oath that he would lead Skeat's raiders back to Lannion in chains. He announced that the Englishmen would be burned in Lannion's marketplace because they were heretics, the devil's men.

Will Skeat was not worried by such a threat. 'I might lose a wink of sleep if the silly bastard had proper archers,' he told Tom, 'but he ain't, so he can blunder about as much as he likes. Is that his real name?'

'Geoffrey of the White Bridge.'

'Daft bastard. Is he Breton or French?'

'I'm told he's French.'

'Have to teach him a lesson then, won't we?'

Sir Geoffrey proved an unwilling pupil. Will Skeat dragged his coat closer and closer to Lannion, burning houses within sight of its walls in an effort to lure Sir Geoffrey out into an ambush of archers, but Sir Geoffrey had seen what English arrows could do to mounted knights and so he refused to lead his men in a wild charge that would inevitably finish as a pile of screaming horses and bleeding men. He stalked Skeat instead, looking for some place where he could ambush the Englishmen, but Skeat was no more of a fool than Sir Geoffrey, and for three weeks the two war bands circled and skirted each other. Sir Geoffrey's presence slowed

Skeat, but did not stop the destruction. The two forces clashed twice, and both times Sir Geoffrey threw his crossbowmen forward on foot, hoping they could finish off Skeat's archers, but both times the longer arrows won and Sir Geoffrey drew off without forcing a fight he knew he must lose. After the second inconclusive clash he even tried appealing to Will Skeat's honour. He rode forward, all alone, dressed in an armour as beautiful as Sir Simon Jekyll's, though Sir Geoffrey's helmet was an old-fashioned pot with perforated eye holes. His surcoat and his horse's trapper were dark blue on which white bridges were embroidered and the same device was blazoned on his shield. He carried a blue-painted lance from which he had hung a white scarf to show he came in peace. Skeat rode forward to meet him with Thomas as interpreter. Sir Geoffrey lifted off his helmet and pushed a hand through his sweat-flattened hair. He was a young fellow, golden-haired and blue-eyed, with a broad, good-humoured face, and Thomas felt he would probably have liked the man if he had not been an enemy. Sir Geoffrey smiled as the two Englishmen curbed their horses.

'It is a dull thing,' he said, 'to shoot arrows at each other's shadows. I suggest you bring your men-at-arms into the field's centre and meet us there on equal terms.'

Thomas did not even bother to translate, for he knew what Skeat's answer would be. 'I have a better idea,' he said, 'you bring your men-at-arms and we'll bring our archers.'

Sir Geoffrey looked puzzled. 'Do you command?' he asked Thomas. He had thought that the older and grizzled Skeat was the captain, but Skeat stayed silent.

'He lost his tongue fighting the Scots,' Thomas said, 'so I speak for him.'

'Then tell him I want an honourable fight,' Sir Geoffrey said spiritedly. 'Let me pit my horsemen against yours.' He smiled as if to suggest his suggestion was as reasonable as it was chivalrous as it was ridiculous.

Thomas translated for Skeat, who twisted in his saddle and spat into the clover.

'He says,' Thomas said, 'that our archers will meet your men. A dozen of our archers against a score of your men-at-arms.'

Sir Geoffrey shook his head sadly. 'You have no sense of sport, you English,' he said, then put his leather-lined pot back on his head and rode away. Thomas told Skeat what had passed between them.

'Silly goddamn bastard,' Skeat said. 'What did he want? A tournament? Who does he think we are? The knights of the round bloody table? I don't know what happens to some folk. They put a sir in front of their names and their brains get addled. Fighting fair! Whoever heard of anything so daft? Fight fair and you lose. Bloody fool.'

Sir Geoffrey of the White Bridge continued to haunt the hellequin, but Skeat gave him no chance for a fight. There was always a large band of archers watching the Frenchman's forces, and whenever the men from Lannion became too bold they were likely to have the goose-feathered arrows thumping into their horses. So Sir Geoffrey was reduced to a shadow, but he was an irritating and persistent shadow, following Skeat's men almost back to the gates of La Roche-Derrien.

The trouble occurred the third time that he trailed

Skeat and so came close to the town. Sir Simon Jekyll had heard of Sir Geoffrey and, warned by a sentinel on the highest church tower that Skeat's men were in sight, he led out a score of the garrison's men-at-arms to meet the hellequin. Skeat was just over a mile from the town and Sir Geoffrey, with fifty men-at-arms and as many mounted crossbowmen, was just another half-mile behind. The Frenchman had caused no great problems to Skeat and if Sir Geoffrey wanted to ride home to Lannion and claim that he had chased the hellequin back to their lair then Skeat was quite happy to give the Frenchman that satisfaction.

Then Sir Simon came and it was all suddenly display and arrogance. The English lances went up, the helmet visors clanged shut and their horses were prancing. Sir Simon rode towards the French and Breton horsemen, bellowing a challenge. Will Skeat followed Sir Simon and advised him to let the bastards be, but the Yorkshireman was wasting his breath.

Skeat's men-at-arms were at the front of the column, escorting the captured livestock and three wagons filled with plunder, while the rearguard was formed by sixty mounted archers. Those sixty men had just reached the big woods where the army had camped during the siege of La Roche-Derrien and, at a signal from Skeat, they split into two groups and rode into the trees either side of the road. They dismounted in the woods, tied their horses' reins to branches, then carried their bows to the edge of the trees. The road ran between the two groups, edged by wide grassy verges.

Sir Simon wheeled his horse to confront Will Skeat. 'I want thirty of your men-at-arms, Skeat,' he demanded peremptorily.

'You can want them,' Will Skeat said, 'but you'll not have them.'

'Good Christ, man, I outrank you!' Sir Simon was incredulous at Skeat's refusal. 'I outrank you, Skeat! I'm not asking, you fool, I'm ordering.'

Skeat looked up at the sky. 'Looks like rain, don't you think? And we could do with a drop. Fields are right dry and streams are low.'

Sir Simon reached out and gripped Skeat's arm, forcing the older man to turn to him. 'He has fifty knights,' Sir Simon spoke of Sir Geoffrey de Pont Blanc, 'and I have twenty. Give me thirty men and I'll take him prisoner. Just give me twenty!' He was pleading, all arrogance gone, for this was a chance for Sir Simon to fight a proper skirmish, horseman against horseman, and the winner would have renown and the prize of captured men and horses.

But Will Skeat knew everything about men, horses and renown. 'I'm not out here to play games,' he said, shaking his arm free, 'and you can order me till the cows sprout wings, but you'll not have a man of mine.'

Sir Simon looked anguished, but then Sir Geoffrey de Pont Blanc decided the matter. He saw how his men-at-arms outnumbered the English horsemen and so he ordered thirty of his followers to ride back and join the crossbowmen. Now the two troops of horsemen were evenly matched and Sir Geoffrey rode forward on his big black stallion that was swathed in its blue and white trapper and had a boiled leather mask for face armour, a chanfron. Sir Simon rode to meet him in his new armour, but his horse had no padded trapper and no chanfron, and he wanted both, just as he wanted this fight. All winter he had endured the misery of a peasant's war, all muck and murder, and now the enemy was offering honour, glory and the chance to capture some fine horses, armour and good weapons. The two men saluted each other by dipping their lances, then exchanged names and compliments.

Will Skeat had joined Thomas in the woods. 'You might be a woolly-headed fool, Tom,' Skeat said, 'but there's plenty more stupid than you. Look at the daft bastards! Not a brain between either of them. You could shake them by the heels and nothing would drop out of their ears but dried muck.' He spat.

Sir Geoffrey and Sir Simon agreed on the rules of the fight. Tournament rules, really, only with death to give the sport spice. An unhorsed man was out of the fight, they agreed, and would be spared, though such a man could be taken prisoner. They wished each other well then turned and rode back to their men.

Skeat tied his horse to a tree and strung his bow. 'There's a place in York,' he said, 'where you can watch the mad folk. They keep them caged up and you pay a farthing to go and laugh at them. They should put those two silly bastards in with them.'

'My father was mad for a time,' Thomas said.

'Don't surprise me, lad, don't surprise me at all.' Skeat said. He looped his bowcord onto a stave that had been carved with crosses.

His archers watched the men-at-arms from the edge of the woods. As a spectacle it was wondrous, like a tournament, only on this spring meadow there were no marshals to save a man's life. The two groups of horsemen readied themselves. Squires tightened girths, men hefted lances and made sure their shield straps were tight. Visors clanged shut, turning the horsemen's world into a dark place slashed with slitted daylight. They dropped their reins, for from now on the well-trained destriers would be guided by the touch of spur and the pressure of knees; the horsemen needed both hands for their shields and weapons. Some men wore two swords, a heavy one for slashing and a thinner blade for stabbing, and they made certain the weapons slid easily from their scabbards. Some gave their lances to squires to leave a hand free to make the sign of the cross, then took the lances back. The horses stamped on the pasture, then Sir Geoffrey lowered his lance in a signal that he was ready and Sir Simon did the same, and the forty men spurred their big horses forward. These were not the light-boned mares and geldings that the archers rode, but the heavy destriers, stallions all, and big enough to carry a man and his armour. The beasts snorted, tossed their heads and lumbered into a trot as the riders lowered their long lances. One of Sir Geoffrey's men made the beginner's mistake of lowering the lance too much so that the point struck the dry turf and he was lucky not be unhorsed. He left the lance behind and drew his sword. The horsemen spurred into the canter and one of Sir Simon's men swerved to the left, probably because his horse was ill trained, and it bumped the next horse and the ripple of colliding horses went down the line as the spurs rowelled back to demand the gallop. Then they struck.

The sound of the wooden lances striking shields and mail was a crunch like splintering bones. Two horsemen were rammed back out of their high saddles, but most of the lance thrusts had been parried by shields and now the horsemen dropped the shivered weapons as they galloped past their opponents. They sawed on the reins and drew their swords, but it was plain to the watching archers that the enemy had gained an advantage. Both of the unhorsed riders were English, and Sir Geoffrey's men were much more closely aligned so that when they turned to bring their swords to the mêlée they came as a disciplined group that struck Sir Simon's men in a clangour of sword against sword. An Englishman reeled from the mêlée with a missing hand. Dust and turf spewed up from hoofs. A riderless horse limped away. The swords clashed like hammers on anvils. Men grunted as they swung. A huge Breton, with no device on his plain shield, was wielding a falchion, a weapon that was half sword and half axe, and he used the broad blade with a terrible skill. An English man-at-arms had his helmet split open and his skull with it, so that he rode wavering from the fight, blood pouring down his mail coat. His horse stopped a few paces from the turmoil and the man-at-arms slowly, so slowly, bent forward and then slumped down from the saddle. One foot was trapped in a stirrup as he died but his horse did not seem to notice. It just went on cropping the grass.

Two of Sir Simon's men yielded and were sent back to be taken prisoner by the French and Breton squires. Sir Simon himself was fighting savagely, turning his horse to beat off two opponents. He sent one reeling out of the fight with a useless arm, then battered the other with swift cuts from his stolen sword. The French had fifteen men still fighting, but the English were down to ten when the great brute with the falchion decided to finish Sir Simon off. He roared as he charged, and Sir Simon caught the falchion on his shield and lunged his sword into the mail under the Breton's armpit. He yanked the sword free and there was blood pouring from the rent in the enemy's mail and leather tunic. The big man twitched in the saddle and Sir Simon hammered the sword onto the back of his head, then turned his horse to beat off another assailant, before wheeling back to drive his heavy weapon in a crushing blow against the big Breton's adam's apple. The man dropped his falchion and clutched his throat as he rode away.

'He's good, isn't he?' Skeat said flatly. 'Got suet for brains, but he knows how to fight.'

But, despite Sir Simon's prowess, the enemy was winning and Thomas wanted to advance the archers. They only needed to run about thirty paces and then would have been in easy range of the rampaging enemy horsemen, but Will Skeat shook his head. 'Never kill two Frenchmen when you can kill a dozen, Tom,' he said reprovingly.

'Our men are getting beat,' Thomas protested.

'Then that'll teach 'em not to be bloody fools, won't it?' Skeat said. He grinned. 'Just wait, lad, just wait, and we'll skin the cat proper.'

The English men-at-arms were being beaten back and only Sir Simon was fighting with spirit. He was indeed good. He had driven the huge Breton from the fight and was now holding off four of the enemy, and doing it with a ferocious skill, but the rest of his men, seeing that their battle was lost and that they could not reach Sir Simon because there were too many enemy horsemen around him, turned and fled.

'Sam!' Will shouted across the road. 'When I give you the word, take a dozen men and run away! You hear me, Sam?'

'I'll run away!' Sam shouted back.

The English men-at-arms, some bleeding and one half falling from his tall saddle, thundered back down the road towards La Roche-Derrien. The French and Bretons had surrounded Sir Simon, but Sir Geoffrey of the White Bridge was a romantic fellow and refused to take the life of a brave opponent, and so he ordered his men to spare the English knight.

Sir Simon, sweating like a pig under the leather and iron plate, pushed up the snoutlike visor of his helmet. 'I don't yield,' he told Sir Geoffrey. His new armour was scarred and his sword edge chipped, but the quality of both had helped him in the fight. 'I don't yield,' he said again, 'so fight on!'

Sir Geoffrey bowed in his saddle. 'I salute your bravery, Sir Simon,' he said magnanimously, 'and you are free to go with all honour.' He waved his men-at-arms aside and Sir Simon, miraculously alive and free, rode away with his head held high. He had led his men into disaster and death, but he had emerged with honour.

Sir Geoffrey could see past Sir Simon, down the long road that was thick with fleeing men-at-arms and, beyond them, the captured livestock and the heaped carts of plunder that were being escorted by Skeat's men. Then Will Skeat shouted at Sam and suddenly Sir Geoffrey could see a bunch of panicked archers riding northwards as hard as they could. 'He'll fall for it,' Skeat said knowingly, 'you just see if he don't.'

Sir Geoffrey had proved in the last few weeks that he was no fool, but he lost his wits that day. He saw a chance to cut down the hated hellequin archers and recapture three carts of plunder and so he ordered his remaining thirty men-at-arms to join him and, leaving his four prisoners and nine captured horses in the care of his crossbowmen, waved his knights forward. Will Skeat had been waiting weeks for this.

Sir Simon turned in alarm as he heard the sound of hooves. Nearly fifty armoured men on big destriers charged towards him and, for a moment, he thought they were trying to capture him and so he spurred his horse towards the woods only to see the French and Breton horsemen crash past him at full gallop. Sir Simon ducked under branches and swore at Will Skeat, who ignored him. He was watching the enemy.

Sir Geoffrey de Pont Blanc led the charge and saw only glory. He had forgotten the archers in the woods, or else believed they had all fled after the defeat of Sir Simon's men. Sir Geoffrey was on the cusp of a great victory. He would take back the plunder and, even better, lead the dreaded hellequin to a fiery fate in Lannion's marketplace.

'Now!' Skeat shouted through cupped hands. 'Now!'

There were archers on both sides of the road and they stepped out from the new spring foliage and loosed their bowstrings. Thomas's second arrow was in the air before the first even struck. Look and loose, he thought, do not think, and there was no need to aim, for the enemy was a tight group and all the archers did was pour their long arrows into the horsemen so that in an eyeblink the charge was reduced to a tangle of rearing stallions, fallen men, screaming horses and splashing blood. The enemy had no chance. A few at the back managed to turn and gallop away, but the majority were trapped in a closing ring of bowmen who drove their arrows mercilessly through mail and leather. Any man who even twitched invited three or four arrows. The pile of iron and flesh was spiked with feathers, and still the arrows came, cutting through mail and driving deep into horseflesh. Only the handful of men at the rear and a single man at the very front of the charge survived.

That man was Sir Geoffrey himself. He had been ten paces in front of his men and maybe that was why he was spared, or perhaps the archers had been impressed by the manner in which he had treated Sir Simon, but for whatever reason he rode ahead of the carnage like a charmed soul. Not an arrow flew close, but he heard the screams and clatter behind and he slowed his horse then turned to see the horror. He watched with disbelief for an instant, then walked his stallion back towards the arrow-stuck pile that had been his men. Skeat shouted at some of his bowmen to turn and face the enemy's crossbowmen, but they, seeing the fate of their men-at-arms, were in no mood to face the English arrows. They retreated southwards.

There was a curious stillness then. Fallen horses twitched and some beat at the road with their hooves. A man groaned, another called on Christ and some just whimpered. Thomas, an arrow still on his bowstring, could hear larks, the call of plovers and the whisper of wind in the leaves. A drop of rain fell, splashing the dust on the road, but it was a lone outrider of a shower that went to the west. Sir Geoffrey stood his horse beside his dead and dying men as if inviting the archers to add his corpse to the heap that was streaked with blood and flecked with goose feathers.

'See what I mean, Tom?' Skeat said. 'Wait long enough and the bloody fools will always oblige you. Right, lads! Finish the bastards off!' Men dropped their bows, drew their knives and ran to the shuddering heap, but Skeat held Thomas back. 'Go and tell that stupid white bridge bastard to make himself scarce.'

Thomas walked to the Frenchman, who must have thought he was expected to surrender for he pulled off his helmet and extended his sword handle. 'My family cannot pay a great ransom,' he said apologetically.

'You're not a prisoner,' Thomas said.

Sir Geoffrey seemed perplexed by the words. 'You release me?'

'We don't want you,' Thomas said. 'You might think about going to Spain,' he suggested, 'or the Holy Land. Not too many hellequin in either place.'

Sir Geoffrey sheathed his sword. 'I must fight against the enemies of my king so I shall fight here. But I thank you.' He gathered his reins and just at that moment Sir Simon Jekyll rode out of the trees, pointing his drawn sword at Sir Geoffrey.

'He's my prisoner!' he called to Thomas. 'My prisoner!'

'He's no one's prisoner,' Thomas said. 'We're letting him go.'

'You're letting him go?' Sir Simon sneered. 'Do you know who commands here?'

'What I know,' Thomas said, 'is that this man is no prisoner.' He thumped the trapper-covered rump of Sir Geoffrey's horse to send it on its way. 'Spain or the Holy Land!' he called after Sir Geoffrey.

Sir Simon turned his horse to follow Sir Geoffrey, then saw that Will Skeat was ready to intervene and stop any such pursuit so he turned back to Thomas. 'You had no right to release him! No right!'

'He released you,' Thomas said.

'Then he was a fool. And because he is a fool, I must

be?' Sir Simon was quivering with anger. Sir Geoffrey might have declared himself a poor man, hardly able to raise a ransom, but his horse alone was worth at least fifty pounds, and Skeat and Thomas had just sent that money trotting southwards. Sir Simon watched him go, then lowered the sword blade so that it threatened Thomas's throat. 'From the moment I first saw you,' he said, 'you have been insolent. I am the highest-born man on this field and it is I who decides the fate of prisoners. You understand that?'

'He yielded to me,' Thomas said, 'not to you. So it don't matter what bed you were born in.'

'You're a pup!' Sir Simon spat. 'Skeat! I want recompense for that prisoner. You hear me?'

Skeat ignored Sir Simon, but Thomas did not have enough sense to do the same.

'Jesus,' he said in disgust, 'that man spared you, and you'd not return the favour? You're not a bloody knight, you're just a bully. Go and boil your arse.'

The sword rose and so did Thomas's bow. Sir Simon looked at the glittering arrow point, its edges feathered white through sharpening and he had just enough wit not to strike with his sword. He sheathed it instead, slamming the blade into the scabbard, then wheeled his destrier and spurred away.

Which left Skeat's men to sort out the enemy's dead. There were eighteen of them and another twenty-three grievously wounded. There were also sixteen bleeding horses and twenty-four dead destriers, and that, as Will Skeat remarked, was a wicked waste of good horseflesh.

And Sir Geoffrey had been taught his lesson.

There was a fuss back in La Roche-Derrien. Sir Simon Jekyll complained to Richard Totesham that Will Skeat had failed to support him in battle, then also claimed to have been responsible for the death or wounding of forty-one enemy men-at-arms. He boasted he had won the skirmish, then returned to his theme of Skeat's perfidy, but Richard Totesham was in no mood to endure Sir Simon's querulousness. 'Did you win the fight or not?'

'Of course we won!' Sir Simon blinked indignantly. 'They're dead, ain't they?'

'So why did you need Will's men-at-arms?' Totesham asked.

Sir Simon searched for an answer and found none. 'He was impertinent,' he complained.

'That's for you and him to settle, not me,' Totesham said in abrupt dismissal, but he was thinking about the conversation and that night he talked with Skeat.

'Forty-one dead or wounded?' he wondered aloud. 'That must be a third of Lannion's men-at-arms.'

'Near as maybe, aye.'

Totesham's quarters were near the river and from his window he could watch the water slide under the bridge arches. Bats flittered about the barbican tower that guarded the bridge's further side, while the cottages beyond the river were lit by a sharp-edged moon. 'They'll be short-handed, Will,' Totesham said.

'They'll not be happy, that's for sure.'

'And the place will be stuffed with valuables.'

'Like as not,' Skeat agreed. Many folk, fearing the hellequin, had taken their belongings to the nearby fortresses, and Lannion must be filled with their goods. More to the point, Totesham would find food there. His garrison received some food from the farms north of La Roche-Derrien and more was brought across the Channel from England, but the hellequin's wastage of the countryside had brought hunger perilously close.

'Leave fifty men here?' Totesham was still thinking aloud, but he had no need to explain his thoughts to an old soldier like Skeat.

'We'll need new ladders,' Skeat said.

'What happened to the old ones?'

'Firewood. It were a cold winter.'

'A night attack?' Totesham suggested.

'Full moon in five or six days.'

'Five days from now, then,' Totesham decided. 'And I'll want your men, Will.'

'If they're sober by then.'

'They deserve their drink after what they did today,' Totesham said warmly, then gave Skeat a smile. 'Sir Simon was complaining about you. Says you were impertinent.'

'That weren't me, Dick, it was my lad Tom. Told the bastard to go and boil his arse.'

'I fear Sir Simon was never one for taking good advice,' Totesham said gravely.

Nor were Skeat's men. He had let them loose in the

135

town, but warned them that they would feel rotten in the morning if they drank too much and they ignored that advice to make celebration in La Roche-Derrien's taverns. Thomas had gone with a score of his friends and their women to an inn where they sang, danced and tried to pick a fight with a group of Duke John's white rats, who were too sensible to rise to the provocation and slipped quietly into the night. A moment later two men-at-arms walked in, both wearing jackets with the Earl of Northampton's badge of the lions and the stars. Their arrival was jeered, but they endured it with patience and asked if Thomas was present.

'He's the ugly bastard over there,' Jake said, pointing to Thomas, who was dancing to the music of a flute and drum. The men-at-arms waited till he had finished his dance, then explained that Will Skeat was with the garrison's commander and wanted to talk with him.

Thomas drained his ale. 'What it is,' he told the other archers, 'is that they can't make a decision without me. Indispensable, that's me.' The archers mocked that, but cheered good-naturedly as Thomas left with the two men-at-arms.

One of them came from Dorset and had actually heard of Hookton. 'Didn't the French land there?' he asked.

'Bastards wrecked it. I doubt there's anything left,' Thomas said. 'So why does Will want me?'

'God knows and He ain't telling,' one of the men said. He had led Thomas towards Richard Totesham's quarters, but now he pointed down a dark alley. 'They're in a tavern at the end there. Place with the anchor hanging over the door.'

'Good for them,' Thomas said. If he had not been half

drunk he might have realized that Totesham and Skeat were unlikely to summon him to a tavern, let alone the smallest one in town at the river end of the darkest alley, but Thomas suspected nothing until he was half-way down the narrow passage and two men stepped from a gateway. The first he knew of them was when a blow landed on the back of his head. He pitched forward onto his knees and the second man kicked him in the face, then both men rained kicks and blows on him until he offered no more resistance and they could seize his arms and drag him through the gate into a small smithy. There was blood in Thomas's mouth, his nose had been broken again, a rib was cracked and his belly was churning with ale.

A fire burned in the smithy. Thomas, through half-closed eyes, could see an anvil. Then more men surrounded him and gave him a second kicking so that he rolled into a ball in a vain attempt to protect himself.

'Enough,' a voice said, and Thomas opened his eyes to see Sir Simon Jekyll. The two men who had fetched him from the tavern, and who had seemed so friendly, now came through the smithy gate and stripped off their borrowed tunics showing the Earl of Northampton's badge. 'Well done,' Sir Simon told them, then looked at Thomas. 'Mere archers,' Sir Simon said, 'do not tell knights to boil their arse.'

A tall man, a huge brute with lank yellow hair and blackened teeth, was standing beside Thomas, wanting to kick him if he offered an insolent reply, so Thomas held his tongue. Instead he offered a silent prayer to St Sebastian, the patron saint of archers. This plight, he reckoned, was too serious to be left to a dog.

'Take his breeches down, Colley,' Sir Simon ordered,

and turned back to the fire. Thomas saw there was a great three-legged pot standing in the red-hot charcoal. He swore under his breath, realizing that he was the one who was to get a boiled arse. Sir Simon peered into the pot. 'You are to be taught a lesson in courtesy,' he told Thomas, who whimpered as the yellow-haired brute cut through his belt, then dragged his breeches down. The other men searched Thomas's pockets, taking what coins they found and a good knife, then they turned him onto his belly so that his naked arse was ready for the boiling water.

Sir Simon saw the first wisps of steam float from the pot. 'Take it to him,' he ordered his men.

Three of Sir Simon's soldiers were holding Thomas down and he was too hurt and too weak to fight them, so he did the only thing he could. He screamed murder. He filled his lungs and bellowed as loud as he could. He reckoned he was in a small town that was crowded with men and someone must hear and so he shrieked the alarm. 'Murder! Murder!' A man kicked his belly, but Thomas went on shouting.

'For Christ's sake, silence him,' Sir Simon snarled, and Colley, the yellow-haired man, kneeled beside Thomas and tried to stuff straw into his mouth, but Thomas managed to spit it out.

'Murder!' he screamed. 'Murder!'

Colley swore, took a handful of filthy mud and slapped it into Thomas's mouth, muffling his noise. 'Bastard,' Colley said, and thumped Thomas's skull. 'Bastard!'

Thomas gagged on the mud, but he could not spit it out.

Sir Simon was standing over him now. 'You are to

be taught good manners,' he said, and watched as the steaming pot was carried across the smithy yard.

Then the gate opened and a newcomer stepped into the yard. 'What in God's name is happening here?' the man asked, and Thomas could have sung a *Te Deum* in praise of St Sebastian if his mouth had not been crammed with mud, for his rescuer was Father Hobbe, who must have heard the frantic shouting and come running down the alley to investigate. 'What are you doing?' the priest demanded of Sir Simon.

'It is not your business, father,' Sir Simon said.

'Thomas, is it you?' He turned back to the knight. 'By God, it is my business!' Father Hobbe had a temper and he lost it now. 'Who the devil do you think you are?'

'Be careful, priest,' Sir Simon snarled.

'Be careful! Me? I will have your soul in hell if you don't leave.' The small priest snatched up the smith's huge poker and wielded it like a sword. 'I'll have all your souls in hell! Leave! All of you! Out of here! Out! In the name of God, get out! Get out!'

Sir Simon backed down. It was one thing to torture an archer, but quite another to get into a fight with a priest whose voice was loud enough to attract still more attention. Sir Simon snarled that Father Hobbe was an interfering bastard, but he retreated all the same.

Father Hobbe knelt beside Thomas and hooked some of the mud from his mouth, along with tendrils of thick blood and a broken tooth. 'You poor lad,' Father Hobbe said, then helped Thomas stand. 'I'll take you home, Tom, take you home and clean you up.'

Thomas had to vomit first, but then, holding his breeches up, he staggered back to Jeanette's house, supported all the way by the priest. A dozen archers greeted him, wanting to know what had happened, but Father Hobbe brushed them aside. 'Where's the kitchen?' he demanded.

'She won't let us in there,' Thomas said, his voice indistinct because of his swollen mouth and bleeding gums.

'Where is it?' Father Hobbe insisted. One of the archers nodded at the door and the priest just pushed it open and half carried Thomas inside. He sat him on a chair and pulled the rush lights to the table's edge so he could see Thomas's face. 'Dear God,' he said, 'what have they done to you?' He patted Thomas's hand, then went to find water.

Jeanette came into the kitchen, full of fury. 'You are not supposed to be here! You will get out!' Then she saw Thomas's face and her voice trailed away. If someone had told her that she would see a badly beaten English archer she would have been cheered, but to her surprise she felt a pang of sympathy. 'What happened?'

'Sir Simon Jekyll did this,' Thomas managed to say.

'Sir Simon?'

'He's an evil man.' Father Hobbe had heard the name and came from the scullery with a big bowl of water. 'He's an evil thing, evil.' He spoke in English. 'You have some cloths?' he asked Jeanette.

'She doesn't speak English,' Thomas said. Blood was trickling down his face.

'Sir Simon attacked you?' Jeanette asked. 'Why?'

'Because I told him to boil his arse,' Thomas said, and was rewarded with a smile.

'Good,' Jeanette said. She did not invite Thomas to stay in the kitchen, but nor did she order him to leave. Instead she stood and watched as the priest washed his

140

face, then took off Thomas's shirt to bind up the cracked rib.

'Tell her she could help me,' Father Hobbe said.

'She's too proud to help,' Thomas said.

'It's a sinful sad world,' Father Hobbe declared, then knelt down. 'Hold still, Tom,' he said, 'for this will hurt like the very devil.' He took hold of the broken nose and there was the sound of cartilage scraping before Thomas shouted in pain. Father Hobbe put a cold wet cloth over his nose. 'Hold that there, Tom, and the pain will go. Well, it won't really, but you'll get used to it.' He sat on an empty salt barrel, shaking his head. 'Sweet Jesus, Tom, what are we going to do with you?'

'You've done it,' Thomas said, 'and I'm grateful. A day or two and I'll be leaping about like a spring lamb.'

'You've been doing that for too long, Tom,' Father Hobbe said earnestly. Jeanette, not understanding a word, just watched the two men. 'God gave you a good head,' the priest went on, 'but you waste your wits, Tom, you do waste them.'

'You want me to be a priest?'

Father Hobbe smiled. 'I doubt you'd be much credit to the Church, Tom. You'd like as not end up as an archbishop because you're clever and devious enough, but I think you'd be happier as a soldier. But you have debts to God, Tom. Remember that promise you made to your father! You made it in a church, and it would be good for your soul to keep that promise, Tom.'

Thomas laughed, and immediately wished he had not, for the pain whipped through his ribs. He swore, apologized to Jeanette, then looked back to the priest. 'And how in the name of God, father, am I supposed to keep that promise? I don't even know what bastard stole the lance.'

'What bastard?' Jeanette asked, for she had picked up that one word. 'Sir Simon?'

'He is a bastard,' Thomas said, 'but he's not the only one,' and he told her about the lance, about the day his village had been murdered, about his father dying, and about the man who carried a banner showing three yellow hawks on a blue field. He told the story slowly, through bloody lips, and when he had finished Jeanette shrugged.

'So you want to kill this man, yes?'

'One day.'

'He deserves to be killed,' Jeanette said.

Thomas stared at her through half-closed eyes, astonished by those words. 'You know him?'

'He is called Sir Guillaume d'Evecque,' Jeanette said.

'What's she saying?' Father Hobbe asked.

'I know him,' Jeanette said grimly. 'In Caen, where he comes from, he is sometimes called the lord of the sea and of the land.'

'Because he fights on both?' Thomas guessed.

'He is a knight,' Jeanette said, 'but he is also a sea-raider. A pirate. My father owned sixteen ships and Guillaume d'Evecque stole three of them.'

'He fought against you?' Thomas sounded surprised.

Jeanette shrugged. 'He thinks any ship that is not French is an enemy. We are Bretons.'

Thomas looked at Father Hobbe. 'There you are, father,' he said lightly, 'to keep my promise all I must do is fight the knight of the sea and of the land.'

Father Hobbe had not followed the French, but he shook his head sadly. 'How you keep the promise,

Thomas, is your business. But God knows you made it, and I know you are doing nothing about it.' He fingered the wooden cross he wore on a leather lace about his neck. 'And what shall I do about Sir Simon?'

'Nothing,' Thomas said.

'I must tell Totesham, at least!' the priest insisted.

'Nothing, father.' Thomas was just as insistent. 'Promise me.'

Father Hobbe looked suspiciously at Thomas. 'You're not thinking of taking your own revenge, are you?'

Thomas crossed himself and hissed because of the pain in his rib. 'Doesn't our Mother Church tell us to turn the other cheek?' he asked.

'It does,' Father Hobbe said dubiously, 'but it wouldn't condone what Sir Simon did tonight.'

'We shall turn away his wrath with a soft answer,' Thomas said, and Father Hobbe, impressed by this display of genuine Christianity, nodded his acceptance of Thomas's decision.

Jeanette had been following the conversation as best she could and had at least gathered the gist of their words. 'Are you discussing what to do to Sir Simon?' she asked Thomas.

'I'm going to murder the bastard,' Thomas said in French.

She offered him a sour grimace. 'That is a very clever idea, Englishman. So you will be a murderer and they will hang you. Then, thanks be to God, there will be two dead Englishmen.'

'What's she saying, Thomas?' Father Hobbe asked.

'She's agreeing that I ought to forgive my enemies, father.'

'Good woman, good woman,' Father Hobbe said.

143

'Do you really want to kill him?' Jeanette demanded coldly.

Thomas shuddered with the pain, but he was not so hurt that he could not appreciate Jeanette's closeness. She was a hard woman, he reckoned, but still as lovely as the spring and, like the rest of Will Skeat's men, he had harboured impossible dreams of knowing her better. Her question gave him that chance. 'I'll kill him,' he assured her, 'and in killing him, my lady, I'll fetch you your husband's armour and sword.'

Jeanette frowned at him. 'You can do that?'

'If you help me.'

She grimaced. 'How?'

So Thomas told her and, to his astonishment, she did not dismiss the idea in horror, but instead nodded a grudging acceptance. 'It might really work,' she said after a while, 'it really might work.'

Which meant that Sir Simon had united his enemies and Thomas had found himself an ally.

Jeanette's life was encompassed by enemies. She had her son, but everyone else she loved was dead, and those who were left she hated. There were the English, of course, occupying her town, but there was also Belas, the lawyer, and the shipmasters who had cheated her, and the tenants who used the presence of the English to default on their rent, and the town's merchants who dunned her for money she did not have. She was a countess, yet her rank counted for nothing. At night, brooding on her plight, she would dream of meeting a great champion, a duke perhaps, who would come to La Roche-Derrien and punish her enemies one by one.

She saw them whimpering with terror, pleading for mercy and receiving none. But in each dawn there was no duke and her enemies did not cringe, and Jeanette's troubles were unrelieved until Thomas promised to help her kill the one enemy she hated above the rest.

To which end, early in the morning after her conversation with Thomas, Jeanette went to Richard Totesham's headquarters. She went early because she hoped Sir Simon Jekyll would still be in bed, and though it was essential he knew the purpose of her visit, she did not want to meet him. Let him learn from others what she planned.

The headquarters, like her own house, fronted the River Jaudy, and the waterfront yard, despite the early hour, already held a score of petitioners seeking favours from the English. Jeanette was told to wait with the other petitioners. 'I am the Countess of Armorica,' she told the clerk.

'You must wait like the rest,' the clerk answered in poor French, then cut another notch in a tally stick on which he was counting arrow sheaves that were being unloaded from a lighter that had come upriver from the deepwater harbour at Tréguier. A second lighter held barrels of red herrings, and the stench of the fish made Jeanette shudder. English food! They did not even gut the herrings before smoking them and the red fish came from the barrels covered in yellow-green mould, yet the archers ate them with relish. She tried to escape the reeking fish by crossing the yard to where a dozen local men trimmed great lengths of timber propped on sawhorses. One of the carpenters was a man who had sometimes worked for Jeanette's father, though he was usually too drunk to hold a job for more than a few days.

He was barefoot, ragged, hump-backed and hare-lipped, though when he was sober he was as good a labourer as any in the town.

'Jacques!' Jeanette called. 'What are you doing?' She spoke in Breton.

Jacques tugged his forelock and bobbed down. 'You're looking well, my lady.' Only a few folk could understand his speech for his split lip mangled the sounds. 'Your father always said you were his angel.'

'I asked what you are doing.'

'Ladders, my lady, ladders.' Jacques cuffed a stream of mucus from his nose. There was a weeping ulcer on his neck and the stink of it was as bad as the red herrings. 'They want six ever so long ladders.'

'Why?'

Jacques looked left and right to make sure no one could overhear him. 'What he says,' he jerked his head at the Englishman who was supposedly supervising the work, 'what he says is that they're taking them to Lannion. And they're long enough for that big wall, ain't they?'

'Lannion?'

'He likes his ale, he does,' Jacques said, explaining the Englishman's indiscretion.

'Hey! Handsome!' the supervisor shouted at Jacques. 'Get to work!' Jacques, with a grin to Jeanette, picked up his tools.

'Make the rungs loose!' Jeanette advised Jacques in Breton, then turned because her name had been called from the house. Sir Simon Jekyll, looking heavy-eyed and sleepy, was standing in the doorway and Jeanette's heart sank at the sight of him.

'My lady,' Sir Simon offered Jeanette a bow, 'you should not be waiting with common folk.'

'Tell that to the clerk,' Jeanette said coldly.

The clerk tallying the arrow sheaves squealed when Sir Simon caught him by the ear. 'This clerk?' he asked.

'He told me to wait out here.'

Sir Simon cuffed the man across the face. 'She's a lady, you bastard! You treat her like a lady.' He kicked the man away, then pulled the door fully open. 'Come, my lady,' he invited her.

Jeanette went to the door and was relieved to see four more clerks busy at tables inside the house. 'The army,' Sir Simon said as she brushed past him, 'has almost as many clerks as archers. Clerks, farriers, masons, cooks, herdsmen, butchers, anything else on two legs that can take the King's coin.' He smiled at her, then brushed a hand down his threadbare wool robe that was trimmed with fur. 'If I had known you were gracing us with a visit, my lady, I would have dressed.'

Sir Simon, Jeanette noted gladly, was in a puppy mood this morning. He was always either boorish or clumsily polite and she hated him in either mood, but at least he was easier to deal with when he tried to impress her with his manners. 'I came,' she told him, 'to request a pass from Monsieur Totesham.' The clerks watched her surreptitiously, their quills scratching and spluttering on the scraped parchment.

'I can give you a pass,' Sir Simon said gallantly, 'though I trust you are not leaving La Roche-Derrien permanently?'

'I just wish to visit Louannec,' Jeanette said.

'And where, dear lady, is Louannec?'

'It is on the coast,' Jeanette said, 'north of Lannion.'

'Lannion, eh?' He perched on a table's edge, his bare

leg swinging. 'Can't have you wandering near Lannion. Not this week. Next, maybe, but only if you can persuade me that you have good reason to travel.' He smoothed his fair moustache. 'And I can be very persuadable.'

'I wish to pray at the shrine there,' Jeanette said.

'I would not keep you from your prayers,' Sir Simon said. He was thinking that he should have invited her through into the parlour, but in truth he had small appetite for love's games this morning. He had consoled himself for his failure to boil Thomas of Hookton's backside by drinking deep into the darkness, and his belly felt liquid, his throat was dry and his head was banging like a kettledrum. 'Which saint will have the pleasure of hearing your voice?' he asked.

'The shrine is dedicated to Yves who protects the sick. My son has a fever.'

'Poor boy,' Sir Simon said in mock sympathy, then peremptorily ordered a clerk to write the pass for her ladyship. 'You will not travel alone, madame?' he asked.

'I shall take servants.'

'You would be better with soldiers. There are bandits everywhere.'

'I do not fear my own countrymen, Sir Simon.'

'Then you should,' he said tartly. 'How many servants?'

'Two.'

Sir Simon told the clerk to note two companions on the pass, then looked back to Jeanette. 'You really would be much safer with soldiers as escort.'

'God will preserve me,' Jeanette said.

Sir Simon watched as the ink on the pass was sanded dry and a blob of hot wax was dropped onto the parchment. He pressed a seal into the wax, then held the document to Jeanette. 'Maybe I should come with you, madame?'

'I would rather not travel at all,' Jeanette said, refusing to take the pass.

'Then I shall relinquish my duties to God,' Sir Simon said.

Jeanette took the pass, forced herself to thank him, then fled. She half expected that Sir Simon would follow her, but he let her go unmolested. She felt dirty, but also triumphant because the trap was baited now. Well and truly baited.

She did not go straight home, but went instead to the house of the lawyer, Belas, who was still eating a breakfast of blood sausage and bread. The aroma of the sausage put an edge to Jeanette's hunger, but she refused his offer of a plate. She was a countess and he was a mere lawyer and she would not demean herself by eating with him.

Belas straightened his robe, apologized that the parlour was cold, and asked whether she had at last decided to sell the house. 'It is the sensible thing to do, madame. Your debts mount.'

'I shall let you know my decision,' she said, 'but I have come on other business.'

Belas opened the parlour shutters. 'Business costs money, madame, and your debts, forgive me, are mounting.'

'It is Duke Charles's business,' Jeanette said. 'Do you still write to his men of business?'

'From time to time,' Belas said guardedly.

'How do you reach them?' Jeanette demanded.

Belas was suspicious of the question, but finally saw

no harm in giving an answer. 'The messages go by boat to Paimpol,' he said, 'then overland to Guingamp.'

'How long does it take?'

'Two days? Three? It depends if the English are riding the country between Paimpol and Guingamp.'

'Then write to the Duke,' Jeanette said, 'and tell him from me that the English will attack Lannion at the end of this week. They are making ladders to scale the wall.' She had decided to send the message through Belas, for her own couriers were two fishermen who only came to sell their wares in La Roche-Derrien on a Thursday, and any message sent through them must arrive too late. Belas's couriers, on the other hand, could reach Guingamp in good time to thwart the English plans.

Belas dabbed egg from his thin beard. 'You are sure, madame?'

'Of course I'm sure!' She told him about Jacques and the ladders and about the indiscreet English supervisor, and how Sir Simon had forced her to wait a week before venturing near Lannion on her expedition to the shrine at Louannec.

'The Duke,' Belas said as he ushered Jeanette to the house door, 'will be grateful.'

Belas sent the message that day, though he did not say it came from the Countess, but instead claimed all the credit for himself. He gave the letter to a shipmaster who sailed that same afternoon, and next morning a horseman rode south from Paimpol. There were no hellequin in the wasted country between the port and the Duke's capital so the message arrived safely. And in Guingamp, which was Duke Charles's headquarters, the farriers checked the war horses' shoes, the crossbowmen greased their weapons, squires scrubbed mail till it shone and a thousand swords were sharpened.

The English raid on Lannion had been betrayed.

Jeanette's unlikely alliance with Thomas had soothed the hostility in her house. Skeat's men now used the river as their lavatory instead of the courtyard, and Jeanette allowed them into the kitchen, which proved useful, for they brought their rations with them and so her household ate better than it had since the town had fallen, though she still could not bring herself to try the smoked herrings with their bright red, mould-covered skins. Best of all was the treatment given to two importunate merchants who arrived demanding payment from Jeanette and were so badly manhandled by a score of archers that both men left hatless, limping, unpaid and bloody.

'I will pay them when I can,' she told Thomas.

'Sir Simon's likely to have money on him,' he told her.

'He is?'

'Only a fool leaves cash where a servant can find it,' he said.

Four days after the beating his face was still swollen and his lips black with blood clots. His rib hurt and his body was a mass of bruises, but he had insisted to Skeat that he was well enough to ride to Lannion. They would leave that afternoon. At midday Jeanette found him in St Renan's church.

'Why are you praying?' she asked him.

'I always do before a fight.'

'There will be a fight today? I thought you were not riding till tomorrow?'

'I love a well-kept secret,' Thomas said, amused. 'We're going a day early. Everything's ready, why wait?'

'Going where?' Jeanette asked, though she already knew.

'To wherever they take us,' Thomas said.

Jeanette grimaced and prayed silently that her message had reached Duke Charles. 'Be careful,' she said to Thomas, not because she cared for him, but because he was her agent for taking revenge on Sir Simon Jekyll. 'Perhaps Sir Simon will be killed?' she suggested.

'God will save him for me,' Thomas said.

'Perhaps he won't follow me to Louannec?'

'He'll follow you like a dog,' Thomas said, 'but it will be dangerous for you.'

'I shall get the armour back,' Jeanette said, 'and that is all that matters. Are you praying to St Renan?'

'To St Sebastian,' Thomas said, 'and to St Guinefort.'

'I asked the priest about Guinefort,' Jeanette said accusingly, 'and he said he had never heard of him.'

'He probably hasn't heard of St Wilgefortis either,' Thomas said.

'Wilgefortis?' Jeanette stumbled over the unfamiliar name. 'Who is he?'

'She,' Thomas said, 'and she was a very pious virgin who lived in Flanders and grew a long beard. She prayed every day that God would keep her ugly so that she could stay chaste.'

Jeanette could not resist laughing. 'That isn't true!'

'It is true, my lady,' Thomas assured her. 'My father was once offered a hair of her holy beard, but he refused to buy it.'

'Then I shall pray to the bearded saint that you survive your raid,' Jeanette said, 'but only so you can help me against Sir Simon. Other than that I hope you all die.'

The garrison at Guingamp had the same wish, and to make it come true they assembled a strong force of crossbowmen and men-at-arms to ambush the Englishmen on their way to Lannion, but they, like Jeanette, were convinced that La Roche-Derrien's garrison would make their sally on the Friday and so they did not leave till late on Thursday, by which time Totesham's force was already within five miles of Lannion. The shrunken garrison did not know the English were coming because Duke Charles's war captains, who commanded his forces in Guingamp while the Duke was in Paris, decided not to warn the town. If too many people knew that the English had been betrayed then the English themselves might hear of it, abandon their plans and so deny the Duke's men the chance of a rare and complete victory.

The English expected victory themselves. It was a dry night and, near midnight, a full moon slid out from behind a silver-edged cloud to cast Lannion's walls in sharp relief. The raiders were hidden in woods from where they watched the few sentinels on the ramparts. Those sentinels grew sleepy and, after a time, went to the bastions where fires burned and so they did not see the six ladder parties creep across the night fields, nor the hundred archers following the ladders. And still they slept as the archers climbed the rungs and Totesham's main force erupted from the woods, ready to burst through the eastern gate that the archers would open.

The sentinels died. The first dogs awoke in the town,

then a church bell began to ring and Lannion's garrison came awake, but too late for the gate was open and Totesham's mail-clad soldiers were crying havoc in the dark alleys while still more men-at-arms and archers were pouring through the narrow gate.

Skeat's men were the rearguard and so waited outside the town as the sack began. Church bells were clanging wildly as the town's parishes woke to nightmare, but gradually the clangour ceased.

Will Skeat stared at the moon-glossed fields south of Lannion. 'I hear it was Sir Simon Jekyll who improved your looks,' he said to Thomas.

'It was.'

'Because you told him to boil his arse?' Skeat grinned. 'You can't blame him for thumping you,' Skeat said, 'but he should have talked to me first.'

'What would you have done?'

'Made sure he didn't thump you too much, of course,' Skeat said, his gaze moving steadily across the landscape. Thomas had acquired the same habit of watchfulness but all the land beyond the town was still. A mist rose from the low ground. 'So what do you plan to do about it?' Skeat asked.

'Talk to you.'

'I don't fight your goddamn battles, boy,' Skeat growled. 'What do you plan to do about it?'

'Ask you to lend me Jake and Sam on Saturday. And I want three crossbows.'

'Crossbows, eh?' Skeat asked flatly. He saw that the rest of Totesham's force had now entered the town so he put two fingers to his lips and sounded a piercing whistle to signal that his own men could follow. 'Onto the walls!' he shouted as the hellequin rode forward.

'Onto the walls!' That was the rearguard's job: to man the fallen town's defences. 'Half the bloody bastards will still get drunk,' Skeat growled, 'so you stay with me, Tom.'

Most of Skeat's men did their duty and climbed the stone steps to the town's ramparts, but a few slipped away in search of plunder and drink, so Skeat, Thomas and a half-dozen archers scoured the town to find those laggards and drive them back to the walls. A score of Totesham's men-at-arms were doing much the same – dragging men out of taverns and setting them to loading the many wagons that had been stored in the town to keep them from the hellequin. Totesham particularly wanted food for his garrison, and his more reliable men-at-arms did their best to keep the English soldiers from drink, women or anything else that would slow the plunder.

The town's garrison, woken and surprised, had done their best to fight back, but they had responded much too late, and their bodies now lay in the moonlit streets. But in the western part of the town, close to the quays which fronted the River Léguer, the battle still went on, and Skeat was drawn to the sound. Most men were ignoring it, too intent on kicking down house doors and ransacking warehouses, but Skeat reckoned no one in town was safe until all the defenders were dead.

Thomas followed him to find a group of Totesham's men-at-arms who had just retreated from a narrow street. 'There's a mad bastard down there,' one of them told Skeat, 'and he's got a dozen crossbowmen.'

The mad bastard and his crossbowmen had already killed their share of Englishmen, for the red-crossed bodies lay where the street bent sharply towards the river.

'Burn them out,' one of the men-at-arms suggested.

'Not before we've searched the buildings,' Skeat said, then sent two of his archers to fetch one of the ladders that had been used to scale the ramparts. Once the ladder was fetched he propped it against the nearest house and looked at Thomas, who grinned, climbed the rungs and then clambered up the steep thatch. His broken rib hurt, but he gained the ridge and there took the bow from his shoulder and fitted an arrow onto the cord. He walked along the rooftop, his mooncast shadow long on the sloping straw. The roof ended just above the place where the enemy waited and so, before reaching the ridge's peak, he drew the bow to its full extent, then took two steps forward.

The enemy saw him and a dozen crossbows jerked up, but so did the unhelmeted face of a fair-haired man who had a long sword in his hand. Thomas recognized him. It was Sir Geoffrey de Pont Blanc, and Thomas hesitated because he admired the man. But then the first bolt whipped so close to his face that he felt the wind of its passing on his cheek and so he loosed, and he knew the arrow would go straight into the open mouth of Sir Geoffrey's upturned face. He did not see it strike, though, for he had stepped back as the other crossbows twanged and their bolts seared up towards the moon.

'He's dead!' Thomas shouted.

There was a tramp of feet as the men-at-arms charged before the crossbowmen could reload their clumsy weapons. Thomas stepped back to the ridge's end and saw the swords and axes rise and fall. He saw the blood splash up onto the plastered house fronts. Saw the men hacking at Sir Geoffrey's corpse just to make certain he was really dead. A woman shrieked in the house that Sir Geoffrey had been defending.

Thomas slithered down the thatch and jumped into the street where Sir Geoffrey had died and there he picked up three of the crossbows and a bag of bolts that he carried back to Will Skeat.

The Yorkshireman grinned. 'Crossbows, eh? That means you'll be pretending to be the enemy, and you can't do that in La Roche-Derrien, so you're waylaying Sir Simon somewhere outside the town. Am I right?'

'Something like that.'

'I could read you like a bloody book, boy, if I could read, which I can't on account of having too much sense.' Skeat walked on towards the river where three ships were being plundered and another two, their holds already emptied, were burning fiercely. 'But how do you get the bastard out of town?' Skeat asked. 'He's not a complete fool.'

'He is when it comes to the Countess.'

'Ah!' Skeat grinned. 'And the Countess, she's suddenly being nice to us all. So it's you and her, is it?'

'It is not her and me, no.'

'Soon will be, though, won't it?' Skeat said.

'I doubt it.'

'Why? Because she's a countess? Still a woman, boy. But I'd be careful of her.'

'Careful?'

'Hard bitch, that one. Looks lovely on the outside, but it's all flint inside. She'll break your heart, boy.'

Skeat had stopped on the wide stone quays where men were emptying warehouses of leather, grain, smoked fish, wine and bolts of cloth. Sir Simon was among them, shouting at his men to commandeer more wagons. The town was yielding a vast fortune. It was a much bigger place than La Roche-Derrien and, because it had successfully fought off the Earl of Northampton's winter siege, it had been reckoned a safe place for Bretons to store their valuables. Now it was being gutted. A man staggered past Thomas with an armload of silver plate, another man was dragging a half-naked woman by the shreds of her nightdress. One group of archers had broken open a vat and were dipping their faces to drink the wine.

'It was easy enough getting in here,' Skeat said, 'but it'll be the devil's own job to get these sodden bastards back out again.'

Sir Simon beat his sword on the backs of two drunks who were getting in the way of his men emptying a storehouse of its bolts of cloth. He saw Thomas and looked surprised, but he was too wary of Will Skeat to say anything. He just turned away.

'Bastard must have paid off his debts by now,' Skeat said, still staring at Sir Simon's back. 'War's a good way to get rich, so long as you ain't taken prisoner and ransomed. Not that they'd ransom you or me, boy. Slit our bellies and prick our eyes out, more like. Have you ever shot a crossbow?'

'No.'

'Ain't quite as easy as it looks. Not as hard as shooting a real bow, of course, but it still takes practice. Goddamn things can pitch a bit high if you're not used to them. Do Jake and Sam want to help you?'

'They say so.'

'Of course they do, evil bastards that they are.' Skeat

still stared at Sir Simon, who was wearing his new, shining armour. 'I reckon the bastard will carry his cash with him.'

'I would think so, yes.'

'Half mine, Tom, and I'll ask no questions come Saturday.'

'Thanks, Will.'

'But do it proper, Tom,' Skeat said savagely, 'do it proper. I don't want to watch you hang. I don't mind watching most fools doing the rope dance with the piss running down their legs, but it'd be a shame to watch you twitching your way to the devil.'

They went back to the walls. Neither man had collected any plunder, but they had already taken more than enough from their raids on the north Breton farms and it was now the turn of Totesham's men to gorge themselves on a captured town.

One by one the houses were searched and the tavern barrels were drained. Richard Totesham wanted his force to leave Lannion at dawn, but there were too many captured carts waiting to get through the narrow eastern gate and not nearly enough horses to pull the carts, so men were harnessing themselves the shafts rather than leave their pickings behind. Other men were drunk and senseless, and Totesham's men-at-arms scoured the town to find them, but it was fire that drove most of the drunks from their refuges. The townsfolk fled south as the English set the thatched roofs alight.

The smoke thickened into a vast dirty pillar that drifted south on the small sea wind. The pillar glowed a lurid red on its underside, and it must have been that sight which first told the approaching force from Guingamp that they had arrived too late to save the town. They had marched through the night, expecting to find some place where they could lay an ambush for Totesham's men, but the damage was already done. Lannion was burning and its wealth was piled on carts that were still being manhandled through the gate. But if the hated English could not be ambushed on their way to the town, then they could be surprised as they left and so the enemy commanders swung their forces eastwards towards the road which led back to La Roche-Derrien.

Cross-eyed Jake saw the enemy first. He was gazing south through the pearly mist that lay over the flat land and he saw the shadows in the vapour. At first he thought it was a herd of cows, then he decided it had to be refugees from the town. But then he saw a banner and a lance and the dull grey of a mail coat, and he shouted to Skeat that there were horsemen in sight.

Skeat peered over the ramparts. 'Can you see anything, Tom?'

It was just before dawn proper and the countryside was suffused with greyness and streaked with mist. Thomas stared. He could see a thick wood a mile or more to the south and a low ridge showing dark above the mist. Then he saw the banners and the grey mail in the grey light, and a thicket of lances.

'Men-at-arms,' he said, 'a lot of the bastards.'

Skeat swore. Totesham's men were either still in the town or else strung along the road to La Roche-Derrien, and strung so far that there could be no hope of pulling them back behind Lannion's walls – though even if that had been possible it was not practical for the whole western side of the town was burning furiously and the flames were spreading fast. To retreat behind the walls

160

was to risk being roasted alive, but Totesham's men were hardly in a fit condition to fight: many were drunk and all were laden with plunder.

'Hedgerow,' Skeat said curtly, pointing to a ragged line of blackthorn and elder that ran parallel to the road where the carts rumbled. 'Archers to the hedge, Tom. We'll look after your horses. Christ knows how we'll stop the bastards,' he made the sign of the cross, 'but we ain't got much choice.'

Thomas bullied a passage at the crowded gate and led forty archers across a soggy pasture to the hedgerow that seemed a flimsy barrier against the enemy massing in the silvery mist. There were at least three hundred horsemen there. They were not advancing yet, but instead grouping themselves for a charge, and Thomas had only forty men to stop them.

'Spread out!' he shouted. 'Spread out!' He briefly went onto one knee and made the sign of the cross. St Sebastian, he prayed, be with us now. St Guinefort, protect me. He touched the desiccated dog's paw, then made the sign of the cross again.

A dozen more archers joined his force, but it was still far too small. A score of pageboys, mounted on ponies and armed with toy swords, could have massacred the men on the road, for Thomas's hedge did not provide a complete screen, but rather straggled into nothingness about half a mile from the town. The horsemen only had to ride round that open end and there would be nothing to stop them. Thomas could take his archers into the open ground, but fifty men could not stop three hundred. Archers were at their best when they were massed together so that their arrows made a hard, steel-tipped rain. Fifty men could make a shower, but they would still be overrun and massacred by the horsemen.

'Crossbowmen,' Jake grunted, and Thomas saw the men in green and red jackets emerging from the woods behind the enemy men-at-arms. The new dawn light reflected cold from mail, swords and helmets. 'Bastards are taking their time,' Jake said nervously. He had planted a dozen arrows in the base of the hedge, which was just thick enough to stop the horsemen, but not nearly dense enough to slow a crossbow bolt.

Will Skeat had gathered sixty of his men-at-arms beside the road, ready to countercharge the enemy whose numbers increased every minute. Duke Charles's men and their French allies were riding eastwards now, looking to advance about the open end of the hedge where there was an inviting swathe of green and open land leading all the way to the road. Thomas wondered why the hell they were waiting. He wondered if he would die here. Dear God, he thought, but there were not nearly enough men to stop this enemy. The fires continued to burn in Lannion, pouring smoke into the pale sky.

He ran to the left of the line, where he found Father Hobbe holding a bow. 'You shouldn't be here, father,' he said.

'God will forgive me,' the priest said. He had tucked his cassock into his belt and had a small stand of arrows stuck into the hedgebank. Thomas gazed at the open land, wondering how long his men would last in that immensity of grass. Just what the enemy wanted, he thought, a stretch of bare flat land on which their horses could run hard and straight. Only the land was not entirely flat for it was dotted with grassy hummocks through which two grey herons walked stiff-legged as they hunted for frogs or ducklings. Frogs, Thomas thought, and ducklings. Sweet God, it was a marsh! The spring had been unusually dry, yet his boots were soaking from the damp field he had crossed to reach the hedgerow. The realization burst on Thomas like the rising sun. The open land was marsh! No wonder the enemy was waiting. They could see Totesham's men strung out for slaughter, but they could see no way across the swampy ground.

'This way!' Thomas shouted at the archers. 'This way! Hurry! Hurry! Come on, you bastards!'

He led them round the end of the hedge into the swamp where they leaped and splashed through a maze of marsh, tussocks and streamlets. They went south towards the enemy and once in range Thomas spread his men out and told them to indulge in target practice. His fear had gone, replaced by exaltation. The enemy was balked by the marsh. Their horses could not advance, but Thomas's light archers could leap across the tussocks like demons. Like hellequin.

'Kill the bastards!' he shouted.

The white-fledged arrows hissed across the wetland to strike horses and men. Some of the enemy tried to charge the archers, but their horses floundered in the soft ground and became targets for volleys of arrows. The crossbowmen dismounted and advanced, but the archers switched their aim to them, and now more archers were arriving, dispatched by Skeat and Totesham, so that the marsh was suddenly swarming with English and Welsh bowmen who poured a steel-tipped hell on the befuddled enemy. It became a game. Men wagered on whether or not they could strike a particular target. The sun rose higher, casting shadows from the dead horses. The enemy was edging back to the trees. One brave group tried a last charge, hoping to skirt the marsh, but their horses stumbled in the soft ground and the arrows spitted and sliced at them so that men and beasts screamed as they fell. One horseman struggled on, flailing his beast with the flat of his sword. Thomas put an arrow into the horse's neck and Jake skewered its haunch, and the animal screeched piteously as it thrashed in pain and collapsed into the swamp. The man somehow extricated his feet from his stirrups and stumbled cursing towards the archers with his sword held low and shield high, but Sam buried an arrow in his groin and then a dozen more bowmen added their arrows before swarming over the fallen enemy. Knives were drawn, throats cut, then the business of plunder could begin. The corpses were stripped of their mail and weapons and the horses of their bridles and saddles, then Father Hobbe prayed over the dead while the archers counted their spoils.

The enemy was gone by mid-morning. They left two score of dead men, and twice that number had been wounded, but not a single Welsh or English archer had died.

Duke Charles's men slunk back to Guingamp. Lannion had been destroyed, they had been humiliated and Will Skeat's men celebrated in La Roche-Derrien. They were the hellequin, they were the best and they could not be beaten.

The following morning Thomas, Sam and Jake left La Roche-Derrien before daybreak. They rode west towards Lannion, but once in the woods they swerved off the road and picketed their horses deep among the trees. Then, moving like poachers, they worked their way back to the wood's edge. Each had his own bow slung on his shoulder, and carried a crossbow too, and they practised with the unfamiliar weapons as they waited in a swathe of bluebells at the wood's margin from where they could see La Roche-Derrien's western gate. Thomas had only brought a dozen bolts, short and stub-feathered, so each of them shot just two times. Will Skeat had been right: the weapons did kick up as the archers loosed so that their first bolts went high on the trunk that was their target. Thomas's second shot was more accurate, but nothing like as true as an arrow shot from a proper bow. The near miss made him apprehensive of the morning's risks, but Jake and Sam were both cheerful at the prospect of larceny and murder.

'Can't really miss,' Sam said after his second shot had also gone high. 'Might not catch the bastard in the belly, but we'll hit him somewhere.' He levered the cord back, grunting with the effort. No man alive could haul a crossbow's string by arm-power alone and so a mechanism had to be employed. The most expensive crossbows, those with the longest range, used a jackscrew. The archer would place a cranked handle on the screw's end and wind the cord back, inch by creaking inch, until the pawl above the trigger engaged the string. Some crossbowmen used their bodies as a lever. They wore thick leather belts to which a hook was attached and by bending down, attaching the hook to the cord and then straightening, they could pull the twisted strings back, but the crossbows Thomas had brought from Lannion used a lever, shaped like a goat's hind leg, that forced the cord and bent the short bow shaft, which was a layered thing of horn, wood and glue. The lever was probably the fastest way of cocking the weapon, though it did not offer the power of a screw-cocked bow and was still slow compared to a yew shaft. In truth there was nothing to compare with the English bow and Skeat's men debated endlessly why the enemy did not adopt the weapon. 'Because they're daft,' was Sam's curt judgement, though the truth, Thomas knew, was that other nations simply did not start their sons early enough. To be an archer meant starting as a boy, then practising and practising until the chest was broad, the arm muscles huge and the arrow seemed to fly without the archer giving its aim any thought.

Jake shot his second bolt into the oak and swore horribly when it missed the mark. He looked at the bow. 'Piece of shit,' he said. 'How close are we going to be?'

'Close as we can get,' Thomas said.

Jake sniffed. 'If I can poke the bloody bow into the bastard's belly I might not miss.'

'Thirty, forty feet should be all right,' Sam reckoned.

'Aim at his crotch,' Thomas encouraged them, 'and we should gut him.'

'It'll be all right,' Jake said, 'three of us? One of us has got to skewer the bastard.'

'In the shadows, lads,' Thomas said, gesturing them deeper into the trees. He had seen Jeanette coming from the gate where the guards had inspected her pass then waved her on. She sat sideways on a small horse that Will Skeat had lent her and was accompanied by two grey-haired servants, a man and a woman, both of whom had grown old in her father's service and now walked beside their mistress's horse. If Jeanette had truly planned to ride to Louannec then such a feeble

166

and aged escort would have been an invitation for trouble, but trouble, of course, was what she intended, and no sooner had she reached the trees than the trouble appeared as Sir Simon Jekyll emerged from the archway's shadow, riding with two other men.

'What if those two bastards stay close to him?' Sam asked.

'They won't,' Thomas said. He was certain of that, just as he and Jeanette had been certain that Sir Simon would follow her and that he would wear the expensive suit of plate he had stolen from her.

'She's a brave lass,' Jake grunted.

'She's got spirit,' Thomas said, 'knows how to hate someone.'

Jake tested the point of a quarrel. 'You and her?' he asked Thomas. 'Doing it, are you?'

'No.'

'But you'd like to. I would.'

'I don't know,' Thomas said. He thought Jeanette beautiful, but Skeat was right, there was a hardness in her that repelled him. 'I suppose so,' he admitted.

'Of course you would,' Jake said, 'be daft not to.'

Once Jeanette was among the trees Thomas and his companions trailed her, staying hidden and always conscious that Sir Simon and his two henchmen were closing quickly. Those three horsemen trotted once they reached the wood and succeeded in catching up with Jeanette in a place that was almost perfect for Thomas's ambush. The road ran within yards of a clearing where a meandering stream had undercut the roots of a willow. The fallen trunk was rotted and thick with disc-like fungi. Jeanette, pretending to make way for the three armoured horsemen, turned into the clearing and

167

waited beside the dead tree. Best of all there was a stand of young alders close to the willow's trunk that offered cover to Thomas.

Sir Simon turned off the road, ducked under the branches and curbed his horse close to Jeanette. One of his companions was Henry Colley, the brutal yellow-haired man who had hurt Thomas so badly, while the other was Sir Simon's slack-jawed squire, who grinned in expectation of the coming entertainment. Sir Simon pulled off the snouted helmet and hung it on his saddle's pommel, then smiled triumphantly.

'It is not safe, madame,' he said, 'to travel without an armed escort.'

'I am perfectly safe,' Jeanette declared. Her two servants cowered beside her horse as Colley and the squire hemmed Jeanette in place with their horses.

Sir Simon dismounted with a clank of armour. 'I had hoped, dear lady,' he said, approaching her, 'that we could talk on our way to Louannec.'

'You wish to pray to the holy Yves?' Jeanette asked. 'What will you beg of him? That he grants you courtesy?'

'I would just talk with you, madame,' Sir Simon said.

'Talk of what?'

'Of the complaint you made to the Earl of North-ampton. You fouled my honour, lady.'

'Your honour?' Jeanette laughed. 'What honour do you have that could be fouled? Do you even know the meaning of the word?'

Thomas, hidden behind the straggle of alders, was whispering a translation to Jake and Sam. All three crossbows were cocked and had their wicked little bolts lying in the troughs.

'If you will not talk to me on the road, madame, then we must have our conversation here,' Sir Simon declared.

'I have nothing to say to you.'

'Then you will find it easy enough to listen,' he said, and reached up to haul her out of the saddle. She beat at his armoured gauntlets, but no resistance of hers could prevent him from dragging her to the ground. The two servants shrieked protests, but Colley and the squire silenced them by grabbing their hair, then pulling them out of the clearing to leave Jeanette and Sir Simon alone.

Jeanette had scrabbled backwards and was now standing beside the fallen tree. Thomas had raised his crossbow, but Jake pushed it down, for Sir Simon's escort was still too near.

Sir Simon pushed Jeanette hard so that she sat down on the rotting trunk, then he took a long dagger from his sword belt and drove its narrow blade hard through Jeanette's skirts so that she was pinned to the fallen willow. He hammered the knife hilt with his steel-shod foot to make sure it was deep in the trunk. Colley and the squire had vanished now and the noise of their horses' hooves had faded among the leaves.

Sir Simon smiled, then stepped forward and plucked the cloak from Jeanette's shoulders. 'When I first saw you, my lady,' he said, 'I confess I thought of marriage. But you have been perverse, so I have changed my mind.' He put his hands at her bodice's neckline and ripped it apart, tearing the laces from their embroidered holes. Jeanette screamed as she tried to cover herself and Jake again held Thomas's arm down.

'Wait till he gets the armour off,' Jake whispered.

They knew the bolts could pierce mail, but none of the three knew how strong the plate armour would prove.

Sir Simon slapped Jeanette's hands away. 'There, madame,' he said, gazing at her breasts, 'now we can have discourse.'

Sir Simon stepped back and began to strip himself of the armour. He pulled off the plated gauntlets first, unbuckled the sword belt, then lifted the shoulder pieces on their leather harness over his head. He fumbled with the side buckles of the breast and back plates that were attached to a leather coat that also supported the rerebraces and vambraces that protected his arms. The coat had a chain skirt, which, because of the weight of the plate and ring mail, made it a struggle for Sir Simon to drag over his head. He staggered as he pulled at the heavy armour and Thomas again raised the crossbow, but Sir Simon was stepping back and forward as he tried to steady himself and Thomas could not be sure of his aim and so kept his finger off the trigger.

The armour-laden coat thumped onto the ground, leaving Sir Simon tousle-haired and bare-chested, and Thomas again put the crossbow stock into his shoulder, but now Sir Simon sat down to strip off the cuisses, greaves, poleyns and boots, and he sat in such a way that his armoured legs were towards the ambush and kept getting in the way of Thomas's aim. Jeanette was struggling with the knife, scared out of her wits that Thomas had not stayed close, but tug as she might the dagger would not move.

Sir Simon pulled off the sollerets that covered his feet, then wriggled out of the leather breeches to which the leg plates were attached. 'Now, madame,' he said, standing whitely naked, 'we can talk properly.'

Jeanette heaved a last time at the dagger, hoping to plunge it into Sir Simon's pale belly, and just then Thomas pulled his trigger.

The bolt scraped across Sir Simon's chest. Thomas had aimed at the knight's groin, hoping to send the short arrow deep into his belly, but the bolt had grazed one of the whiplike alder boughs and been deflected. Blood streaked on Sir Simon's skin and he dropped to the ground so fast that Jake's bolt whipped over his head. Sir Simon scrambled away, going first to his discarded armour. Then he realized he had no time to save the plate and so he ran for his horse, and it was then that Sam's bolt caught him in the flesh of his right thigh so that he yelped, half fell and decided there was no time to rescue his horse either and just limped naked and bleeding into the woods. Thomas loosed a second bolt that rattled past Sir Simon to whack into a tree, and then the naked man vanished. Thomas swore. He had meant to kill, but Sir Simon was all too alive.

'I thought you weren't here!' Jeanette said as Thomas appeared. She was clutching her torn clothing to her breasts.

'We missed the bastard,' Thomas said angrily. He heaved the dagger free of her skirts while Jake and Sam thrust the armour into two sacks. Thomas threw down the crossbow and took his own black bow from his shoulder. What he should do now, he thought, was track Sir Simon through the trees and kill the bastard. He could pull out the white-feathered arrow and put a crossbow bolt into the wound so that whoever found him would believe that bandits or the enemy had killed the knight.

'Search the bastard's saddle pouches,' he told Jake

and Sam. Jeanette had tied the cloak round her neck and her eyes widened as she saw the gold pour from the pouches. 'You're going to stay here with Jake and Sam,' Thomas told her.

'Where are you going?' she asked.

'To finish the job,' Thomas said grimly. He loosed the laces of his arrow bag and dropped one crossbow bolt in among the longer arrows. 'Wait here,' he told Jake and Sam.

'I'll help you,' Sam said.

'No,' Thomas insisted, 'wait here and look after the Countess.' He was angry with himself. He should have used his own bow from the start and simply removed the telltale arrow and shot a bolt into Sir Simon's corpse, but he had fumbled the ambush. But at least Sir Simon had fled westwards, away from his two men-at-arms, and he was naked, bleeding and unarmed. Easy prey, Thomas told himself as he followed the blood drops among the trees. The trail went west and then, as the blood thinned, southwards. Sir Simon was obviously working his way back towards his companions and Thomas abandoned caution and just ran, hoping to cut the fugitive off. Then, bursting through some hazels, he saw Sir Simon, limping and bent. Thomas pulled the bow back, and just then Colley and the squire came into view, both with swords drawn and both spurring their horses at Thomas. He switched his aim to the nearest and loosed without thinking. He loosed as a good archer should, and the arrow went true and fast, smack into the mailed chest of the squire, who was thrown back in his saddle. His sword dropped to the ground as his horse swerved hard to its left, going in front of Sir Simon.

Colley wrenched his reins and reached for Sir Simon, who clutched at his outstretched hand and then half ran and was half carried away into the trees. Thomas had dragged a second arrow from the bag, but by the time he loosed it the two men were half hidden by trees and the arrow glanced off a branch and was lost among the leaves.

Thomas swore. Colley had stared straight at Thomas for an instant. Sir Simon had also seen him and Thomas, a third arrow on his string, just stared at the trees as he understood that everything had just fallen apart. In one instant. Everything.

He ran back to the clearing by the stream. 'You're to take the Countess to the town,' he told Jake and Sam, 'but for Christ's sake go carefully. They'll be searching for us soon. You'll have to sneak back.'

They stared at him, not understanding, and Thomas told them what had happened. How he had killed Sir Simon's squire, and how that made him both a murderer and a fugitive. He had been seen by Sir Simon and by the yellow-haired Colley, and they would both be witnesses at his trial and celebrants at his execution.

He told Jeanette the same in French. 'You can trust Jake and Sam,' he told her, 'but you mustn't be caught going home. You have to go carefully!'

Jake and Sam argued, but Thomas knew well enough what the consequences of the killing arrow were. 'Tell Will what happened,' he told them. 'Blame it all on me and say I'll wait for him at Quatre Vents.' That was a village the hellequin had laid waste south of La Roche-Derrien. 'Tell him I'd like his advice.'

Jeanette tried to persuade him that his panic was

unnecessary. 'Perhaps they did not recognize you?' she suggested.

'They recognized me, my lady,' Thomas said grimly. He smiled ruefully. 'I am sorry, but at least you have your armour and sword. Hide them well.' He pulled himself into Sir Simon's saddle. 'Quatre Vents,' he told Jake and Sam, then spurred southwards through the trees.

He was a murderer, a wanted man and a fugitive, and that meant he was any man's prey, alone in the wilderness made by the hellequin. He had no idea what he should do or where he could go, only that if he was to survive then he must ride like the devil's horseman that he was.

So he did.

Quatre Vents had been a small village, scarce larger than Hookton, with a gaunt barn-like church, a cluster of cottages where cows and people had shared the same thatched roofs, a water mill, and some outlying farms crouched in sheltered valleys. Only the stone walls of the church and mill were left now, the rest was just ashes, dust and weeds. The blossom was blowing from the untended orchards when Thomas arrived on a horse sweated white by its long journey. He released the stallion to graze in a well-hedged and overgrown pasture, then took himself into the woods above the church. He was shaken, nervous and frightened, for what had seemed like a game had twisted his life into darkness. Not a few hours before he had been an archer in England's army and, though his future might not have appealed to the young men with whom he had rioted in Oxford, Thomas had been certain he would at least rise as high as Will Skeat. He had imagined himself leading a band of soldiers, becoming wealthy, following his black bow to fortune and even rank, but now he was a hunted man. He was in such panic that he began to doubt Will Skeat's reaction, fearing that Skeat would be so disgusted at the failure of the ambush that he would arrest Thomas and lead him back to a rope-dancing end in La Roche-Derrien's marketplace. He worried that Jeanette would have been caught going back to the town. Would they charge her with murder too? He shivered as night fell. He was twenty-two years old, he had failed utterly, he was alone and he was lost.

He woke in a cold, drizzling dawn. Hares raced across the pasture where Sir Simon Jekyll's destrier cropped the grass. Thomas opened the purse he kept under his mail coat and counted his coins. There was the gold from Sir Simon's saddle pouch and his own few coins, so he was not poor, but like most of the hellequin he left the bulk of his money in Will Skeat's keeping; even when they were out raiding, there were always some men left in La Roche-Derrien to keep an eye on the hoard. What would he do? He had a bow and some arrows, and perhaps he could walk to Gascony, though he had no idea how far that was, but at least he knew there were English garrisons there who would surely welcome another trained archer. Or perhaps he could find a way to cross the Channel? Go home, find another name, start again – except he had no home. What he must never do was find himself within a hanging rope's distance of Sir Simon Jekyll.

The hellequin arrived shortly after midday. The archers rode into the village first, followed by the men-at-arms, who were escorting a one-horse wagon that had wooden hoops supporting a flapping cover of brown cloth. Father Hobbe and Will Skeat rode beside the wagon, which puzzled Thomas, for he had never known the hellequin use such a vehicle before. But then Skeat and the priest broke away from the men-at-arms and spurred their horses towards the field where the stallion grazed.

The two men stopped by the hedge, and Skeat cupped his hands and shouted towards the woods, 'Come on out, you daft bastard!' Thomas emerged very sheepishly, to be greeted with an ironic cheer from the archers. Skeat regarded him sourly. 'God's bones, Tom,' he said, 'but the devil did a bad thing when he humped your mother.'

Father Hobbe tutted at Will's blasphemy, then raised a hand in blessing. 'You missed a fine sight, Tom,' he said cheerfully: 'Sir Simon coming home to La Roche, half naked and bleeding like a stuck pig. I'll hear your confession before we go.'

'Don't grin, you stupid bastard,' Skeat snapped. 'Sweet Christ, Tom, but if you do a job, do it proper. Do it proper! Why did you leave the bastard alive?'

'I missed.'

'Then you go and kill some poor bastard squire instead. Sweet Christ, but you're a goddamn bloody fool.'

'I suppose they want to hang me?' Thomas asked.

'Oh no,' Skeat said in feigned surprise, 'of course not! They want to feast you, hang garlands round your neck and give you a dozen virgins to warm your bed. What the hell do you think they want to do with you? Of course they want you dead and I swore on my mother's life I'd bring you back if I found you alive. Does he look alive to you, father?'

Father Hobbe examined Thomas. 'He looks very dead to me, Master Skeat.'

'He bloody deserves to be dead, the daft bastard.'

'Did the Countess get safe home?' Thomas asked.

'She got home, if that's what you mean,' Skeat said, 'but what do you think Sir Simon wanted the moment he'd covered up his shrivelled prick? To have her house searched, Tom, for some armour and a sword that were legitimately his. He's not such a daft fool; he knows you and she were together.' Thomas cursed and Skeat repeated the blasphemy. 'So they pressed her two servants and they admitted the Countess planned everything.'

'They did what?' Thomas asked.

'They pressed them,' Skeat repeated, which meant that the old couple had been put flat on the ground and had stones piled on their chests. 'The old girl squealed everything at the first stone, so they were hardly hurt,' Skeat went on, 'and now Sir Simon wants to charge her ladyship with murder. And naturally he had her house searched for the sword and armour, but they found nowt because I had them and her hidden well away, but she's still as deep in the shit as you are. You can't just go about sticking crossbow bolts into knights and slaughtering squires, Tom! It upsets the order of things!'

'I'm sorry, Will,' Thomas said.

'So the long and the brief of it,' Skeat said, 'is that the Countess is seeking the protection of her husband's uncle.' He jerked a thumb at the cart. 'She's in that, together with her bairn, two bruised servants, a suit of armour and a sword.'

'Sweet Jesus,' Thomas said, staring at the cart.

'You put her there,' Skeat growled, 'not Him. And I had the devil's own business keeping her hid from Sir Simon. Dick Totesham suspects I'm up to no good and he don't approve, though he took my word in the end, but I still had to promise to drag you back by the scruff of your miserable neck. But I haven't seen you, Tom.'

'I'm sorry, Will,' Thomas said again.

'You bloody well should be sorry,' Skeat said, though he was exuding a quiet satisfaction that he had managed to clean up Thomas's mess so efficiently. Jake and Sam had not been seen by Sir Simon or his surviving man-at-arms, so they were safe, Thomas was a fugitive and Jeanette had been safely smuggled out of La Roche-Derrien before Sir Simon could make her life into utter misery. 'She's travelling to Guingamp,' Skeat went on, 'and I'm sending a dozen men to escort her and God only knows if the enemy will respect their flag of truce. If I had a lick of bloody sense I'd skin you alive and make a bow-cover out of your hide.'

'Yes, Will,' Thomas said meekly.

'Don't bloody "yes, Will" me,' Skeat said. 'What are you going to do with the few days you've got left to live?'

'I don't know.'

Skeat sniffed. 'You could grow up, for a start, though there's probably scant chance of that happening. Right, lad.' He braced himself, taking charge. 'I took your money from the chest, so here it is.' He handed Thomas a leather pouch. 'And I've put three sheaves of arrows in the lady's cart and that'll keep you for a few days. If you've got any sense, which you ain't, then you'd go south or north. You could go to Gascony, but it's a hell of a long walk. Flanders is closer and has plenty of English troops who'll probably take you in if they're desperate. That's my advice, lad. Go north and hope Sir Simon never goes to Flanders.'

'Thank you,' Thomas said.

'But how do you get to Flanders?' Skeat asked.

'Walk?' Thomas suggested.

'God's bones,' Will said, 'but you're a useless worm-eaten piece of lousy meat. Walk dressed like that and carrying a bow, and you might just as well just cut your own throat. It'll be quicker than letting the French do it.'

'You might find this useful,' Father Hobbe intervened, and offered Thomas a black cloth bundle which, on unrolling, proved to be the robe of a Dominican friar. 'You speak Latin, Tom,' the priest said, 'so you could pass for a wandering preacher. If anyone challenges you, say you're travelling from Avignon to Aachen.'

Thomas thanked him. 'Do many Dominicans travel with a bow?' he asked.

'Lad,' Father Hobbe said sadly, 'I can unbutton your breeches and I can point you down wind, but even with the Good Lord's help I can't piss for you.'

'In other words,' Skeat said, 'work it out for yourself. You got yourself in this bloody mess, Tom, so you get yourself out. I enjoyed your company, lad. Thought you'd be useless when I first saw you and you weren't, but you are now. But be lucky, boy.' He held out his hand and Thomas shook it. 'You might as well go to Guingamp with the Countess,' Skeat finished, 'and then find your own way, but Father Hobbe wants to save your soul first. God knows why.'

Father Hobbe dismounted and led Thomas into the roofless church where grass and weeds now grew between the flagstones. He insisted on hearing a confession and Thomas was feeling abject enough to sound contrite.

Father Hobbe sighed when it was done. 'You killed a man, Tom,' he said heavily, 'and it is a great sin.'

'Father –' Thomas began.

'No, no, Tom, no excuses. The Church says that to

kill in battle is a duty a man owes to his lord, but you killed outside the law. That poor squire, what offence did he give you? And he had a mother, Tom; think of her. No, you've sinned grievously and I must give you a grievous penance.'

Thomas, on his knees, looked up to see a buzzard sliding between the thinning clouds above the church's scorched walls. Then Father Hobbe stepped closer, looming above him. 'I'll not have you muttering paternosters, Tom,' the priest said, 'but something hard. Something very hard.' He put his hand on Thomas's hair. 'Your penance is to keep the promise you made to your father.' He paused to hear Thomas's response, but the young man was silent. 'You hear me?' Father Hobbe demanded fiercely.

'Yes, father.'

'You will find the lance of St George, Thomas, and return it to England. That is your penance. And now,' he changed into execrable Latin, 'in the name of the Father, and of the Son, and of the Holy Spirit, I absolve you.' He made the sign of the cross. 'Don't waste your life, Tom.'

'I think I already have, father.'

'You're just young. It seems like that when you're young. Life's nothing but joy or misery when you're young.' He helped Thomas up from his knees. 'You're not hanging from a gibbet, are you? You're alive, Tom, and there's a deal of life in you yet.' He smiled. 'I have a feeling we shall meet again.'

Thomas made his farewells, then watched as Will Skeat collected Sir Simon Jekyll's horse and led the hellequin eastwards, leaving the wagon and its small escort in the ruined village.

The leader of the escort was called Hugh Boltby, one

of Skeat's better men-at-arms, and he reckoned they would likely meet the enemy the next day somewhere close to Guingamp. He would hand the Countess over, then ride back to join Skeat. 'And you'd best not be dressed as an archer, Tom,' he added.

Thomas walked beside the wagon that was driven by Pierre, the old man who had been pressed by Sir Simon. Jeanette did not invite Thomas inside, indeed she pretended he did not exist, though next morning, after they had camped in an abandoned farm, she laughed at the sight of him dressed in the friar's robe.

'I'm sorry about what happened,' Thomas said to her.

Jeanette shrugged. 'It may be for the best. I probably should have gone to Duke Charles last winter.'

'Why didn't you, my lady?'

'He hasn't always been kind to me,' she said wistfully, 'but I think that might have changed by now.' She had persuaded herself that the Duke's attitude might have altered because of the letters she had sent to him, letters that would help him when he led his troops against the garrison at La Roche-Derrien. She also needed to believe the Duke would welcome her, for she desperately needed a safe home for her son, Charles, who was enjoying the adventure of riding in a swaying, creaking wagon. Together they would both start a new life in Guingamp and Jeanette had woken with optimism about that new life. She had been forced to leave La Roche-Derrien in a frantic hurry, putting into the cart just the retrieved armour, the sword and some clothes, though she had some money that Thomas suspected Will had given to her, but her real hopes were pinned on Duke Charles who, she told Thomas, would surely find her a house and lend her money in advance of the missing rents from Plabennec. 'He is sure to like Charles, don't you think?' she asked Thomas.

'I'm sure,' Thomas said, glancing at Jeanette's son, who was shaking the wagon's reins and clicking his tongue in a vain effort to make the horse go quicker.

'But what will you do?' Jeanette asked.

'I'll survive,' Thomas said, unwilling to admit that he did not know what he would do. Go to Flanders, probably, if he could ever reach there. Join another troop of archers and pray nightly that Sir Simon Jekyll never came his way again. As for his penance, the lance, he had no idea how he was to find it or, having found it, retrieve it.

Jeanette, on that second day of the journey, decided Thomas was a friend after all.

'When we get to Guingamp,' she told him, 'you find somewhere to stay and I shall persuade the Duke to give you a pass. Even a wandering friar will be helped by a pass from the Duke of Brittany.'

But no friar ever carried a bow, let alone a long English war bow, and Thomas did not know what to do with the weapon. He was loath to abandon it, but the sight of some charred timbers in the abandoned farmhouse gave him an idea. He broke off a short length of blackened timber and lashed it crosswise to the unstrung bowstave so that it resembled a pilgrim's crossstaff. He remembered a Dominican visiting Hookton with just such a staff. The friar, his hair cropped so short he looked bald, had preached a fiery sermon outside the church until Thomas's father became tired of his ranting and sent him on his way, and Thomas now reckoned he would have to pose as just such a man. Jeanette suggested he tied flowers to the staff to disguise it further, and so he wrapped it with clovers that grew tall and ragged in the abandoned fields.

The wagon, hauled by a bony horse that had been plundered from Lannion, lurched and lumbered southwards. The men-at-arms became ever more cautious as they neared Guingamp, fearing an ambush of crossbow bolts from the woods that pressed close to the deserted road. One of the men had a hunting horn that he sounded constantly to warn the enemy of their approach and to signal that they came in peace, while Boltby had a strip of white cloth hanging from the tip of his lance. There was no ambush, but a few miles short of Guingamp they came in sight of a ford where a band of enemy soldiers waited. Two men-at-arms and a dozen crossbowmen ran forward, their weapons cocked, and Boltby summoned Thomas from the wagon. 'Talk to them,' he ordered.

Thomas was nervous. 'What do I say?'

'Give them a bloody blessing, for Christ's sake,' Boltby said, disgusted, 'and tell them we're here in peace.'

So, with a beating heart and a dry mouth, Thomas walked down the road. The black gown flapped awkwardly about his ankles as he waved his hands at the crossbowmen. 'Lower your weapons,' he called in French, 'lower your weapons. The Englishmen come in peace.'

One of the horsemen spurred forward. His shield bore the same white ermine badge that Duke John's men carried, though these supporters of Duke Charles had surrounded the ermine with a blue wreath on which fleurs-de-lis had been painted.

'Who are you, father?' the horseman demanded.

Thomas opened his mouth to answer, but no words

came. He gaped up at the horseman, who had a reddish moustache and oddly yellow eyes. A hard-looking bastard, Thomas thought, and he raised a hand to touch St Guinefort's paw. Perhaps the saint inspired him, for he was suddenly possessed of devilment and began to enjoy playing a priest's role. 'I am merely one of God's humbler children, my son,' he answered unctuously.

'Are you English?' the man-at-arms demanded suspiciously. Thomas's French was near perfect, but it was the French spoken by England's rulers rather than the language of France itself.

Thomas again felt panic fluttering in his breast, but he bought time by making the sign of the cross, and as his hand moved so inspiration came to him. 'I am a Scotsman, my son,' he said, and that allayed the yellow-eyed man's suspicions; the Scots had ever been France's ally. Thomas knew nothing of Scotland, but doubted many Frenchmen or Bretons did either, for it was far away and, by all accounts, a most uninviting place. Skeat always said it was a country of bog, rock and heathen bastards who were twice as difficult to kill as any Frenchman. 'I am a Scotsman,' Thomas repeated, 'who brings a kinswoman of the Duke out of the hands of the English.'

The man-at-arms glanced at the wagon. 'A kinswoman of Duke Charles?'

'Is there another duke?' Thomas asked innocently. 'She is the Countess of Armorica,' he went on, 'and her son, who is with her, is the Duke's grandnephew and a count in his own right. The English have held them prisoner these six months, but by God's good grace they have relented and set her free. The Duke, I know, will want to welcome her.'

Thomas laid on Jeanette's rank and relationship to the Duke as thick as newly skimmed cream and the enemy swallowed it whole. They allowed the wagon to continue, and Thomas watched as Hugh Boltby led his men away at a swift trot, eager to put as much distance as possible between themselves and the crossbowmen. The leader of the enemy's men-at-arms talked with Jeanette and seemed impressed by her hauteur. He would, he said, be honoured to escort the Countess to Guingamp, though he warned her that the Duke was not there, but was still returning from Paris. He was said to be at Rennes now, a city that lay a good day's journey to the east.

'You will take me as far as Rennes?' Jeanette asked Thomas.

'You want me to, my lady?'

'A young man is useful,' she said. 'Pierre is old,' she gestured at the servant, 'and has lost his strength. Besides, if you're going to Flanders then you will need to cross the river at Rennes.'

So Thomas kept her company for the three days that it took the painfully slow wagon to make the journey. They needed no escort beyond Guingamp for there was small danger of any English raiders this far east in Brittany and the road was well patrolled by the Duke's forces. The countryside looked strange to Thomas, for he had become accustomed to rank fields, untended orchards and deserted villages, but here the farms were busy and prosperous. The churches were bigger and had stained glass, and fewer and fewer folk spoke Breton. This was still Brittany, but the language was French.

They stayed in country taverns that had fleas in the straw. Jeanette and her son were given what passed for

186

the best room while Thomas shared the stables with the two servants. They met two priests on the road, but neither suspected that Thomas was an imposter. He greeted them in Latin, which he spoke better than they did, and both men wished him a good day and a fervent Godspeed. Thomas could almost feel their relief when he did not engage them in further conversation. The Dominicans were not popular with parish priests. The friars were priests themselves, but were charged with the suppression of heresy so a visitation by the Dominicans suggested that a parish priest has not been doing his duty and even a rough, wild and young friar like Thomas was unwelcome.

They reached Rennes in the afternoon. There were dark clouds in the east against which the city loomed larger than any place Thomas had ever seen. The walls were twice as high as those at Lannion or La Roche-Derrien, and had towers with pointed roofs every few yards to serve as buttresses from which crossbowmen could pour bolts on any attacking force. Above the walls, higher even than the turrets, the church towers or the cathedral, was the citadel, a stronghold of pale stone hung with banners. The smell of the city wafted westwards on a chill wind, a stink of sewage, tanneries and smoke.

The guards at the western gate became excited when they discovered the arrows in the wagon, but Jeanette persuaded them that they were trophies she was taking to the Duke. Then they wanted to levy a custom's duty on the fine armour and Jeanette harangued them again, using her title and the Duke's name liberally. The soldiers eventually gave in and allowed the wagon into the narrow streets where shopwares protruded onto the roadway. Beggars ran beside the wagon and soldiers jostled Thomas, who was leading the horse. The city was crammed with soldiers. Most of the men-at-arms were wearing the wreathed white ermine badge, but many had the green grail of Genoa on their tunics, and the presence of so many troops confirmed that the Duke was indeed in the city and readying himself for the campaign that would eject the English from Brittany.

They found a tavern beneath the cathedral's looming twin towers. Jeanette wanted to ready herself for her audience with the Duke and demanded a private room, though all she got for her cash was a spider-haunted space beneath the tavern's eaves. The innkeeper, a sallow fellow with a twitch, suggested Thomas would be happier in the Dominican friary that lay by the church of St Germain, north of the cathedral, but Thomas declared his mission was to be among sinners, not saints, and so the innkeeper grudgingly said he could sleep in Jeanette's wagon that was parked in the inn yard.

'But no preaching, father,' the man added, 'no preaching. There's enough of that in the city without spoiling the Three Keys.'

Jeanette's maid brushed her mistress's hair, then coiled and pinned the black tresses into ram's horns that covered her ears. Jeanette put on a red velvet dress that had escaped the sack of her house and which had a skirt that fell from just beneath her breasts to the floor, while the bodice, intricately embroidered with cornflowers and daisies, hooked tight up to her neck. Its sleeves were full, trimmed with fox fur, and dropped to her red shoes, which had horn buckles. Her hat matched the dress and was trimmed with the same fur and a blue-black veil of lace. She spat on her son's face and rubbed off the dirt, then led him down to the tavern yard.

'Do you think the veil is right?' she asked Thomas anxiously.

Thomas shrugged. 'It looks right to me.'

'No, the colour! Is it right with the red?'

He nodded, hiding his astonishment. He had never seen her dressed so fashionably. She looked like a countess now, while her son was in a clean smock and had his hair wetted and smoothed.

'You're to meet your great-uncle!' Jeanette told Charles, licking a finger and rubbing at some more dirt on his cheek. 'And he's nephew to the King of France. Which means you're related to the King! Yes, you are! Aren't you a lucky boy?'

Charles recoiled from his mother's fussing, but she did not notice for she was busy instructing Pierre, her manservant, to stow the armour and sword in a great sack. She wanted the duke to see the armour. 'I want him to know,' she told Thomas, 'that when my son comes of age he will fight for him.'

Pierre, who claimed to be seventy years old, lifted the sack and almost fell over with the weight. Thomas offered to carry it to the citadel instead, but Jeanette would not hear of it.

'You might pass for a Scotsman among the common folk, but the Duke's entourage will have men who may have visited the place.' She smoothed wrinkles from the red velvet skirt. 'You wait here,' she told Thomas, 'and I'll send Pierre back with a message, maybe even some money. I'm sure the Duke is going to be generous. I shall demand a pass for you. What name shall I use? A Scot's name? Just Thomas the friar? As soon as he sees you,' she was now talking to her son, 'he'll open his purse, won't he? Of course he will.'

Pierre managed to hoist the armour onto his shoulder without falling over and Jeanette took her son's hand. 'I shall send you a message,' she promised Thomas.

'God's blessing, my child,' Thomas said, 'and may the blessed St Guinefort watch over you.'

Jeanette wrinkled her nose at that mention of St Guinefort, who, she had learned from Thomas, was really a dog. 'I shall put my trust in St Renan,' she said reprovingly, and with those words she left. Pierre and his wife followed her, and Thomas waited in the yard, offering blessings to ostlers, stray cats and tapmen. Be mad enough, his father had once said, and they will either lock you away or make you a saint.

The night fell, damp and cold, with a gusting wind sighing in the cathedral's towers and rustling the tavern's thatch. Thomas thought of the penance that Father Hobbe had demanded.

Was the lance real? Had it truly smashed through a dragon's scales, pierced the ribs and riven a heart in which cold blood flowed? He thought it was real. His father had believed and his father, though he might have been mad, had been no fool. And the lance had looked old, so very old. Thomas had used to pray to St George, but he no longer did and that made him feel guilty so that he dropped to his knees beside the wagon and asked the saint to forgive him his sins, to forgive him for the squire's murder and for impersonating a friar. I do not mean to be a bad person, he told the dragon killer, but it is so easy to forget heaven and the saints. And if you wish, he prayed, I will find the lance, but you must tell me what to do with it. Should he restore it to Hookton that, so far as Thomas knew, no longer existed? Or should he return it to whoever had owned it before his grandfather stole it? And who was his grandfather? And why had his father hidden from his family? And why had the family sought him out to take the lance back? Thomas did not know and, for the past three years, he had not cared, but suddenly, in the tavern yard, he found himself consumed by curiosity. He did have a family somewhere. His grandfather had been a soldier and a thief, but who was he? He added a prayer to St George to allow him to discover them.

'Praying for rain, father?' one of the ostlers suggested. 'I reckon we're going to get it. We need it.'

Thomas could have eaten in the tavern, but he was suddenly nervous of the crowded room where the Duke's soldiers and their women sang, boasted and brawled. Nor could he face the landlord's sly suspicions. The man was curious why Thomas did not go to the friary, and even more curious why a friar should travel with a beautiful woman. 'She is my cousin,' Thomas had told the man, who had pretended to believe the lie, but Thomas had no desire to face more questions and so he stayed in the yard and made a poor meal from the dry bread, sour onions and hard cheese that was the only food left in the wagon.

It began to rain and he retreated into the wagon and listened to the drops patter on the canvas cover. He thought of Jeanette and her little son being fed sugared delicacies on silver plates before sleeping between clean linen sheets in some tapestry-hung bedchamber, and then began to feel sorry for himself. He was a fugitive, Jeanette was his only ally and she was too high and mighty for him.

Bells announced the shutting of the city's gates. Watchmen walked the streets, looking for fires that could destroy a city in a few hours. Sentries shivered on the walls and Duke Charles's banners flew from the citadel's summit. Thomas was among his enemies, protected by nothing more than wit and a Dominican's robe. And he was alone.

Jeanette became increasingly nervous as she approached the citadel, but she had persuaded herself that Charles of Blois would accept her as a dependant once he met her son who was named for him, and Jeanette's husband had always said that the Duke would like Jeanette if only he could get to know her better. It was true that the Duke had been cold in the past, but her letters must have convinced him of her allegiance and, at the very least, she was certain he would possess the chivalry to look after a woman in distress.

To her surprise it was easier to enter the citadel than it had been to negotiate the city gate. The sentries waved her across the drawbridge, beneath the arch and so into a great courtyard ringed with stables, mews and storehouses. A score of men-at-arms were practising with their swords which, in the gloom of the late afternoon, generated bright sparks. More sparks flowed from a smithy where a horse was being shoed, and Jeanette caught the whiff of burning hoof mingling with the stink of a dungheap and the reek of a decomposing corpse, which hung in chains high on the courtyard wall. A laconic and misspelled placard pronounced the man to have been a thief.

A steward guided her through a second arch and so

into a great cold chamber where a score of petitioners waited to see the Duke. A clerk took her name, raising an eyebrow in silent surprise when she announced herself. 'His grace will be told of your presence,' the man said in a bored voice, then dismissed Jeanette to a stone bench that ran along one of the hall's high walls.

Pierre lowered the armour to the floor and squatted beside it while Jeanette sat. Some of the petitioners paced up and down, clutching scrolls and silently mouthing the words they would use when they saw the Duke, while others complained to the clerks that they had already been waiting three, four or even five days. How much longer? A dog lifted its leg against a pillar, then two small boys, six or seven years old, ran into the hall with mock wooden swords. They gazed at the petitioners for a second, then ran up some stairs that were guarded by men-at-arms. Were they the Duke's sons, Jeanette wondered, and she imagined Charles making friends with the boys.

'You're going to be happy here,' she told him.

'I'm hungry, Mama.'

'We shall eat soon.'

She waited. Two women strolled along the gallery at the head of the stairs wearing pale dresses made of expensive linen that seemed to float as they walked and Jeanette suddenly felt shabby in her wrinkled red velvet. 'You must be polite to the Duke,' she told Charles, who was getting fretful from hunger. 'You kneel to him, can you do that? Show me how you kneel.'

'I want to go home,' Charles said.

'Just for Mama, show me how you kneel. That's good!'

Jeanette ruffled her son's hair in praise, then immediately tried to stroke it back into place. From upstairs came the sound of a sweet harp and a breathy flute, and Jeanette thought longingly of the life she wanted. A life fit for a countess, edged with music and handsome men, elegance and power. She would rebuild Plabennec, though with what she did not know, but she would make the tower larger and have a staircase like the one in this hall. An hour passed, then another. It was dark now and the hall was dimly lit by two burning torches that sent smoke into the fan tracery of the high roof. Charles became ever more petulant so Jeanette took him in her arms and tried to rock him to sleep. Two priests, arm in arm, came slowly down the stairs, laughing, and then a servant in the Duke's livery ran down and all the petitioners straightened and looked at the man expectantly. He crossed to the clerk's table, spoke there for a moment, then turned and bowed to Jeanette.

She stood. 'You will wait here,' she told her two servants.

The other petitioners stared at her resentfully. She had been the last to enter the hall, yet she was the first to be summoned. Charles dragged his feet and Jeanette struck him lightly on the head to remind him of his manners. The servant walked silently beside her. 'His grace is in good health?' Jeanette asked nervously.

The servant did not reply, but just led her up the stairs, then turned right down the gallery where rain spat through open windows. They went under an arch and up a further flight of steps at the top of which the servant threw open a high door. 'The Count of Armorica,' he announced, 'and his mother.'

The room was evidently in one of the citadel's turrets

for it was circular. A great fireplace was built into one side, while cruciform arrow slits opened onto the grey wet darkness beyond the walls. The circular chamber itself was brilliantly lit by forty or fifty candles that cast their light over hanging tapestries, a great polished table, a chair, a prie-dieu carved with scenes from Christ's passion, and a fur-covered couch. The floor was soft with deerskins. Two clerks worked at a smaller table, while the Duke, gorgeous in a deep blue robe edged with ermine and with a cap to match, sat at the great table. A middle-aged priest, gaunt, white-haired and narrow faced, stood beside the prie-dieu and watched Jeanette with an expression of distaste.

Jeanette curtsied to the Duke and nudged Charles. 'Kneel,' she whispered.

Charles began crying and hid his face in his mother's skirts.

The Duke flinched at the child's noise, but said nothing. He was still young, though closer to thirty than to twenty, and had a pale, watchful face. He was thin, had a fair beard and moustache, and long, bony white hands that were clasped in front of his down-turned mouth. His reputation was that of a learned and pious man, but there was a petulance in his expression that made Jeanette wary. She wished he would speak, but all four men in the room just watched her in silence.

'I have the honour of presenting your grace's grand-nephew,' Jeanette said, pushing her crying son forward, 'the Count of Armorica.'

The Duke looked at the boy. His face betrayed nothing.

'He is named Charles,' Jeanette said, but she might as well have stayed silent for the Duke still said nothing.

The silence was broken only by the child's whimpering and the crackle of flames in the great hearth. 'I trust your grace received my letters,' Jeanette said nervously.

The priest suddenly spoke, making Jeanette jump with surprise. 'You came here,' he said in a high voice, 'with a servant carrying a burden. What is in it?'

Jeanette realized they must have thought she had brought the Duke a gift and she blushed for she had not thought to bring one. Even a small token would have been a tactful gesture, but she had simply not remembered that courtesy. 'It contains my dead husband's armour and sword,' she said, 'which I rescued from the English who have otherwise left me with nothing. Nothing. I am keeping the armour and sword for my son, so that one day he can use them to fight for his liege lord.' She bowed her head to the Duke.

The Duke steepled his fingers. To Jeanette it seemed he never blinked and that was as unsettling as his silence.

'His grace would like to see the armour,' the priest announced, though the Duke had shown no sign of wishing anything at all. The priest snapped his fingers and one of the clerks left the room. The second clerk, armed with a small pair of scissors, went round the big chamber trimming the wicks of the many candles in their tall iron holders. The Duke and the priest ignored him.

'You say,' the priest spoke again, 'that you wrote letters to his grace. Concerning what?'

'I wrote about the new defences at La Roche-Derrien, father, and I warned his grace of the English attack on Lannion.'

'So you say,' the priest said, 'so you say.' Charles was

still crying and Jeanette jerked his hand hard in the hope of stilling him, but he just whined more. The clerk, head averted from the Duke, went from candle to candle. The scissors snipped, a puff of smoke would writhe for a heartbeat, then the flame would brighten and settle. Charles began crying louder.

'His grace,' the priest said, 'does not like snivelling infants.'

'He is hungry, father,' Jeanette explained nervously.

'You came with two servants?'

'Yes, father,' Jeanette said.

'They can eat with the boy in the kitchens,' the priest said, and snapped his fingers towards the candle-trimming clerk, who, abandoning his scissors on a rug, took the frightened Charles by the hand. The boy did not want to leave his mother, but he was dragged away and Jeanette flinched as the sound of his crying receded down the stairs.

The Duke, other than steepling his fingers, had not moved. He just watched Jeanette with an unreadable expression.

'You say,' the priest took up the questioning again, 'that the English left you with nothing?'

'They stole all I had!'

The priest flinched at the passion in her voice. 'If they left you destitute, madame, then why did you not come for our help earlier?'

'I did not wish to be a burden, father.'

'But now you do wish to become a burden?'

Jeanette frowned. 'I have brought his grace's nephew, the Lord of Plabennec. Or would you rather that he grew up among the English?'

'Do not be impertinent, child,' the priest said placidly.

The first clerk re-entered the room carrying the sack, which he emptied on the deerskins in front of the Duke's table. The Duke gazed at the armour for a few seconds, then settled back in his high carved chair.

'It is very fine,' the priest declared.

'It is most precious,' Jeanette agreed.

The Duke peered again at the armour. Not a muscle of his face moved.

'His grace approves,' the priest said, then gestured with a long white hand and the clerk, who seemed to understand what was wanted without words, gathered up the sword and armour and carried them from the room.

'I am glad your grace approves,' Jeanette said, and dropped another curtsy. She had a confused idea that the Duke, despite her earlier words, had assumed the armour and sword were a gift, but she did not want to enquire. It could all be cleared up later. A gust of cold wind came through the arrow slits to bring spots of rain and to flicker the candles in wild shudders.

'So what,' the priest asked, 'do you require of us?'

'My son needs shelter, father,' Jeanette said nervously. 'He needs a house, a place to grow and learn to be a warrior.'

'His grace is pleased to grant that request,' the priest said.

Jeanette felt a great wash of relief. The atmosphere in the room was so unfriendly that she had feared she would be thrown out as destitute as she had arrived, but the priest's words, though coldly stated, told her that she need not have worried. The Duke was taking his responsibility and she curtsied for a third time. 'I am grateful, your grace.'

The priest was about to respond, but, to Jeanette's surprise, the Duke held up one long white hand and the priest bowed. 'It is our pleasure,' the Duke said in an oddly high-pitched voice, 'for your son is dear to us and it is our desire that he grows to become a warrior like his father.' He turned to the priest and inclined his head, and the priest gave another stately bow then left the room.

The Duke stood and walked to the fire where he held his hands to the small flames. 'It has come to our notice,' he said distantly, 'that the rents of Plabennec have not been paid these twelve quarters.'

'The English are in possession of the domain, your grace.'

'And you are in debt to me,' the Duke said, frowning at the flames.

'If you protect my son, your grace, then I shall be for ever in your debt,' Jeanette said humbly.

The Duke took off his cap and ran a hand through his fair hair. Jeanette thought he looked younger and kinder without the hat, but his next words chilled her. 'I did not want Henri to marry you.' He stopped abruptly.

For a heartbeat Jeanette was struck dumb by his frankness. 'My husband regretted your grace's disapproval,' she finally said in a small voice.

The Duke ignored Jeanette's words. 'He should have married Lisette of Picard. She had money, lands, tenants. She would have brought our family great wealth. In times of trouble wealth is a . . .' he paused, trying to find the right word, 'it is a cushion. You, madame, have no cushion.'

'Only your grace's kindness,' Jeanette said.

'Your son is my charge,' the Duke said. 'He will be raised in my household and trained in the arts of war and civilization as befits his rank.'

'I am grateful.' Jeanette was tired of grovelling. She wanted some sign of affection from the Duke, but ever since he had walked to the hearth he would not meet her eyes.

Now, suddenly, he turned on her. 'There is a lawyer called Belas in La Roche-Derrien?'

'Indeed, your grace.'

'He tells me your mother was a Jewess.' He spat the last word.

Jeanette gaped at him. For a few heartbeats she was unable to speak. Her mind was reeling with disbelief that Belas would say such a thing, but at last she managed to shake her head. 'She was not!' she protested.

'He tells us, too,' the Duke went on, 'that you petitioned Edward of England for the rents of Plabennec?'

'What choice did I have?'

'And that your son was made a ward of Edward's?' the Duke asked pointedly.

Jeanette opened and closed her mouth. The accusations were coming so thick and fast she did not know how to defend herself. It was true that her son had been named a ward of King Edward's, but it had not been Jeanette's doing; indeed, she had not even been present when the Earl of Northampton made that decision, but before she could protest or explain the Duke spoke again.

'Belas tells us,' he said, 'that many in the town of La Roche-Derrien have expressed satisfaction with the English occupiers?'

'Some have,' Jeanette admitted.

'And that you, madame, have English soldiers in your own house, guarding you.'

'They forced themselves on my house!' she said indignantly. 'Your grace must believe me! I did not want them there!'

The Duke shook his head. 'It seems to us, madame, that you have given a welcome to our enemies. Your father was a vintner, was he not?'

Jeanette was too astonished to say anything. It was slowly dawning on her that Belas had betrayed her utterly, yet she still clung to the hope that the Duke would be convinced of her innocence. 'I offered them no welcome,' she insisted. 'I fought against them!'

'Merchants,' the Duke said, 'have no loyalties other than to money. They have no honour. Honour is not learned, madame. It is bred. Just as you breed a horse for bravery and speed, or a hound for agility and ferocity, so you breed a nobleman for honour. You cannot turn a plough-horse into a destrier, nor a merchant into a gentleman. It is against nature and the laws of God.' He made the sign of the cross. 'Your son is Count of Armorica, and we shall raise him in honour, but you, madame, are the daughter of a merchant and a Jewess.'

'It is not true!' Jeanette protested.

'Do not shout at me, madame,' the Duke said icily. 'You are a burden on me. You dare to come here, tricked out in fox fur, expecting me to give you shelter? What else? Money? I will give your son a home, but you, madame, I shall give you a husband.' He walked towards her, his feet silent on the deerskin rugs. 'You are not fit to be the Count of Armorica's mother. You have offered comfort to the enemy, you have no honour.'

'I –' Jeanette began to protest again, but the Duke slapped her hard across the cheek.

'You will be silent, madame,' he commanded, 'silent.' He pulled at the laces of her bodice and, when she dared to resist, he slapped her again. 'You are a whore, madame,' the Duke said, then lost patience with the intricate cross-laces, retrieved the discarded scissors from the rug and used them to cut through the laces to expose Jeanette's breasts. She was so astonished, stunned and horrified that she made no attempt to protect herself. This was not Sir Simon Jekyll, but her liege lord, the King's nephew and her husband's uncle. 'You are a pretty whore, madame,' the Duke said with a sneer. 'How did you enchant Henri? Was it Jewish witchcraft?'

'No,' Jeanette whimpered, 'please, no!'

The Duke unhooked his gown and Jeanette saw he was naked beneath.

'No,' she said again, 'please, no.'

The Duke pushed her hard so that she fell on the bed. His face still showed no emotion – not lust, not pleasure, not anger. He hauled her skirts up, then knelt on the bed and raped her with no sign of enjoyment. He seemed, if anything, angry, and when he was done he collapsed on her, then shuddered. Jeanette was weeping. He wiped himself on her velvet skirt. 'I shall take that experience,' he said, 'as payment of the missing rents from Plabennec.' He crawled off her, stood and hooked the ermine edges of his gown. 'You will be placed in a chamber here, madame, and tomorrow I shall give you in marriage to one of my men-at-arms. Your son will stay here, but you will go wherever your new husband is posted.'

Jeanette was whimpering on the bed. The Duke grimaced with distaste, then crossed the room and kneeled on the prie-dieu. 'Arrange your gown, madame,' he said coldly, 'and compose yourself.'

Jeanette rescued enough of the cut laces to tie her bodice into place, then looked at the Duke through the candle flames. 'You have no honour,' she hissed, 'you have no honour.'

The Duke ignored her. He rang a small handbell, then clasped his hands and closed his eyes in prayer. He was still praying when the priest and a servant came and, without a word, took Jeanette by her arms and walked her to a small room on the floor beneath the Duke's chamber. They thrust her inside, shut the door and she heard a bolt slide into place on the far side. There was a straw-filled mattress and a stack of brooms in the makeshift cell, but no other furnishing.

She lay on the mattress and sobbed till her broken heart was raw.

The wind howled at the window and rain beat on its shutters, and Jeanette wished she was dead.

The city's cockerels woke Thomas to a brisk wind and pouring rain that beat on the cart's leaking cover. He opened the flap and sat watching the puddles spread across the cobbles of the inn yard. No message had come from Jeanette, nor, he thought, would there be one. Will Skeat had been right. She was as hard as mail and, now she was in her proper place – which, in this cold, wet dawn, was probably a deep bed in a room warmed by a fire tended by the Duke's servants – she would have forgotten Thomas.

And what message, Thomas asked himself, had he been expecting? A declaration of affection? He knew that was what he wanted, but he persuaded himself he merely waited so Jeanette could send him the pass signed by the Duke, yet he knew he did not need a pass. He must just walk east and north, and trust that the Dominican's robe protected him. He had little idea how to reach Flanders, but had a notion that Paris lay somewhere close to that region so he reckoned he would start by following the River Seine, which would lead him from Rennes to Paris. His biggest worry was that he would meet some real Dominican on the road, who would quickly discover Thomas had only the haziest notion of the brotherhood's rules and no knowledge at all of their hierarchy, but he consoled himself that Scottish Dominicans were probably so far from civilization that such ignorance would be expected of them. He would survive, he told himself.

He stared at the rain spattering in the puddles. Expect nothing from Jeanette, he told himself, and to prove that he believed that bleak prophecy he readied his small baggage. It irked him to leave the mail coat behind, but it weighed too much, so he stowed it in the wagon, then put the three sheaves of arrows into a sack. The seventy-two arrows were heavy and their points threatened to tear open the sack, but he was reluctant to travel without the sheaves that were wrapped in hempen bowstring cord and he used one cord to tie his knife to his left leg where, like his money pouch, it was hidden by the black robe.

He was ready to go, but the rain was now hammering the city like an arrow storm. Thunder crackled to the west, the rain pelted on the thatch, poured off the roofs and overflowed the water butts to wash the inn's night-soil out of the yard. Midday came, heralded by the city's rain-muffled bells, and still the city drowned. Wind-driven dark clouds wreathed the cathedral's towers and Thomas told himself he would leave the moment the rain slackened, but the storm just became fiercer. Lightning flickered above the cathedral and a clap of thunder rocked the city. Thomas shivered, awed by the sky's fury. He watched the lightning reflected in the cathedral's great west window and was amazed by the sight. So much glass! Still it rained and he began to fear that he would be trapped in the cart till the next day. And then, just after a peal of thunder seemed to stun the whole city with its violence, he saw Jeanette.

He did not know her at first. He just saw a woman standing in the arched entrance to the inn's yard with the water flowing about her shoes. Everyone else in Rennes was huddling in shelter, but this woman suddenly appeared, soaked and miserable. Her hair, which had been looped so carefully over her ears, hung lank and black down the sopping red velvet dress, and it was that dress that Thomas recognized, then he saw the grief on her face. He clambered out of the wagon.

'Jeanette!'

She was weeping, her mouth distorted by grief. She seemed incapable of speaking, but just stood and cried.

'My lady!' Thomas said. 'Jeanette!'

'We must go,' she managed to say, 'we must go.' She had used soot as a cosmetic about her eyes and it had run to make grey streaks down her face.

'We can't go in this!' Thomas said.

'We must go!' she screamed at him angrily. 'We must go!'

'I'll get the horse,' Thomas said.

'There's no time! There's no time!' She plucked at his robe. 'We must go. Now!' She tried to tug him through the arch into the street.

Thomas pulled away from her and ran to the wagon where he retrieved his disguised bow and the heavy sack. There was a cloak of Jeanette's there and he took that too and wrapped it about her shoulders, though she did not seem to notice.

'What's happening?' Thomas demanded.

'They'll find me here, they'll find me!' Jeanette declared in a panic, and she pulled him blindly out of the tavern's archway. Thomas turned her eastwards onto a crooked street that led to a fine stone bridge across the Seine and then to a city gate. The big gates were barred, but a small door in one of the gates was open and the guards in the tower did not care if some fool of a drenched friar wanted to take a madly sobbing woman out of the city. Jeanette kept looking back, fearing pursuit, but still did not explain her panic or her tears to Thomas. She just hurried eastwards, insensible to the rain, wind and thunder.

The storm eased towards dusk, by which time they were close to a village that had a poor excuse for a tavern. Thomas ducked under the low doorway and asked for shelter. He put coins on a table.

'I need shelter for my sister,' he said, reckoning that anyone would be suspicious of a friar travelling with a woman. 'Shelter, food and a fire,' he said, adding another coin.

'Your sister?' The tavern-keeper, a small man with a face scarred by the pox and bulbous with wens, peered at Jeanette, who was crouched in the tavern's porch.

Thomas touched his head, suggesting she was mad. 'I am taking her to the shrine of St Guinefort,' he explained.

The tavern-keeper looked at the coins, glanced again at Jeanette, then decided the strange pair could have the use of an empty cattle byre. 'You can put a fire there,' he said grudgingly, 'but don't burn the thatch.'

Thomas lit a fire with embers from the tavern's kitchen, then fetched food and ale. He forced Jeanette to eat some of the soup and bread, then made her go close to the fire. It took over two hours of coaxing before she would tell him the story, and telling it only made her cry again. Thomas listened, appalled.

'So how did you escape?' he asked when she was finished.

A woman had unbolted the room, Jeanette said, to fetch a broom. The woman had been astonished to see Jeanette there, and even more astonished when Jeanette ran past her. Jeanette had fled the citadel, fearing the soldiers would stop her, but no one had taken any notice of her and now she was running away. Like Thomas she was a fugitive, but she had lost far more than he. She had lost her son, her honour and her future.

'I hate men,' she said. She shivered, for the miserable fire of damp straw and rotted wood had scarcely dried her clothes. 'I hate men,' she said again, then looked at Thomas. 'What are we going to do?'

'You must sleep,' he said, 'and tomorrow we'll go north.'

She nodded, but he did not think she had understood his words. She was in despair. The wheel of fortune that had once raised her so high had taken her into the utter depths.

She slept for a time, but when Thomas woke in the grey dawn he saw she was crying softly and he did not know what to do or say, so he just lay in the straw until he heard the tavern door creak open, then went to fetch some food and water. The tavern-keeper's wife cut some bread and cheese while her husband asked Thomas how far he had to walk.

'St Guinefort's shrine is in Flanders,' Thomas said.

'Flanders!' the man said, as though it was on the far side of the moon.

'The family doesn't know what else to do with her,' Thomas explained, 'and I don't know how to reach Flanders. I thought to go to Paris first.'

'Not Paris,' the tavern-keeper's wife said scornfully, 'you must go to Fougères.' Her father, she said, had often traded with the north countries and she was sure that Thomas's route lay through Fougères and Rouen. She did not know the roads beyond Rouen, but was certain he must go that far, though to begin, she said, he must take a small road that went north from the village. It went through woods, her husband added, and he must be careful for the trees were hiding places for terrible men escaping justice, but after a few miles he would come to the Fougères highway, which was patrolled by the Duke's men.

Thomas thanked her, offered a blessing to the house, then took the food to Jeanette, who refused to eat. She seemed drained of tears, almost of life, but she followed Thomas willingly enough as he walked north. The road, deep rutted by wagons and slick with mud from the previous day's rain, twisted into deep woods that dripped with water. Jeanette stumbled for a few miles, then began to cry. 'I must go back to Rennes,' she insisted. 'I want to go back to my son.'

Thomas argued, but she would not be moved. He finally gave in, but when he turned to walk south she just began to cry even harder. The Duke had said she was not a fit mother! She kept repeating the words, 'Not fit! Not fit!' She screamed at the sky. 'He made me his whore!' Then she sank onto her knees beside the road and sobbed uncontrollably. She was shivering again and Thomas thought that if she did not die of an ague then the grief would surely kill her.

'We're going back to Rennes,' Thomas said, trying to encourage her.

'I can't!' she wailed. 'He'll just whore me! Whore

me!' She shouted the words, then began rocking back and forwards and shrieking in a terrible high voice. Thomas tried to raise her up, tried to make her walk, but she fought him. She wanted to die, she said, she just wanted to die. 'A whore,' she screamed, and tore at the fox-fur trimmings of her red dress, 'a whore! He said I shouldn't wear fur. He made me a whore.' She threw the tattered fur into the undergrowth.

It had been a dry morning, but the rain clouds were heaping in the east again, and Thomas was nervously watching as Jeanette's soul unravelled before his eyes. She refused to walk, so he picked her up and carried her until he saw a well-trodden path going into the trees. He followed it to find a cottage so low, and with its thatch so covered with moss that at first he thought it was just a mound among the trees until he saw blue-grey woodsmoke seeping from a hole at its top. Thomas was worried about the outlaws who were said to haunt these woods, but it was beginning to rain again and the cottage was the only refuge in sight, so Thomas lowered Jeanette to the ground and shouted through the burrow-like entrance. An old man, white-haired, red-eyed and with skin blackened by smoke, peered back at Thomas. The man spoke a French so thick with local words and accent that Thomas could scarcely understand him, but he gathered the man was a forester and lived here with his wife, and the forester looked greedily at the coins Thomas offered, then said that Thomas and his woman could use an empty pig shelter. The place stank of rotted straw and shit, but the thatch was almost rainproof and Jeanette did not seem to care. Thomas raked out the old straw, then cut Jeanette a bed of bracken. The forester, once the money was in his hands, seemed little interested in his guests, but in the middle of the afternoon, when the rain had stopped, Thomas heard the forester's wife hissing at him and, a few moments later, the old man left and walked towards the road, but without any of the tools of his trade; no axe, billhook or saw.

Jeanette was sleeping, exhausted, so Thomas stripped the dead clover plants from his black bow, unlashed the crosspiece and put back the horn tips. He strung the yew, thrust half a dozen arrows into his belt and followed the old man as far as the road, and there he waited in a thicket.

The forester returned towards evening with two young men whom Thomas presumed were the outlaws of whom he had been warned. The old man must have reckoned that Thomas and his woman were fugitives, for though they carried bags and money, they had sought a hiding place and that was enough to raise anyone's suspicions. A friar did not need to skulk in the trees, and women wearing dresses trimmed with torn remnants of fur did not seek a forester's hospitality. So doubtless the two young men had been fetched to help slit Thomas's throat and then divide whatever coins they found on his body. Jeanette's fate would be similar, but delayed.

Thomas put his first arrow into the ground between the old man's feet and the second into a tree close by. 'The next arrow kills,' he said, though they could not see him for he was in the thicket's shadows. They just stared wide-eyed at the bushes where he was hiding and Thomas made his voice deep and slow. 'You come with murder in your souls,' he said, 'but I can raise the hellequin from the deeps of hell. I can make the devil's claws cut to your heart and have the dead haunt your daylight. You will leave the friar and his sister alone.'

The old man dropped to his knees. His superstitions were as old as time and scarcely touched by Christianity. He believed there were trolls in the forest and giants in the mist. He knew there were dragons. He had heard of black-skinned men who lived on the moon and who dropped to earth when their home shrank to a sickle. He understood there were ghosts who hunted among the trees. All this he knew as well as he knew ash and larch, oak and beech, and he did not doubt that it was a demon who had spat the strangely long arrow from the thicket.

'You must go,' he told his companions, 'you must go!' The two fled and the old man touched his forehead to the leaf mould. 'I meant no harm!'

'Go home,' Thomas said.

He waited till the old man had gone, then he dug the arrow out of the tree and that night he went to the forester's cottage, crawled through the low doorway and sat on the earthen floor facing the old couple.

'I shall stay here,' he told them, 'until my sister's wits are recovered. We wish to hide her shame from the world, that is all. When we go we shall reward you, but if you try to kill us again I shall summon demons to torment you and I will leave your corpses as a feast for the wild things that lurk in the trees.' He put another small coin on the earth floor. 'You will bring us food each night,' he told the woman, 'and you will thank God that though I can read your hearts I still forgive you.'

They had no more trouble after that. Every day the old man went off into the trees with his billhook and axe, and every night his wife brought her visitors gruel or bread. Thomas took milk from their cow, shot a deer and thought Jeanette would die. For days she refused to eat, and sometimes he would find her rocking back and forth in the noxious shed and making a keening noise. Thomas feared she had gone mad for ever. His father would sometimes tell him how the mad were treated, how he himself had been treated, how starvation and beating were the only cures. 'The devil gets into the soul,' Father Ralph had said, 'and he can be starved out or he can be thrashed out, but there is no way he will be coaxed out. Beat and starve, boy, beat and starve, it is the only treatment the devil understands.' But Thomas could neither starve nor beat Jeanette, so he did his best by her. He kept her dry, he persuaded her to take some warm milk fresh from the cow, he talked with her through the nights, he combed her hair and washed her face and sometimes, when she was sleeping and he was sitting by the shed and staring at the stars through the tangled trees, he would wonder whether he and the hellequin had left other women as broken as Jeanette. He prayed for forgiveness. He prayed a lot in those days, and not to St Guinefort, but to the Virgin and to St George.

The prayers must have worked for he woke one dawn to see Jeanette sitting in the shed's doorway with her thin body outlined by the bright new day. She turned to him and he saw there was no madness in her face any more, just a profound sorrow. She looked at him a long time before she spoke.

'Did God send you to me, Thomas?'

'He showed me great favour if He did,' Thomas replied.

She smiled at that, the first smile he had seen on her face since Rennes. 'I have to be content,' she said very earnestly, 'because my son is alive and he will be properly cared for and one day I shall find him.'

'We both shall,' Thomas said.

'Both?'

He grimaced. 'I have kept none of my promises,' he said. 'The lance is still in Normandy, Sir Simon lives, and how I shall find your son for you, I do not know. I think my promises are worthless, but I shall do my best.'

She held out her hand so he could take it and she let it stay there. 'We have been punished, you and I,' she said, 'probably for the sin of pride. The Duke was right. I am no aristocrat. I am a merchant's daughter, but thought I was higher. Now look at me.'

'Thinner,' Thomas said, 'but beautiful.'

She shuddered at that compliment. 'Where are we?'

'Just a day outside Rennes.'

'Is that all?'

'In a pig shed,' Thomas said, 'a day out of Rennes.'

'Four years ago I lived in a castle,' she said wistfully. 'Plabennec wasn't large, but it was beautiful. It had a tower and a courtyard and two mills and a stream and an orchard that grew very red apples.'

'You will see them again,' Thomas said, 'you and your son.'

He regretted mentioning her son for tears came to her eyes, but she cuffed them away. 'It was the lawyer,' she said.

'Lawyer?'

'Belas. He lied to the Duke.' There was a kind of wonderment in her voice that Belas had proved so

214

traitorous. 'He told the Duke I was supporting Duke Jean. Then I will, Thomas, I will. I will support your duke. If that is the only way to regain Plabennec and find my son then I shall support Duke Jean.' She squeezed Thomas's hand. 'I'm hungry.'

They spent another week in the forest while Jeanette recovered her strength. For a while, like a beast struggling to escape a trap, she devised schemes that would give her instant revenge on Duke Charles and restore her son, but the schemes were wild and hopeless and, as the days passed, she accepted her fate.

'I have no friends,' she said to Thomas one night.

'You have me, my lady.'

'They died,' she said, ignoring him. 'My family died. My husband died. Do you think I am a curse on those I love?'

'I think,' Thomas said, 'that we must go north.'

She was irritated by his practicality. 'I'm not sure I want to go north.'

'I do,' Thomas said stubbornly.

Jeanette knew that the further north she went, the further she went from her son, but she did not know what else to do, and that night, as if accepting that she would now be guided by Thomas, she came to his bracken bed and they were lovers. She wept afterwards, but then made love to him again, this time fiercely, as though she could slake her misery in the consolations of the flesh.

Next morning they left, going north. Summer had come, clothing the countryside in thick green. Thomas had disguised the bow again, lashing the crosspiece to the stave and hanging it with bindweed and willowherb instead of clover. His black robe had become ragged and no one would have taken him for a friar, while Jeanette had stripped the remains of the fox fur from the red velvet, which was dirty, creased and threadbare. They looked like vagabonds, which they were, and they moved like fugitives, skirting the towns and bigger villages to avoid trouble. They bathed in streams, slept beneath the trees and only ventured into the smallest villages when hunger demanded they buy a meal and cider in some slatternly tavern. If they were challenged they claimed to be Bretons, brother and sister, going to join their uncle who was a butcher in Flanders, and if anyone disbelieved the tale they were unwilling to cross Thomas, who was tall and strong and always kept his knife visible. By preference, though, they avoided villages and stayed in the woods where Thomas taught Jeanette how to tickle the trout out of their streams. They would light fires, cook their fish and cut bracken for a bed.

They kept close to the road, though they were forced to a long detour to avoid the drum-like fortress of St-Aubin-du-Cormier, and another to skirt the city of Fougères, and somewhere north of that city they entered Normandy. They milked cows in their pastures, stole a great cheese from a wagon parked outside a church and slept under the stars. They had no idea what day of the week it was, nor even what month it was any more. Both were browned by the sun and made ragged by travelling. Jeanette's misery was dissolved in a new happiness, and nowhere more than when they discovered an abandoned cottage – merely cob walls of mud and straw decaying without a roof – in a spinney of hazel trees. They cleared away the nettles and brambles and lived in the cottage for more than a week, seeing no one, wanting to see no one, delaying their future because the present was so blissful. Jeanette could still weep for her son and spent hours devising exquisite revenges to be taken against the Duke, against Belas and against Sir Simon Jekyll, but she also revelled in that summer's freedom. Thomas had fitted his bow again so he could hunt and Jeanette, growing ever stronger, had learned to pull it back almost to her chin.

Neither knew where they were and did not much care. Thomas's mother used to tell him a tale of children who ran away into the forest and were reared by the beasts. 'They grow hair all over their bodies,' she would tell him, 'and have claws and horns and teeth,' and now Thomas would sometimes examine his hands to see if claws were coming. He saw none. Yet if he was becoming a beast then he was happy. He had rarely been happier, but he knew that the winter, even though far off, was nevertheless coming and so, perhaps a week after midsummer, they moved gently north again in search of something that neither of them could quite imagine.

Thomas knew he had promised to retrieve a lance and restore Jeanette's son, but he did not know how he was to do either of those things. He only knew he must go to a place where a man like Will Skeat would employ him, though he could not talk of such a future with Jeanette. She did not want to hear about archers or armies, or of men and mail coats, but she, like him, knew they could not stay for ever in their refuge.

'I shall go to England,' she told him, 'and appeal to your king.' Out of all the schemes she had dreamed of, this was the only one that made sense. The Earl of Northampton had placed her son under the King of

England's protection, so she must appeal to Edward and hope he would support her.

They walked north, still keeping the road to Rouen in sight. They forded a river and climbed into a broken country of small fields, deep woods and abrupt hills, and somewhere in that green land, unheard by either of them, the wheel of fortune creaked again. Thomas knew that the great wheel governed mankind, it turned in the dark to determine good or evil, high or low, sickness or health, happiness or misery. Thomas reckoned God must have made the wheel to be the mechanism by which He ruled the world while He was busy in heaven, and in that midsummer, when the harvest was being flailed on the threshing floors, and the swifts were gathering in the high trees, and the rowan trees were in scarlet berry, and the pastures were white with ox-eye daisies, the wheel lurched for Thomas and Jeanette.

They walked to the wood's edge one day to check that the road was still in view. They usually saw little more than a man driving some cows to market, a group of women following with eggs and vegetables to sell. A priest might pass on a poor horse, and once they had seen a knight with his retinue of servants and men-at-arms, but most days the road lay white, dusty and empty under the summer sun. Yet this day it was full. Folk were walking southwards, driving cows and pigs and sheep and goats and geese. Some pushed handcarts, others had wagons drawn by oxen or horses, and all the carts were loaded high with stools, tables, benches and beds. Thomas knew he was seeing fugitives.

They waited till it was dark, then Thomas beat the worst dirt off the Dominican's gown and, leaving Jeanette in the trees, walked down to the road where some of the travellers were camping beside small, smoky fires.

'God's peace be on you,' Thomas said to one group.

'We have no food to spare, father,' a man answered, eyeing the stranger suspiciously.

'I am fed, my son,' Thomas said, and squatted near their fire.

'Are you a priest or a vagabond?' the man asked. He had an axe and he drew it towards him protectively, for Thomas's tangled hair was wildly long and his face as dark as any outlaw's.

'I am both,' Thomas said with a smile. 'I have walked from Avignon,' he explained, 'to do penance at the shrine of St Guinefort.'

None of the refugees had ever heard of the Blessed Guinefort, but Thomas's words convinced them, for the idea of pilgrimage explained his woebegone condition while their own sad condition, they made clear, was caused by war. They had come from the coast of Normandy, only a day's journey away, and in the morning they must be up early and travelling again to escape the enemy.

Thomas made the sign of the cross. 'What enemy?' he asked, expecting to hear that two Norman lords had fallen out and were ravaging each other's estates.

But the ponderous wheel of fortune had turned unexpectedly. King Edward III of England had crossed the Channel. Such an expedition had long been expected, but the King had not gone to his lands in Gascony, as many had thought he would, nor to Flanders where other Englishmen fought, but had come to Normandy. His army was just a day away and, at the news, Thomas's mouth dropped open.

'You should flee them, father,' one of the women advised Thomas. 'They know no pity, not even for friars.'

Thomas assured them he would, thanked them for their news, then walked back up the hill to where Jeanette waited. All had changed.

His king had come to Normandy.

They argued that night. Jeanette was suddenly convinced they should turn back to Brittany and Thomas could only stare at her in astonishment.

'Brittany?' he asked faintly.

She would not meet his eyes, but stubbornly stared at the campfires that burned all along the road, while further north, on the night's horizon, great red glows showed where larger fires burned, and Thomas knew that English soldiers must have been ravaging the fields of Normandy just as the hellequin had harrowed Brittany. 'I can be near Charles if I'm in Brittany,' Jeanette said.

Thomas shook his head. He was dimly aware that the sight of the army's destruction had forced them both into a reality from which they had been escaping in these last weeks of freedom, but he could not connect that with her sudden wish to head back to Brittany.

'You can be near Charles,' he said carefully, 'but can you see him? Will the Duke let you near him?'

'Maybe he will change his mind,' Jeanette said without much conviction.

'And maybe he'll rape you again,' Thomas said brutally.

'And if I don't go,' she said vehemently, 'maybe I will never see Charles again. Never!'

'Then why come this far?'

'I don't know, I don't know.' She was angry as she used to be when Thomas first met her in La Roche-Derrien. 'Because I was mad,' she said sullenly.

'You say you want to appeal to the King,' Thomas said, 'and he's here!' He flung a hand towards the livid glow of the fires. 'So appeal to him here.'

'Maybe he won't believe me,' Jeanette said stubbornly.

'And what will we do in Brittany?' Thomas asked, but Jeanette would not answer. She looked sulky and still avoided his gaze. 'You can marry one of the Duke's men-at-arms,' Thomas went on, 'that's what he wanted, isn't it? A pliant wife of a pliant follower so that when he feels like taking his pleasure, he can.'

'Isn't that what you do?' she challenged him, looking him in the face at last.

'I love you,' Thomas said.

Jeanette said nothing.

'I do love you,' Thomas said, and felt foolish for she had never said the same to him.

Jeanette looked at the glowing horizon that was tangled by the leaves of the forest. 'Will your king believe me?' she asked him.

'How can he not?'

'Do I look like a countess?'

She looked ragged, poor and beautiful. 'You speak like a countess,' Thomas said, 'and the King's clerks will make enquiries of the Earl of Northampton.' He did not know if that was true, but he wanted to encourage her.

Jeanette sat with her head bowed. 'Do you know

what the Duke told me? That my mother was a Jewess!' She looked up at him, expecting him to share her indignation.

Thomas frowned. 'I've never met a Jew,' he said.

Jeanette almost exploded. 'You think I have? You need to meet the devil to know he is bad? A pig to discover he stinks?' She began to weep. 'I don't know what to do.'

'We shall go to the King,' Thomas said, and next morning he walked north and, after a few heartbeats, Jeanette followed him. She had tried to clean her dress, though it was so filthy that all she could manage was to brush the twigs and leaf mould from the velvet. She coiled her hair and pinned it with slivers of wood.

'What kind of man is the King?' she asked Thomas.

'They say he's a good man.'

'Who says?'

'Everyone. He's straightforward.'

'He's still English,' Jeanette said softly, and Thomas pretended not to hear. 'Is he kind?' she asked him.

'No one says he's cruel,' Thomas said, then held up a hand to silence Jeanette.

He had seen horsemen in mail.

Thomas had often found it strange that when the monks and scriveners made their books they painted warfare as gaudy. Their squirrel-hair brushes showed men in brightly coloured surcoats or jupons, and their horses in brilliantly patterned trappers. Yet for most of the time war was grey until the arrows bit, when it became shot through with red. Grey was the colour of a mail coat, and Thomas was seeing grey among the green leaves. He did not know if they were Frenchmen or Englishmen, but he feared both. The French were his enemy, but so were the English until they were convinced that he was English too, and convinced, moreover, that he was not a deserter from their army.

More horsemen came from the distant trees and these men were carrying bows, so they had to be English. Still Thomas hesitated, reluctant to face the problems of persuading his own side that he was not a deserter. Beyond the horsemen, hidden by the trees, a building must have been set on fire for smoke began to thicken above the summer leaves. The horsemen were looking towards Thomas and Jeanette, but the pair were hidden by a bank of gorse and after a while, satisfied that no enemy threatened, the troops turned and rode eastwards.

Thomas waited till they were out of sight, then led Jeanette across the open land, into the trees and out to where a farm burned. The flames were pale in the bright sun. No one was in sight. There was just a farm blazing and a dog lying next to a duck pond that was surrounded by feathers. The dog was whimpering and Jeanette cried out for it had been stabbed in the belly. Thomas stooped beside the beast, stroked its head and fondled its ears and the dying dog licked his hand and tried to wag its tail and Thomas rammed his knife deep into its heart so that it died swiftly.

'It would not have lived,' he told Jeanette. She said nothing, just stared at the burning thatch and rafters. Thomas pulled out the knife and patted the dog's head. 'Go to St Guinefort,' he said, cleaning the blade. 'I always wanted a dog when I was a child,' he told Jeanette, 'but my father couldn't abide them.'

'Why?'

'Because he was strange.' He sheathed the knife and

stood. A track, imprinted with hoofmarks, led north from the farm, and they followed it cautiously between hedges thick with cornflowers, ox-eye and dogwood. They were in a country of small fields, high banks, sudden woods and lumpy hills, a country for ambush, but they saw no one until, from the top of a low hill, they glimpsed a squat stone church tower in a valley and then the unburned roofs of a village and after that the soldiers. There were hundreds of them camped in the fields beyond the cottages, and more in the village itself. Some large tents had been raised close to the church and they had the banners of nobles planted by their entrances.

Thomas still hesitated, reluctant to finish these good days with Jeanette, yet he knew there was no choice and so, bow on his shoulder, he took her down to the village. Men saw them coming and a dozen archers, led by a burly man in a mail hauberk, came to meet them.

'What the hell are you?' was the burly man's first question. His archers grinned wolfishly at the sight of Jeanette's ragged dress. 'You're either a bleeding priest who stole a bow,' the man went on, 'or an archer who filched a priest's robe.'

'I'm English,' Thomas said.

The big man seemed unimpressed. 'Serving who?'

'I was with Will Skeat in Brittany,' Thomas said.

'Brittany!' The big man frowned, not certain whether or not to believe Thomas.

'Tell them I'm a countess,' Jeanette urged Thomas in French.

'What's she saying?'

'Nothing,' Thomas said.

'So what are you doing here?' the big man asked.

'I got cut off from my troop in Brittany,' Thomas said weakly. He could hardly tell the truth – that he was a fugitive from justice – but he had no other tale prepared. 'I just walked.'

It was a lame explanation and the big man treated it with the scorn it deserved. 'What you mean, lad,' he said, 'is that you're a bloody deserter.'

'I'd hardly come here if I was, would I?' Thomas asked defiantly.

'You'd hardly come here from Brittany if you just got lost!' the man pointed out. He spat. 'You'll have to go to Scoresby, let him decide what you are.'

'Scoresby?' Thomas asked.

'You've heard of him?' the big man asked belligerently.

Thomas had heard of Walter Scoresby who, like Skeat, was a man who led his own band of men-at-arms and archers, but Scoresby did not have Skeat's good reputation. He was said to be a dark-humoured man, but he was evidently to decide Thomas's fate, for the archers closed around him and walked the pair towards the village. 'She your woman?' one of them asked Thomas.

'She's the Countess of Armorica,' Thomas said.

'And I'm the bloody Earl of London,' the archer retorted.

Jeanette clung to Thomas's arm, terrified of the unfriendly faces. Thomas was equally unhappy. When things had been at their worst in Brittany, when the hellequin were grumbling and it was cold, wet and miserable, Skeat liked to say 'be happy you're not with Scoresby' and now, it seemed, Thomas was.

'We hang deserters,' the big man said with relish.

225

Thomas noted that the archers, like all the troops he could see in the village, wore the red cross of St George on their tunics. A great crowd of them were gathered in a pasture that lay between the small village church and a Cistercian monastery or priory that had somehow escaped destruction, for the white-robed monks were assisting a priest who said Mass for the soldiers. 'Is it Sunday?' Thomas asked one of the archers.

'Tuesday,' the man said, taking off his hat in honour of the sacraments, 'St James's day.'

They waited at the pasture's edge, close to the village church where a row of new graves suggested that some villagers had died when the army came, but most had probably fled south or west. One or two remained. An old man, bent double from work and with a white beard that almost reached the ground, mumbled along with the distant priest while a small boy, perhaps six or seven years old, tried to draw an English bow to the amusement of its owner.

The Mass ended and the mail-clad men climbed from their knees and walked towards the tents and houses. One of the archers from Thomas's escort had gone into the dispersing crowd and he now reappeared with a group of men. One stood out because he was taller than the others and had a new coat of mail that had been polished so it seemed to shine. He had long boots, a green cloak and a gold-hilted sword with a scabbard wrapped in red cloth. The finery seemed at odds with the man's face, which was pinched and gloomy. He was bald, but had a forked beard, which he had twisted into plaits. 'That's Scoresby,' one of the archers muttered and Thomas had no need to guess which of the approaching soldiers he meant.

Scoresby stopped a few paces away and the big archer who had arrested Thomas smirked. 'A deserter,' he announced proudly, 'says he walked here from Brittany.'

Scoresby gave Thomas a hard glance and Jeanette a much longer look. Her ragged dress revealed a length of thigh and a ripped neckline and Scoresby clearly wanted to see more. Like Will Skeat he had begun his military life as an archer and had risen by dint of shrewdness, and Thomas guessed there was not much mercy in his soul's mix.

Scoresby shrugged. 'If he's a deserter,' he said, 'then hang the bastard.' He smiled. 'But we'll keep his woman.'

'I'm not a deserter,' Thomas said, 'and the woman is the Countess of Armorica, who is related to the Count of Blois, nephew to the King of France.'

Most of the archers jeered at this outrageous claim, but Scoresby was a cautious man and he was aware of a small crowd that had gathered at the churchyard's edge. Two priests and some men-at-arms wearing noblemen's escutcheons were among the spectators, and Thomas's confidence had put just enough doubt in Scoresby's mind. He frowned at Jeanette, seeing a girl who looked at first glance like a peasant, but despite her tanned face she was undoubtedly beautiful and the remnants of her dress suggested she had once known elegance.

'She's who?' Scoresby demanded.

'I told you who she was,' Thomas said belligerently, 'and I will tell you more. Her son has been stolen from her, and her son is a ward of our king's. She has come for His Majesty's help.' Thomas hastily told Jeanette what he had said and, to his relief, she nodded her agreement.

Scoresby gazed at Jeanette and something about her increased his doubt. 'Why are you with her?' he asked Thomas.

'I rescued her,' Thomas said.

'He says,' a voice spoke in French from the crowd and Thomas could not see the speaker, who was evidently surrounded by men-at-arms, all wearing a green and white livery. 'He says that he rescued you, madame, is that true?'

'Yes,' Jeanette said. She frowned, unable to see who was questioning her.

'Tell us who you are,' the unseen man demanded.

'I am Jeanette, dowager Countess of Armorica.'

'Your husband was who?' The voice suggested a young man, but a very confident young man.

Jeanette bridled at the tone of the question, but answered it. 'Henri Chenier, Comte d'Armorique.

'And why are you here, madame?'

'Because Charles of Blois has kidnapped my child!' Jeanette answered angrily. 'A child who was placed under the protection of the King of England.'

The young man said nothing for a while. Some in the crowd were edging nervously away from the liveried men-at-arms who surrounded him, and Scoresby was looking apprehensive. 'Who placed him under that protection?' he eventually asked.

'William Bohun,' Jeanette said, 'Earl of Northampton.'

'I believe her,' the voice said, and the men-at-arms stepped aside so that Thomas and Jeanette could see the speaker, who proved to be scarce more than a boy.

Indeed, Thomas doubted he had even begun to shave, though he was surely full grown for he was tall – taller even than Thomas – and had only stayed hidden because his men-at-arms had been wearing green and white plumes in their helmets. The young man was fair-haired, had a face slightly burned by the sun, was dressed in a green cloak, plain breeches and a linen shirt, and nothing except his height explained why men were suddenly kneeling on the grass. 'Down,' Scoresby hissed at Thomas who, perplexed, went on one knee. Now only Jeanette, the boy and his escort of eight tall men-at-arms were standing.

The boy looked at Thomas. 'Did you really walk here from Brittany?' he asked in English, though, like many noblemen, his English was touched with a French accent.

'We both did, sire,' Thomas said in French.

'Why?' he demanded harshly.

'To seek the protection of the King of England,' Thomas said, 'who is the guardian of my lady's son, who has been treacherously taken prisoner by England's enemies.'

The boy looked at Jeanette with much the same wolfish appreciation that Scoresby had shown. He might not shave, but he knew a beautiful woman when he saw one. He smiled. 'You are most welcome, madame,' he said. 'I knew of your husband's reputation, I admired him, and I regret that I will never have a chance to meet him in combat.' He bowed to Jeanette, then untied his cloak and walked to her. He placed the green cape over her shoulders to cover the torn dress. 'I shall ensure, madame,' he said, 'that you are treated with the courtesy your rank demands and will vow to keep whatever promises England made on your son's behalf.' He bowed again.

Jeanette, astonished and pleased by the young man's manner, put the question that Thomas had been wanting answered. 'Who are you, my lord?' she asked, offering a curtsey.

'I am Edward of Woodstock, madame,' he said, offering her his arm.

It meant nothing to Jeanette, but it astonished Thomas. 'He is the King's eldest son,' he whispered to her.

She dropped to one knee, but the smooth-cheeked boy raised her and walked her towards the priory. He was Edward of Woodstock, Earl of Chester, Duke of Cornwall and Prince of Wales. And the wheel of fate had once again spun Jeanette high.

The wheel seemed indifferent towards Thomas. He was left alone, abandoned. Jeanette walked away on the Prince's arm and did not so much as glance back at Thomas. He heard her laugh. He watched her. He had nursed her, fed her, carried her and loved her, and now, without a thought, she had discarded him. No one else was interested in him. Scoresby and his men, cheated of a hanging, had gone to the village, and Thomas wondered just what he was supposed to do.

'Goddamn,' he said aloud. He felt conspicuously foolish in his tattered robe. 'Goddamn,' he said again. Anger, thick as the black humour that could make a man sick, rose in him, but what he could do? He was a fool in a ragged robe and the Prince was the son of a king.

The Prince had taken Jeanette to the low grassy ridge

where the big tents stood in a colourful row. Each tent had a flagpole, and the tallest flew the quartered banner of the Prince of Wales, which showed the golden lions of England on the two red quarters and golden fleur-de-lis on the two blue. The fleur-de-lis were there to show the King's claim to the French throne while the whole flag, which was that of England's king, was crossed with a white-toothed bar to show that this was the banner of the King's eldest son. Thomas was tempted to follow Jeanette, to demand the Prince's help, but then one of the lower banners, the one furthest away from him, caught the small warm wind and sluggishly lifted its folds. He stared at it.

The banner had a blue field and was slashed diagonally with a white band. Three rampant yellow lions were emblazoned on either side of the bar, which was decorated with three red stars that had green centres. It was a flag Thomas knew well, but he scarcely dared believe that he was seeing it here in Normandy, for the arms were those of William Bohun, Earl of Northampton. Northampton was the King's deputy in Brittany, yet his flag was unmistakable and Thomas walked towards it, fearing that the wind-rippled flag would turn out to be a different coat of arms, similar to the Earl's, but not the same.

But it was the Earl's banner, and the Earl's tent, in contrast to the other stately pavilions on the low ridge, was still the grubby shelter made from two worn-out sails. A half-dozen men-at-arms wearing the Earl's livery barred Thomas's way as he neared the tent. 'Have you come to hear his lordship's confession or put an arrow in his belly?' one asked.

'I would speak to his lordship,' Thomas said, barely

suppressing the anger provoked by Jeanette's abandonment of him.

'But will he talk to you?' the man asked, amused at the ragged archer's pretensions.

'He will,' Thomas said with a confidence he did not entirely feel. 'Tell him the man who gave him La Roche-Derrien is here,' he added.

The man-at-arms looked startled. He frowned, but just then the tent flap was thrown back and the Earl himself appeared, stripped to the waist to reveal a muscled chest covered in tight red curls. He was chewing on a goose-bone and peered up at the sky as though fearing rain. The man-at-arms turned to him, indicated Thomas, then shrugged as if to say he was not responsible for a madman showing up unannounced.

The Earl stared at Thomas. 'Good God,' he said after a while, 'have you taken orders?'

'No, my lord.'

The Earl stripped a piece of flesh from the bone with his teeth. 'Thomas, ain't that right?'

'Yes, my lord.'

'Never forget a face,' the Earl said, 'and I have cause to remember yours, though I hardly expected you to fetch up here. Did you walk?'

Thomas nodded. 'I did, my lord.' Something about the Earl's demeanour was puzzling, almost as though he was not really surprised to see Thomas in Normandy.

'Will told me about you,' the Earl said, 'told me all about you. So Thomas, my modest hero from La Roche-Derrien, is a murderer, eh?' He spoke grimly.

'Yes, my lord,' Thomas said humbly.

The Earl threw away the stripped bone, then snapped his fingers and a servant tossed him a shirt from within the tent. He pulled it on and tucked it into his hose. 'God's teeth, boy, do you expect me to save you from Sir Simon's vengeance? You know he's here?'

Thomas gaped at the Earl. Said nothing. Sir Simon Jekyll was here? And Thomas had just brought Jeanette to Normandy. Sir Simon could hardly hurt her so long as she was under the Prince's protection, but Sir Simon could harm Thomas well enough. And delight in it.

The Earl saw Thomas blanch and he nodded. 'He's with the King's men, because I didn't want him, but he insisted on travelling because he reckons there's more plunder to be had in Normandy than in Brittany and I dare say he's right, but what will truly put a smile on his face is the sight of you. Ever been hanged, Thomas?'

'Hanged, my lord?' Thomas asked vaguely. He was still reeling from the news that Sir Simon had sailed to Normandy. He had just walked all this way to find his enemy waiting?

'Sir Simon will hang you,' the Earl said with indecent relish. 'He'll let you strangle on the rope and there'll be no kindly soul tugging on your ankles to make it quick. You could last an hour, two hours, in utter agony. You could choke for even longer! One fellow I hanged lasted from matins till prime and still managed to curse me. So I suppose you want my help, yes?'

Thomas belatedly went onto one knee. 'You offered me a reward after La Roche-Derrien, my lord. Can I claim it now?'

The servant brought a stool from the tent and the Earl sat, his legs set wide. 'Murder is murder,' he said, picking his teeth with a sliver of wood.

'Half Will Skeat's men are murderers, my lord,' Thomas pointed out.

The Earl thought about that, then reluctantly nodded. 'But they're pardoned murderers,' he answered. He sighed. 'I wish Will was here,' he said, evading Thomas's demand. 'I wanted him to come, but he can't come until Charles of Blois is put back into his cage.' He scowled at Thomas. 'If I give you a pardon,' the Earl went on, 'then I make an enemy out of Sir Simon. Not that he's a friend now, but still, why spare you?'

'For La Roche-Derrien,' Thomas said.

'Which is a great debt,' the Earl agreed, 'a very great debt. We'd have looked bloody fools if we hadn't taken that town, miserable goddamn place though it be. God's teeth, boy, but why didn't you just walk south? Plenty of bastards to kill in Gascony.' He looked at Thomas for a while, plainly irritated by the undeniable debt he owed the archer and the nuisance of paying it. He finally shrugged. 'I'll talk to Sir Simon, offer him money, and if it's enough he'll pretend you're not here. As for you,' he paused, frowning as he remembered his earlier meetings with Thomas, 'you're the one who wouldn't tell me who your father was, ain't I right?'

'I didn't tell you, my lord, because he was a priest.'

The Earl thought that was a fine jest. 'God's teeth! A priest? So you're a devil's whelp, are you? That's what they say in Guyenne, that the children of priests are the devil's whelps.' He looked Thomas up and down, amused again at the ragged robe. 'They say the devil's whelps make good soldiers,' he said, 'good soldiers and better whores. I suppose you've lost your horse?'

'Yes, my lord.'

'All my archers are mounted,' the Earl said, then turned to one of his men-at-arms. 'Find the bastard a sway-backed nag till he can filch something better, then give him a tunic and offer him to John Armstrong.' He looked back to Thomas. 'You're joining my archers, which means you'll wear my badge. You're my man, devil's whelp, and perhaps that will protect you if Sir Simon wants too much money for your miserable soul.'

'I shall try to repay your lordship,' Thomas said.

'Pay me, boy, by getting us into Caen. You got us into La Roche-Derrien, but that little place is nothing compared to Caen. Caen is a true bastard. We go there tomorrow, but I doubt we'll see the backside of its walls for a month or more, if ever. Get us into Caen, Thomas, and I'll forgive you a score of murders.' He stood, nodded a dismissal and went back into the tent.

Thomas did not move. Caen, he thought, Caen. Caen was the city where Sir Guillaume d'Evecque lived, and he made the sign of the cross for he knew fate had arranged all this. Fate had determined that his crossbow arrow would miss Sir Simon Jekyll and it had brought him to the edge of Caen. Because fate wanted him to do the penance that Father Hobbe had demanded. God, Thomas decided, had taken Jeanette from him because he had been slow to keep his promise.

But now the time for the keeping of promises had come, for God had brought Thomas to Caen.

PART TWO

Normandy

The Earl of Northampton had been summoned from Brittany to be one of the Prince of Wales's advisers. The Prince was just sixteen, though John Armstrong reckoned the boy was as good as any grown man. 'Ain't nothing wrong with young Edward,' he told Thomas. 'Knows his weapons. Headstrong, maybe, but brave.'

That, in John Armstrong's world, was high praise. He was a forty-year-old man-at-arms who led the Earl's personal archers and was one of those hard, common men that the Earl liked so much. Armstrong, like Skeat, came from the north country and was said to have been fighting the Scots since he had been weaned. His personal weapon was a falchion, a curved sword with a heavy blade as broad as an axe, though he could draw a bow with the best of his troop. He also commanded three score of hobelars, light horsemen mounted on shaggy ponies and carrying spears.

'They don't look up to much,' he said to Thomas, who was gazing at the small horsemen, who all had long shaggy hair and bent legs, 'but they're rare at scouting. We send swarms of yon bastards into the Scottish hills to find the enemy. Be dead else.' Armstrong had been at La Roche-Derrien and remembered Thomas's achievement in turning the town's river flank and, because of that, he accepted Thomas readily enough. He gave him a lice-ridden hacqueton – a padded jacket that might stop a feeble sword cut – and a short surcoat, a jupon, that had the Earl's stars and lions on its breast and bore the cross of St George on its right sleeve. The hacqueton and jupon, like the breeches and arrow bag that completed Thomas's outfit, had belonged to an archer who had died of the fever shortly after reaching Normandy. 'You can find yourself better stuff in Caen,' Armstrong told him, 'if we ever get into Caen.'

Thomas was given a sway-backed grey mare that had a hard mouth and an awkward gait. He watered the beast, rubbed her down with straw, then ate red herrings and dry beans with Armstrong's men. He found a stream and washed his hair, then twisted the bowcord round the wet pigtail. He borrowed a razor and scraped off his beard, tossing the stiff hairs into the stream so that no one could work a spell on them. It seemed strange to spend the night in a soldiers' encampment and to sleep without Jeanette. He still felt bitter about her and that bitterness was like a sliver of iron in his soul when he was roused in the night's dark heart. He felt lonely, chill and unwanted as the archers began their march. He thought of Jeanette in the Prince's tent, and remembered the jealousy he had felt in Rennes when she had gone to the citadel to meet Duke Charles. She was like a moth, he thought, flying to the brightest candle in the room. Her wings had been scorched once, but the flame drew her still.

The army advanced on Caen in three battles, each of about four thousand men. The King commanded one, the Prince of Wales the second while the third was under the orders of the Bishop of Durham, who much preferred slaughter to sanctity. The Prince had left the encampment early to stand his horse beside the road where he could watch his men pass in the summer dawn. He was in black armour, with a lion crest on his helm, and escorted by a dozen priests and fifty knights. As Thomas approached, he saw Jeanette was among those green-and-white-blazoned horsemen. She was wearing the same colours, a dress of pale green cloth with white cuffs, hems and bodice, and was mounted on a palfrey that had silver curb chains, green and white ribbons plaited into its mane and a white saddle cloth embroidered with the lions of England. Her hair had been washed, brushed and coiled, then decorated with cornflowers, and as Thomas came nearer he thought how ravishing she looked. There was a radiant happiness on her face and her eyes were bright. She was just to one side of the Prince and a pace or so behind him, and Thomas noted how often the boy turned to speak to her. The men in front of Thomas were pulling off their helmets or caps to salute the Prince, who looked from Jeanette to them, sometimes nodding or calling out to a knight he recognized.

Thomas, riding his borrowed horse that was so small his long legs hung almost to the ground, raised a hand to greet Jeanette. She stared into his smiling face, then looked away without showing any expression. She spoke with a priest who was evidently the Prince's chaplain. Thomas let his hand drop. 'If you're a bloody prince,' the man beside Thomas said, 'you get the cream, don't you? We get lice and he gets that.'

Thomas said nothing. Jeanette's dismissal had left him embarrassed. Had the last weeks been a dream? He twisted in his saddle to look at her and saw she was laughing at some comment of the Prince's. You are a fool, Thomas told himself, a fool, and he wondered why he felt so hurt. Jeanette had never declared any love for him, yet her abandonment bit his heart like a snake. The road dropped into a hollow where sycamore and ash grew thick and Thomas, turning again, could not see Jeanette.

'There'll be plenty of women in Caen,' an archer said with relish.

'If we ever get in,' another commented, using the five words that were always spoken whenever the city was named.

The previous night Thomas had listened to the campfire talk that had all been about Caen. It was, he gathered, a huge city, one of the biggest in France, and protected by a massive castle and a great wall. The French, it seemed, had adopted a strategy of retreating into such citadels rather than face England's bowmen in the open fields, and the archers feared they could be stranded in front of Caen for weeks. The city could not be ignored, for if it was left untaken its huge garrison would threaten the English supply lines. So Caen had to fall and no one believed it would be easy, though some men reckoned the new guns that the King had fetched to France would knock down the city's ramparts as easily as Joshua's trumpets had felled the walls of Jericho.

The King himself must have been sceptical of the guns' power for he had decided to scare the city into surrender by the sheer numbers of his army. The three English battles moved eastward on every road, track or stretch of meadow that offered a path, but an hour or two after dawn the men-at-arms who served as marshals began halting the various contingents. Sweaty horsemen galloped up and down the masses of men, shouting at them to move into a rough line. Thomas, wrestling with his stubborn mare, understood that the whole army was being formed into a huge crescent. A low hill lay in front and a hazy smear beyond the hill betrayed the thousands of cooking fires in Caen. When the signal was given the whole clumsy crescent of mailed men would be advanced to the hilltop so that the defenders, instead of seeing a few English scouts trickle from the woods, would be presented with an overwhelming host and, to make the army seem double its real size, the marshals were pushing and shouting the camp followers into the curved line. Cooks, clerks, women, masons, farriers, carpenters, scullions, anyone who could walk, crawl, ride or stand was being added to the crescent, and a host of bright flags were raised over those bemused masses. It was a hot morning and the leather and mail made men and horses sweat. Dust blew in the wind. The Earl of Warwick, Marshal of the Host, was galloping up and down the crescent, red-faced and cursing, but slowly the cumbersome line formed to his satisfaction.

'When the trumpet sounds,' a knight shouted at Armstrong's men, 'advance to the hilltop. When the trumpet sounds! Not before!'

That army of England must have looked like twenty thousand men when the trumpets tore the summer sky with their massed defiance. To Caen's defenders it was a nightmare. One moment the horizon was empty, even though the sky beyond had long been blanched by the dust kicked up by hoofs and boots, and then there was a sudden host, a horde, a swarm of men glinting iron-hard in the sun and topped by a forest of raised lances and flags. The whole north and east of the city was ringed with men who, when they saw Caen, gave a great roar of incoherent scorn. There was plunder ahead of them, a whole rich city waiting to be taken.

It was a fine and famous city, bigger even than London and that was the biggest city in England. Caen, indeed, was one of the great cities of France. The Conqueror had endowed it with the wealth he stole from England, and it still showed. Within the city walls the church spires and towers stood as close as the lances and flags in Edward's army, while on either side of the city were two vast abbeys. The castle lay to the north, its ramparts, like the pale stone of the city's high walls, hung with war banners. The English roar was answered with a defiant cheer from the defenders, who clustered thick on the ramparts. So many crossbows, Thomas thought, remembering the heavy bolts thumping from La Roche-Derrien's embrasures.

The city had spread beyond its walls, but instead of placing the new houses beside the ramparts, as most towns did, here they had been built on a sprawling island that lay to the south of the old city. Formed by a maze-like tangle of tributaries that fed the two main rivers which flowed by Caen, the island had no walls, for it was protected by the waterways. It needed such protection, for even from the hilltop Thomas could see that the island was where the wealth of Caen lay. The old city within its high walls would be a labyrinth of narrow alleys and cramped houses, but the island was filled with large mansions, big churches and wide gardens. But even though it appeared to be the wealthiest part of Caen, it did not seem to be defended. No troops were visible there. Instead they were all on the ramparts of the old city. The town's boats had been moored on the island's bank, opposite the city wall, and Thomas wondered if any of them belonged to Sir Guillaume d'Evecque.

The Earl of Northampton, released from the Prince's entourage, joined John Armstrong at the head of the archers and nodded towards the city walls.

'Brute of a place, John!' the Earl said cheerfully.

'Formidable, my lord,' Armstrong grunted.

'The island's named for you,' the Earl said glibly.

'For me?' Armstrong sounded suspicious.

'It's the Île St Jean,' the Earl said, then pointed to the nearer of the two abbeys, a great monastery that was surrounded by its own ramparts, which were joined to the city's higher walls. 'The Abbaye aux Hommes,' the Earl said. 'You know what happened when they buried the Conqueror there? They left him in the abbey for too long and when the time came to put him in the vault he was rotted and swollen. His body burst and they reckon the stench of it drove the congregation out of the abbey.'

'God's vengeance, my lord,' Armstrong said stoically.

The Earl gave him a quizzical look. 'Maybe,' he said uncertainly.

'There's no love of William in the north country,' Armstrong said.

'Long time ago, John.'

'Not so long that I won't spit on his grave,' Armstrong declared, then explained himself. 'He might have been our king, my lord, but he were no Englishman.'

'I suppose he wasn't,' the Earl allowed.

'Time for revenge,' Armstrong said loudly enough for the nearest archers to hear. 'We'll take him, we'll take his city and we'll take his goddamn women!'

The archers cheered, though Thomas did not see how the army could possibly take Caen. The walls were huge and well-buttressed with towers, and the ramparts were thick with defenders who looked as confident as the attackers. Thomas was searching the banners for the one showing three yellow hawks on a blue field, but there were so many flags and the wind was stirring them so briskly that he could not pick Sir Guillaume d'Evecque's three hawks from the other gaudy ripples that swirled beneath the embrasures.

'So what are you, Thomas?' The Earl had dropped back to ride beside him. His horse was a big destrier so that the Earl, despite being much shorter than Thomas, towered above him. He spoke in French. 'English or Norman?'

Thomas grimaced. 'English, my lord. Right to my sore arse.' It had been so long since he had ridden that his thighs were chafed raw.

'We're all English now, aren't we?' The Earl sounded mildly surprised.

'Would you want to be anything else?' Thomas asked, and looked around at the archers. 'God knows, my lord, I wouldn't want to fight them.'

'Nor me,' the Earl grunted, 'and I've saved you a fight with Sir Simon. Or rather I've saved your miserable life. I talked to him last night. I can't say he was very willing to spare you a throttling and I can't blame him for that.' The Earl slapped at a horsefly. 'But in the end his greed overcame his hatred of you. You've cost me my share of the prize money for the Countess's two ships, young Thomas. One ship for his dead squire and the other for the hole you put in his leg.'

'Thank you, my lord,' Thomas said effusively. He felt the relief surge through him. 'Thank you,' he said again.

'So you're a free man,' the Earl said. 'Sir Simon shook on it, a clerk made a note of it and a priest witnessed it. Now for God's sake don't go and kill another of his fellows.'

'I won't, sir,' Thomas promised.

'And you're in my debt now,' the Earl said.

'I acknowledge it, my lord.'

The Earl made a dismissive noise, suggesting it was unlikely Thomas could ever pay such a debt, then he shot the archer a suspicious look. 'And speaking of the Countess,' he went on, 'you never mentioned that you brought her north.'

'It didn't seem important, my lord.'

'And last night,' the Earl continued, 'after I'd growled at Jekyll for you, I met her ladyship in the Prince's quarters. She says you treated her with complete chivalry. It seems you behaved with discretion and respect. Is that really true?'

Thomas reddened. 'If she says so, my lord, it must be true.'

The Earl laughed, then touched his spurs to his destrier. 'I've bought your soul,' he said cheerfully, 'so fight well for me!' He curved away to rejoin his men-at-arms.

'He's all right, our Billy,' an archer said, nodding at the Earl, 'a good one.'

'If only they were all like him,' Thomas agreed.

'How come you talk French?' the archer asked suspiciously.

'Picked it up in Brittany,' Thomas said vaguely.

The army's vanguard had now reached the cleared

space in front of the walls and a crossbow bolt slammed into the turf as a warning. The camp followers, who had helped give the illusion of overwhelming force, were pitching tents on the hills to the north, while the fighting men spread out in the plain that surrounded the city. Marshals were galloping between the units, shouting that the Prince's men were to go clear about the walls to the Abbaye aux Dames on the city's further side. It was still early, about mid-morning, and the wind brought the smell of Caen's cooking fires as the Earl's men marched past deserted farms. The castle loomed above them.

They went to the western side of the town. The Prince of Wales, mounted on a big black horse and followed by a standard-bearer and a troop of men-at-arms, galloped to the convent, which, because it lay well outside the city walls, had been abandoned. He would make it his home for the duration of the siege and Thomas, dismounting where Armstrong's men would camp, saw Jeanette following the Prince. Following him like a puppy, he thought sourly, then chided himself for jealousy. Why be jealous of a prince? A man might as well resent the sun or curse the ocean. There are other women, he told himself as he hobbled his horse in one of the abbey pastures.

A group of archers was exploring the deserted buildings that lay close to the convent. Most were cottages, but one had been a carpenter's workshop and was piled with wood-shavings and sawdust, while beyond it was a tannery, still stinking of the urine, lime and dung that cured the leather. Beyond the tannery was nothing but a waste ground of thistles and nettles that ran clear to the city's great wall, and Thomas saw that dozens of archers were venturing into the weeds to stare at the ramparts. It was a hot day so that the air in front of the walls seemed to shiver. A small north wind drifted some high clouds and rippled the long grass that grew in the ditch at the base of the battlements. About a hundred archers were in the waste ground now and some were within long crossbow range, though no Frenchman shot at them. A score of the inquisitive bowmen were carrying axes to cut firewood, but morbid curiosity had driven them towards the ramparts instead of outwards to the woods and Thomas now followed them, wanting to judge for himself what horrors the besiegers faced. The screeching sound of ungreased axles made him turn to see two farm wagons being dragged towards the convent. They both held guns, great bulbous things with swollen metal bellies and gaping mouths. He wondered if the guns' magic could blast a hole through the city's ramparts, but even if it did then men would still have to fight through the breach. He made the sign of the cross. Maybe he would find a woman inside the city. He had almost everything a man needed. He had a horse, he had a hacqueton, he had his bow and arrow bag. He just needed a woman.

Yet he did not see how an army twice the size could cross Caen's great walls. They reared up from their boggy ditch like cliffs, and every fifty paces there was a conical roofed bastion that would give the garrison's crossbowmen the chance to slash their quarrels into the flanks of the attackers. It would be carnage, Thomas thought, far worse than the slaughter that had occurred each time the Earl of Northampton's men had assailed the southern wall at La Roche-Derrien.

More and more archers came into the waste ground

to stare at the city. Most were just inside crossbow range, but the French still ignored them. Instead the defenders began hauling in the gaudy banners that hung from the embrasures. Thomas looked for Sir Guillaume's three hawks, but could not see them. Most of the banners were decorated with crosses or the figures of saints. One showed the keys of heaven, another the lion of St Mark and a third had a winged angel scything down English troops with a flaming sword. That banner disappeared.

'What the hell are the goddamn bastards doing?' an archer asked.

'The bastards are running away!' another man said. He was staring at the stone bridge that led from the old city to the Île St Jean.

That bridge was thronged with soldiers, some mounted, most on foot, and all of them streaming out of the walled city onto the island of big houses, churches and gardens. Thomas walked a few paces southwards to get a better view and saw crossbowmen and men-at-arms appear in the alleys between the island's houses.

'They're going to defend the island,' he said to anyone in earshot.

By now carts were being pushed over the bridge and he could see women and children being chivvied on their way by men-at-arms.

More defenders crossed the bridge and still more banners vanished from the walls until there was only a handful left. The big flags of the great lords still flew from the castle's topmost towers, and pious banners hung down the keep's long walls, but the city ramparts were almost bare and there must have been a thousand archers from the Prince of Wales's battle watching those walls now. They should have been cutting firewood, building shelters or digging latrines, but a slow suspicion was dawning on them that the French were not planning to defend both the city and the island, but only the island. Which meant the city had been abandoned. That seemed so unlikely that no one even dared mention it. They just watched the city's inhabitants and defenders crowd across the stone bridge and then, as the last banner was hauled from the ramparts, someone began walking towards the nearest gate.

No one gave any orders. No prince, earl, constable or knight ordered the archers forward. They simply decided to approach the city themselves. Most wore the Prince of Wales's green and white livery, but a good few, like Thomas, had the Earl of Northampton's stars and lions. Thomas half expected crossbowmen to appear and greet the straggling advance with a terrible volley of spitting quarrels, but the embrasures stayed empty and that emboldened the archers who saw birds settling on the crenellations, a sure sign that the defenders had abandoned the wall. The men with axes ran to the gate and started to hack at its timbers, and no crossbow bolts flew from the flanking bastions. The great walled city of William the Conqueror had been left unguarded.

The axemen broke through the iron-studded planks, lifted the bar and pulled the big gates open to reveal an empty street. A handcart with one broken wheel was abandoned on the cobbles, but no Frenchmen were visible. There was a pause as the archers stared in disbelief, then the shouting began. 'Havoc! Havoc!' The first thought was plunder, and men eagerly broke into the houses, but found little except chairs, tables and cupboards. Everything of real value, like every person in the city, was gone to the island.

Still more archers were coming into the city. A few climbed towards the open ground surrounding the castle where two died from crossbow bolts spat from the high ramparts, but the rest spread through the city to find it bare, and so more and more men were drawn towards the bridge that spanned the River Odon and led to the Île St Jean. At the bridge's southern end, where it reached the island, there was a barbican tower that was thick with crossbows, but the French did not want the English getting close to the barbican and so they had hastily thrown up a barricade on the bridge's northern side out of a great heap of wagons and furniture and they had garrisoned the barrier with a score of men-at-arms reinforced by as many crossbowmen. There was another bridge at the island's further side, but the archers did not know of its existence and, besides, it was a long way off and the barricaded bridge was the quickest route to the enemy's riches.

The first white-fledged arrows began to fly. Then came the harder sounds of the enemy's crossbows discharging and the crack of bolts striking the stones of the church beside the bridge. The first men died.

There were still no orders. No man of rank was inside the city yet, just a mass of archers as mindless as wolves smelling blood. They poured arrows at the barricade, forcing its defenders to crouch behind the overturned wagons, then the first group of English gave a cheer and charged at the barricade with swords, axes and spears. More men followed as the first tried to climb the ungainly pile. The crossbows banged from the barbican and men were thrown back by the heavy bolts. The

French men-at-arms stood to repel the survivors and swords clashed on axes. Blood was slick on the bridge approach and one archer slipped and was trampled underfoot by his colleagues going to the fight. The English were howling, the French were shouting, a trumpet was calling from the barbican and every church bell on the Île St Jean was tolling the alarm.

Thomas, having no sword of his own, was standing in the porch of a church which stood hard beside the bridge from where he was shooting arrows up at the barbican tower, but his aim was obscured because a thatch in the old city was on fire and the smoke was curling over the river like a low cloud.

The French held all the advantages. Their crossbowmen could shoot from the barbican and from the shelter of the barricade, and to attack them the English had to funnel onto the narrow bridge approach, which was littered with bodies, blood and bolts. Still more enemy crossbowmen were stationed in the line of boats that was moored along the island's bank, stranded there by the falling tide, and the defenders of those boats, sheltered by the stout wooden gunwales, could shoot up at any archer foolish enough to show himself on those parts of the city wall that were not smoke-shrouded. More and more crossbowmen were coming to the bridge until it seemed as if the air above the river was as thick with quarrels as a flock of starlings.

Another rush of archers charged from the alleys to fill the narrow street leading to the barricade. They screamed as they charged. They were not fighting with their bows, but rather with axes, swords, billhooks and spears. The spears were mostly carried by the hobelars, many of them Welshmen who uttered a high-shrieked howl as they ran with the archers. A dozen of the new attackers must have fallen to crossbow bolts, but the survivors leaped the bodies and closed right up to the barricade that was now defended by at least thirty men-at-arms and as many crossbowmen. Thomas ran and picked up the arrow bag of a dead man. The attackers were crammed up against the arrow-stuck barricade with little room to wield their axes, swords and spears. The French men-at-arms stabbed with lances, hacked with swords and flailed with maces, and as the front rank of archers died, the next rank was pushed onto the enemy weapons, and all the time the crossbow quarrels thumped down from the barbican's crenellated tower and flew up from the grounded ships in the river. Thomas saw a man reeling from the bridge with a crossbow bolt buried in his helmet. Blood poured down his face as he made a strange incoherent mewing before falling to his knees and then, slowly, collapsing on the road where he was trampled by another rush of attackers. A few English archers found their way onto the roof of the church and they killed a half-dozen of the barricade's defenders before the crossbowmen on the barbican swept them away with stinging volleys. The bridge approach was thick with bodies now, so many corpses that they obstructed the charging English, and a half-dozen men began heaving the dead over the parapet. A tall archer, armed with a long-handled axe, managed to reach the barricade's summit, where he chopped the heavy blade again and again, beating down at a Frenchman who had ribbons on his helmet, but then he was struck by two crossbow bolts and he folded over, letting the axe fall and clutching at his belly, and the French hauled him down to their side of the barricade where three men hacked at him with swords, then used the archer's own axe to sever his head. They thrust the bloody trophy onto a spear and waved it above the barricade to taunt their attackers.

A mounted man-at-arms, wearing the Earl of Warwick's badge of a bear and ragged staff, shouted at the archers to retreat. The Earl himself was in the city now, sent by the King to pull his bowmen back from their unequal fight, but the archers were not willing to listen. The French were jeering them, killing them, but still the archers wanted to break through the bridge's defences and slake themselves on Caen's wealth. And so still more blood-maddened men charged at the barricade – so many that they filled the road as the bolts whipped down from the smoky sky. The attackers at the back heaved forward and the men at the front died on French lances and blades.

The French were winning. Their crossbow bolts were smacking into the crush of men and those at the front began to push backwards to escape the slaughter while those at the back still shoved forward and the ones in between, threatened with a crushing death, broke through a stout wooden fence that let them spill off the bridge's approach onto a narrow strip of ground that lay between the river and the city walls. More men followed them.

Thomas was still crouching in the church porch. He sent an occasional arrow up towards the barbican, but the thickening smoke hung like fog and he could scarcely see his targets. He watched the men streaming off the bridge onto the narrow riverbank, but did not follow, for that seemed just another way of committing suicide. They were trapped there with the high city wall at their backs and the swirling river in front, and the far bank of the river was lined with boats from which crossbowmen poured quarrels into these new and inviting targets.

The spillage of men off the bridge opened the roadway to the barricade again and newly arrived men, who had not experienced the carnage of the first attacks, took up the fight. A hobelar managed to climb onto an overturned wagon and stabbed down with his short spear. There were crossbow bolts sticking from his chest, but still he screeched and stabbed and tried to go on fighting even when a French man-at-arms disembowelled him. His guts spilled out, but somehow he found the strength to raise the spear and give one last lunge before he fell into the defenders. A half-dozen archers were trying to dismantle the barricade, while others were throwing the dead off the bridge to clear the roadway. At least one living man, wounded, was thrown into the river. He screamed as he fell.

'Get back, you dogs, get back!' The Earl of Warwick had come to the chaos and he flailed at men with his marshal's staff. He had a trumpeter sounding the four falling notes of the retreat while the French trumpeter was blasting out the attack signal, brisk couplets of rising notes that stirred the blood, and the English and Welsh were obeying the French rather than the English trumpet. More men – hundreds of them – were streaming into the old city, dodging the Earl of Warwick's constables and closing on the bridge where, unable to get past the barricade, they followed the men down to the riverbank from where they shot their arrows at the crossbowmen in the barges. The Earl of Warwick's men started pulling archers away from the street that led to the bridge, but for every one they hauled away another two slipped past.

A crowd of Caen's menfolk, some armed with nothing more than staves, waited beyond the barbican, promising yet another fight if the barricade was ever overcome. A madness had gripped the English army, a madness to attack a bridge that was too well defended. Men went screaming to their deaths and still more followed. The Earl of Warwick was bellowing at them to pull back, but they were deaf to him. Then a great roar of defiance sounded from the riverbank and Thomas stepped out from the porch to see that groups of men were now trying to wade the River Odon. And they were succeeding. It had been a dry summer, the river was low and the falling tide made it lower still, so that at its deepest the water only came up to a man's chest. Scores of men were now plunging into the river. Thomas, dodging two of the Earl's constables, leaped the remnants of the fence and slithered down the bank, which was studded with embedded crossbow quarrels. The place stank of shit, for this was where the city emptied its nightsoil. A dozen Welsh hobelars waded into the river and Thomas joined them, holding his bow high above his head to keep its string dry. The crossbowmen had to stand up from their shelter behind the barge gunwales to shoot down at the attackers in the river, and once they were standing they made easy targets for those archers who had stayed on the city bank.

The current was strong and Thomas could only take short steps. Bolts splashed about him. A man just in front was hit in the throat and was snatched down by the weight of his mail coat to leave nothing but a swirl of bloody water. The ships' gunwales were stuck with white-feathered arrows. A Frenchman was draped over the side of one boat and his body twitched whenever an arrow hit his corpse. Blood trickled from a scupper.

'Kill the bastards, kill the bastards,' a man muttered next to Thomas, who saw it was one of the Earl of Warwick's constables; finding he could not stop the attack, he had decided to join it. The man was carrying a curved falchion, half sword and half butcher's cleaver.

The wind flattened the smoke from the burning houses, dipping it close to the river and filling the air with scraps of burning straw. Some of those scraps had lodged in the furled sails of two of the ships that were now burning fiercely. Their defenders had scrambled ashore. Other enemy bowmen were retreating from the first mud-streaked English and Welsh soldiers who clambered up the bank between the grounded boats. The air was filled with the quick-fluttering hiss of arrows flying overhead. The island's bells still clamoured. A Frenchman was shouting from the barbican's tower, ordering men to spread along the river and attack the groups of Welsh and English who struggled and slithered in the river mud.

Thomas kept wading. The water reached his chest, then began to recede. He fought the clinging mud of the riverbed and ignored the crossbow bolts that drove into the water about him. A crossbowman stood up from behind a boat's gunwale and aimed straight at Thomas's chest, but then two arrows struck the man and he fell backwards. Thomas pushed on, climbing now. Then suddenly he was out of the river, and he stumbled up the slick mud into the shelter of the overhanging stern of the closest barge. He could see that men were still fighting at the barricade, but he could also see that the river was now swarming with archers and hobelars who, mud-spattered and soaking, began to haul themselves onto the boats. The remaining defenders had few weapons other than their crossbows, while most of the archers had swords or axes. The fight on the moored boats was one-sided, the slaughter brief, and then the disorganized and leaderless mass of attackers surged off the blood-soaked decks and up from the river onto the island.

The Earl of Warwick's man-at-arms went ahead of Thomas. He clambered up the steep grassy bank and was immediately hit in the face by a crossbow bolt so that he jerked backwards with a fine mist of blood encircling his helmet. The bolt had driven clean through the bridge of his nose, killing him instantly and leaving him with an offended expression. His falchion landed in the mud at Thomas's feet, so he slung his bow and picked the weapon up. It was surprisingly heavy. There was nothing sophisticated about a falchion; it was simply a killing tool with an edge designed to cut deep because of the weight of the broad blade. It was a good weapon for a mêlée. Will Skeat had once told Thomas how he had seen a Scottish horse decapitated with a single blow of a falchion, and just to see one of the brutal blades was to feel terror in the gut.

The Welsh hobelars were on the barge, finishing off its defenders, then they gave a shout in their strange language and leaped ashore and Thomas followed them, to find himself in a loose rank of crazed attackers who ran towards a row of tall and wealthy houses defended by the men who had escaped from the barges and by the citizens of Caen. The crossbowmen had time to loose one bolt apiece, but they were nervous and most shot wide, and then the attackers were onto them like hounds onto a wounded deer.

Thomas wielded the falchion two-handed. A crossbowman tried to defend himself with his bow but the heavy blade sliced through the weapon's stock as if it had been made of ivory, then buried itself in the Frenchman's neck. A spurt of blood jetted over Thomas's head as he wrenched the heavy sword free and kicked the crossbowman between the legs. A Welshman was grinding a spear blade into a Frenchman's ribs. Thomas stumbled on the man he had struck down, caught his balance and shouted the English war cry. 'St George!' He swung the blade again, chopping through the forearm of a man wielding a club. He was close enough to smell the man's breath and the stink of his clothes. A Frenchman was swinging a sword while another was beating at the Welsh with an iron-studded mace. This was tavern fighting, outlaw fighting, and Thomas was screaming like a fiend. God damn them all. He was spattered with blood as he kicked and clawed and slashed his way down the alley. The air seemed unnaturally thick, moist and warm; it stank of blood. The iron-studded mace missed his head by a finger's breadth and struck the wall instead, and Thomas swung the falchion upwards so it cut into the man's groin. The man yelled out and Thomas kicked the back of the blade to drive it home. 'Bastard,' he said, kicking the blade again, 'bastard.' A Welshman speared the man and two more leaped his body and, their long hair and beards smeared with blood, lunged their red-bladed spears at the next rank of defenders.

There must have been twenty or more enemy in the alley, and Thomas and his companions were fewer than a dozen, but the French were nervous and the attackers were confident and so they ripped into them with spear and sword and falchion; just hacking and stabbing, slicing and cursing them, killing in a welter of summer hatred. More and more English and Welsh were swarming up from the river, and the sound they made was a keening noise, a howl for blood and a wail of derision for a wealthy enemy. These were the hounds of war that had escaped from their kennels and they were taking this great city that the lords of the army had supposed would hold the English advance for a month.

The defenders in the alley broke and ran. Thomas hacked a man down from behind and wrenched the blade free with a scraping noise of steel on bone. The hobelars kicked in a door, claiming the house beyond as their property. A rush of archers in the Prince of Wales's green and white livery poured down the alley, following Thomas into a long and pretty garden where pear trees grew about neat plots of herbs. Thomas was struck by the incongruity of such a beautiful place under a sky filled with smoke and terrible with screams. The garden had a border of sweet rocket, wallflowers and peonies, and seats under a vine trellis and for an instant it looked like a scrap of heaven, but then the archers trampled the herbs, threw down the grape arbour and ran across the flowers.

A group of Frenchmen tried to drive the invaders out of the garden. They approached from the east, from out of the mass of men waiting behind the bridge's barbican. They were led by three mounted men-at-arms, who all wore blue surcoats decorated with yellow stars. They jumped their horses over the low fences and shouted as they raised their long swords ready to strike.

The arrows smacked into the horses. Thomas had not unslung his bow, but some of the Prince's archers had arrows on their cords and they aimed at the horses instead of the riders. The arrows bit deep, the horses screamed, reared and fell, and the archers swarmed over the fallen men with axes and swords. Thomas went to the right, heading off the Frenchmen on foot, most of whom seemed to be townsfolk armed with anything from small axes to thatch-hooks to ancient two-handed swords. He cut the falchion through a leather coat, kicked the blade free, swung it so that blood streamed in droplets from the blade, then hacked again. The French wavered, saw more archers coming from the alley and fled back to the barbican.

The archers were hacking at the unsaddled horsemen. One of the fallen men screamed as the blades chopped at his arms and trunk. The blue and yellow surcoats were soaked in blood. Then Thomas saw that it was not yellow stars on a blue field, but hawks. Hawks with their wings raised and their claws outstretched. Sir Guillaume d'Evecque's men! Maybe Sir Guillaume himself! But when he looked at the grimacing, blood-spattered faces Thomas saw that all three had been young men. But Sir Guillaume was here in Caen, and the lance, Thomas thought, must be near. He broke through the fence and headed down another alley. Behind him, in the house that the hobelars had commandeered, a woman cried, the first of many. The church bells were falling silent.

Edward the Third, by the Grace of God, King of England, led close to twelve thousand fighting men and by now a fifth of them were on the island and still more were coming. No one had led them there. The only orders they had received were to retreat. But they had disobeyed and so they had captured Caen, though the enemy still held the bridge barbican from where they were spitting crossbow bolts.

Thomas emerged from the alley into the main street, where he joined a group of archers who swamped the crenellated tower with arrows and, under their cover, a howling mob of Welsh and English overwhelmed the Frenchmen cowering under the barbican's arch before charging the defenders of the bridge barricade, who were now assailed on both sides. The Frenchmen, seeing their doom, threw down their weapons and shouted that they yielded, but the archers were in no mood for quarter. They just howled and attacked. Frenchmen were tossed into the river, and then scores of men hauled the barricade apart, tipping its furniture and wagons over the parapet.

The great mass of Frenchmen who had been waiting behind the barbican scattered into the island, most, Thomas assumed, going to rescue their wives and daughters. They were pursued by the vengeful archers who had been waiting at the bridge's far side, and the grim crowd went past Thomas, going into the heart of the Île St Jean where the screams were now constant. The cry of havoc was everywhere. The barbican tower was still held by the French, though they were no longer using their crossbows for fear of retaliation by the English arrows. No one tried to take the tower, though a small group of archers stood in the bridge's centre and stared up at the banners hanging from the ramparts.

Thomas was about to go into the island's centre when he heard the clash of hooves on stone and he looked back to see a dozen French knights who must have been concealed behind the barbican. Those men now erupted from a gate and, with visors closed and lances couched, spurred their horses towards the bridge. They plainly wanted to charge clean through the old city to reach the greater safety of the castle.

Thomas took a few steps towards the Frenchmen, then thought better of it. No one wanted to resist a dozen fully armoured knights. But he saw the blue and yellow surcoat, saw the hawks on a knight's shield and he unslung his bow and took an arrow from the bag. He hauled the cord back. The Frenchmen were just spurring onto the bridge and Thomas shouted, 'Evecque! Evecque!' He wanted Sir Guillaume, if it was he, to see his killer, and the man in the blue and yellow surcoat did half turn in the saddle though Thomas could not see his enemy's face because the visor was down. He loosed, but even as he let the cord snap he saw that the arrow was warped. It flew low, smacking into the man's left leg instead of the small of his back where Thomas had aimed. He pulled a second arrow out, but the dozen knights were on the bridge now, their horses' hooves striking sparks from the cobbles, and the leading men lowered their lances to batter the handful of archers aside, and then they were through and galloping up the further streets towards the castle. The white-fledged arrow still jutted from the knight's thigh where it had sunk deep and Thomas sent a second arrow after it, but that one vanished in the smoke as the French fugitives disappeared in the old city's tight streets.

The castle had not fallen, but the city and the island belonged to the English. They did not belong to the King yet, because the great lords – the earls and the barons – had not captured either place. They belonged to the archers and the hobelars, and they now set about plundering the wealth of Caen.

The Île St Jean was, other than Paris itself, the fairest, plumpest and most elegant city in northern France. Its houses were beautiful, its gardens fragrant, its streets wide, its churches wealthy and its citizens, as they should be, civilized. Into that pleasant place came a savage horde of muddy, bloody men who found riches beyond their dreams. What the hellequin had done to countless Breton villages was now visited on a great city. It was a time for killing, for rape and wanton cruelty. Any Frenchman was an enemy, and every enemy was cut down. The leaders of the city garrison, magnates of France, were safe in the upper floors of the barbican tower and they stayed there until they recognized some English lords to whom they could safely surrender, while a dozen knights had escaped to the castle. A few other lords and knights managed to outgallop the invading English and flee across the island's southern bridge, but at least a dozen titled men whose ransoms could have made a hundred archers rich as princelings were cut down like dogs and reduced to mangled meat and weltering blood. Knights and men-at-arms, who could have paid a hundred or two hundred pounds for their freedom, were shot with arrows or clubbed down in the mad rage which possessed the army. As for the humbler men, the citizens armed with lengths of timber, mattocks or mere knives, they were just slaughtered. Caen, the city of the Conqueror that had become rich on English plunder, was killed that day and the wealth of it was given back to Englishmen.

And not just its wealth, its women too. To be a

woman in Caen that day was to be given a foretaste of hell. There was little fire, for men wanted the houses to be plundered rather than burned, but there were devils aplenty. Men begged for the honour of their wives and daughters, then were forced to watch that honour being trampled. Many women hid, but they were found soon enough by men accustomed to riddling out hiding places in attics or under stairs. The women were driven to the streets, stripped bare and paraded as trophies. One merchant's wife, monstrously fat, was harnessed to a small cart and whipped naked up and down the main street which ran the length of the island. For an hour or more the archers made her run, some men laughing themselves to tears at the sight of her massive rolls of fat, and when they were bored with her they tossed her into the river where she crouched, weeping and calling for her children until an archer, who had been trying out a captured crossbow on a pair of swans, put a quarrel through her throat. Men laden with silver plate were staggering over the bridge, others were still searching for riches and instead found ale, cider or wine, and so the excesses grew worse. A priest was hanged from a tavern sign after he tried to stop a rape. Some men-at-arms, very few, tried to stem the horror, but they were hugely outnumbered and driven back to the bridge. The church of St Jean, which was said to contain the fingerbones of St John the Divine, a hoof of the horse St Paul was riding to Damascus and one of the baskets that had held the miraculous loaves and fishes, was turned into a brothel where the women who had fled to the church for sanctuary were sold to grinning soldiers. Men paraded in silks and lace and threw dice for the women from whom they had stolen the finery.

Thomas took no part. What happened could not be stopped, not by one man nor even by a hundred men. Another army could have quelled the mass rape, but in the end Thomas knew it would be the stupor of drunkenness that would finish it. Instead he searched for his enemy's house, wandering from street to street until he found a dying Frenchman and gave him a drink of water before asking where Sir Guillaume d'Evecque lived. The man rolled his eyes, gasped for breath and stammered that the house was in the southern part of the island. 'You cannot miss it,' the man said, 'it is stone, all stone, and has three hawks carved above the door.'

Thomas walked south. Bands of the Earl of Warwick's men-at-arms were coming in force to the island to restore order, but they were still struggling with the archers close to the bridge, and Thomas was going to the southern part of the island which had not suffered as badly as the streets and alleys closer to the bridge. He saw the stone house above the roofs of some plundered shops. Most other buildings were half-timbered and straw-roofed, but Sir Guillaume d'Evecque's two-storey mansion was almost a fortress. Its walls were stone, its roof tiled and its windows small, but still some archers had got inside, for Thomas could hear screams. He crossed a small square where a large oak grew through the cobbles, strode up the house steps and under an arch that was surmounted by the three carved hawks. He was surprised by the depth of anger that the sight of the escutcheon gave him. This was revenge, he told himself, for Hookton.

He went through the hallway to find a group of archers and hobelars squabbling over the kitchen pots.

Two menservants lay dead by the hearth in which a fire still smouldered. One of the archers snarled at Thomas that they had reached the house first and its contents were theirs, but before Thomas could answer he heard a scream from the upper floor and he turned and ran up the big wooden stairway. Two rooms opened from the upper hallway and Thomas pushed open one of the doors to see an archer in the Prince of Wales's livery struggling with a girl. The man had half torn off her pale blue dress, but she was fighting back like a vixen, clawing at his face and kicking his shins. Then, just as Thomas came into the room, the man managed to subdue her with a great clout to the head. The girl gasped and fell back into the wide and empty hearth as the archer turned on Thomas. 'She's mine,' he said curtly, 'go and find your own.'

Thomas looked at the girl. She was fair-haired, thin and weeping. He remembered Jeanette's anguish after the Duke had raped her and he could not stomach seeing such pain inflicted on another girl, not even a girl in Sir Guillaume d'Evecque's mansion.

'I think you've hurt her enough,' he said. He crossed himself, remembering his sins in Brittany. 'Let her go,' he added.

The archer, a bearded man a dozen years older than Thomas, drew his sword. It was an old weapon, broadbladed and sturdy, and the man hefted it confidently. 'Listen, boy,' he said, 'I'm going to watch you go through that door, and if you don't I'll string your goddamn guts from wall to wall.'

Thomas hefted the falchion. 'I've sworn an oath to St Guinefort,' he told the man, 'to protect all women.'

'Goddamn fool.'

The man leaped at Thomas, lunged, and Thomas stepped back and parried so that the blades struck sparks as they rang together. The bearded man was quick to recover, lunged again, and Thomas took another backwards step and swept the sword aside with the falchion. The girl was watching from the hearth with wide blue eyes. Thomas swung his broad blade, missed and was almost skewered by the sword, but he stepped aside just in time, then kicked the bearded man in the knee so that he hissed with pain, then Thomas swept the falchion in a great haymaking blow that cut into the bearded man's neck. Blood arced across the room as the man, without a sound, dropped to the floor. The falchion had very nearly severed his head and the blood still pulsed from the open wound as Thomas knelt beside his victim.

'If anyone asks,' he said to the girl in French, 'your father did this, then ran away.' He had got into too much trouble after murdering a squire in Brittany and did not want to compound the crime by the death of an archer. He took four small coins from the archer's pouch then smiled at the girl, who had remained remarkably calm while a man was almost decapitated in front of her eyes. 'I'm not going to hurt you,' Thomas said, 'I promise.'

She watched him from the hearth. 'You won't?'

'Not today,' he said gently.

She stood, shaking the dizziness from her head. She pulled her dress close at her neck and tied the torn parts together with loose threads. 'You may not hurt me,' she said, 'but others will.'

'Not if you stay with me,' Thomas said. 'Here,' he took the big black bow from his shoulder, unstrung it and tossed it to her. 'Carry that,' he said, 'and everyone will know you're an archer's woman. No one will touch you then.'

She frowned at the weight of the bow. 'No one will hurt me?'

'Not if you carry that,' Thomas promised her again. 'Is this your house?'

'I work here,' she said.

'For Sir Guillaume d'Evecque?' he asked and she nodded. 'Is he here?'

She shook her head. 'I don't know where he is.'

Thomas reckoned his enemy was in the castle where he would be trying to extricate an arrow from his thigh. 'Did he keep a lance here?' he asked, 'a great black lance with a silver blade?'

She shook her head quickly. Thomas frowned. The girl, he could see, was trembling. She had shown bravery, but perhaps the blood seeping from the dead man's neck was unsettling her. He also noted she was a pretty girl despite the bruises on her face and the dirt in her tangle of fair hair. She had a long face made solemn by big eyes. 'Do you have family here?' Thomas asked her.

'My mother died. I have no one except Sir Guillaume.'

'And he left you here alone?' Thomas asked scornfully.

'No!' she protested. 'He thought we'd be safe in the city, but then, when your army came, the men decided to defend the island instead. They left the city! Because all the good houses are here.' She sounded indignant.

'So what do you do for Sir Guillaume?' Thomas asked her.

'I clean,' she said, 'and milk the cows on the other

side of the river.' She flinched as men shouted angrily from the square outside.

Thomas smiled. 'It's all right, no one will hurt you. Hold on to the bow. If anyone looks at you, say, "I am an archer's woman."' He repeated it slowly, then made her say the phrase over and over till he was satisfied. 'Good!' He smiled at her. 'What's your name?'

'Eleanor.'

He doubted it would serve much purpose to search the house, though he did, but there was no lance of St George hidden in any of the rooms. There was no furniture, no tapestries, nothing of any value except the spits and pots and dishes in the kitchen. Everything precious, Eleanor said, had gone to the castle a week before. Thomas looked at the shattered dishes on the kitchen flagstones.

'How long have you worked for him?' he asked.

'All my life,' Eleanor said, then added shyly, 'I'm fifteen.'

'And you never saw a great lance that he brought back from England?'

'No,' she said, eyes wide, but something about her expression made Thomas think she was lying, though he did not challenge her. He decided he would question her later, when she had learned to trust him.

'You'd better stay with me,' he told Eleanor, 'then you won't get hurt. I'll take you to the encampment and when our army moves on you can come back here.' What he really meant was that she could stay with him and become a true archer's woman, but that, like the lance, could wait a day or two.

She nodded, accepting that fate with equanimity. She must have prayed to be spared the rape that tortured

271

Caen and Thomas was her prayer's answer. He gave her his arrow bag so that she looked even more like an archer's woman. 'We'll have to go through the city,' he told Eleanor as he led her down the staircase, 'so stay close.'

He went down the house's outer steps. The small square was now crowded with mounted men-at-arms wearing the badge of the bear and ragged staff. They had been sent by the Earl of Warwick to stop the slaughter and robbery, and they stared hard at Thomas, but he lifted his hands to show he was carrying nothing, then threaded between the horses. He had gone perhaps a dozen paces when he realized that Eleanor was not with him. She was terrified of the horsemen in dirty mail, their grim faces framed in steel and so she had hesitated at the house door.

Thomas opened his mouth to call her and just then a horseman spurred at him from under the branches of the oak. Thomas looked up, then the flat of a sword blade hammered into the side of his head and he was pitched forward, his ear bleeding, onto the cobblestones. The falchion fell from his hand, then the man's horse stepped on his forehead and Thomas's vision was seared with lightning.

The man climbed from the saddle and stamped his armoured foot on Thomas's head. Thomas felt the pain, heard the protests from the other men-at-arms, then felt nothing as he was kicked a second time. But in the few heartbeats before he lost consciousness he had recognized his assailant.

Sir Simon Jekyll, despite his agreement with the Earl, wanted revenge.

Perhaps Thomas was lucky. Perhaps his guardian saint, whether dog or man, was looking after him, for if he had been conscious he would have suffered torture. Sir Simon might have put his signature to the agreement with the Earl the previous night, but the sight of Thomas had driven any mercy from his mind. He remembered the humiliation of being hunted naked through the trees and he recalled the pain of the crossbow bolt in his leg, a wound that still made him limp, and those memories provoked nothing except a wish to give Thomas a long, slow hurting that would leave the archer screaming. But Thomas had been stunned by the flat of the sword and by the kicks to his head and he did not know a thing as two men-at-arms dragged him towards the oak. At first the Earl of Warwick's men had tried to protect Thomas from Sir Simon, but when he assured them that the man was a deserter, a thief and a murderer they had changed their minds. They would hang him.

And Sir Simon would let them. If these men hanged Thomas as a deserter then no one could accuse Sir Simon of executing the archer. He would have kept his word and the Earl of Northampton would still have to forfeit his share of the prize money. Thomas would be dead and Sir Simon would be both richer and happier.

The men-at-arms were willing enough once they heard Thomas was a murderous thief. They had orders to hang enough rioters, thieves and rapists to cool the army's ardour, but this quarter of the island, being furthest from the old city, had not seen the same atrocities as the northern half and so these men-at-arms had been denied the opportunity to use the ropes which the Earl had issued. Now they had a victim and so one man tossed the rope over an oak branch.

Thomas was aware of little of it. He felt nothing as Sir Simon searched him and cut away the money pouch from under his tunic; he did not know a thing when the rope was knotted about his neck, but then he was dimly aware of the stench of horse urine and suddenly there was a tightening at his gullet and his slowly recovering sight was sheeted with red. He felt himself hauled into the air, then tried to gasp because of a dreadful gripping pain in his throat, but he could not gasp and he could scarcely breathe; he could only feel a burning and choking as the smoky air scraped in his windpipe. He wanted to scream in terror but his lungs could do nothing except give him agony. He had an instant's lucidity as he realized he was dangling and jerking and twitching, and though he scrabbled at his neck with his hooked fingers he could not loosen the rope's strangling grip. Then, in terror, he pissed himself.

'Yellow bastard,' Sir Simon sneered, and he struck at Thomas's body with his sword, though the blow did little more than slice the flesh at Thomas's waist and swing his body on the rope.

'Leave him be,' one of the men-at-arms said. 'He's a dead 'un,' and they watched until Thomas's movements became spasmodic. Then they mounted and rode on. A group of archers also watched from one of the houses in the square, and their presence scared Sir Simon, who feared they might be friends of Thomas and so, when the Earl's men left the square, he rode with them. His own followers were searching the nearby church of St Michael, and Sir Simon had only come to the square because he had seen the tall stone house and wondered if it contained plunder. Instead he had found Thomas and now Thomas was hanged. It was not the revenge Sir Simon had dreamed of, but there had been pleasure in it and that was a compensation.

Thomas felt nothing now. It was all darkness and no pain. He was dancing the rope to hell, his head to one side, body still swinging slightly, legs twitching, hands curling and feet dripping.

The army stayed five days in Caen. Some three hundred Frenchmen of rank, all of whom could yield ransoms, had been taken prisoner, and they were escorted north to where they could take ship for England. The injured English and Welsh soldiers were carried to the Abbaye aux Dames where they lay in the cloisters, their wounds stinking so high that the Prince and his entourage moved to the Abbaye aux Hommes where the King had his quarters. The bodies of the massacred citizens were cleared from the streets. A priest of the King's household tried to bury the dead decently, as befitted Christians, but when a common grave was dug in the churchyard of St Jean it could hold only five hundred bodies, and no one had time or spades enough to bury the rest, so four and a half thousand corpses were tipped into the rivers. The city's survivors, creeping out of their hiding places when the madness of the sack was over, wandered along the riverbanks to search for their relatives among the corpses that were stranded by the falling tide. Their searches disturbed the wild dogs and the screeching flocks of ravens and gulls that squabbled as they feasted on the bloated dead.

The castle was still in French hands. Its walls were high and thick, and no ladder could scale them. The King sent a herald to demand the garrison's surrender, but the French lords in the great keep politely refused and then invited the English to do their worst, confident that no mangonel or catapult could hurl a stone high enough to breach their lofty walls. The King reckoned they were right, so instead ordered his gunners to break down the castle's stones, and the army's five largest cannon were trundled through the old city on their wagons. Three of the guns were long tubes made from wrought-iron strips bound by steel hoops, while two had been cast in brass by bell-founders and looked like bulbous jars with swollen oval bellies, narrow necks and flaring mouths. All were around five feet long and needed shear-legs to be swung from their wagons onto wooden cradles.

The cradles were set on planks of wood. The ground under the gun carriages had been graded so that the guns could point up towards the castle's gate. Bring down the gate, the King had ordered, and he could release his archers and men-at-arms in an assault. So the gunners, most of them men from Flanders or Italy who were skilled in this work, mixed their gunpowder. It was made from saltpetre, sulphur and charcoal, but the saltpetre was heavier than the other ingredients and always settled to the bottom of the barrels while the charcoal rose to the top so the gunners had to stir the mix thoroughly before they ladled the deadly powder into the bellies of the jars. They placed a shovelful of loam, made from water and clay soil, in the narrow part of each gun's neck before loading the crudely sculpted stone balls that were the missiles. The loam was to seal the firing chamber so that the power of the explosion did not leak away before all the powder had caught the fire. Still more loam was packed about the stone balls to fill the space between the missiles and the barrels, then the gunners had to wait while the loam hardened to make a firmer seal.

The other three guns were quicker to load. Each iron tube was lashed to a massive wooden cradle that ran the length of the gun, then turned in a right angle so that the gun's breech rested against a baulk of solid oak. That breech, a quarter of the gun's length, was separate from the barrel, and was lifted clean out of the cradle and set upright on the ground where it was filled with the precious black powder. Once the three breech chambers were filled they were sealed by willow plugs to contain the explosion, then slotted back into their cradles. The three tube barrels had already been loaded, two with stone balls and the third with a yard-long garro, a giant arrow made of iron.

The three breech chambers had to be worked firmly against the barrels so that the force of the explosion did not escape through the joint between the gun's two parts. The gunners used wooden wedges that they hammered between the breech and the oak at the back of the cradle, and every blow of the mauls sealed the joints imperceptibly tighter. Other gunners were ladling powder into the spare breech chambers that would fire the next shots. It all took time – well over an hour for the loam in the two bulbous guns to set firm enough – and the work attracted a huge crowd of curious onlookers who stood a judicious distance away to be safe from fragments should any of the strange machines explode. The French, just as curious, watched from the castle battlements. Once in a while a defender would shoot a crossbow quarrel, but the range was too long. One bolt came within a dozen yards of the guns, but the rest fell well short and each failure provoked a jeer from the watching archers. Finally the French abandoned the provocation and just watched.

The three tube guns could have been fired first, for they had no loam to set, but the King wanted the first volley to be simultaneous. He envisaged a mighty blow in which the five missiles would shatter the castle gate and, once the gate was down, he would have his gunners gnaw at the gate's arch. The master gunner, a tall and lugubrious Italian, finally declared the weapons ready and so the fuses were fetched. These were short lengths of hollow straw filled with gunpowder, their ends sealed with clay, and the fuses were pushed down through the narrow touchholes. The master gunner pinched the clay seal from each fuse's upper end, then made the sign of the cross. A priest had already blessed the guns, sprinkling them with holy water, and now the master gunner knelt and looked at the King, who was mounted on a tall grey stallion.

The King, yellow-bearded and blue-eyed, looked up at the castle. A new banner had been hung from the ramparts, showing God holding a hand in blessing over a fleur-de-lis. It was time, he thought, to show the

French whose side God was really on. 'You may fire,' he said solemnly.

Five gunners armed themselves with linstocks – long wands that each held a length of glowing linen. They stood well to the side of the guns and, at a signal from the Italian, they touched the fire to the exposed fuses. There was a brief fizzing, a puff of smoke from the touchholes, then the five mouths vanished in a cloud of grey-white smoke in which five monstrous flames stabbed and writhed as the guns themselves, firm-gripped by their cradles, slammed back along their plank bedding to thud against the mounds of earth piled behind each breech. The noise of the weapons hammered louder than the loudest thunder. It was a noise that physically pounded the eardrums and echoed back from the pale castle walls, and when the sound at last faded the smoke still hung in a shabby screen in front of the guns that now lay askew on their carriages with gently smoking muzzles.

The noise had startled a thousand nesting birds up from the old city's roofs and the castle's higher turrets, yet the gate appeared undamaged. The stone balls had shattered themselves against the walls, while the garro had done nothing except gouge a furrow in the approach road. The French, who had ducked behind the battlements when the noise and smoke erupted, now stood and called insults as the gunners stoically began to realign their weapons.

The King, thirty-four years old and not as confident as his bearing suggested, frowned as the smoke cleared. 'Did we use enough powder?' he demanded of the master gunner. The question had to be translated into Italian by a priest.

'Use more powder, sire,' the Italian said, 'and the guns will shatter.' He spoke regretfully. Men always expected his machines to work miracles and he was tired of explaining that even black powder needed time and patience to do its work.

'You know best,' the King said dubiously, 'I'm sure you know best.' He was hiding his disappointment for he had half hoped that the whole castle would shatter like glass when the missiles struck. His entourage, most of them older men, were looking contemptuous for they had little faith in guns and even less in Italian gunners.

'Who,' the King asked a companion, 'is that woman with my son?'

'The Countess of Armorica, sire. She fled from Brittany.'

The King shuddered, not because of Jeanette, but because the rotten smell of the powder smoke was pungent. 'He grows up fast,' he said, with just a touch of jealousy in his voice. He was bedding some peasant girl, who was pleasant enough and knew her business, but she was not as beautiful as the black-haired Countess who accompanied his son.

Jeanette, unaware that the King watched her, gazed at the castle in search of any sign that it had been struck by gunfire. 'So what happened?' she asked the Prince.

'It takes time,' the Prince said, hiding his surprise that the castle gate had not magically vanished in an eruption of splinters. 'But they do say,' he went on, 'that in the future we shall fight with nothing but guns. Myself, I cannot imagine it.'

'They are amusing,' Jeanette said as a gunner carried a bucket of puddled loam to the nearest gun. The grass in front of the guns was burning in a score of places and the air was filled with a stench like rotted eggs that was even more repugnant than the smell of the corpses in the river.

'If it amuses you, my dear, then I am glad we have the machines,' the Prince said, then frowned because a group of his white-and-green-clad archers were jeering the gunners. 'Whatever happened to the man who brought you from Normandy?' he asked. 'I should have thanked him for his services to you.'

Jeanette feared she was blushing, but made her voice careless. 'I have not seen him since we came here.'

The Prince twisted in his saddle. 'Bohun!' he called to the Earl of Northampton. 'Didn't my lady's personal archer join your fellows?'

'He did, sire.'

'So where is he?'

The Earl shrugged. 'Vanished. We think he must have died crossing the river.'

'Poor fellow,' the Prince said, 'poor fellow.'

And Jeanette, to her surprise, felt a pang of sorrow. Then thought it was probably for the best. She was the widow of a count and now the lover of a prince, and Thomas, if he was on the river's bed, could never tell the truth. 'Poor man,' she said lightly, 'and he behaved so gallantly to me.' She was looking away from the Prince in case he saw her flushed face and she found herself staring, to her utter astonishment, at Sir Simon Jekyll, who, with another group of knights, had come for the entertainment of the guns. Sir Simon was laughing, evidently amused that so much noise and smoke had produced so little effect. Jeanette, disbelieving her eyes, just stared at him. She had gone pale. The sight of Sir Simon had brought back the memories of her worst days in La Roche-Derrien, the days of fear, poverty, humiliation and the uncertainty of knowing to whom she could turn for help.

'I fear we never rewarded the fellow,' the Prince said, still speaking of Thomas, then he saw that Jeanette was taking no notice. 'My dear?' the Prince prompted, but she still looked away from him. 'My lady?' The Prince spoke louder, touching her arm.

Sir Simon had noticed there was a woman with the Prince, but he had not realized it was Jeanette. He only saw a slender lady in a pale gold dress, seated side-saddle on an expensive palfrey that was hung with green and white ribbons. The woman wore a tall hat from which a veil stirred in the wind. The veil had concealed her profile, but now she was staring directly at him, indeed she was pointing at him and, to his horror, he recognized the Countess. He also recognized the banner of the young man beside her though at first he could not believe she was with the Prince. Then he saw the grim entourage of mailed men behind the fair-haired youth and he had an impulse to flee, but instead nervelessly dropped to his knees. As the Prince, Jeanette and the horsemen approached him, he fell full length on the ground. His heart was beating wildly, his mind a whirl of panic.

'Your name?' the Prince demanded curtly.

Sir Simon opened his mouth, but no words would come.

'His name,' Jeanette said vengefully, 'is Sir Simon Jekyll. He tried to strip me naked, sire, and then he would have raped me if I had not been rescued. He stole my money, my armour, my horses, my ships and he would have taken my honour with as much delicacy as a wolf stealing a lamb.'

'Is it true?' the Prince demanded.

Sir Simon still could not speak, but the Earl of Northampton intervened. 'The ships, armour and horses, sire, were spoils of war. I granted them to him.'

'And the rest, Bohun?'

'The rest, sire?' The Earl shrugged. 'The rest Sir Simon must explain for himself.'

'But it seems he is speechless,' the Prince said. 'Have you lost your tongue, Jekyll?'

Sir Simon raised his head and caught Jeanette's gaze, and it was so triumphant that he dropped his head again. He knew he should say something, anything, but his tongue seemed too big for his mouth and he feared he would merely stammer nonsense, so he kept silent.

'You tried to smirch a lady's honour,' the Prince accused Sir Simon. Edward of Woodstock had high ideas of chivalry, for his tutors had ever read to him from the romances. He understood that war was not as gentle as the hand-written books liked to suggest, but he believed that those who were in places of honour should display it, whatever the common man might do. The Prince was also in love, another ideal encouraged by the romances. Jeanette had captivated him, and he was determined that her honour would be upheld. He spoke again, but his words were drowned by the sound of a tube gun firing. Everyone turned to stare at the castle, but the stone ball merely shattered against the gate tower, doing no damage.

'Would you fight me for the lady's honour?' the Prince demanded of Sir Simon.

Sir Simon would have been happy to fight the Prince so long as he could have been assured that his victory would bring no reprisals. He knew the boy had a reputation as a warrior, yet the Prince was not full grown and nowhere near as strong or experienced as Sir Simon, but only a fool fought against a prince and expected to win. The King, it was true, entered tournaments, but he did so disguised in plain armour, without a surcoat, so that his opponents had no idea of his identity, but if Sir Simon fought the Prince then he would not dare use his full strength, for any injury done would be repaid a thousandfold by the prince's supporters, and indeed, even as Sir Simon hesitated, the grim men behind the Prince spurred their horses forward as if offering themselves as champions for the fight. Sir Simon, overwhelmed by reality, shook his head.

'If you will not fight,' the Prince said in his high, clear voice, 'then we must assume your guilt and demand recompense. You owe the lady armour and a sword.'

'The armour was fairly taken, sire,' the Earl of Northampton pointed out.

'No man can take armour and weapons from a mere woman fairly,' the Prince snapped. 'Where is the armour now, Jekyll?'

'Lost, sir,' Sir Simon spoke for the first time. He wanted to tell the Prince the whole story, how Jeanette had arranged an ambush, but that tale ended with his own humiliation and he had the sense to keep quiet.

'Then that mail coat will have to suffice,' the Prince declared. 'Take it off. And the sword too.'

Sir Simon gaped at the Prince, but saw he was serious. He unbuckled the sword belt and let it drop, then hauled the mail coat over his head so that he was left in his shirt and breeches.

'What is in the pouch?' the Prince demanded,

pointing at the heavy leather bag suspended about Sir Simon's neck.

Sir Simon sought an answer and found none but the truth, which was that the pouch was the heavy money bag he had taken from Thomas. 'It is money, sire.'

'Then give it to her ladyship.'

Sir Simon lifted the bag over his head and held it out to Jeanette, who smiled sweetly. 'Thank you, Sir Simon,' she said.

'Your horse is forfeit too,' the Prince decreed, 'and you will leave this encampment by midday for you are not welcome in our company. You may go home, Jekyll, but in England you will not have our favour.'

Sir Simon looked into the Prince's eyes for the first time. You damned miserable little pup, he thought, with your mother's milk still sour on your unshaven lips, then he shook as he was struck by the coldness of the Prince's eyes. He bowed, knowing he was being banished, and he knew it was unfair, but there was nothing he could do except appeal to the King, yet the King owed him no favours and no great men of the realm would speak for him, and so he was effectively an outcast. He could go home to England, but there men would soon learn he had incurred royal disfavour and his life would be endless misery. He bowed, he turned and he walked away in his dirty shirt as silent men opened a path for him.

The cannon fired on. They fired four times that day and eight the next, and at the end of the two days there was a splintered rent in the castle gate that might have given entrance to a starved sparrow. The guns had done nothing except hurt the gunners' ears and shatter stone balls against the castle's ramparts. Not a Frenchman had died, though one gunner and an archer had been killed when one of the brass guns exploded into a myriad red-hot scraps of metal. The King, realizing that the attempt was ridiculous, ordered the guns taken away and the siege of the castle abandoned.

And the next day the whole army left Caen. They marched eastwards, going towards Paris, and after them crawled their wagons and their camp followers and their herds of beef cattle, and for a long time afterwards the eastern sky showed white where the dust of their marching hazed the air. But at last the dust settled and the city, ravaged and sacked, was left alone. The folk who had succeeded in escaping from the island crept back to their homes. The splintered door of the castle was pushed open and its garrison came down to see what was left of Caen. For a week the priests carried an image of St Jean about the littered streets and sprinkled holy water to get rid of the lingering stink of the enemy. They said Masses for the souls of the dead, and prayed fervently that the wretched English would meet the King of France and have their own ruin visited on them.

But at least the English were gone, and the violated city, ruined, could stir again.

Light came first. A hazy light, smeared, in which Thomas thought he could see a wide window, but a shadow moved against the window and the light went. He heard voices, then they faded. *In pascuis herbarum adclinavit me*. The words were in his head. He makes me lie down in leafy pastures. A psalm, the same psalm from which his father had quoted his dying words. *Calix meus inebrians*. My cup makes me drunk. Only he was not drunk. Breathing hurt, and his chest felt as though he was being pressed by the torture of the stones. Then there was blessed darkness and oblivion once more.

The light came again. It wavered. The shadow was there, the shadow moved towards him and a cool hand was laid on his forehead.

'I do believe you are going to live,' a man's voice said in a tone of surprise.

Thomas tried to speak, but only managed a strangled, grating sound.

'It astonishes me,' the voice went on, 'what young men can endure. Babies too. Life is marvellously strong. Such a pity we waste it.'

'It's plentiful enough,' another man said.

'The voice of the privileged,' the first man, whose hand was still on Thomas's forehead, answered. 'You take life,' he said, 'so value it as a thief values his victims.'

'And you are a victim?'

'Of course. A learned victim, a wise victim, even a valuable victim, but still a victim. And this young man, what is he?'

'An English archer,' the second voice said sourly, 'and if we had any sense we'd kill him here and now.'

'I think we shall try and feed him instead. Help me raise him.'

Hands pushed Thomas upright in the bed, and a spoonful of warm soup was put into his mouth, but he could not swallow and so spat the soup onto the blankets. Pain seared through him and the darkness came again.

The light came a third time or perhaps a fourth, he

could not tell. Perhaps he dreamed it, but this time an old man stood outlined against the bright window. The man had a long black robe, but he was not a priest or monk, for the robe was not gathered at the waist and he wore a small square black hat over his long white hair.

'God,' Thomas tried to say, though the word came out as a guttural grunt.

The old man turned. He had a long, forked beard and was holding a jordan jar. It had a narrow neck and a round belly, and the bottle was filled with a pale yellow liquid that the man held up to the light. He peered at the liquid, then swilled it about before sniffing the jar's mouth.

'Are you awake?'

'Yes.'

'And you can speak! What a doctor I am! My brilliance astonishes me; if only it would persuade my patients to pay me. But most believe I should be grateful that they don't spit at me. Would you say this urine is clear?'

Thomas nodded and wished he had not for the pain jarred through his neck and down his spine.

'You do not consider it turgid? Not dark? No, indeed not. It smells and tastes healthy too. A good flask of clear yellow urine, and there is no better sign of good health. Alas, it is not yours.' The doctor pushed open the window and poured the urine away. 'Swallow,' he instructed Thomas.

Thomas's mouth was dry, but he obediently tried to swallow and immediately gasped with pain.

'I think,' the doctor said, 'that we had best try a thin gruel. Very thin, with some oil, I believe, or better still, butter. That thing tied about your neck is a strip of cloth which has been soaked in holy water. It was not my doing, but I did not forbid it. You Christians believe in magic – indeed you could have no faith without a trust in magic – so I must indulge your beliefs. Is that a dog's paw about your neck? Don't tell me, I'm sure I don't want to know. However, when you recover, I trust you will understand that it was neither dog paws nor wet cloths that healed you, but my skill. I have bled you, I have applied poultices of dung, moss and clove, and I have sweated you. Eleanor, though, will insist it was her prayers and that tawdry strip of wet cloth that revived you.'

'Eleanor?'

'She cut you down, dear boy. You were half dead. By the time I arrived you were more dead than alive and I advised her to let you expire in peace. I told her you were halfway in what you insist is hell and that I was too old and too tired to enter into a tugging contest with the devil, but Eleanor insisted and I have ever found it difficult to resist her entreaties. Gruel with rancid butter, I think. You are weak, dear boy, very weak. Do you have a name?'

'Thomas.'

'Mine is Mordecai, though you may call me Doctor. You won't, of course. You'll call me a damned Jew, a Christ murderer, a secret worshipper of pigs and a kidnapper of Christian children.' This was all said cheerfully. 'How absurd! Who would want to kidnap children, Christian or otherwise? Vile things. The only mercy of children is that they grow up, as my son has but then, tragically, they beget more children. We do not learn life's lessons.'

'Doctor?' Thomas croaked.

'Thomas?'

'Thank you.'

'An Englishman with manners! The world's wonders never cease. Wait there, Thomas, and do not have the bad manners to die while I'm gone. I shall fetch gruel.'

'Doctor?'

'I am still here.'

'Where am I?'

'In the house of my friend, and quite safe.'

'Your friend?'

'Sir Guillaume d'Evecque, knight of the sea and of the land, and as great a fool as any I know, but a good-hearted fool. He does at least pay me.'

Thomas closed his eyes. He did not really understand what the doctor had said, or perhaps he did not believe it. His head was aching. There was pain all through his body, from his aching head down to his throbbing toes. He thought of his mother, because that was comforting, then he remembered being hauled up the tree and he shivered. He wished he could sleep again, for in sleep there was no pain, but then he was made to sit up and the doctor forced a pungent, oily gruel into his mouth and he managed not to spit it out or throw it up. There must have been mushrooms in the gruel, or else it had been infused with the hemp-like leaves that the Hookton villagers had called angel salad, for after he had eaten he had vivid dreams, but less pain. When he awoke it was dark and he was alone, but he managed to sit up and even stand, though he tottered and had to sit again.

Next morning, when the birds were calling from the oak branches where he had so nearly died, a tall man came into the room. The man was on crutches and his left thigh was swathed in bandages. He turned to look at Thomas and showed a face that was horribly scarred. A blade had cut him from the forehead to the jaw, taking the man's left eye in its savage chop. He had long yellow hair, very shaggy and full, and Thomas guessed the man had been handsome once, though now he looked like a thing of nightmare.

'Mordecai,' the man growled, 'tells me you will live.'

'With God's help,' Thomas said.

'I doubt God's interested in you,' the man said sourly. He looked to be in his thirties and had the bowed legs of a horseman and the deep chest of a man who practises hard with weapons. He swung on the crutches to the window, where he sat on the sill. His beard was streaked with white where the blade had chopped into his jaw and his voice was uncommonly deep and harsh. 'But you might live with Mordecai's help. There isn't a physician to touch him in all Normandy, though Christ alone knows how he does it. He's been squinting at my piss for a week now. I'm crippled, you Jewish halfwit, I tell him, not wounded in the bladder, but he just tells me to shut my mouth and squeeze out more drops. He'll start on you soon.' The man, who wore nothing except a long white shirt, contemplated Thomas moodily. 'I have a notion,' he growled, 'that you are the godforsaken bastard who put an arrow into my thigh. I remember seeing a son of a whore with long hair like yours, then I was hit.'

'You're Sir Guillaume?'

'I am.'

'I meant to kill you,' Thomas said.

'So why shouldn't I kill you?' Sir Guillaume asked.

'You lie in my bed, drink my gruel and breathe my air. English bastard. Worse, you're a Vexille.'

Thomas turned his head to stare at the forbidding Sir Guillaume. He said nothing, for the last three words had mystified him.

'But I choose not to kill you,' Sir Guillaume said, 'because you saved my daughter from rape.'

'Your daughter?'

'Eleanor, you fool. She's a bastard daughter, of course,' Sir Guillaume said. 'Her mother was a servant to my father, but Eleanor is all I've got left and I'm fond of her. She says you were kind to her, which is why she cut you down and why you're lying in my bed. She always was overly sentimental.' He frowned. 'But I still have a mind to slice your damned throat.'

'For four years,' Thomas said, 'I have dreamed of slitting yours.'

Sir Guillaume's one eye gazed at him balefully. 'Of course you have. You're a Vexille.'

'I've never heard of the Vexilles,' Thomas said. 'My name is Thomas of Hookton.'

Thomas half expected Sir Guillaume to frown as he tried to remember Hookton, but his recognition of the name was instant.

'Hookton,' he said, 'Hookton. Good sweet Christ, Hookton.' He was silent for a few heartbeats. 'And of course you're a damned Vexille. You have their badge on your bow.'

'My bow?'

'You gave it to Eleanor to carry! She kept it.'

Thomas closed his eyes. There was pain in his neck and down his back and in his head. 'I think it was my father's badge,' he said, 'but I don't really know because he would never talk of his family. I know he hated his own father. I wasn't very fond of my own, but your men killed him and I swore to avenge him.'

Sir Guillaume turned to gaze out of the window. 'You have truly never heard of the Vexilles?'

'Never.'

'Then you are fortunate.' He stood. 'They are the devil's offspring, and you, I suspect, are one of their pups. I would kill you, boy, with as little conscience as if I stamped on a spider, but you were kind to my bastard daughter and for that I thank you.' He limped from the room.

Leaving Thomas in pain and utterly confused.

Thomas recovered in Sir Guillaume's garden, shaded from the sun by two quince trees under which he waited anxiously for Dr Mordecai's daily verdict on the colour, consistency, taste and smell of his urine. It did not seem to matter to the doctor that Thomas's grotesquely swollen neck was subsiding, nor that he could swallow bread and meat again. All that mattered was the state of his urine. There was, the doctor declared, no finer method of diagnosis. 'The urine betrays all. If it smells rank, or if it is dark, if it tastes of vinegar or should it be cloudy then it is time for vigorous doctoring. But good, pale, sweet-smelling urine like this is the worst news of all.'

'The worst?' Thomas asked, alarmed.

'It means fewer fees for a physician, dear boy.'

The doctor had survived the sack of Caen by hiding in a neighbour's pig shed. 'They slaughtered the pigs, but missed the Jew. Mind you, they broke all my instruments, scattered my medicines, shattered all but three of my bottles and burned my house. Which is why I am forced to live here.' He shuddered, as though living in Sir Guillaume's mansion was a hardship. He smelled Thomas's urine and then, uncertain of his diagnosis, spilled a drop onto a finger and tasted it. 'Very fine,' he said, 'lamentably fine.' He poured the jar's contents onto a bed of lavender where bees were at work. 'So I lost everything,' he said, 'and this after we were assured by our great lords that the city would be safe!' Originally, the doctor had told Thomas, the leaders of the garrison had insisted on defending only the walled city and the castle, but they needed the help of the townsfolk to man the walls and those townsfolk had insisted that the Île St Jean be defended, for that was where the city's wealth lay, and so, at the very last minute, the garrison had streamed across the bridge to disaster. 'Fools,' Mordecai said scornfully, 'fools in steel and glory. Fools.'

Thomas and Mordecai were sharing the house while Sir Guillaume visited his estate in Evecque, some thirty miles south of Caen, where he had gone to raise more men. 'He will fight on,' the doctor said, 'wounded leg or not.'

'What will he do with me?'

'Nothing,' the doctor said confidently. 'He likes you, despite all his bluster. You saved Eleanor, didn't you? He's always been fond of her. His wife wasn't, but he is.'

'What happened to his wife?'

'She died,' Mordecai said, 'she just died.'

Thomas could eat properly now and his strength returned fast so that he could walk about the Île St Jean with Eleanor. The island looked as though a plague had struck, for over half the houses were empty and even those that were occupied were still blighted by the sack. Shutters were missing, doors splintered and the shops had no goods. Some country folk were selling beans, peas and cheeses from wagons, and small boys were offering fresh perch taken from the rivers, but they were still hungry days. They were also nervous days, for the city's survivors feared that the hated English might return and the island was still haunted by the sickly smell of the corpses in the two rivers where the gulls, rats and dogs grew fat.

Eleanor hated walking about the city, preferring to go south into the countryside where blue dragonflies flew above water lilies in the streams that twisted between fields of overripe rye, barley and wheat.

'I love harvest time,' she told Thomas. 'We used to go into the fields and help.' There would be little harvest this year, for there were no folk to cut the grain and so the corn buntings were stripping the heads and pigeons were squabbling over the leavings. 'There should be a feast at harvest's end,' Eleanor said wistfully.

'We had a feast too,' Thomas said, 'and we used to hang corn dollies in the church.'

'Corn dollies?'

He made her a little doll from straw. 'We used to hang thirteen of these above the altar,' he told her, 'one for Christ and one each for the Apostles.' He picked some cornflowers and gave them to Eleanor, who threaded them into her hair. It was very fair hair, like sunlit gold.

They talked incessantly and one day Thomas asked her again about the lance and this time Eleanor nodded.

'I lied to you,' she said, 'because he did have it, but it was stolen.'

'Who stole it?'

She touched her face. 'The man who took his eye.'

'A man called Vexille?'

She nodded solemnly. 'I think so. But it wasn't here, it was in Evecque. That's his real home. He got the Caen house when he married.'

'Tell me about the Vexilles,' Thomas urged her.

'I know nothing of them,' Eleanor said, and he believed her.

They were sitting by a stream where two swans floated and a heron stalked frogs in a reedbed. Thomas had talked earlier of walking away from Caen to find the English army and his words must have been weighing on Eleanor's mind for she frowned at him.

'Will you really go?'

'I don't know.' He wanted to be with the army, for that was where he belonged, though he did not know how he was to find it, nor how he was to survive in a countryside where the English had made themselves hated, but he also wanted to stay. He wanted to learn more about the Vexilles and only Sir Guillaume could satisfy that hunger. And, day by day, he wanted to be with Eleanor. There was a calm gentleness in her that Jeanette had never possessed, a gentleness that made him treat her with tenderness for fear that otherwise he would break her. He never tired of watching her long face with its slightly hollow cheeks and bony nose and big eyes. She was embarrassed by his scrutiny, but did not tell him to stop.

'Sir Guillaume,' she told him, 'tells me I look like my mother, but I don't remember her very well.'

Sir Guillaume came back to Caen with a dozen men-at-arms whom he had hired in northern Alençon. He would lead them to war, he said, along with the half-dozen of his men who had survived the fall of Caen. His leg was still sore, but he could walk without crutches and on the day of his return he summarily ordered Thomas to go with him to the church of St Jean. Eleanor, working in the kitchen, joined them as they left the house and Sir Guillaume did not forbid her to come.

Folk bowed as Sir Guillaume passed and many sought his assurance that the English were truly gone.

'They are marching towards Paris,' he would answer, 'and our king will trap them and kill them.'

'You think so?' Thomas asked after one such assurance.

'I pray so,' Sir Guillaume growled. 'That's what the King is for, isn't it? To protect his people? And God knows, we need protection. I'm told that if you climb that tower,' he nodded towards the church of St Jean that was their destination, 'you can see the smoke from the towns your army has burned. They are conducting a *chevauchée.*'

'*Chevauchée?*' Eleanor asked.

Her father sighed. 'A *chevauchée*, child, is when you march in a great line through your enemy's country and you burn, destroy and break everything in your path. The object of such barbarity is to force your enemy to come out from his fortresses and fight, and I think our king will oblige the English.'

'And the English bows,' Thomas said, 'will cut his army down like hay.'

Sir Guillaume looked angry at that, but then

shrugged. 'A marching army gets worn down,' he said. 'The horses go lame, the boots wear out and the arrows run out. And you haven't seen the might of France, boy. For every knight of yours we have six. You can shoot your arrows till your bows break, but we'll still have enough men left to kill you.' He fished in a pouch hanging at his belt and gave some small coins to the beggars at the churchyard gate, which lay close to the new grave where the five hundred corpses had been buried. It was now a mound of raw earth dotted with dandelions and it stank, for when the English had dug the grave they had struck water not far beneath the surface and so the pit was too shallow and the earth covering was too thin to contain the corruption the grave concealed.

Eleanor clapped a hand to her mouth, then hurried up the steps into the church where the archers had auctioned the town's wives and daughters. The priests had thrice exorcized the church with prayers and holy water, but it still had a sad air, for the statues were broken and the windows shattered. Sir Guillaume genuflected towards the main altar, then led Thomas and Eleanor up a side aisle where a painting on the limewashed wall showed St John escaping from the cauldron of boiling oil that the Emperor Domitian had prepared for him. The saint was shown as an ethereal form, half smoke and half man, floating away in the air while the Roman soldiers looked on in perplexity.

Sir Guillaume approached a side altar where he dropped to his knees beside a great black flagstone and Thomas, to his surprise, saw that the Frenchman was weeping from his one eye. 'I brought you here,' Sir Guillaume said, 'to teach you a lesson about your family.'

Thomas did not contradict him. He did not know that he was a Vexille, but the yale on the silver badge suggested he was.

'Beneath that stone,' Sir Guillaume said, 'lies my wife and my two children. A boy and a girl. He was six, she was eight and their mother was twenty-five years old. The house here belonged to her father. He gave me his daughter as ransom for a boat I captured. It was mere piracy, not war, but I gained a good wife from it.' The tears were flowing now and he closed his eye. Eleanor stood beside him, a hand on his shoulder, while Thomas waited. 'Do you know,' Sir Guillaume asked after a while, 'why we went to Hookton?'

'We thought because the tide took you away from Poole.'

'No, we went to Hookton on purpose. I was paid to go there by a man who called himself the Harlequin.'

'Like hellequin?' Thomas asked.

'It is the same word, only he used the Italian form. A devil's soul, laughing at God, and he even looked like you.' Sir Guillaume crossed himself, then reached out to trace a finger down the edge of the stone. 'We went to fetch a relic from the church. You knew that already, surely?'

Thomas nodded. 'And I have sworn to get it back.'

Sir Guillaume seemed to sneer at that ambition. 'I thought it was all foolishness, but in those days I thought all life was foolishness. Why would some miserable church in an insignificant English village have a precious relic? But the Harlequin insisted he was right, and when we took the village we found the relic.'

'The lance of St George,' Thomas said flatly.

'The lance of St George,' Sir Guillaume agreed. 'I had

a contract with the Harlequin. He paid me a little money, and the balance was kept by a monk in the abbey here. He was a monk that everyone trusted, a scholar, a fierce man whom folk said would become a saint, but when we returned I found that Brother Martin had fled and he had taken the money with him. So I refused to give the lance to the Harlequin. Bring me nine hundred livres in good silver, I told him, and the lance is yours, but he would not pay. So I kept the lance. I kept it in Evecque and the months passed and I heard nothing and I thought the lance had been forgotten. Then, two years ago, in the spring, the Harlequin returned. He came with men-at-arms and he captured the manor. He slaughtered everyone – everyone – and took the lance.'

Thomas stared at the black flagstone. 'You lived?'

'Scarcely,' Sir Guillaume said. He hauled up his black jacket and showed a terrible scar on his belly. 'They gave me three wounds,' he went on. 'One to the head, one to the belly and one to the leg. They told me the one to the head was because I was a fool with no brains, the one in the guts was a reward for my greed and the one to the leg was so I would limp down to hell. Then they left me to watch the corpses of my wife and children while I died. But I lived, thanks to Mordecai.' He stood, wincing as he put his weight onto his left leg. 'I lived,' he said grimly, 'and I swore I would find the man who did that,' he pointed at the flagstone, 'and send his soul screaming into the pit. It took me a year to discover who he was, and you know how I did it? When he came to Evecque he had his men's shields covered with black cloth, but I slashed the cloth of one with my sword and saw the yale. So I asked men about the yale. I asked them in Paris and Anjou, in Burgundy and the Dauphiné, and in the end I found my answer. And where did I find it? After asking the length and breadth of France I found it here, in Caen. A man here knew the badge. The Harlequin is a man called Vexille. I do not know his first name, I do not know his rank, I just know he is a devil called Vexille.'

'So the Vexilles have the lance?'

'They have. And the man who killed my family killed your father.' Sir Guillaume looked ashamed for a brief instant. 'I killed your mother. I think I did, anyway, but she attacked me and I was angry.' He shrugged. 'But I did not kill your father, and in killing your mother I did nothing more than you have done in Brittany.'

'True,' Thomas admitted. He looked into Sir Guillaume's eye and could feel no hatred for his mother's death. 'So we share an enemy,' Thomas said.

'And that enemy,' Sir Guillaume said, 'is the devil.'

He said it grimly, then crossed himself. Thomas suddenly felt cold, for he had found his enemy, and his enemy was Lucifer.

That evening Mordecai rubbed a salve into Thomas's neck. 'It is almost healed, I think,' he said, 'and the pain will go, though perhaps a little will remain to remind you of how close you came to death.' He sniffed the garden scents. 'So Sir Guillaume told you the story of his wife?'

'Yes.'

'And you are related to the man who killed his wife?'

'I don't know,' Thomas said, 'truly I don't, but the yale suggests I am.'

301

'And Sir Guillaume probably killed your mother, and the man who killed his wife killed your father, and Sir Simon Jekyll tried to kill you.' Mordecai shook his head. 'I nightly lament that I was not born a Christian. I could carry a weapon and join the sport.' He handed Thomas a bottle. 'Perform,' he commanded, 'and what, by the by, is a yale?'

'A heraldic beast,' Thomas explained.

The doctor sniffed. 'God, in His infinite wisdom, made the fishes and the whales on the fifth day, and on the sixth he made the beasts of the land, and He looked at what He had done and saw that it was good. But not good enough for the heralds, who have to add wings, horns, tusks and claws to His inadequate work. Is that all you can do?'

'For the moment.'

'I'd get more juice from squeezing a walnut,' he grumbled, and shuffled away.

Eleanor must have been watching for his departure, for she appeared from under the pear trees that grew at the garden's end and gestured towards the river gate. Thomas followed her down to the bank of the River Orne where they watched an excited trio of small boys trying to spear a pike with English arrows left after the city's capture.

'Will you help my father?' Eleanor asked.

'Help him?'

'You said his enemy was your enemy.'

Thomas sat on the grass and she sat beside him. 'I don't know,' he said. He still did not really believe in any of it. There was a lance, he knew that, and a mystery about his family, but he was reluctant to admit that the lance and the mystery must govern his whole life.

'Does that mean you'll go back to the English army?' Eleanor asked in a small voice.

'I want to stay here,' Thomas said after a pause, 'to be with you.'

She must have known he was going to say something of the sort, but she still blushed and gazed at the swirling water where fish rose to the swarms of insects, and the three boys vainly splashed. 'You must have a woman,' she said softly.

'I did,' Thomas said, and he told her about Jeanette and how she had found the Prince of Wales and so abandoned him without a glance. 'I will never understand her,' he admitted.

'But you love her?' Eleanor asked directly.

'No,' Thomas said.

'You say that because you're with me,' Eleanor declared.

He shook his head. 'My father had a book of St Augustine's sayings and there was one that always puzzled me.' He frowned, trying to remember the Latin. '*Nondum amabam, et amare amabam.* I did not love, but yearned to love.'

Eleanor gave him a sceptical look. 'A very elaborate way of saying you're lonely.'

'Yes,' Thomas agreed.

'So what will you do?' she asked.

Thomas did not speak for a while. He was thinking of the penance he had been given by Father Hobbe. 'I suppose one day I must find the man who killed my father,' he said after a while.

'But what if he is the devil?' she asked seriously.

'Then I shall wear garlic,' Thomas said lightly, 'and pray to St Guinefort.'

303

She looked at the darkening water. 'Did St Augustine really say that thing?'

'*Nondum amabam, et amare amabam*?' Thomas said. 'Yes, he did.'

'I know how he felt,' Eleanor said, and rested her head on his shoulder.

Thomas did not move. He had a choice. Follow the lance or take his black bow back to the army. In truth he did not know what he should do. But Eleanor's body was warm against his and it was comforting and that, for the moment, was enough and so, for the moment, he would stay.

Next morning Sir Guillaume, escorted now by a half-dozen men-at-arms, took Thomas to the Abbaye aux Hommes. A crowd of petitioners stood at the gates, wanting food and clothing that the monks did not have, though the abbey itself had escaped the worst of the plundering because it had been the quarters of the King and of the Prince of Wales. The monks themselves had fled at the approach of the English army. Some had died on the Île St Jean, but most had gone south to a brother house and among those was Brother Germain who, when Sir Guillaume arrived, had just returned from his brief exile.

Brother Germain was tiny, ancient and bent, a wisp of a man with white hair, myopic eyes and delicate hands with which he was trimming a goose quill.

'The English,' the old man said, 'use these feathers for their arrows. We use them for God's word.' Brother Germain, Thomas was told, had been in charge of the monastery's scriptorium for more than thirty years. 'In the course of copying books,' the monk explained, 'one discovers knowledge whether one wishes it or not. Most of it is quite useless, of course. How is Mordecai? He lives?'

'He lives,' Sir Guillaume said, 'and sends you this.' He

put a clay pot, sealed with wax, on the sloping surface of the writing desk. The pot slid down until Brother Germain trapped it and pushed it into a pouch. 'A salve,' Sir Guillaume explained to Thomas, 'for Brother Germain's joints.'

'Which ache,' the monk said, 'and only Mordecai can relieve them 'Tis a pity he will burn in hell, but in heaven, I am assured, I shall need no ointments. Who is this?' He peered at Thomas.

'A friend,' Sir Guillaume said, 'who brought me this.' He was carrying Thomas's bow, which he now laid across the desk and tapped the silver plate. Brother Germain stooped to inspect the badge and Thomas heard a sharp intake of breath.

'The yale,' Brother Germain said. He pushed the bow away, then blew the scraps from his sharpened quill off the desk. 'The beast was introduced by the heralds in the last century. Back then, of course, there was real scholarship in the world. Not like today. I get young men from Paris whose heads are stuffed with wool, yet they claim to have doctorates.'

He took a sheet of scrap parchment from a shelf, laid it on the desk and dipped his quill in a pot of vermilion ink. He let a glistening drop fall onto the parchment and then, with the skill gained in a lifetime, drew the ink out of the drop in quick strokes. He hardly seemed to be taking notice of what he was doing, but Thomas, to his amazement, saw a yale taking shape on the parchment.

'The beast is said to be mythical,' Brother Germain said, flicking the quill to make a tusk, 'and maybe it is. Most heraldic beasts seem to be inventions. Who has seen a unicorn?' He put another drop of ink on the parchment, paused a heartbeat, then began on the beast's raised paws. 'There is, however, a notion that the yale exists in Ethiopia. I could not say, not having travelled east of Rouen, nor have I met any traveller who has been there, if indeed Ethiopia even exists.' He frowned. 'The yale is mentioned by Pliny, however, which suggests it was known to the Romans, though God knows they were a credulous race. The beast is said to possess both horns and tusks, which seems extravagant, and is usually depicted as being silver with yellow spots. Alas, our pigments were stolen by the English, but they left us the vermilion which, I suppose, was kind of them. It comes from cinnabar, I'm told. Is that a plant? Father Jacques, rest his soul, always claimed it grows in the Holy Land and perhaps it does. Do I detect that you are limping, Sir Guillaume?'

'A bastard English archer put an arrow in my leg,' Sir Guillaume said, 'and I pray nightly that his soul will roast in hell.'

'You should, instead, give thanks that he was inaccurate. Why do you bring me an English war bow decorated with a yale?'

'Because I thought it would interest you,' Sir Guillaume said, 'and because my young friend here,' he touched Thomas's shoulder, 'wants to know about the Vexilles.'

'He would do much better to forget them,' Brother Germain grumbled.

He was perched on a tall chair and now peered about the room where a dozen young monks tidied the mess left by the monastery's English occupiers. Some of them chattered as they worked, provoking a frown from Brother Germain.

'This is not Caen marketplace!' he snapped. 'If you want to gossip, go to the lavatories. I wish I could. Ask Mordecai if he has an unguent for the bowels, would you?' He glowered about the room for an instant, then struggled to pick up the bow that he had propped against the desk. He looked intently at the yale for an instant, then put the bow down. 'There was always a rumour that a branch of the Vexille family went to England. This seems to confirm it.'

'Who are they?' Thomas asked.

Brother Germain seemed irritated by the direct question, or perhaps the whole subject of the Vexilles made him uncomfortable. 'They were the rulers of Astarac,' he said, 'a county on the borders of Languedoc and the Agenais. That, of course, should tell you all you need to know of them.'

'It tells me nothing,' Thomas confessed.

'Then you probably have a doctorate from Paris!' The old man chuckled at this jest. 'The Counts of Astarac, young man, were Cathars. Southern France was infested by that damned heresy, and Astarac was at the centre of the evil.' He made the sign of the cross with fingers deep-stained by pigments. '*Habere non potest*,' he said solemnly, '*Deum patrem qui ecclesiam non habet matrem.*'

'St Cyprian,' Thomas said. '"He cannot have God as his father who does not have the Church as his mother."'

'I see you are not from Paris after all,' Brother Germain said. 'The Cathars rejected the Church, looking for salvation within their own dark souls. What would become of the Church if we all did that? If we all pursued our own whims? If God is within us then we need no Church and no Holy Father to lead us to His mercy, and that notion is the most pernicious of heresies, and where did it lead the Cathars? To a life of dissipation, of fleshly lust, of pride and of perversion. They denied the divinity of Christ!' Brother Germain made the sign of the cross again.

'And the Vexilles were Cathars?' Sir Guillaume prompted the old man.

'I suspect they were devil worshippers,' Brother Germain retorted, 'but certainly the Counts of Astarac protected the Cathars, they and a dozen other lords. They were called the dark lords and very few of them were Perfects. The Perfects were the sect leaders, the heresiarchs, and they abstained from wine, intercourse and meat, and no Vexille would willingly abandon those three joys. But the Cathars allowed such sinners to be among their ranks and promised them the joys of heaven if they recanted before their deaths. The dark lords liked such a promise and, when the heresy was assailed by the Church, they fought bitterly.' He shook his head. 'This was a hundred years ago! The Holy Father and the King of France destroyed the Cathars, and Astarac was one of the last fortresses to fall. The fight was dreadful, the dead innumerable, but the heresiarchs and the dark lords were finally scotched.'

'Yet some escaped?' Sir Guillaume suggested gently.

Brother Germain was silent for a while, gazing at the drying vermilion ink. 'There was a story,' he said, 'that some of the Cathar lords did survive, and that they took their riches to countries all across Europe. There is even a rumour that the heresy yet survives, hidden in the lands where Burgundy and the Italian states meet.' He made the sign of the cross. 'I think a part of the Vexille family went to England, to hide there, for it was in England, Sir Guillaume, that you found the lance of St George. Vexille . . .' He said the name thoughtfully. 'It derives, of course, from *vexillaire*, a standard-bearer, and it is said that an early Vexille discovered the lance while on the crusades and thereafter carried it as a standard. It was certainly a symbol of power in those old days. Myself? I am sceptical of these relics. The abbot assures me he has seen three foreskins of the infant Jesus and even I, who hold Him blessed above all things, doubt He was so richly endowed, but I have asked some questions about this lance. There is a legend attached to it. It is said that the man who carries the lance into battle cannot be defeated. Mere legend, of course, but belief in such nonsense inspires the ignorant, and there are few more ignorant than soldiers. What troubles me most, though, is their purpose.'

'Whose purpose?' Thomas asked.

'There is a story,' Brother Germain said, ignoring the question, 'that before the fall of the last heretic fortresses, the surviving dark lords made an oath. They knew the war was lost, they knew their strongholds must fall and that the Inquisition and the forces of God would destroy their people, and so they made an oath to visit vengeance on their enemies. One day, they swore, they would bring down the Throne of France and the Holy Mother Church, and to do it they would use the power of their holiest relics.'

'The lance of St George?' Thomas asked.

'That too,' Brother Germain said.

'That too?' Sir Guillaume repeated the words in a puzzled tone.

Brother Germain dipped his quill and put another

glistening drop of ink on the parchment. Then, deftly, he finished his copy of the badge on Thomas's bow. 'The yale,' he said, 'I have seen before, but the badge you showed me is different. The beast is holding a chalice. But not any chalice, Sir Guillaume. You are right, the bow interests me, and frightens me, for the yale is holding the Grail. The holy, blessed and most precious Grail. It was always rumoured that the Cathars possessed the Grail. There is a tawdry lump of green glass in Genoa Cathedral that is said to be the Grail, but I doubt our dear Lord drank from such a bauble. No, the real Grail exists, and whoever holds it possesses power above all men on earth.' He put down the quill. 'I fear, Sir Guillaume, that the dark lords want their revenge. They gather their strength. But they hide still and the Church has not yet taken notice. Nor will it until the danger is obvious, and by then it will be too late.' Brother Germain lowered his head so that Thomas could only see the bald pink patch among the white hair. 'It is all prophesied,' the monk said; 'it is all in the books.'

'What books?' Sir Guillaume asked.

'*Et confortabitur rex austri et de principibus eius praevalebit super eum,*' Brother Germain said softly.

Sir Guillaume looked quizzically at Thomas. 'And the King from the south will be mighty,' Thomas reluctantly translated, 'but one of his princes will be stronger than him.'

'The Cathars are of the south,' Brother Germain said, 'and the prophet Daniel foresaw it all.' He raised his pigment-stained hands. 'The fight will be terrible, for the soul of the world is at stake, and they will use any weapon, even a woman. *Filiaque regis austri veniet ad regem aquilonis facere amicitiam.*'

311

'The daughter of the King of the south,' Thomas said, 'shall come to the King of the north and make a treaty.'

Brother Germain heard the distaste in Thomas's voice. 'You don't believe it?' he hissed. 'Why do you think we keep the scriptures from the ignorant? They contain all sorts of prophecies, young man, and each of them given direct to us by God, but such knowledge is confusing to the unlearned. Men go mad when they know too much.' He made the sign of the cross. 'I thank God I shall be dead soon and taken to the bliss above while you must struggle with this darkness.'

Thomas walked to the window and watched two wagons of grain being unloaded by novices. Sir Guillaume's men-at-arms were playing dice in the cloister. That was real, he thought, not some babbling prophet. His father had ever warned him against prophecy. It drives men's minds awry, he had said, and was that why his own mind had gone astray?

'The lance,' Thomas said, trying to cling to fact instead of fancy, 'was taken to England by the Vexille family. My father was one of them, but he fell out with the family and he stole the lance and hid it in his church. He was killed there, and at his death he told me it was his brother's son who did it. I think it is that man, my cousin, who called himself the Harlequin.' He turned to look at Brother Germain. 'My father was a Vexille, but he was no heretic. He was a sinner, yes, but he struggled against his sin, he hated his own father, and he was a loyal son of the Church.'

'He was a priest,' Sir Guillaume explained to the monk.

'And you are his son?' Brother Germain asked in a

disapproving tone. The other monks had abandoned their tidying and were listening avidly.

'I am a priest's son,' Thomas said, 'and a good Christian.'

'So the family discovered where the lance was hidden,' Sir Guillaume took up the story, 'and hired me to retrieve it. But forgot to pay me.'

Brother Germain appeared not to have heard. He was staring at Thomas. 'You are English?'

'The bow is mine,' Thomas acknowledged.

'So you are a Vexille?'

Thomas shrugged. 'It would seem so.'

'Then you are one of the dark lords,' Brother Germain said.

Thomas shook his head. 'I am a Christian,' he said firmly.

'Then you have a God-given duty,' the small man said with surprising force, 'which is to finish the work that was left undone a hundred years ago. Kill them all! Kill them! And kill the woman. You hear me, boy? Kill the daughter of the King of the south before she seduces France to heresy and wickedness.'

'If we can even find the Vexilles,' Sir Guillaume said dubiously, and Thomas noted the word 'we'. 'They don't display their badge. I doubt they use the name Vexille. They hide.'

'But they have the lance now,' Brother Germain said, 'and they will use it for the first of their vengeances. They will destroy France, and in the chaos that ensues, they will attack the Church.' He moaned, as if he was in physical pain. 'You must take away their power, and their power is the Grail.'

So it was not just the lance that Thomas must save.

313

To Father Hobbe's charge had been added all of Christendom. He wanted to laugh. Catharism had died a hundred years before, scourged and burned and dug out of the land like couch grass grubbed from a field! Dark lords, daughters of kings and princes of darkness were figments of the troubadours, not the business of archers. Except that when he looked at Sir Guillaume he saw that the Frenchman was not mocking the task. He was staring at a crucifix hanging on the scriptorium wall and mouthing a silent prayer. God help me, Thomas thought, God help me, but I am being asked to do what all the great knights of Arthur's round table failed to do: to find the Grail.

Philip of Valois, King of France, ordered every Frenchman of military age to gather at Rouen. Demands went to his vassals and appeals were carried to his allies. He had expected the walls of Caen to hold the English for weeks, but the city had fallen in a day and the panicked survivors were spreading across northern France with terrible stories of devils unleashed.

Rouen, nestled in a great loop of the Seine, filled with warriors. Thousands of Genoese crossbowmen came by galley, beaching their ships on the river's bank and thronging the city's taverns, while knights and men-at-arms arrived from Anjou and Picardy, from Alençon and Champagne, from Maine, Touraine and Berry. Every blacksmith's shop became an armoury, every house a barracks and every tavern a brothel. More men arrived, until the city could scarce contain them, and tents had to be set up in the fields south of the city. Wagons crossed the bridge, loaded with hay and newly harvested grain from the rich farmlands north of the river, while from the Seine's southern bank came rumours. The English had taken Evreux, or perhaps it was Bernay? Smoke had been seen at Lisieux, and archers were swarming through the forest of Brotonne. A nun in Louviers had a dream in which the dragon killed St George. King Philip ordered the woman brought to Rouen, but she had a harelip, a hunchback and a stammer, and when she was presented to the King she proved unable to recount the dream, let alone confide God's strategy to His Majesty. She just shuddered and wept and the King dismissed her angrily, but took consolation from the bishop's astrologer who said Mars was in the ascendant and that meant victory was certain.

Rumour said the English were marching on Paris, then another rumour claimed they were going south to protect their territories in Gascony. It was said that every person in Caen had died, that the castle was rubble; then a story went about that the English themselves were dying of a sickness. King Philip, ever a nervous man, became petulant, demanding news, but his advisers persuaded their irritable master that wherever the English were they must eventually starve if they were kept south of the great River Seine that twisted like a snake from Paris to the sea. Edward's men were wasting the land, so needed to keep moving if they were to find food, and if the Seine was blocked then they could not go north towards the harbours on the Channel coast where they might expect supplies from England.

'They use arrows like a woman uses money,' Charles, the Count of Alençon and the King's younger brother, advised Philip, 'but they cannot fetch their arrows from

France. They are brought to them by sea, and the further they go from the sea, the greater their problems.' So if the English were kept south of the Seine then they must eventually fight or make an ignominious retreat to Normandy.

'What of Paris? Paris? What of Paris?' the King demanded.

'Paris will not fall,' the Count assured his brother. The city lay north of the Seine, so the English would need to cross the river and assault the largest ramparts in Christendom, and all the while the garrison would be showering them with crossbow bolts and the missiles from the hundreds of small iron guns that had been mounted on the city walls.

'Maybe they will go south?' Philip worried. 'To Gascony?'

'If they march to Gascony,' the Count said, 'then they will have no boots by the time they arrive, and their arrow store will be gone. Let us pray they do go to Gascony, but above all things pray they do not reach the Seine's northern bank.' For if the English crossed the Seine they would go to the nearest Channel port to receive reinforcements and supplies and, by now, the Count knew, the English would be needing supplies. A marching army tired itself, its men became sick and its horses lame. An army that marched too long would eventually wear out like a tired crossbow.

So the French reinforced the great fortresses that guarded the Seine's crossings and where a bridge could not be guarded, such as the sixteen-arched bridge at Poissy, it was demolished. A hundred men with sledge-hammers broke down the parapets and hammered the stonework of the arches into the river to leave the fifteen stumps of the broken piers studding the Seine like the stepping stones of a giant, while Poissy itself, which lay south of the Seine and was reckoned indefensible, was abandoned and its people evacuated to Paris. The wide river was being turned into an impassable barrier to trap the English in an area where their food must eventually run short. Then, when the devils were weakened, the French would punish them for the terrible damage they had wrought on France. The English were still burning towns and destroying farms so that, in those long summer days, the western and southern horizons were so smeared by smoke plumes that it seemed as if there were permanent clouds on the skylines. At night the world's edge glowed and folk fleeing the fires came to Rouen where, because so many could not be housed or fed, they were ordered across the river and away to wherever they might find shelter.

Sir Simon Jekyll, and Henry Colley, his man-at-arms, were among the fugitives, and they were not refused admittance, for they both rode destriers and were in mail. Colley wore his own mail and rode his own horse, but Sir Simon's mount and gear had been stolen from one of his other men-at-arms before he fled from Caen. Both men carried shields, but they had stripped the leather covers from the willow boards so that the shields bore no device, thus declaring themselves to be masterless men for hire. Scores like them came to the city, seeking a lord who could offer food and pay, but none arrived with the anger that filled Sir Simon.

It was the injustice that galled him. It burned his soul, giving him a lust for revenge. He had come so close to paying all his debts – indeed, when the money from the sale of Jeanette's ships was paid from England he had expected to be free of all encumbrances – but now he was a fugitive. He knew he could have slunk back to England, but any man out of favour with the King or the King's eldest son could expect to be treated as a rebel, and he would be fortunate if he kept an acre of land, let alone his freedom. So he had preferred flight, trusting that his sword would win back the privileges he had lost to the Breton bitch and her puppy lover, and Henry Colley had ridden with him in the belief that any man as skilled in arms as Sir Simon could not fail.

No one questioned their presence in Rouen. Sir Simon's French was tinged with the accent of England's gentry, but so was the French of a score of other men from Normandy. What Sir Simon needed now was a patron, a man who would feed him and give him the chance to fight back against his persecutors, and there were plenty of great men looking for followers. In the fields south of Rouen, where the looping river narrowed the land, a pasture had been set aside as a tourney ground where, in front of a knowing crowd of men-at-arms, anyone could enter the lists to show their prowess. This was not a serious tournament – the swords were blunt and lances were tipped with wooden blocks – but rather it was a chance for masterless men to show their prowess with weapons, and a score of knights, the champions of dukes, counts, viscounts and mere lords, were the judges. Dozens of hopeful men were entering the lists, and any horseman who could last more than a few minutes against the well-mounted and superbly armed champions was sure to find a place in the entourage of a great nobleman.

Sir Simon, on his stolen horse and with his ancient

battered sword, was one of the least impressive men to ride into the pasture. He had no lance, so one of the champions drew a sword and rode to finish him off. At first no one took particular notice of the two men for other combats were taking place, but when the champion was sprawling on the grass and Sir Simon, untouched, rode on, the crowd took notice.

A second champion challenged Sir Simon and was startled by the fury which confronted him. He called out that the combat was not to the death, but merely a demonstration of swordplay, but Sir Simon gritted his teeth and hacked with the sword so savagely that the champion spurred and wheeled his horse away rather than risk injury. Sir Simon turned his horse in the pasture's centre, daring another man to face him, but instead a squire trotted a mare to the field's centre and wordlessly offered the Englishman a lance.

'Who sent it?' Sir Simon demanded.

'My lord.'

'Who is?'

'There,' the squire said, pointing to the pasture's end where a tall man in black armour and riding a black horse waited with his lance.

Sir Simon sheathed his sword and took the lance. It was heavy and not well balanced, and he had no lance rest in his armour that would cradle the long butt to help keep the point raised, but he was a strong man and an angry one, and he reckoned he could manage the cumbersome weapon long enough to break the stranger's confidence.

No other men fought on the field now. They just watched. Wagers were being made and all of them favoured the man in black. Most of the onlookers had seen him fight before, and his horse, his armour and his weapons were all plainly superior. He wore plate mail and his horse stood at least a hand's breadth taller than Sir Simon's sorry mount. His visor was down, so Sir Simon could not see the man's face, while Sir Simon himself had no faceplate, merely an old, cheap helmet like those worn by England's archers. Only Henry Colley laid a bet on Sir Simon, though he had difficulty in doing it for his French was rudimentary, but the money was at last taken.

The stranger's shield was black and decorated with a simple white cross, a device unknown to Sir Simon, while his horse had a black trapper that swept the pasture as the beast began to walk. That was the only signal the stranger gave and Sir Simon responded by lowering the lance and kicking his own horse forward. They were a hundred paces apart and both men moved swiftly into the canter. Sir Simon watched his opponent's lance, judging how firmly it was held. The man was good, for the lance tip scarcely wavered despite the horse's uneven motion. The shield was covering his trunk, as it should be.

If this had been a battle, if the man with the strange shield had not offered Sir Simon a chance of advancement, he might have lowered his own lance to strike his opponent's horse. Or, a more difficult strike, thrust the weapon's tip into the high pommel of his saddle. Sir Simon had seen a lance go clean through the wood and leather of a saddle to gouge into a man's groin, and it was ever a killing blow. But today he was required to show the skill of a knight, to strike clean and hard, and at the same time defend himself from the oncoming lance. The skill of that was to deflect the thrust which, having the weight of a horse behind it, could break a man's back by throwing him against the high cantle. The shock of two heavy horsemen meeting, and with all their weight concentrated into lance points, was like being hit by a cannon's stone.

Sir Simon was not thinking about any of this. He was watching the oncoming lance, glancing at the white cross on the shield where his own lance was aimed, and guiding his horse with pressure from his knees. He had trained to this from the time he could first sit on a pony. He had spent hours tilting at a quintain in his father's yard, and more hours schooling stallions to endure the noise and chaos of battle. He moved his horse slightly to the left like a man wanting to widen the angle at which the lances would strike and so deflect some of their force, and he noted that the stranger did not follow the move to straighten the line, but seemed happy to accept the lesser risk. Then both men rowelled back their spurs and the destriers went into the gallop. Sir Simon touched the horse's right side and straightened the line himself, driving hard at the stranger now, and leaning slightly forward to ready himself for the blow. His opponent was trying to swing towards him, but it was too late. Sir Simon's lance cracked against the black and white shield with a thump that hurled Sir Simon back, but the stranger's lance was not centred and banged against Sir Simon's plain shield and glanced off.

Sir Simon's lance broke into three pieces and he let it fall as he pressed his knee to turn the horse. His opponent's lance was across his body now and was encumbering the black-armoured knight. Sir Simon drew his sword and, while the other man was still trying to rid himself of the lance, gave a backswing that struck his opponent like a hammer blow.

The field was still. Henry Colley held out a hand for his winnings. The man pretended not to understand his crude French, but he understood the knife that the yellow-eyed Englishman suddenly produced and the coins, just as suddenly, appeared.

The knight in the black armour did not continue the fight, but instead curbed his horse and pushed up his visor. 'Who are you?'

'My name is Sir Simon Jekyll.'

'English?'

'I was.'

The two horses stood beside each other. The stranger threw down his lance and hung the shield from his pommel. He had a sallow face with a thin black moustache, clever eyes and a broken nose. He was a young man, not a boy, but a year or two older than Sir Simon.

'What do you want?' he asked Sir Simon.

'A chance to kill the Prince of Wales.'

The man smiled. 'Is that all?'

'Money, food, land, women,' Sir Simon said.

The man gestured to the side of the pasture. 'There are great lords here, Sir Simon, who will offer you pay, food and girls. I can pay you too, but not so well; I can feed you, though it will be common stuff; and the girls you must find for yourself. What I will promise you is that I shall equip you with a better horse, armour and weapons. I lead the best knights in this army and we are sworn to take captives who will make us rich. And none, I think, so rich as the King of England and his whelp. Not kill, mark you, but capture.'

Sir Simon shrugged. 'I'll settle for capturing the bastard,' he said.

'And his father,' the man said, 'I want his father too.'

There was something vengeful in the man's voice that intrigued Sir Simon. 'Why?' he asked.

'My family lived in England,' the man said, 'but when this king took power we supported his mother.'

'So you lost your land?' Sir Simon asked. He was too young to remember the turmoil of those times – when the King's mother had tried to keep power for herself and for her lover and the young Edward had struggled to break free. Young Edward had won and some of his old enemies had not forgotten.

'We lost everything,' the man said, 'but we shall get it back. Will you help?'

Sir Simon hesitated, wondering whether he would not do better with a wealthier lord, but he was intrigued by the man's calmness and by his determination to tear the heart out of England. 'Who are you?' he asked.

'I am sometimes called the Harlequin,' the man said.

The name meant nothing to Sir Simon. 'And you employ only the best?' he asked.

'I told you so.'

'Then you had best employ me,' Sir Simon said, 'with my man.' He nodded towards Henry Colley.

'Good,' the Harlequin said.

So Sir Simon had a new master and the King of France had gathered an army. The great lords: Alençon, John of Hainault, Aumale, the Count of Blois, who was brother to the aspiring Duke of Brittany, the Duke of Lorraine, the Count of Sancerre – all were in Rouen with their vast retinues of heavily armoured men. The army's numbers became so large that men could not count the ranks, but clerks reckoned there were at least eight thousand men-at-arms and five thousand cross-bowmen in Rouen, and that meant that Philip of Valois's army already outnumbered Edward of England's forces, and still more men were coming. John, Count of Luxembourg and King of Bohemia, a friend of Philip of France, was bringing his formidable knights. The King of Majorca came with his famed lances, and the Duke of Normandy was ordered to abandon the siege of an English fortress in the south and bring his army north. The priests blessed the soldiers and promised them that God would recognize the virtue of France's cause and crush the English mercilessly.

The army could not be fed in Rouen, so at last it crossed the bridge to the north bank of the Seine, leaving a formidable garrison behind to guard the river crossing. Once out of the city and on the long roads stretching through the newly harvested fields, men could dimly comprehend just how vast their army was. It stretched for miles in long columns of armed men, troops of horsemen, battalions of crossbowmen and, trailing behind, the innumerable host of infantry armed with axes, billhooks and spears. This was the might of France, and France's friends had rallied to the cause. There was a troop of knights from Scotland – big, sav-age-looking men who nourished a rare hatred of the English. There were mercenaries from Germany and Italy, and there were knights whose names had become famous in Christendom's tournaments, the elegant kil-lers who had become rich in the sport of war. The French knights spoke not just of defeating Edward of England, but of carrying the war to his kingdom, fore-seeing earldoms in Essex and dukedoms in Devonshire.

The Bishop of Meaux encouraged his cook to think of a recipe for archers' fingers, a *daube* perhaps, seasoned with thyme? He would, the bishop insisted, force the dish down Edward of England's throat.

Sir Simon rode a seven-year-old destrier now, a fine grey that must have cost the Harlequin close to a hundred pounds. He wore a hauberk of close-ringed mail covered with a surcoat that bore the white cross. His horse had a chanfron of boiled leather and a black trapper, while at Sir Simon's waist hung a sword made in Poitiers. Henry Colley was almost as well equipped, though in place of a sword he carried a four-foot-long shaft of oak topped with a spiked metal ball.

'They're a solemn bunch,' he complained to Sir Simon about the other men who followed the Harlequin. 'Like bloody monks.'

'They can fight,' Sir Simon said, though he himself was also daunted by the grim dedication of the Harlequin's men.

The men were all confident, but none took the English as lightly as the rest of the army, which had convinced itself that any battle would be won by numbers alone. The Harlequin quizzed Sir Simon and Henry Colley about the English way of fighting, and his questions were shrewd enough to force both men to drop their bombast and think.

'They'll fight on foot,' Sir Simon concluded. He, like all knights, dreamed of a battle conducted on horseback, of swirling men and couched lances, but the English had learned their business in the wars against the Scots and knew that men on foot defended territory much more effectively than horsemen. 'Even the knights will fight on foot,' Sir Simon forecast, 'and for every man-at-arms they'll have two or three archers. Those are the bastards to watch.'

The Harlequin nodded. 'But how do we defeat the archers?'

'Let them run out of arrows,' Sir Simon said. 'They must, eventually. So let every hothead in the army attack, then wait till the arrow bags are empty. Then you'll get your revenge.'

'It is more than revenge I want,' the Harlequin said quietly.

'What?'

The Harlequin, a handsome man, smiled at Sir Simon, though there was no warmth in the smile. 'Power,' he answered very calmly. 'With power, Sir Simon, comes privilege and with privilege, wealth. What are kings,' he asked, 'but men who have risen high? So we shall rise too, and use the defeat of kings as the rungs of our ladder.'

Such talk impressed Sir Simon, though he did not wholly understand it. It seemed to him that the Harlequin was a man of high fancies, but that did not matter because he was also unswervingly dedicated to the defeat of men who were Sir Simon's enemies. Sir Simon daydreamed of the battle; he saw the English prince's frightened face, heard his scream and revelled in the thought of taking the insolent whelp prisoner. Jeanette too. The Harlequin could be as secretive and subtle as he wished so long as he led Sir Simon to those simple desires.

And so the French army marched, and still it grew as men came from the outlying parts of the kingdom and from the vassal states beyond France's frontiers. It marched to seal off the Seine and so trap the English, and its confidence soared when it was learned that the King had made his pilgrimage to the Abbey of St Denis to fetch the oriflamme. It was France's most sacred symbol, a scarlet banner kept by the Benedictines in the abbey where the Kings of France lay entombed, and every man knew that when the oriflamme was unfurled no quarter would be given. It was said to have been carried by Charlemagne himself, and its silk was red as blood, promising carnage to the enemies of France. The English had come to fight, the oriflamme had been released and the dance of the armies had begun.

Sir Guillaume gave Thomas a linen shirt, a good mail coat, a leather-lined helmet and a sword. 'It's old, but good,' he said of the sword, 'a cutter rather than a piercer.' He provided Thomas with a horse, a saddle, a bridle and gave him money. Thomas tried to refuse the last gift, but Sir Guillaume brushed his protest aside. 'You've taken what you wanted from me, I might as well give you the rest.'

'Taken?' Thomas was puzzled, even hurt, by the accusation.

'Eleanor.'

'I've not taken her,' Thomas protested.

Sir Guillaume's ravaged face broke into a grin. 'You will, boy,' he said, 'you will.'

They rode next day, going eastwards in the wake of the English army that was now far off. News had come to Caen of burned towns, but no one knew where the enemy had gone and so Sir Guillaume planned to lead his twelve men-at-arms, his squire and his servant to

Paris. 'Someone will know where the King is,' he said. 'And you, Thomas, what will you do?'

Thomas had been wondering the same ever since he woke to the light in Sir Guillaume's house, but now he must make the decision and, to his surprise, there was no conflict at all. 'I shall go to my king,' he said.

'And what of this Sir Simon? What if he hangs you again?'

'I have the Earl of Northampton's protection,' Thomas said, though he reflected it had not worked before.

'And what of Eleanor?' Sir Guillaume turned to look at his daughter who, to Thomas's surprise, had accompanied them. Her father had given her a small palfrey and, unused to riding, she sat its saddle awkwardly, clutching the high pommel. She did not know why her father had let her come, suggesting to Thomas that perhaps he wanted her to be his cook.

The question made Thomas blush. He knew he could not fight against his own friends, but nor did he want to leave Eleanor. 'I shall come looking for her,' he told Sir Guillaume.

'If you still live,' the Frenchman growled. 'Why don't you fight for me?'

'Because I'm English.'

Sir Guillaume sneered. 'You're Cathar, you're French, you're from Languedoc, who knows what you are? You're a priest's son, a mongrel bastard of heretic stock.'

'I'm English,' Thomas said.

'You're a Christian,' Sir Guillaume retorted, 'and God has given you and me a duty. How are you to fulfil that duty by joining Edward's army?'

Thomas did not answer at once. Had God given him a duty? If so he did not want to accept it, for acceptance meant believing in the legends of the Vexilles. Thomas, in the evening after he had met Brother Germain, had talked with Mordecai in Sir Guillaume's garden, asking the old man if he had ever read the book of Daniel.

Mordecai had sighed, as if he found the question wearisome. 'Years ago,' he'd said, 'many years ago. It is part of the Ketuvim, the writings that all Jewish youths must read. Why?'

'He's a prophet, yes? He tells the future.'

'Dear me,' Mordecai had said, sitting on the bench and dragging his thin fingers through his forked beard. 'You Christians,' he had said, 'insist that prophets tell the future, but that wasn't really what they did at all. They warned Israel. They told us that we would be visited by death, destruction and horror if we did not mend our ways. They were preachers, Thomas, just preachers, though, God knows, they were right about the death, destruction and horror. As for Daniel . . . He is very strange, very strange. He had a head filled with dreams and visions. He was drunk on God, that one.'

'But do you think,' Thomas had asked, 'that Daniel could foretell what is happening now?'

Mordecai had frowned. 'If God wished him to, yes, but why should God wish that? And I assume, Thomas, that you think Daniel might foretell what happens here and now in France, and what possible interest could that hold for the God of Israel? The Ketuvim are full of fancy, vision and mystery, and you Christians see more in them than we ever did. But would I make a decision because Daniel ate a bad oyster and had a vivid dream all those years ago? No, no, no.' He stood and held a jordan bottle high. 'Trust what is before your eyes,

Thomas, what you can smell, hear, taste, touch and see. The rest is dangerous.'

Thomas now looked at Sir Guillaume. He had come to like the Frenchman whose battle-hardened exterior hid a wealth of kindness, and Thomas knew he was in love with the Frenchman's daughter, but, even so, he had a greater loyalty.

'I cannot fight against England,' he said, 'any more than you would carry a lance against King Philip.'

Sir Guillaume dismissed that with a shrug. 'Then fight against the Vexilles.'

But Thomas could not smell, hear, taste, touch or see the Vexilles. He did not believe the king of the south would send his daughter to the north. He did not believe the Holy Grail was hidden in some heretic's fastness. He believed in the strength of a yew bow, the tension of a hemp cord and the power of a white-feathered arrow to kill the King's enemies. To think of dark lords and of heresiarchs was to flirt with the madness that had harrowed his own father.

'If I find the man who killed my father,' he evaded Sir Guillaume's demand, 'then I will kill him.'

'But you will not search for him?'

'Where do I look? Where do you look?' Thomas asked, then offered his own answer. 'If the Vexilles really still exist, if they truly want to destroy France, then where would they begin? In England's army. So I shall look for them there.' That answer was an evasion, but it half convinced Sir Guillaume, who grudgingly conceded that the Vexilles might indeed take their forces to Edward of England.

That night they sheltered in the scorched remains of a farm where they gathered about a small fire on which they roasted the hind legs of a boar that Thomas had shot. The men-at-arms treated Thomas warily. He was, after all, one of the hated English archers whose bows could pierce even plate mail. If he had not been Sir Guillaume's friend they would have wanted to slice off his string fingers in revenge for the pain that the white-fledged arrows had given to the horsemen of France, but instead they treated him with a distant curiosity. After the meal Sir Guillaume gestured to Eleanor and Thomas that they should both accompany him outside. His squire was keeping watch, and Sir Guillaume led them away from the young man, going to the bank of a stream where, with an odd formality, he looked at Thomas. 'So you will leave us,' he said, 'and fight for Edward of England.'

'Yes.'

'But if you see my enemy, if you see the lance, what will you do?'

'Kill him,' Thomas said. Eleanor stood slightly apart, watching and listening.

'He will not be alone,' Sir Guillaume warned, 'but you assure me he is your enemy?'

'I swear it,' Thomas said, puzzled that the question even needed to be asked.

Sir Guillaume took Thomas's right hand. 'You have heard of a brotherhood in arms?'

Thomas nodded. Men of rank frequently made such pacts, swearing to aid each other in battle and share each other's spoils.

'Then I swear a brotherhood to you,' Sir Guillaume said, 'even if we will fight on opposing sides.'

'I swear the same,' Thomas said awkwardly.

Sir Guillaume let Thomas's hand go. 'There,' he said

331

to Eleanor, 'I'm safe from one damned archer.' He paused, still looking at Eleanor. 'I shall marry again,' he said abruptly, 'and have children again and they will be my heirs. You know what I'm saying, don't you?'

Eleanor's head was lowered, but she looked up at her father briefly, then dropped her gaze again. She said nothing.

'And if I have more children, God willing,' Sir Guillaume said, 'what does that leave for you, Eleanor?'

She gave a very small shrug as if to suggest that the question was not of great interest to her. 'I have never asked you for anything.'

'But what would you have asked for?'

She stared into the ripples of the stream. 'What you gave me,' she said after a while, 'kindness.'

'Nothing else?'

She paused. 'I would have liked to call you Father.'

Sir Guillaume seemed uncomfortable with that answer. He stared northwards. 'You are both bastards,' he said after a while, 'and I envy that.'

'Envy?' Thomas asked.

'A family serves like the banks of a stream. They keep you in your place, but bastards make their own way. They take nothing and they can go anywhere.' He frowned, then flicked a pebble into the water. 'I had always thought, Eleanor, that I would marry you to one of my men-at-arms. Benoit asked me for your hand and so did Fossat. And it's past time you were married. What are you? Fifteen?'

'Fifteen,' she agreed.

'You'll rot away, girl, if you wait any longer,' Sir Guillaume said gruffly, 'so who shall it be? Benoit? Fossat?' He paused. 'Or would you prefer Thomas?'

Eleanor said nothing and Thomas, embarrassed, kept silent.

'You want her?' Sir Guillaume asked him brutally.

'Yes.'

'Eleanor?'

She looked at Thomas, then back to the stream. 'Yes,' she said simply.

'The horse, the mail, the sword and the money,' Sir Guillaume said to Thomas, 'are my bastard daughter's dowry. Look after her, or else become my enemy again.' He turned away.

'Sir Guillaume?' Thomas asked. The Frenchman turned back. 'When you went to Hookton,' Thomas went on, wondering why he asked the question now, 'you took a dark-haired girl prisoner. She was pregnant. Her name was Jane.'

Sir Guillaume nodded. 'She married one of my men. Then died in childbirth. The child too. Why?' He frowned. 'Was the child yours?'

'She was a friend,' Thomas evaded the question.

'She was a pretty friend,' Sir Guillaume said, 'I remember that. And when she died we had twelve Masses said for her English soul.'

'Thank you.'

Sir Guillaume looked from Thomas to Eleanor, then back to Thomas. 'A good night for sleeping under the stars,' he said, 'and we shall leave at dawn.' He walked away.

Thomas and Eleanor sat by the stream. The sky was still not wholly dark, but had a luminous quality like the glow of a candle behind horn. An otter slid down the far side of the stream, its fur glistening where it showed above the water. It raised its head, looked briefly at Thomas, then dived out of sight, to leave a trickle of silver bubbles breaking the dark surface.

Eleanor broke the silence, speaking the only English words she knew. 'I am an archer's woman,' she said.

Thomas smiled. 'Yes,' he said.

And in the morning they rode on and next evening they saw the smear of smoke on the northern horizon and knew it was a sign that the English army was going about its business. They parted in the next dawn.

'How you reach the bastards, I do not know,' Sir Guillaume said, 'but when it is all over, look for me.'

He embraced Thomas, kissed Eleanor, then pulled himself into his saddle. His horse had a long blue trapper decorated with yellow hawks. He settled his right foot into its stirrup, gathered the reins and pushed back his spurs.

A track led north across a heath that was fragrant with thyme and fluttering with blue butterflies. Thomas, his helmet hanging from the saddle's pommel and the sword thumping at his side, rode towards the smoke, and Eleanor, who insisted on carrying his bow because she was an archer's woman, rode with him. They looked back from the low crest of the heath, but Sir Guillaume was already a half-mile westwards, not looking back, hurrying towards the oriflamme.

So Thomas and Eleanor rode on.

The English marched east, ever further from the sea, searching for a place to cross the Seine, but every bridge was broken or else was guarded by a fortress. They still destroyed everything they touched. Their *chevauchée* was a line twenty miles wide and behind it was a charred trail a hundred miles long. Every house was burned and every mill destroyed. The folk of France fled from the army, taking their livestock and the newly gathered harvest with them so that Edward's men had to range ever further to find food. Behind them was desolation while in front lay the formidable walls of Paris. Some men thought the King would assault Paris, others reckoned he would not waste his troops on those great walls, but instead attack one of the strongly fortified bridges that could lead him north of the river. Indeed, the army tried to capture the bridge at Meulan, but the stronghold which guarded its southern end was too massive and its crossbowmen were too many, and the assault failed. The French stood on the ramparts and bared their backsides to insult the defeated English. It was said that the King, confident of crossing the river, had ordered supplies sent to the port of Le Crotoy that lay far to the north, beyond both the Seine and the River Somme, but if the supplies were waiting then they were unreachable because the Seine was a wall behind which the English were penned in a land they had themselves emptied of food. The first horses began to go lame and men, their boots shredded by marching, went barefoot.

The English came closer to Paris, entering the wide lands that were the hunting grounds of the French kings. They took Philip's lodges and stripped them of tapestries and plate, and it was while they hunted his royal deer that the French King sent Edward a formal offer of battle. It was the chivalrous thing to do, and it would, by God's grace, end the harrowing of his farmlands. So Philip of Valois sent a bishop to the English, courteously suggesting that he would wait with his army south of Paris, and the English King graciously accepted the invitation and so the French marched their army through the city and arrayed it among the vine-yards on a hillcrest by Bourg-la-Reine. They would make the English attack them there, forcing the archers and men-at-arms to struggle uphill into massed Genoese crossbows, and the French nobles estimated the value of the ransoms they would fetch for their prisoners.

The French battleline waited, but no sooner had Philip's army settled in its positions than the English treacherously turned about and marched in the other direction, going to the town of Poissy where the bridge across the Seine had been destroyed and the town evacuated. A few French infantrymen, poor soldiers armed with spears and axes, had been left to guard the northern bank, but they could do nothing to stop the swarm of archers, carpenters and masons who used tim-bers ripped from the roofs of Poissy to make a new bridge on the fifteen broken piers of the old. It took two days to repair the bridge and the French were still waiting for their arranged battle among the ripening grapes at Bourg-la-Reine as the English crossed the Seine and started marching northwards. The devils had escaped the trap and were loose again.

It was at Poissy that Thomas, with Eleanor beside him, rejoined the army.

And it was there, by God's Grace, that the hard times began.

Eleanor had been apprehensive about joining the English army. 'They won't like me because I'm French,' she said.

'The army's full of Frenchmen,' Thomas had told her. 'There are Gascons, Bretons, even some Normans, and half the women are French.'

'The archers' women?' she asked, giving him a wry smile. 'But they are not good women?'

'Some are good, some are bad,' Thomas said vaguely, 'but you I shall make into a wife and everyone will know you're special.'

If Eleanor was pleased she showed no sign, but they were now in the broken streets of Poissy, where a rearguard of English archers shouted at them to hurry. The makeshift bridge was about to be destroyed and the army's laggards were being chivvied across its planks. The bridge had no parapets and had been hurriedly made from whatever timbers the army had found in the abandoned town, and the uneven planking swayed, creaked and bent as Thomas and Eleanor led their horses onto the roadway. Eleanor's palfrey became so scared of the uncertain footing that it refused to move until Thomas put a blindfold over its eyes and then, still shaking, it trod slowly and steadily across the planks, which had gaps between them through which Thomas could see the river sliding. They were among the last to cross. Some of the army's wagons had been abandoned in Poissy, their loads distributed onto the hundreds of horses that had been captured south of the Seine.

Once the last stragglers had crossed the bridge the archers began hurling the planks into the river, breaking down the fragile link that had let the English escape across the river. Now, King Edward hoped, they would find new land to waste in the wide plains that lay between the Seine and the Somme and the three battles spread into the twenty-mile-wide line of the *chevauchée* and advanced northwards, camping that night just a short march from the river.

Thomas looked for the Prince of Wales's troops while Eleanor tried to ignore the dirty, tattered and sun-browned archers, who looked more like outlaws than soldiers. They were supposed to be making their shelters for the coming night, but preferred to watch the women and call obscene invitations. 'What are they saying?' Eleanor asked Thomas.

'That you are the most beautiful creature in all France,' he said.

'You lie,' she said, then flinched as a man shouted at her. 'Have they never seen a woman before?'

'Not like you. They probably think you're a princess.'

She scoffed at that, but was not displeased. There were, she saw, women everywhere. They gathered firewood while their men made the shelters and most, Eleanor noted, spoke French. 'There will be many babies next year,' she said.

'True.'

'They will go back to England?' she asked.

'Some, perhaps.' Thomas was not really sure. 'Or they'll go to their garrisons in Gascony.'

'If I marry you,' she asked, 'will I become English?'

'Yes,' Thomas said.

It was getting late and cooking fires were smoking across the stubble fields, though there was precious little to cook. Every pasture held a score of horses and Thomas knew they needed to rest, feed and water their own animals. He had asked many soldiers where the Prince of Wales's men could be found, but one man said west, another east, so in the dusk Thomas simply turned their tired horses towards the nearest village for he did not know where else to go. The place was swarming with troops, but Thomas and Eleanor found a quiet enough spot in the corner of a field where Thomas made a fire while Eleanor, the black bow prominent on her shoulder to demonstrate that she belonged to the army, watered the horses in a stream. They cooked the last of their food and afterwards sat under the hedge and watched the stars brighten above a dark wood. Voices sounded from the village where some women were singing a French song and Eleanor crooned the words softly.

'I remember my mother singing it to me,' she said, plucking strands of grass that she wove into a small bracelet. 'I was not his only bastard,' she said ruefully. 'There were two others I know of. One died when she was very small, and the other is now a soldier.'

'He's your brother.

'Half-brother.' She shrugged. 'I don't know him. He went away.' She put the bracelet on her thin wrist. 'Why do you wear a dog's paw?' she asked.

'Because I'm a fool,' he said, 'and mock God.' That was the truth, he thought ruefully, and he pulled the dry paw hard to break its cord, then tossed it into the field. He did not really believe in St Guinefort; it was an affectation. A dog would not help him recover the lance, and that duty made him grimace, for the penance weighed on his conscience and soul.

'Do you really mock God?' Eleanor asked, worried.

'No. But we jest about the things we fear.'

'And you fear God?'

'Of course,' Thomas said, then stiffened because there had been a rustle in the hedge behind him and a cold blade was suddenly pressed against the back of his neck. The metal felt very sharp.

'What we should do,' a voice said, 'is hang the bastard properly and take his woman. She's pretty.'

'She's pretty,' another man agreed, 'but he ain't good for anything.'

'You bastards!' Thomas said, turning to stare into two grinning faces. It was Jake and Sam. He did not believe it at first, just gazed for a while. 'It is you! What are you doing here?'

Jake slashed at the hedge with his billhook, pushed through and gave Eleanor what he thought was a reassuring grin, though with his scarred face and crossed eyes he looked like something from nightmare. 'Charlie Blois got his face smacked,' Jake said, 'so Will brought us here to give the King of France a bloody nose. She your woman?'

'She's the Queen of bloody Sheba,' Thomas said.

'And the Countess is humping the Prince, I hear,' Jake grinned. 'Will saw you earlier, only you didn't see us. Got your nose in the air. We heard you were dead.'

'I nearly was.'

'Will wants to see you.'

The thought of Will Skeat, of Jake and Sam, came as a vast relief to Thomas, for such men lived in a world far removed from dire prophecies, stolen lances and dark lords. He told Eleanor these men were his friends, his best friends, and that she could trust them, though she looked alarmed at the ironic cheer which greeted Thomas when they ducked into the village tavern. The archers put their hands at their throats and contorted their faces to imitate a hanged man while Will Skeat shook his head in mock despair.

'God's belly,' he said, 'but they can't even hang you properly.' He looked at Eleanor. 'Another countess?'

'The daughter of Sir Guillaume d'Evecque, knight of the sea and of the land,' Thomas said, 'and she's called Eleanor.'

'Yours?' Skeat asked.

'We shall marry.'

'Bloody hellfire,' Skeat said, 'you're still daft as a carrot! You don't marry them, Tom, that's not what they're for. Still, she ain't a bad looker, is she?' He courteously made space for Eleanor on the bench. 'There wasn't much ale,' he went on, 'so we drank it all.' He looked about the tavern. It was so bare there was not even a bunch of herbs hanging from the rafters. 'Bastards cleaned up before they left,' he said sourly, 'and there's about as much plunder here as you'd get hairs off a bald man.'

'What happened in Brittany?' Thomas asked.

Will shrugged. 'Nowt to do with us. Duke Charles led his men into our territory and trapped Tommy Dugdale on a hilltop. Three thousand of them and three hundred

341

with Tommy, and at the end of the day Duke Charles was running like a scalded hare. Arrows, boy, arrows.'

Thomas Dugdale had taken over the Earl of Northampton's responsibilities in Brittany and had been travelling between the English fortresses when the Duke's army caught him, but his archers and men-at-arms, ensconced behind the thick hedge of a hilltop pasture, had cut the enemy into shreds.

'All day they fought,' Skeat said, 'morning to night, and the bastards wouldn't learn their lesson and kept sending men up the hill. They reckoned Tommy had to run out of arrows soon enough, but he was carrying carts of spares to the fortresses, see, so he had enough to last him till doomsday. So Duke Charles lost his best men, the fortresses are safe till he gets some more, and we're up here. The Earl sent for us. Just bring fifty archers, he told me, so I did. And Father Hobbe, of course. We sailed to Caen and joined the army just as it marched out. So what the hell happened to you?'

Thomas told his tale. Skeat shook his head when he heard about the hanging. 'Sir Simon's gone,' he said. 'Probably joined the French.'

'He's done what?'

'Vanished. Your countess caught up with him and pissed all over him from what we hear.' Skeat grinned. 'Luck of the devil, you've got. God knows why I saved you this.' He put a clay jar of ale on the table, then nodded at Thomas's bow that Eleanor was carrying. 'Can you still shoot that thing? I mean you've been bollocking about with the aristocracy for so long that you might have forgotten why God put you on the earth?'

'I can still use it.'

'Then you might as well ride with us,' Skeat said, but confessed he knew little of what the army was doing. 'No one tells me,' he said scornfully, 'but they say there's another river up north and we've got to cross it. Sooner the better, I reckon, as the Frenchies have skimmed this land proper. Couldn't feed a kitten up here.'

It was indeed a bare land. Thomas saw that for himself next day as Will Skeat's men moved slowly north across harvested fields, but the grain, instead of lying in the barns, had already been taken for the French army, just as the livestock had all been driven away. South of the Seine the English had cut grain from abandoned fields and their advance guards had moved swiftly enough to capture thousands of cattle, pigs and goats, but here the land had been scraped bare by an even larger army and so the King ordered haste. He wanted his men to cross the next river, the Somme, to where the French army might not have stripped the land and where, at Le Crotoy, he hoped a fleet would be waiting with supplies, but despite the royal orders the army went painfully slowly. There were fortified towns that promised food and men insisted on trying to assault their walls. They captured some, were repulsed at others, but it all took time that the King did not have, and while he was trying to discipline an army more interested in plunder than progress, the King of France led his army back across the Seine, through Paris and north to the Somme.

A new trap was set, an even deadlier one, for the English were now penned in a land that had been stripped of food. Edward's army at last reached the Somme, but found it was blocked just as the Seine had been barred. Bridges were destroyed or guarded by grim forts with heavy garrisons that would take weeks to dislodge, and the English did not have weeks. They were weakening daily. They had marched from Normandy to the edge of Paris, then they had crossed the Seine and left a path of destruction to the Somme's southern bank and the long journey had abraded the army. Hundreds of men were now barefoot while others hobbled on disintegrating shoes. They had horses enough, but few spare horseshoes or nails, and so men led their animals to save their hooves.

There was grass to feed horses, but little grain for men, and so the foraging parties had to travel long distances to find villages where the peasants might have hidden some of the harvest. The French were becoming bolder now and there were frequent skirmishes at the edges of the army as the French sensed the English vulnerability. Men ate unripe fruit that soured their bellies and loosened their bowels. Some reckoned they had no choice but to march all the way back to Normandy, but others knew the army would fall apart long before they reached the safety of the Norman harbours. The only course was to cross the Somme and march to the English strongholds in Flanders, but the bridges were gone or garrisoned, and when the army crossed desolate marshlands to find fords they discovered the enemy ever waiting on the far bank. They twice tried to force a passage, but both times the French, secure on the higher dry land, were able to cut down the archers in the river by crowding the bank with Genoese crossbows. And so the English retreated and marched westwards, getting ever nearer to the river's mouth, and every step reduced the number of possible crossing places as the river grew wider and deeper. They marched for eight days between the rivers, eight days of increasing hunger and frustration.

'Save your arrows,' a worried Will Skeat warned his men late one afternoon. They were making their camp by a small, deserted village which was as bare as every other place they had found since crossing the Seine. 'We'll need every arrow we've got for a battle,' Skeat went on, 'and Christ knows we've none to waste.'

An hour later, when Thomas was searching a hedge-row for blackberries, a voice called from on high. 'Thomas! Get your evil bones up here!'

Thomas turned to see Will Skeat on the small tower of the village church. He ran to the church, climbed the ladder, past a beam where a bell had hung till the villagers took it away to prevent the English from stealing it, then pulled himself through the hatch and onto the tower's flat roof where a half-dozen men were crowded, among them the Earl of Northampton, who gave Thomas a very wry look.

'I heard you were hanged!'

'I lived, my lord,' Thomas said grimly.

The Earl hesitated, wondering whether to ask if Sir Simon Jekyll had been the hangman, but there was no point in continuing that feud. Sir Simon had fled and the Earl's agreement with him was void. He grimaced instead. 'No one can kill a devil's whelp, eh?' he said, then pointed eastwards, and Thomas stared through the twilight and saw an army on the march.

It was a long way off, on the far northern bank of the river that here flowed between vast reedbeds, but Thomas could still see that the lines of horsemen, wagons, infantry and crossbowmen were filling every lane and track of that distant bank. The army was approaching a walled town, Abbeville, the Earl said, where a bridge crossed the river, and Thomas, gazing at the black lines twisting towards the bridge, felt as though the gates of hell had opened and spewed out a vast horde of lances, swords and crossbows. Then he remembered Sir Guillaume was there and he made the sign of the cross and mouthed a silent prayer that Eleanor's father would survive.

'Sweet Christ,' Will Skeat said, mistaking Thomas's gesture for fear, 'but they want our souls bad.'

'They know we're tired,' the Earl said, 'and they know the arrows must run out in the end, and they know they have more men than we do. Far more.' He turned westwards. 'And we can't run much further.' He pointed again and Thomas saw the flat sheen of the sea. 'They've caught us,' the Earl said. 'They'll cross at Abbeville and attack tomorrow.'

'So we fight,' Will Skeat growled.

'On this ground, Will?' the Earl asked. The land was flat, ideal for cavalry, and with few hedgerows or coppices to protect archers. 'And against so many?' he added. He stared at the distant enemy. 'They outnumber us. Will, they outnumber us. By God, they outnumber us.' He shrugged. 'Time to move on.'

'Move on where?' Skeat asked. 'Why not find our ground and stand?'

'South?' The Earl sounded unsure. 'Maybe we can cross the Seine again and take ships home from Normandy? God knows we can't cross the Somme.' He shaded his eyes as he stared at the river. 'Christ,' he blasphemed, 'but why the hell isn't there a ford? We could have raced the bastards back to our fortresses in Flanders and left Philip stranded like the damned fool he is.'

'Not fight him?' Thomas asked, sounding shocked.

The Earl shook his head. 'We've hurt him. We've robbed him blind. We've marched through his kingdom and left it smouldering, so why fight him? He's spent a fortune on hiring knights and crossbowmen, so why not let him waste that money? Then we come back next year and do it again.' He shrugged. 'Unless we can't escape him.' With those grim words he backed down through the hatch and his entourage followed, leaving Skeat and Thomas alone.

'The real reason they don't want to fight,' Skeat said sourly when the Earl was safe out of earshot, 'is that they're scared of being taken prisoner. A ransom can wipe out a family's fortune in the blink of an eye.' He spat over the tower parapet, then drew Thomas to its northern edge. 'But the real reason I brought you up here, Tom, is because your eyes are better than mine. Can you see a village over there?' He pointed northwards.

It took Thomas a while, but eventually he spotted a group of low roofs amidst the reeds. 'Bloody poor village,' he said sourly.

'But it's still a place we haven't searched for food,' Skeat said, 'and being on a marsh they might have some smoked eels. I like a smoked eel, I do. Better than sour apples and nettle soup. You can go and have a look.'

'Tonight?'

'Why not next week?' Skeat said, going to the roof hatch, 'or next year? Of course I mean tonight, you toad. Hurry yourself.'

Thomas took twenty archers. None of them wanted to go, for it was late in the day and they feared that French patrols might be waiting on the track that twisted endlessly through the dunes and reedbeds that stretched towards the Somme. It was a desolate country. Birds flew from the reeds as the horses picked their way along a track that was so low-lying that in places there were battens of elm to give footing, and all about them the water gurgled and sucked between banks of green-scummed mud.

'Tide's going out,' Jake commented.

Thomas could smell the salt water. They were near enough to the sea for the tides to flow and ebb through this tangle of reeds and marshgrass, though in places the road found a firmer footing on great drifted banks of sand where stiff pale grasses grew. In winter, Thomas thought, this would be a godforsaken place with the cold winds driving the spume across the frozen marsh.

It was very nearly dark when they reached the village, which proved to be a miserable settlement of just a dozen reed-thatched cottages, which were deserted. The folk must have left just before Thomas's archers arrived, for there were still fires in the small rock hearths.

'Look for food,' Thomas said, 'especially smoked eels.'

'Be quicker to catch the bloody eels and smoke them ourselves,' Jake said.

'Get on with it,' Thomas said, then took himself to the end of the village where there was a small wooden church which had been pushed by the wind into a permanently lopsided stance. The church was little more than a shed – maybe it was a shrine to some saint of this misbegotten marshland – but Thomas reckoned the wooden structure would just about bear his weight so he scrambled off the horse onto the moss-thick thatch and then crawled up to the ridge where he clung to the nailed cross that decorated one gable.

He saw no movement in the marshes, though he could see the smear of smoke coming from the French camp-fires that misted the fading light north of Abbeville. Tomorrow, he thought, the French would cross the bridge and file through the town's gates to confront the English army whose fires burned to the south, and the size of the smoke plumes witnessed how much larger the French army was than the English.

Jake appeared from a nearby cottage with a sack in his hand. 'What is it?' Thomas called.

'Grain!' Jake hefted the sack. 'Bloody damp. Sprouting.'

'No eels?'

'Of course there are no bloody eels,' Jake grumbled. 'Bloody eels got more sense than to live in a hovel like this.'

Thomas grinned and looked off to the sea that lay like a blood-reddened swordblade to the west. There was one distant sail, a speck of white, on the clouded horizon. Gulls wheeled and soared above the river that here was a great wide channel, broken by reeds and banks, sliding towards the sea. It was hard to distinguish between river and marsh, so tangled was the landscape. Then Thomas wondered why the gulls were screaming and diving. He stared at them and saw what at first looked like a dozen cattle on the riverbank. He opened his mouth to call that news to Jake, then he saw that there were men with the cattle. Men and women, per-haps a score of them? He frowned, staring, realizing that the folk must have come from this village. They had presumably seen the English archers approaching and they had fled with their livestock, but to where? The marsh? That was sensible, for the wetlands probably had a score of secret paths where folk could hide, but why had they risked going onto the sand ridge where Thomas could see them? Then he saw that they were not trying to hide, but to escape, for the villagers were now wading across the wide waters towards the northern bank.

Sweet Jesus, he thought, but there was a ford! He stared, not daring to believe his own eyes, but the folk were forging steadily across the river and dragging their cows with them. It was a deep ford, and he guessed it could only be crossed at low tide, but it was there. 'Jake!' he shouted. 'Jake!'

Jake ran across to the church and Thomas leaned far down and hauled him onto the rotting thatch. The building swayed perilously under their weight as Jake scrambled to the ridge, took hold of the sun-bleached wooden cross and looked where Thomas was pointing.

'God's arse,' he said, 'there's a bloody ford!'

'And there are bloody Frenchmen,' Thomas said, for on the river's far bank where firmer land rose from the tangle of marsh and water there were now men in grey mail. They were newly arrived, or else Thomas would have seen them earlier, and their first cooking fires pricked the dark stand of trees where they camped. Their presence showed that the French knew of the ford's existence and wanted to stop the English crossing, but that was none of Thomas's business. His only duty was to let the army know that there was a ford; a possible way out of the trap.

Thomas slid down the church's thatch and jumped to the ground. 'You go back to Will,' he told Jake, 'and tell him there's a ford. And tell him I'll burn the cottages one at a time to serve as a beacon.' It would be dark soon and without a light to guide them no one would be able to find the village.

Jake took six men and rode back to the south. Thomas waited. Every now and then he climbed back to the church roof and stared across the ford and each time he thought he saw more fires among the trees. The French, he reckoned, had placed a formidable force there, and no wonder, for it was the last escape route and they were blocking it. But Thomas still fired the cottages one by one to show the English where that escape might lie.

The flames roared into the night, scattering sparks across the marshes. The archers had found some dried fish concealed in a hut wall and that, with brackish water, was their supper. They were disconsolate, and no wonder.

'We should have stayed in Brittany,' one man said.

'They're going to corner us,' another suggested. He had made a flute from a dried reed and had been playing a melancholy air.

'We've got arrows,' a third man said.

'Enough to kill all those bastards?'

'Have to be enough.'

The flute player blew some faint notes, then became bored and tossed the instrument into the closest fire. Thomas, the night dragging hard on his patience, strolled back to the church, but instead of climbing onto the roof he pushed open the ramshackle door and then opened the one window's shutters to let in the firelight. Then he saw it was not a proper church, but a fishermen's shrine. There was an altar made from sea-whitened planks balanced on two broken barrels, and on the altar was a crude doll-like figure draped with strips of white cloth and crowned with a band of dried seaweed. The fishermen at Hookton had sometimes made such places, especially if a boat was lost at sea, and Thomas's father had always hated them. He had burned one to the ground, calling it a place of idols, but Thomas reckoned fishermen needed the shrines. The sea was a cruel place and the doll, he thought it was female, perhaps represented some saint of the area. Women whose men were long gone to sea could come to pray to the saint, begging that the ship would come home.

The shrine's roof was low and it was more comfortable to kneel. Thomas said a prayer. Let me live, he prayed, let me live, and he found himself thinking of the lance, thinking of Brother Germain and Sir Guillaume and of their fears that a new evil, born of the dark lords, was brewing in the south. It is none of your business, he told himself. It is superstition. The Cathars are dead, burned in the church's fires and gone to hell. Beware of madmen, his father had told him, and who better than his father to know that truth? But was he a Vexille? He bowed his head and prayed that God would keep him from the madness.

'And what are you praying for now?' a voice suddenly asked, startling Thomas, who turned to see Father Hobbe grinning from the low doorway. He had chatted with the priest during the last few days, but he had never been alone with him. Thomas was not even sure he wanted to be, for Father Hobbe's presence was a reminder of his conscience.

'I'm praying for more arrows, father.'

'Please God the prayer's answered,' Father Hobbe said, then settled on the church's earthen floor. 'I had the devil's own task finding my way across the swamp, but I had a mind to talk with you. I have this feeling you've been avoiding me.'

'Father!' Thomas said chidingly.

'So here you are, and with a beautiful girl as well! I tell you, Thomas, if they forced you to lick a leper's arse you'd taste nothing but sweetness. Charmed, you are. They can't even hang you!'

'They can,' Thomas said, 'but not properly.'

'Thank God for that,' the priest said, then smiled. 'So how is the penance going?'

'I haven't found the lance,' Thomas answered curtly.

'But have you even looked for it?' Father Hobbe asked, then drew a piece of bread from his pouch. He broke the small loaf and tossed half to Thomas. 'Don't ask where I got it, but I didn't steal it. Remember, Thomas, you can fail in a penance and still have absolution if you have made a sincere effort.'

Thomas grimaced, not at Father Hobbe's words, but because he had bitten down on a scrap of millstone grit caught in the bread. He spat it out. 'My soul isn't so black as you make it sound, Father.'

'How would you know? All our souls are black.'

'I've made an effort,' Thomas said, then found himself telling the whole tale of how he had gone to Caen and sought out Sir Guillaume's house, and how he had been a guest there, and about Brother Germain and the Cathar Vexilles, and about the prophecy from Daniel and the advice of Mordecai.

Father Hobbe made the sign of the cross when Thomas talked of Mordecai. 'You can't take the word of such a man,' the priest said sternly. 'He may or may not be a good doctor, but the Jews have ever been

Christ's enemy. If he is on anyone's side it must be the devil's.'

'He's a good man,' Thomas insisted.

'Thomas! Thomas!' Father Hobbe said sadly, then frowned for a few heartbeats. 'I have heard,' he said after a while, 'that the Cathar heresy still lives.'

'But it can't challenge France and the Church!'

'You would know?' Father Hobbe asked. 'It reached out across the sea to steal the lance from your father, and you say it reached across France to kill Sir Guillaume's wife. The devil works his business in the dark, Thomas.'

'There's more,' Thomas said, and told the priest the story that the Cathars had the Grail. The light of the burning cottages flickered on the walls and gave the seaweed-crowned image on the altar a sinister cast. 'I don't think I believe any of it,' Thomas concluded.

'And why not?'

'Because if the story is true,' Thomas said, 'then I am not Thomas of Hookton, but Thomas Vexille. I'm not English, but some half-breed Frenchman. I'm not an archer, but noble born.'

'It gets worse,' Father Hobbe said with a smile. 'It means that you have been given a task.'

'They're just stories,' Thomas said scornfully. 'Give me another penance, Father. I'll make a pilgrimage for you, I'll go to Canterbury on my knees if that's what you want.'

'I want nothing of you, Thomas, but God wants a lot from you.'

'Then tell God to choose someone else.'

'I'm not in the habit of giving advice to the Almighty,'

Father Hobbe said, 'though I do listen to His. You think there is no Grail?'

'Men have sought it for a thousand years,' Thomas said, 'and no one has found it. Unless the thing in Genoa is real.'

Father Hobbe leaned his head against the wattle wall. 'I have heard,' he said quietly, 'that the real Grail is made of common clay. A simple peasant dish like the one my mother treasured, God rest her soul, for she could only afford the one good dish and then, clumsy fool that I am, I broke it one day. But the Grail, I am told, cannot be broken. You could put it in one of those guns that amused everyone at Caen and it would not break even if you dashed it against a castle wall. And when you place the bread and wine, the blood and flesh, of the Mass in that common piece of clay, Thomas, it turns to gold. Pure, shining gold. That is the Grail and, God help me, it does exist.'

'So you would have me wander the earth looking for a peasant's dish?' Thomas asked.

'God would,' Father Hobbe said, 'and for good reason.' He looked saddened. 'There is heresy everywhere, Thomas. The Church is besieged. The bishops and the cardinals and the abbots are corrupted by wealth, the village priests stew in ignorance and the devil is brewing his evil. Yet there are some of us, a few, who believe that the Church can be refreshed, that it can glow with God's glory again. I think the Grail could do that. I think God has chosen you.'

'Father!'

'And perhaps me,' Father Hobbe said, ignoring Thomas's protest. 'When this is all over,' he waved a hand to encompass the army and its plight, 'I think I

355

may join you. We shall seek your family together.'

'You?' Thomas asked. 'Why?'

'Because God calls,' Father Hobbe said simply, then jerked his head. 'You must go, Thomas, you must go. I shall pray for you.'

Thomas had to go because the night had been disturbed by the sound of horses' hooves and the strident voices of men. Thomas seized his bow and ducked out of the church to find that a score of men-at-arms were now in the village. Their shields carried the lions and stars of the Earl of Northumberland and their commander was demanding to know who was in charge of the archers.

'I am,' Thomas said.

'Where's this ford?'

Thomas made himself a torch from a sheaf of thatch lashed to a pole and, while its flame lasted, he led them across the marsh towards the distant ford. The flames flickered out after a while, but he was close enough to find his way to where he had seen the cattle. The tide had risen again and black water seeped and flooded all about the horsemen, who huddled on a shrinking ridge of sand.

'You can see where the other side is,' Thomas told the men-at-arms, pointing to the fires of the French, which looked to be about a mile away.

'Bastards are waiting for us?'

'Plenty of them too.'

'We're crossing anyway,' the leading man-at-arms said. 'The King's decided it, and we're doing it when the tide falls.' He turned to his men. 'Off your horses. Find the path. Mark it.' He pointed to some pollarded willows. 'Cut staves off them, use them as markers.'

Thomas groped his way back to the village, sometimes wading through water up to his waist. A thin mist was seeping from the flooding tide, and had it not been for the blazing huts in the village he could easily have got lost.

The village, built on the highest piece of land in all the marsh, had attracted a crowd of horsemen by the time Thomas returned. Archers and men-at-arms gathered there and some had already pulled down the shrine to make fires from its timbers.

Will Skeat had come with the rest of his archers. 'The women are with the baggage,' he told Thomas. 'Bloody chaos back there, it is. They're hoping to cross everyone in the morning.'

'Be a fight first,' Thomas said.

'Either that or fight their whole damn army later in the day. Did you find any eels?'

'We ate them.'

Skeat grinned, then turned as a voice hailed him. It was the Earl of Northampton, his horse's trapper spattered with mud almost to the saddle.

'Well done, Will!'

'Weren't me, my lord, it was this clever bastard.' Skeat jerked a thumb at Thomas.

'Hanging did you good, eh?' the Earl said, then watched as a file of men-of-arms climbed onto the village's sand ridge. 'Be ready to move at dawn, Will, and we'll be crossing when the tide falls. I want your boys in front. Leave your horses here; I'll have good men watch them.'

There was small sleep that night, though Thomas did doze as he lay on the sand and waited for the dawn, which brought a pale, misty light. Willow trees loomed in the vapour, while men-at-arms crouched at the tide's edge and stared north to where the mist was thickened by smoke from the enemy's fires. The river ran deceptively quick, hastened by the ebbing tide, but it was still too high to cross.

The sandbank by the ford held Skeat's fifty archers and another fifty under John Armstrong. There were the same number of men-at-arms, all on foot, led by the Earl of Northampton, who had been given the job of leading the crossing. The Prince of Wales had wanted to lead the fight himself, but his father had forbidden it. The Earl, far more experienced, had the responsibility and he was not happy. He would have liked many more men, but the sandbank would hold no more and the paths through the marshland were narrow and treacherous, making it difficult to bring reinforcements.

'You know what to do,' the Earl told Skeat and Armstrong.

'We know.'

'Maybe another two hours?' The Earl was judging the fall of the tide. The two hours crept by and the English could only stare through the thinning mist at the enemy, who formed their battleline at the ford's further side. The receding water let more men come to the sandbank, but the Earl's force was still pitifully small – perhaps two hundred men at most – while the French had double that number of men-at-arms alone. Thomas counted them as best he could, using the method Will Skeat had taught him: to divide the enemy in two, divide again, then count the small unit and multiply it by four, and he wished he had not done it for there were so many, and as well as the men-at-arms there had to be five or six hundred infantry, probably a levy from the country north of Abbeville. They were not a serious threat for, like most infantry, they would be ill-trained and badly armed with ancient weapons and farming tools, but they could still cause trouble if the Earl's men got into difficulties. The only blessing Thomas could find in the misty dawn was that the French seemed to have very few crossbowmen, but why would they need them when they had so many men-at-arms? And the formidable force that now gathered on the river's northern bank would be fighting in the knowledge that if they repelled the English attack then they would have their enemy pinned by the sea where the greater French army could crush them.

Two packhorses brought sheaves of precious arrows that were distributed among the archers. 'Ignore the goddamn peasants,' Skeat told his men. 'Kill the men-at-arms. I want the bastards crying for the goats they call their mothers.'

'There's food on the far side,' John Armstrong told his hungry men. 'Those goddamn bastards will have meat, bread and beer, and it'll be yours if you get through them.'

'And don't waste your arrows,' Skeat growled. 'Shoot proper! Aim, boys, aim. I want to see the bastards bleeding.'

'Watch the wind!' John Armstrong shouted. 'It'll carry arrows to the right.'

Two hundred of the French men-at-arms were on foot at the river's edge, while the other two hundred were mounted and waiting a hundred paces behind. The rabble of infantry was split into two vast lumps, one on each flank. The dismounted men-at-arms were there to stop the English at the water's edge and the mounted men would charge if any did break through, while the infantry was present to give the appearance of numbers and to help in the massacre that would follow the French victory. The French must have been confident for they had stopped every other attempt to ford the Somme.

Except at the other fords the enemy had possessed crossbowmen who had been able to keep the archers in deep water where they could not use their bows properly for fear of soaking the strings and here there were no crossbows.

The Earl of Northampton, on foot like his men, spat towards the river. 'He should have left his foot soldiers behind and brought a thousand Genoese,' he remarked to Will Skeat. 'We'd be in trouble then.'

'They'll have some crossbows,' Skeat said.

'Not enough, Will, not enough.' The Earl was wearing an old helmet, one without any face plate. He was accompanied by a grey-bearded man-at-arms with a deeply lined face, who wore a much-mended coat of mail. 'You know Reginald Cobham, Will?' the Earl asked.

'I've heard of you, Master Cobham,' Will said respectfully.

'And I of you. Master Skeat,' Cobham answered. A whisper went through Skeat's archers that Reginald Cobham was at the ford and men turned to look at the greybeard whose name was celebrated in the army. A common man, like themselves, but old in war and feared by England's enemies.

The Earl looked at a pole which marked one edge of the ford. 'Reckon the water's low enough,' he said, then patted Skeat's shoulder. 'Go and kill some, Will.'

Thomas took one glance behind and saw that every dry spot of the marsh was now crowded with soldiers, horses and women. The English army had come into the lowlands, depending on the Earl to force the crossing.

Off to the east, though none at the ford knew it, the main French army was filing across the bridge at Abbeville, ready to fall on the English rear.

There was a brisk wind coming from the sea, bringing a morning chill and the smell of salt. Gulls called forlorn above the pale reeds. The river's main channel was a half-mile wide and the hundred archers looked a puny force as they spread into a line and waded into the tide. Armstrong's men were on the left, Skeat's on the right, while behind them came the first of the earl's men-at-arms. Those men-at-arms were all on foot and their job was to wait till the arrows had weakened the enemy, then charge into the French with swords, axes and falchions. The enemy had two drummers, who began thumping their goatskins, then a trumpeter startled birds from the trees where the French had camped.

'Note the wind,' Skeat shouted at his men. 'Gusting hard, she is, gusting hard.'

The wind was blowing against the ebbing tide, forcing the river into small waves that whipped white at their tops. The French infantry were shouting. Grey clouds scudded above the green land. The drummers kept up a threatening rhythm. Banners flew above the waiting men-at-arms and Thomas was relieved that none of them showed yellow hawks on a blue field. The water was cold and came to his thighs. He held his bow high, watching the enemy, waiting for the first crossbow bolts to whip across the water.

No bolts came. The archers were within long bowshot

range now, but Will Skeat wanted them closer. A French knight on a black horse caparisoned with a green and blue trapper rode to where his comrades were on foot, then swerved off to one side and splashed into the river.

'Silly bastard wants to make a name,' Skeat said. 'Jake! Dan! Peter! Settle the bastard for me.' The three bows were drawn back and three arrows flew.

The French knight was hurled back in his saddle and his fall provoked the French to fury. They gave their war shout, *'Montjoie St Denis!'* and the men-at-arms came splashing into the river, ready to challenge the archers, who drew back their bows.

'Hold hard!' Skeat shouted. 'Hold hard! Closer, get closer!' The drumbeats were louder. The dead knight was being carried away by his horse as the other French edged back to the dry land. The water only reached to Thomas's knees now and the range was shortening. A hundred paces, no more, and Will Skeat was at last satisfied. 'Start putting them down!' he shouted.

The bowcords were drawn back to men's ears, then loosed. The arrows flew, and while the first flight was still whispering over the wind-flecked water the second flight was released, and as the men put their third arrows on the strings the first whipped home. The sound was of metal striking metal, like a hundred light hammers tapping, and the French ranks were suddenly crouching with shields held high.

'Pick your men!' Skeat shouted. 'Pick your men!' He was using his own bow, shooting it infrequently, always waiting for an enemy to lower a shield before loosing an arrow. Thomas was watching the rabble of infantry to his right. They looked as though they were ready to make a wild charge and he wanted to plant some arrows in their bellies before they reached the water.

A score of French men-at-arms were dead or wounded and their leader was shouting at the others to lock their shields. A dozen of the rearward men-at-arms had dismounted and were hurrying forward to reinforce the riverbank.

'Steady, boys, steady,' John Armstrong called. 'Make the arrows count.'

The enemy shields were quilled with arrows. The French were relying on those shields that were thick enough to slow an arrow, and they were staying low, waiting for the arrows to run out or for the English men-at-arms to come close. Thomas reckoned some of the arrows would have driven clean through the shields to inflict wounds, but they were mostly wasted. He glanced back to the infantry and saw they were not moving yet. The English bows were firing less frequently, waiting for their targets, and the Earl of Northampton must have tired of the delay, or else he feared the turn of the tide for he shouted his men forward. 'St George! St George!'

'Spread wide!' Will Skeat shouted, wanting his men to be on the flanks of the Earl's attack so they could use their arrows when the French stood to receive the charge, but the water rapidly grew deeper as Thomas moved upstream and he could not go as far as he wanted.

'Kill them! Kill them!' The Earl was wading up to the bank now.

'Keep ranks!' Reginald Cobham shouted.

The French men-at-arms gave a cheer, for the proximity of the English charge meant the archers' aim would be blocked, though Thomas did manage to loose two arrows as the defenders stood and before the two groups of men-at-arms met at the river's edge with a clash of steel and shield. Men roared their war cries, St Denis contending with St George.

'Watch right! Watch right!' Thomas shouted, for the peasant infantrymen had started forward and he sent two arrows whistling at them. He was plucking shafts from the arrow bag as fast as he could.

'Take the horsemen!' Will Skeat bellowed, and Thomas changed his aim to send an arrow over the heads of the fighting men at the French horsemen who were advancing down the bank to help their comrades. Some English horsemen had entered the ford now, but they could not ride to meet their French counterparts because the ford's northern exit was blocked by the wild mêlée of men-at-arms.

Men slashed and hacked. Swords met axes, falchions split helmets and skulls. The noise was like the devil's blacksmith shop and blood was swirling down tide in the shallows. A Englishman screamed as he was cut down into the water, then screamed again as two Frenchmen drove axes into his legs and trunk. The Earl was thrusting his sword in short hard lunges, ignoring the hammer blows on his shield.

'Close up! Close up!' Reginald Cobham shouted. A man tripped on a body, opening a gap in the English line, and three howling Frenchmen tried to exploit it, but were met by a man with a double-headed axe who struck down so hard that the heavy blade split a helmet and skull from nape to neck.

'Flank them! Flank them!' Skeat bellowed, and his archers waded closer to the shore to drive their arrows into the sides of the French formation. Two hundred French knights were fighting eighty or ninety English men-at-arms, a brawl of swords and shields and monstrous clangour. Men grunted as they swung. The two front ranks were locked together now, shields against shields, and it was the men behind who did the killing, swinging their blades over the front rank to kill the men beyond. Most of the archers were pouring arrows into the French flanks while a few, led by John Armstrong, had closed up behind the men-at-arms to shoot into the enemy's faces.

The French infantry, thinking the English charge stalled, gave a cheer and began to advance. 'Kill them! Kill them!' Thomas shouted. He had used a whole sheaf of arrows, twenty-four shafts, and had only one sheaf more. He drew the bow back, released, drew again. Some of the French infantry had padded jackets, but they were no protection against the arrows. Sheer numbers was their best defence and they screamed a wild war cry as they pounded down the bank. But then a score of English horsemen came from behind the archers, pushing through them to meet the mad charge. The mailed riders chopped hard into the infantry's front ranks, swords flailing left and right as the peasants hacked back. The horses bit at the enemy, and always kept moving so that no one could slash their hamstrings. A man-at-arms was hauled from his saddle and screamed terribly as he was chopped to death in the shallows. Thomas and his archers drove their arrows into the mob, more horsemen rode to help slaughter them, but still the wild rabble crowded the bank and suddenly Thomas had no arrows left and so he hung the bow round his neck, drew his sword and ran to the river's edge.

A Frenchman lunged at Thomas with a spear. He knocked it aside and brought the sword's tip flashing round to rip the man's gullet. Blood spilled bright as dawn, vanishing into the river. He hacked at a second man. Sam, baby-faced Sam, was beside him with a billhook that he sliced into a skull. It stuck there and Sam kicked the man in frustration, then took an axe from the dying enemy and, leaving his billhook in its victim, swung his new weapon in a great arc to drive the enemy back. Jake still had arrows and was shooting them fast.

A splashing and a cheer announced the arrival of more mounted men-at-arms, who drove into the infantry with heavy lances. The big horses, trained to this carnage, rode over the living and dead while the men-at-arms discarded the spears and started hacking with swords. More archers had come with fresh arrows and were shooting from the river's centre.

Thomas was on the bank now. The front of his mail coat was red with blood, none of it his, and the infantry was retreating. Then Will Skeat gave a great shout that more arrows had come, and Thomas and his archers ran back into the river to find Father Hobbe with a pack mule loaded with two panniers of arrow sheaves.

'Do the Lord's work,' Father Hobbe said, tossing a sheaf to Thomas, who undid its binding and spilled the arrows into his bag. A trumpet sounded from the northern bank and he whirled round to see that the French horsemen were riding to join the fight.

'Put them down!' Skeat shouted. 'Put those bastards down!'

Arrows slashed and sliced at horses. More English men-at-arms were wading the river to thicken the Earl's force and, inch by inch, yard by yard, they were making progress up the bank, but then the enemy horsemen drove into the mêlée with lances and swords. Thomas put an arrow through the mail covering a Frenchman's throat, drove another through a leather chanfron so that the horse reared and screamed and spilled its rider.

'Kill! Kill! Kill!' The Earl of Northampton, bloodied from his helmet to his mailed boots, rammed the sword again and again. He was bone tired and deafened by the crack of steel, but he was climbing the bank and his men were pressed close about him. Cobham was killing with a calm certainty, years of experience behind every blow. English horsemen were in the mêlée now, using their lances over the heads of their compatriots to drive the enemy horses back, but they were also blocking the aim of the archers and Thomas again hung his bow round his neck and drew his sword. 'St George! St George!' The Earl was standing on grass now, out of the reeds, above the high-water mark and behind him the river's edge was a charnel house of dead men, wounded men, blood and screaming.

Father Hobbe, his cassock skirts hitched up to his waist, was fighting with a quarterstaff, ramming the pole into French faces. 'In the name of the Father,' he shouted, and a Frenchmen reeled back with a pulped eye, 'and of the Son,' Father Hobbe snarled as he broke a man's nose, 'and of the Holy Ghost!'

A French knight broke through the English ranks, but a dozen archers swarmed over the horse, hamstrung it and hauled its rider down to the mud where they hacked at him with axe, billhook and sword.

'Archers!' the Earl shouted. 'Archers!' The last of the French horsemen had formed into a charge that threatened to sweep the whole ragged mess of brawling men, both English and French, into the river, but a score of archers, the only ones with arrows now, drove their missiles up the bank to bring the leading rank of horsemen down in a tangle of horses' legs and tumbling weapons.

Another trumpet sounded, this one from the English side, and reinforcements were suddenly streaming over the ford and spurring up onto the higher ground.

'They're breaking! They're breaking.' Thomas did not know who shouted that news, but it was true. The French were shuffling backwards. The infantry, their stomach for battle slaked by the deaths they had suffered, had already retreated, but now the French knights, the men-at-arms, were backing away from the fury of the English assault.

'Just kill them! Kill them! No prisoners! No prisoners!' the Earl of Northampton shouted in French, and his men-at-arms, bloody and wet and tired and angry, shoved up the bank and hacked again at the French, who stepped another pace back.

And then the enemy did break. It was sudden. One moment the two forces were locked in grunting, shoving, hacking battle, and then the French were running and the ford was streaming with mounted men-at-arms who crossed from the southern bank to pursue the broken enemy.

'Jesus,' Will Skeat said, and dropped to his knees and made the sign of the cross. A dying Frenchman groaned nearby, but Skeat ignored him. 'Jesus,' he said again. 'You got any arrows, Tom?'

'Two left.'

'Jesus.' Skeat looked up. There was blood on his

cheeks. 'Those bastards,' he said vengefully. He was speaking of the newly arrived English men-at-arms who crashed past the remnants of the battle to harry the fleeing enemy. 'Those bastards! They get into their camp first, don't they? They'll take all the bloody food!'

But the ford was taken, the trap was broken and the English were across the Somme.

PART THREE

Crécy

The whole English army had crossed before the tide rose again. Horses, wagons, men and women – they all crossed safe so that the French army, marching from Abbeville to trap them, found the corner of land between the river and the sea empty.

All next day the armies faced each other across the ford. The English were drawn up for battle with their four thousand archers lining the river's bank and, behind them, three great blocks of men-at-arms on the higher ground, but the French, strung out on the paths to the ford, were not tempted to force the crossing. A handful of their knights rode into the water and shouted challenges and insults, but the King would not let any English knight respond and the archers, knowing they must conserve their arrows, endured the insults without responding.

'Let the bastards shout,' Will Skeat growled, 'shouting never hurt a man yet.' He grinned at Thomas. 'Depends on the man, of course. Upset Sir Simon, didn't it?'

'He was just a bastard.'

'No, Tom,' Skeat corrected him, 'you're the bastard, and he was a gentleman.' Skeat looked across at the French, who showed no sign of trying to contest the ford. 'Most of them are all right,' he went on, evidently talking of knights and nobles. 'Once they've fought with the archers for a while they learn to look after us on account of us being the mucky bastards what keeps them alive, but there's always a few goddamn idiots. Not our Billy, though.' He turned and looked at the Earl of Northampton, who was pacing up and down by the shallows, itching for the French to come and fight. 'He's a proper gentleman. Knows how to kill the goddamn French.'

Next morning the French were gone, the only sign of them the white cloud of dust hanging over the road which was taking their huge army back to Abbeville. The English went north, slowed by hunger and the lame horses that men were reluctant to abandon. The army climbed from the Somme marshes into a heavily wooded country that yielded no grain, livestock or plunder, while the weather, which had been dry and warm, turned cold and wet during the morning. Rain spat from the east and dripped incessantly from the trees to increase men's misery so that what had seemed like a victorious campaign south of the Seine now felt like an ignominious retreat. Which is what it was, for the English were running from the French and all the men knew it, just as they knew that unless they found food soon their weakness would make them easy pickings for the enemy.

The King had sent a strong force to the mouth of the Somme where, at the small port of Le Crotoy, he expected reinforcements and supplies to be waiting, but instead the small port proved to be held by a garrison of Genoese crossbowmen. The walls were in bad repair, the attackers were hungry and so the Genoese died under a hail of arrows and a storm of men-at-arms.

The English emptied the port's storehouses of food and found a herd of beef cattle collected for the French army's use, but when they climbed the church tower they saw no ships moored in the river's mouth nor any fleet waiting at sea. The arrows, the archers and the grain that should have replenished the army were still in England.

The rain became heavier on the first night that the army camped in the forest. Rumour said that the King and his great men were in a village at the forest's edge, but most of the men were forced to shelter under the dripping trees and eat what little they could scavenge.

'Acorn stew,' Jake grumbled.

'You've eaten worse,' Thomas said.

'And a month ago we ate it off silver plates.' Jake spat out a gritty mouthful. 'So why don't we bloody fight the bastards?'

'Because they're too many,' Thomas said wearily, 'because we've only so many arrows. Because we're worn out.'

The army had marched itself into the ground. Jake, like a dozen other of Will Skeat's archers, had no boots any more. The wounded limped because there were not enough carts and the sick were left behind if they could not walk or crawl. The living stank.

Thomas had made Eleanor and himself a shelter from boughs and turf. It was dry inside the little hut where a small fire spewed a thick smoke.

'What happens to me if you lose?' Eleanor asked him.

'We won't lose,' Thomas said, though there was little conviction in his voice.

'What happens to me?' she asked again.

'You thank the Frenchmen who find you,' he said,

'and tell them you were forced to march with us against your will. Then you send for your father.'

Eleanor thought about those answers for a while, but did not look reassured. She had learned in Caen how men after victory are not amenable to reason, but slaves to their appetites. She shrugged. 'And what happens to you?'

'If I live?' Thomas shook his head. 'I'll be a prisoner. They send us to the galleys in the south, I hear. If they let us live.'

'Why shouldn't they?'

'They don't like archers. They hate archers.' He pushed a pile of wet bracken closer to the fire, trying to dry the fronds before they became their bed. 'Maybe there won't be a battle,' he said, 'because we've stolen a day's march on them.' The French were said to have gone back to Abbeville and to be crossing the river there, which meant that the hunters were coming, but the English were still a day ahead and could, perhaps, reach their fortresses in Flanders. Perhaps.

Eleanor blinked from the smoke. 'Have you seen any knight carrying the lance?'

Thomas shook his head. 'I haven't even looked,' he confessed. The last thing on his mind this night was the mysterious Vexilles. Nor, indeed, did he expect to see the lance. That was Sir Guillaume's fancy and now Father Hobbe's enthusiasm, but it was not Thomas's obsession. Staying alive and finding enough to eat were what consumed him.

'Thomas!' Will Skeat called from outside.

Thomas pushed his head through the hut opening to see a cloaked figure was standing next to Skeat. 'I'm here,' he said.

'You've got company,' Skeat said sourly, turning away.

The cloaked figure stooped to enter the hut and, to Thomas's surprise, it was Jeanette. 'I shouldn't be here,' she greeted him, pushing into the smoky interior where, throwing the hood from her hair, she stared at Eleanor. 'Who's that?'

'My woman,' Thomas spoke in English.

'Tell her to go,' Jeanette said in French.

'Stay here,' Thomas told Eleanor. 'This is the Countess of Armorica.'

Jeanette bridled when Thomas contradicted her, but did not insist that Eleanor left. Instead she pushed a bag at Thomas that proved to contain a leg of ham, a loaf of bread and a stone bottle of wine. The bread, Thomas saw, was the fine white bread that only the rich could afford, while the ham was studded with cloves and sticky with honey.

He handed the bag to Eleanor. 'Food fit for a prince,' he told her.

'I should take it to Will?' Eleanor asked, for the archers had agreed to share all their food.

'Yes, but it can wait,' Thomas said.

'I shall take it now,' Eleanor said, and pulled a cloak over her head before vanishing into the wet darkness.

'She's pretty enough,' Jeanette said in French.

'All my women are pretty,' Thomas said. 'Fit for princes, they are.'

Jeanette looked angry, or perhaps it was just the smoke from the small fire irritating her. She prodded the hut's side. 'This reminds me of our journey.'

'It wasn't cold or wet.' Thomas said. And you were mad, he wanted to add, and I nursed you and you walked away from me without looking back.

Jeanette heard the hostility in his voice. 'He thinks,' she said, 'that I am saying confession.'

'Then tell me your sins,' Thomas responded, 'and you won't have lied to His Highness.'

Jeanette ignored that. 'You know what is going to happen now?'

'We run away, they chase us, and either they catch us or they don't.' He spoke brusquely. 'And if they catch us there'll be a blood-letting.'

'They will catch us,' Jeanette said confidently, 'and there will be a battle.'

'You know that?'

'I listen to what is reported to the Prince,' she said, 'and the French are on the good roads. We are not.'

That made sense. The ford by which the English army had crossed the Seine led only into marshland and forest. It was a link between villages, it lay on no great trading route and so no good roads led from its banks, but the French had crossed the river at Abbeville, a city of merchants, and so the enemy army would have wide roads to hasten their march into Picardy. They were well fed, they were fresh and now they had the good roads to speed them.

'So there'll be a battle,' Thomas said, touching his black bow.

'There is to be a battle,' Jeanette confirmed. 'It's been decided. Probably tomorrow or the next day. The King says there is a hill just outside the forest where we can fight. Better that, he says, than letting the French get ahead and block our road. But either way,' she paused, 'they will win.'

'Maybe,' Thomas allowed.

'They will win,' Jeanette insisted. 'I listen to the conversations, Thomas! They are too many.'

Thomas made the sign of the cross. If Jeanette was right, and he had no reason to think she was deceiving him, then the army's leaders had already given up hope, but that did not mean he had to despair. 'They have to beat us first,' he said stubbornly.

'They will,' Jeanette said brutally, 'and what happens to me then?'

'What happens to you?' Thomas asked in surprise. He leaned cautiously against the fragile wall of his shelter. He sensed that Eleanor had already delivered the food and hurried back to eavesdrop. 'Why should I care,' he asked loudly, 'what happens to you?'

Jeanette shot him a vicious look. 'You once swore to me,' she said, 'that you would help restore my son to me.'

Thomas made the sign of the cross again. 'I did, my lady,' he admitted, reflecting that he made his oaths too easily. One oath was enough for a lifetime and he had made more then he could recall or keep.

'Then help me do that,' Jeanette demanded.

Thomas smiled. 'There's a battle to be won first, my lady.'

Jeanette scowled at the smoke that churned in the small shelter. 'If I am found in the English camp after the battle, Thomas, then I will never see Charles again. Never.'

'Why not?' Thomas demanded. 'It's not as if you'll be in danger, my lady. You're not a common woman. There might not be much chivalry when armies meet, but it just about reaches into the tents of royalty.'

Jeanette shook her head impatiently. 'If the English

win,' she said, 'then I might see Charles again because the Duke will want to curry favour with the King. But if they lose, then he will have no need to make any gesture. And if they lose, Thomas, then I lose everything.'

That, Thomas reckoned, was closer to the nub. If the English lost then Jeanette risked losing whatever wealth she had accumulated in the last weeks, wealth that came from the gifts of a prince. He could see a necklace of what looked like rubies half hidden by her swathing cloak, and doubtless she had dozens of other precious stones set in gold.

'So what do you want of me?' he asked.

She leaned forward and lowered her voice. 'You,' she said, 'and a handful of men. Take me south. I can hire a ship at Le Crotoy and sail to Brittany. I have money now. I can pay my debts in La Roche-Derrien and I can deal with that evil lawyer. No one need know I was even here.'

'The Prince will know,' Thomas said.

She bridled at that. 'You think he will want me for ever?'

'What do I know of him?'

'He will tire of me,' Jeanette said. 'He's a prince. He takes what he wants and when he is tired of it he moves on. But he has been good to me, so I cannot complain.'

Thomas said nothing for a while. She had not been this hard, he reflected, in those lazy summer days when they had lived as vagabonds. 'And your son?' he asked. 'How will you get him back? Pay for him?'

'I will find a way,' she said evasively.

Probably, Thomas thought, she would try to kidnap

the boy, and why not? If she could raise some men then it would be possible. Maybe she would expect Thomas himself to do it and as that thought occurred to him so Jeanette looked into his eyes.

'Help me,' she said, 'please.'

'No,' Thomas said, 'not now.' He held up a hand to ward off her protests. 'One day, God willing,' he went on, 'I'll help find your son, but I'll not leave this army now. If there's to be a battle, my lady, then I'm in it with the rest.'

'I am begging you,' she said.

'No.'

'Then damn you,' she spat, pulled the hood over her black hair and went out into the darkness. There was a short pause, then Eleanor came through the entrance.

'So what did you think?' Thomas asked.

'I think she is pretty,' Eleanor said evasively, then she frowned at him, 'and I think that in battle tomorrow a man could seize you by the hair. I think you should cut it.'

Thomas seemed to flinch. 'You want to go south? Escape battle?'

Eleanor gave him a reproachful look. 'I am an archer's woman,' she said, 'and you will not go south. Will says you are a goddamn fool,' she said the last two words in clumsy English, 'to give up such good food, but thanks you anyway. And Father Hobbe tells you that he is saying Mass tomorrow morning and expects you to be there.'

Thomas drew his knife and gave it to her, then bent his head. She sawed at his pigtail, then at handfuls of black hair that she tossed onto the fire. Thomas said nothing as she cut, but just thought about Father

Hobbe's Mass. A Mass for the dead, he thought, or for those about to die.

For in the wet dark, beyond the forest, the might of France was drawing close. The English had escaped the enemy twice, crossing rivers that were supposed to be impassable, but they could not escape a third time. The French had caught them at last.

The village lay only a short walk north of the forest's edge from which it was separated by a small river that twisted through placid water meadows. The village was an unremarkable place: a duckpond, a small church and a score of cottages with thick thatched roofs, small gardens and high dungheaps. The village, like the forest, was called Crécy.

The fields north of the village rose to a long hill that ran north and south. A country road, rutted by farm carts, ran along the hill's crest, going from Crécy to another village, just as unremarkable, called Wadicourt. If an army had marched from Abbeville and skirted the Forest of Crécy it would come westwards in search of the English and, after a while, they would see the hill between Crécy and Wadicourt rearing in front of them. They would see the stump-like church towers in the two small villages, and between the villages, but much closer to Crécy and high on the ridge top where its sails could catch the winds, a mill. The slope facing the French was long and smooth, untroubled by hedge or ditch, a playground for knights on horseback.

The army was woken before dawn. It was a Saturday, 26 August, and men grumbled at the unseasonable chill. Fires were stirred to life, reflecting flame light from the waiting mail and plate armour. The village of Crécy had been occupied by the King and his great lords, some of whom had slept in the church, and those men were still arming themselves when a chaplain of the royal household came to say a Mass. Candles were lit, a hand-bell sounded and the priest, ignoring the clank of armour that filled the small nave, called on the help of St Zephyrinus, St Gelasinus and both the saints called Genesius, all of whom had their feasts on this day, and the priest also sought aid from Little Sir Hugh of Lincoln, a child who had been murdered by the Jews on this same day nearly two hundred years before. The boy, who was said to have shown a remarkable piety, had been found dead, and no one understood how God could have allowed such a paragon to be snatched from earth so young, but there were Jews in Lincoln and their presence had provided a convenient answer. The priest prayed to them all. St Zephyrinus, he prayed, give us victory. St Gelasinus, he pleaded, be with our men. St Genesius, look after us, and St Genesius, give us strength. Little Sir Hugh, he begged, thou child in God's arms, intercede for us. Dear God, he prayed, in Thy great mercy, spare us. The knights came to the altar in their linen shirts to receive the Sacraments.

In the forest the archers knelt to other priests. They made confession and took the dry, stale bread that was the body of Christ. They made the sign of the cross. No one knew there was to be a battle that day, but they sensed the campaign had come to its end and they must either fight today or the next. Give us enough arrows, the archers prayed, and we shall make the earth red, and they held their yew staves towards the priests who touched the bows and said prayers over them.

Lances were unwrapped. They had been carried on packhorses or wagons and had hardly been used in the campaign, but the knights all dreamed of a proper battle of swirling horsemen punctuated by the shock of lances striking shields. The older and wiser men knew they would fight on foot and that their weapons would mostly be swords or axes or falchions, but still the painted lances were taken from their cloth or leather coverings that protected them from being dried by the sun or warped by rain. 'We can use them as pikes,' the Earl of Northampton suggested.

Squires and pages armed their knights, helping them with the heavy coats of leather, mail and plate. Straps were buckled tight. Destriers were brushed with straw while the smiths dragged sharpening stones down the swords' long blades. The King, who had begun arming himself at four in the morning, knelt and kissed a reliquary which contained a feather from the wing of the angel Gabriel and, when he had crossed himself, told the priest to carry the reliquary to his son. Then, with a golden crown surrounding his helmet, he was helped up onto a grey mare and rode north from the village.

It was dawn and the ridge between the two villages was empty. The mill, its linen sails neatly furled and tethered, creaked in the wind that stirred the long grasses where hares grazed but now cocked their ears and raced away as the horsemen climbed the track to the mill.

The King led, mounted on the mare that was swathed in a trapper bright with the royal arms. The scabbard of his sword was red velvet and encrusted with golden fleur-de-lis, while the hilt was decorated with a dozen great rubies. He carried a long white staff and had brought a dozen companions and a score of knights as escorts, but as his companions were all great lords then they were duly followed by their entourages so that close to three hundred men trailed up the winding track. The higher a man's rank, the closer he rode to the King, while the pages and squires were at the back where they tried to hear the conversation of their betters.

A man-at-arms dismounted and went into the mill. He climbed the ladders, opened the small door that gave access to the sails and there straddled the axle as he peered eastwards.

'See anything?' the King called up cheerfully, but the man was so overcome by being addressed by his king that he could only shake his head dumbly.

The sky was half covered in clouds and the country looked dark. From the mill's height the man-at-arms could see down the long slope to the small fields at its foot, then up another slope to a wood. An empty road ran eastwards beyond the wood. The river, filled with English horses being watered, twisted grey on the right to mark the forest's edge. The King, his visor jammed up against the crown's frontal, stared at the same view. A local man, discovered hiding in the forest, had confirmed that the road from Abbeville came from the east, which meant that the French must cross the small fields at the foot of the slope if they were to make a frontal attack on the hill. The fields had no hedges, merely shallow ditches that would offer no obstacle to a mounted knight.

'If I was Philip,' the Earl of Northampton suggested, 'I'd ride round our north flank, sire.'

'You're not Philip, and I thank God you're not,' Edward of England said. 'He's not clever.'

'And I am?' The Earl sounded surprised.

'You are clever at war, William,' the King said. He stared down the slope for a long time. 'If I was Philip,' he said at last, 'I would be mightily tempted by those fields,' he pointed to the foot of the slope, 'especially if I saw our men waiting on this hill.' The long green slope of the open pastureland was perfect for a cavalry charge. It was an invitation for lances and glory, a place made by God for the lords of France to tear an impudent enemy to ragged shreds.

'The hill's steep, sire,' the Earl of Warwick warned.

'I warrant it won't look so from the foot,' the King said, then turned his horse and spurred northwards along the ridge. The mare trotted easily, revelling in the morning air. 'She's Spanish,' the King told the Earl, 'bought off Grindley. D'you use him?'

'If I can afford his prices.'

'Of course you can, William! A rich man like you? I'll breed her. She might make fine destriers.'

'If she does, sire, I'll buy one from you.'

'If you can't afford Grindley's prices,' the King teased, 'how will you pay mine?'

He spurred the mare into a canter, his plate armour clanking, and the long train of men hurried after him along the track which led north on the ridge's summit. Green shoots of wheat and barley, doomed to die in the winter, grew where the grains had fallen from the carts carrying the harvest to the mill. The King stopped at the ridge's end, just above the village of Wadicourt, and stared northwards. His cousin was right, he thought. Philip should march into that empty countryside and cut him off from Flanders. The French, if they did but know it, were the masters here. Their army was larger, their men fresher and they could dance rings about their tired enemy until the English were forced to a desperate attack or were trapped in a place that offered them no advantage. But Edward knew better than to let every fear prey on his mind. The French were also desperate. They had suffered the humiliation of watching an enemy army wreak havoc across their land and they were in no mood to be clever. They wanted revenge. Offer them a chance, he reckoned, and the odds were good that they would snatch at it, and so the King dismissed his fears and rode down into the village of Wadicourt. A handful of the villagers had dared to stay and those folk, seeing the golden crown encircling the King's helmet and the silver curb chains on his mare, went onto their knees.

'We mean you no harm,' the King called airily, but by morning's end, he knew, their houses would have been ransacked thoroughly.

He turned southwards again, riding along the ground at the foot of the ridge. The valley's turf was soft, but not treacherous. A horse would not flounder here, a charge would be possible and – better still, just as he had reckoned – the hill did not look so steep from this angle. It was deceptive. The long stretch of rising grass looked gentle even, though in truth it would sap the horses' lungs by the time they reached the English men-at-arms. If they ever did reach them.

'How many arrows do we have?' he asked every man in earshot.

'Twelve hundred sheaves,' the Bishop of Durham said.

'Two carts full,' the Earl of Warwick answered.

'Eight hundred and sixty sheaves,' the Earl of Northampton said.

There was silence for a while. 'The men have some themselves?' the King asked.

'Perhaps a sheaf apiece,' the Earl of Northampton said gloomily.

'It will just have to be enough,' the King said bleakly. He would have liked twice as many arrows, but then he would have liked a lot of things. He could have wished for twice as many men and a hill twice as steep and an enemy led by a man twice as nervous as Philip of Valois who, God knows, was nervous enough anyway, but it was no good wishing. He had to fight and win. He frowned at the southern end of the ridge where it fell away to the village of Crécy. That would be the easiest place for the French to attack, and the closest too, which meant the fight would be hard there. 'Guns, William,' he said to the Earl of Northampton.

'Guns, sire?'

'We'll have the guns on the flanks. Bloody things have to be useful some time!'

'We could roll the things down the hill, sire, perhaps? Maybe crush a man or two?'

The King laughed and rode on. 'Looks like rain.'

'It should hold off a while,' the Earl of Warwick answered. 'And the French may hold off too, sire.'

'You think they won't come, William?'

The Earl shook his head. 'They'll come, sire, but it'll take them time. A lot of time. We might see their vanguard by noon, but their rearguard will still be crossing the bridge in Abbeville. I'll wager they'll wait till tomorrow morning to make a fight.'

'Today or tomorrow,' the King said carelessly, 'it's all the same.'

'We could march on,' the Earl of Warwick suggested.

'And find a better hill?' The King smiled. He was younger and less experienced than many of the earls, but he was also the King and so the decision must rest with him. He was, in truth, filled with doubts, but knew that he must look confident. He would fight here. He said as much and said it firmly.

'We fight here,' the King said again, staring up the slope. He was imagining his army there, seeing it as the French would see it, and he knew his suspicion was right that the lowest part of the ridge, close to Crécy, would be the dangerous ground. That would be his right flank, close under the mill. 'My son will command on the right,' he said, pointing, 'and you, William, will be with him.'

'I will, sire,' the Earl of Northampton agreed.

'And you, my lord, on the left,' the King said to the Earl of Warwick. 'We shall make our line two-thirds of the way up the hill with archers in front and on the flanks.'

'And you, sire?' the Earl of Warwick asked.

'I shall be at the mill,' the King said, then urged his horse up the hill. He dismounted two-thirds of the way up the slope and waited for a squire to take the mare's reins, then he began the morning's real work. He paced along the hill, marking places by prodding the turf with his white staff and instructing the lords who accompanied him that their men would be here, or there, and those lords sent men to summon their commanders so that when the army marched to the long green slope they would know where to go.

'Bring the banners here,' the King ordered, 'and place them where the men are to assemble.'

He kept his army in the three battles that had marched all the way from Normandy. Two, the largest, would make a long, thick line of men-at-arms stretching across the upper reaches of the slope. 'They'll fight on foot,' the King ordered, confirming what every man had expected though one or two of the younger lords still groaned for there was more honour to be gained by fighting from horseback. But Edward cared more about victory than honour. He knew only too well that if his men-at-arms were mounted then the fools would make a charge as soon as the French attacked and his battle would degenerate into a brawl at the hill's foot that the French must win because they had the advantage of numbers. But if his men were on foot then they could not make a crazed charge against horsemen, but must wait behind their shields to be attacked. 'The horses are to be kept at the rear, beyond the ridge,' he commanded. He himself would command the third and smallest battle on the ridge's summit where it would be a reserve.

'You will stay with me, my lord bishop,' the King told the Bishop of Durham.

The bishop, armoured from nape to toes and carrying a massive spiked mace, bridled. 'You'll deny me a chance to break French heads, sire?'

'I shall let you weary God with your prayers instead,' the King said, and his lords laughed. 'And our archers,' the King went on, 'will be here, and here, and here.' He was pacing the turf and ramming the white staff into the grass every few paces. He would cover his line with archers, and mass more at the two flanks. The archers, Edward knew, were his one advantage. Their long, white-fledged arrows would do murder in this place that invited the enemy horsemen into the glorious charge. 'Here,' he stepped on and gouged the turf again, 'and here.'

'You want pits, sire?' the Earl of Northampton asked.

'As many as you like, William,' the King said. The archers, once they were gathered in their groups all along the face of the line, would be told to dig pits in the turf some yards down the slope. The pits did not have to be large, just big enough to break a horse's leg if it did not see the hole. Make enough pits and the charge must be slowed and thrown into disarray. 'And here,' the King had reached the southern end of the ridge, 'we'll park some empty wagons. Put half the guns here, and the other half at the other end. And I want more archers here.'

'If we've any left,' the Earl of Warwick grumbled.

'Wagons?' the Earl of Northampton asked.

'Can't charge a horse across a line of wagons, William,' the King said cheerfully, then beckoned his horse forward and, because his plate armour was so heavy, two pages had to half lift and half push him into the saddle. It meant an undignified scramble, but once he was settled in the saddle he looked back along the ridge that was no longer empty, but was dotted with the first banners showing where men would assemble. In an hour or two, he thought, his whole army would be here to lure the French into the archers' arrows. He wiped the earth from the butt of the staff, then spurred his horse towards Crécy. 'Let's see if there's any food,' he said.

The first flags fluttered on the empty ridge. The sky

pressed grey across distant fields and woods. Rain fell to the north and the wind felt cold. The eastern road, along which the French must come, was deserted still. The priests prayed.

Take pity on us, O Lord, in Thy great mercy, take pity on us.

The man who called himself the Harlequin was in the woods on the hill that lay to the east of the ridge that ran between Crécy and Wadicourt. He had left Abbeville in the middle of the night, forcing the sentries to open the northern gate, and he had led his men through the dark with the help of an Abbeville priest who knew the local roads. Then, hidden by beeches, he had watched the King of England ride and walk the far ridge. Now the King was gone, but the green turf was speckled with banners and the first English troops were straggling up from the village. 'They expect us to fight here,' he remarked.

'It's as good a place as any,' Sir Simon Jekyll observed grumpily. He did not like being roused in the middle of the night. He knew that the strange black-clad man who called himself the Harlequin had offered to be a scout for the French army, but he had not thought that all the Harlequin's followers would be expected to miss their breakfast and grope through a black and empty countryside for six cold hours.

'It is a ridiculous place to fight,' the Harlequin responded. 'They will line that hill with archers and we will have to ride straight into their points. What we should do is go round their flank.' He pointed to the north.

'Tell His Majesty that,' Sir Simon said spitefully.

'I doubt he will listen to me.' The Harlequin heard the scorn, but did not rise to it. 'Not yet. When we have made our name, then he will listen.' He patted his horse's neck. 'I have only faced English arrows once, and then it was merely a single archer, but I saw an arrow go clean through a mail coat.'

'I've seen an arrow go through two inches of oak,' Sir Simon said.

'Three inches,' Henry Colley added. He, like Sir Simon, might have to face those arrows today, but he was still proud of what English weapons could do.

'A dangerous weapon,' the Harlequin acknowledged, though in an unworried voice. He was ever unworried, always confident, perpetually calm, and that self-control irritated Sir Simon, though he was even more annoyed by the Harlequin's faintly hooded eyes which, he realized, reminded him of Thomas of Hookton. He had the same good looks, but at least Thomas of Hookton was dead, and that was one less archer to face this day. 'But archers can be beaten,' the Harlequin added.

Sir Simon reflected that the Frenchman had faced one archer in his whole life, yet had already worked out how to beat them. 'How?'

'You told me how,' the Harlequin reminded Sir Simon. 'You exhaust their arrows, of course. You send them lesser targets, let them kill peasants, fools and mercenaries for an hour or two, then release your main force. What we shall do,' he turned his horse away, 'is charge with the second line. It does not matter what orders we receive, we shall wait till the arrows are running out. Who wants to be killed by some dirty peasant? No glory there, Sir Simon.'

That, Sir Simon acknowledged, was true enough. He followed the Harlequin to the further side of the beech wood where the squires and servants waited with the packhorses. Two messengers were sent back with news of the English dispositions while the rest dismounted and unsaddled their horses. There was time for men and beasts to rest and feed, time to don the battle armour and time for prayer.

The Harlequin prayed frequently, embarrassing Sir Simon, who considered himself a good Christian but one who did not dangle his soul from God's apron strings. He said confession once or twice a year, went to Mass and bared his head when the Sacraments passed by, but otherwise he spared little thought for the pieties. The Harlequin, on the other hand, confided every day to God, though he rarely stepped into a church and had little time for priests. It was as though he had a private relationship with heaven, and that was both annoying and comforting to Sir Simon. It annoyed him because it seemed unmanly, and it comforted him because if God was of any use to a fighting man then it was on a day of battle.

This day, though, seemed special for the Harlequin, for after going down on one knee and praying silently for a while, he stood and ordered his squire to bring him the lance. Sir Simon, wishing they could stop the pious foolery and eat instead, presumed that they were expected to arm themselves and sent Colley to fetch his own lance, but the Harlequin stopped him. 'Wait,' he ordered.

The lances, wrapped in leather, were carried on a packhorse, but the Harlequin's squire fetched a separate lance, one that had travelled on its own horse and was wrapped in linen as well as leather. Sir Simon had assumed it was the Harlequin's personal weapon, but instead, when the linen was pulled from the shaft, he saw it was an ancient and warped spear made from a timber so old and dark that it would surely splinter if it was subjected to the smallest strain. The blade looked to be made of silver, which was foolish, for the metal was too weak to make a killing blade.

Sir Simon grinned. 'You're not fighting with that!'

'We are all fighting with that,' the Harlequin said and, to Sir Simon's surprise, the black-dressed man fell to his knees again. 'Down,' he instructed Sir Simon.

Sir Simon knelt, feeling like a fool.

'You are a good soldier, Sir Simon,' the Harlequin said. 'I have met few men who can handle weapons as you do and I can think of no man I would rather have fighting at my side, but there is more to fighting than swords and lances and arrows. You must think before you fight, and you must always pray, for if God is on your side then no man can beat you.'

Sir Simon, obscurely aware that he was being criticized, made the sign of the cross. 'I pray,' he said defensively.

'Then give thanks to God that we will carry that lance into battle.'

'Why?'

'Because it is the lance of St George, and the man who fights under the protection of that lance will be cradled in God's arms.'

Sir Simon stared at the lance, which had been laid reverently on the grass. There had been a few times in his life, usually when he was half drunk, when he would glimpse something of the mysteries of God. He had once been reduced to tears by a fierce Dominican, though the effect had not lasted beyond his next visit to a tavern, and he had felt shrunken the first time he had stepped into a cathedral and seen the whole vault dimly lit by candles, but such moments were few, infrequent and unwelcome. Yet now, suddenly, the mystery of Christ reached down to touch his heart. He stared at the lance and did not see a tawdry old weapon tricked with an impractical silver blade, but a thing of God-given power. It had been given by Heaven to make men on earth invincible, and Sir Simon was astonished to feel tears prick at his eyes.

'My family brought it from the Holy Land,' the Harlequin said, 'and they claimed that men who fought under the lance's protection could not be defeated, but that was not true. They were beaten, but when all their allies died, when the very fires of hell were lit to burn their followers to death, they lived. They left France and took the lance with them, but my uncle stole it and concealed it from us. Then I found it, and now it will give its blessings to our battle.'

Sir Simon said nothing. He just gazed at the weapon with a look close to awe.

Henry Colley, untouched by the moment's fervour, picked his nose.

'The world,' the Harlequin said, 'is rotting. The Church is corrupt and kings are weak. We have it in our power, Sir Simon, to make a new world, loved by God, but to do it we must destroy the old. We must take power ourselves, then give the power to God. That is why we fight.'

Henry Colley thought the Frenchman was plain crazy, but Sir Simon had an enraptured expression.

'Tell me,' the Harlequin looked at Sir Simon, 'what is the battle flag of the English King?'

'The dragon banner,' Sir Simon said.

The Harlequin offered one his rare smiles. 'Is that not an omen?' he asked, then paused. 'I shall tell you what will happen this day,' he went on. 'The King of France will come and he will be impatient and he will attack. The day will go badly for us. The English will jeer us because we cannot break them, but then we shall carry the lance into battle and you will see God turn the fight. We shall snatch victory from failure. You will take the English King's son as a prisoner and maybe we will even capture Edward himself, and our reward will be Philip of Valois's favour. That is why we fight, Sir Simon – for the King's favour, because that favour means power, riches and land. You will share that wealth, but only so long as you understand that we shall use our power to purge the rot from Christendom. We shall be a scourge against the wicked.'

Mad as a brush, Henry Colley thought. Daft as lights. He watched as the Harlequin stood and went to a pack-horse's pannier from which he took a square of cloth which, unfolded, proved to be a red banner on which a strange beast with horns, tusks and claws reared on its hind legs while clasping a cup in its forepaws.

'This is my family's banner,' the Harlequin said, tying the flag to the lance's long silver head with black ribbons, 'and for many years, Sir Simon, this banner was forbidden in France because its owners had fought against the King and against the Church. Our lands were wasted and our castle is still slighted, but today we shall be heroes and this banner will be back in favour.' He rolled the flag about the lance-head so that the yale was hidden. 'Today,' he said fervently, 'my family is resurrected.'

'What is your family?' Sir Simon asked.

'My name is Guy Vexille,' the Harlequin admitted, 'and I am the Count of Astarac.'

Sir Simon had never heard of Astarac, but he was pleased to learn that his master was a proper nobleman and, to signify his obedience, he held his praying hands towards Guy Vexille in homage. 'I will not disappoint you, my lord,' Sir Simon said with an unaccustomed humility.

'God will not disappoint us today,' Guy Vexille said. He took Sir Simon's hands in his own. 'Today,' he raised his voice to speak to all his knights, 'we shall destroy England.'

For he had the lance.

And the royal army of France was coming.

And the English had offered themselves for slaughter.

'Arrows,' Will Skeat said. He was standing at the wood's edge beside a pile of sheaves unloaded from a wagon, but suddenly paused. 'Good God.' He was staring at Thomas. 'Looks like a rat got your hair.' He frowned. 'Suits you, though. You look grown up at long last. Arrows!' he said again. 'Don't waste them.' He tossed the sheaves one by one to the archers. 'It looks like a lot, but most of you godforsaken lepers have never been in a proper battle and battles swallow arrows like whores swallowing – Good morning, Father Hobbe!'

'You'll spare me a sheaf, Will?'

'Don't waste it on sinners, father,' Will said, throwing

a bundle to the priest. 'Kill some God-fearing Frenchmen.'

'There's no such thing, Will. They're all spawn of Satan.'

Thomas emptied a sheaf into his arrow bag and tucked another into his belt. He had a pair of bowcords in his helmet, safe from the rain that threatened. A smith had come to the archers' encampment and had hammered the nicks from their swords, axes, knives and billhooks, then sharpened the blades with his stones. The smith, who had been wandering the army, said the King had ridden north to look for a battlefield, but he himself reckoned the French would not come that day. 'It's a lot of sweat for nothing,' he had grumbled as he smoothed a stone down Thomas's sword. 'This is French work,' he said, peering at the long blade.

'From Caen.'

'You could sell this for a penny or two,' the praise was grudging, 'good steel. Old, of course, but good.'

Now, with their arrows replenished, the archers placed their belongings into a wagon that would join the rest of the army's baggage and one man, who was sick in his belly, would guard it through the day while a second invalid would stand sentry on the archers' horses. Will Skeat ordered the wagon away, then cast an eye over his assembled archers. 'The bastards are coming,' he growled, 'if not today, then tomorrow, and there are more of them than there are of us, and they ain't hungry and they've all got boots and they think their shit smells of roses because they're bloody Frenchmen, but they die just like anyone else. Shoot their horses and you'll live to see sundown. And remember, they ain't got proper archers so they're going to lose. It ain't difficult to understand. Keep your heads, aim at the horses, don't waste shafts and listen for orders. Let's go, boys.'

They waded the shallow river, one of the many bands of archers who emerged from the trees to file into the village of Crécy where knights were pacing up and down, then stamping their feet and calling on squires or pages to tighten a strap or loosen a buckle to make their armour comfortable. Bunches of horses, tied bridle to bridle, were being led to the back of the hill where, with the army's women, children and baggage, they would stay inside a ring of wagons. The Prince of Wales, armoured from the waist down, was eating a green apple beside the church and he nodded distractedly when Skeat's men respectfully pulled off their helmets. There was no sign of Jeanette, and Thomas wondered if she had fled on her own, then decided he did not care.

Eleanor walked beside him. She touched his arrow bag. 'Do you have enough arrows?'

'Depends how many Frenchmen come,' Thomas said.

'How many Englishmen are there?' Rumour said the army had eight thousand men now, half of them archers, and Thomas reckoned that was probably about right. He gave that figure to Eleanor, who frowned. 'And how many Frenchmen?' she asked.

'The good Lord knows,' Thomas said, but he reckoned it had to be far more than eight thousand, a lot more, but he could do nothing about that now and so he tried to forget the disparity in numbers as the archers climbed towards the windmill.

They crossed the crest to see the long forward slope, and for an instant Thomas had the impression that a great fair was just beginning. Gaudy flags dotted the hill and bands of men wandered between them, and all it needed was some dancing bears and a few jugglers and it would have looked just like the Dorchester fair.

Will Skeat had stopped to search for the Earl of Northampton's banner, then spotted it on the right of the slope, straight down from the mill. He led the men down and a man-at-arms showed them the sticks marking the spot where the archers would fight. 'And the Earl wants horse-pits dug,' the man-at-arms said.

'You heard him!' Will Skeat shouted. 'Get digging!'

Eleanor helped Thomas make the pits. The soil was thick and they used knives to loosen the earth that they scooped out with their hands.

'Why do you dig pits?' Eleanor asked.

'To trip the horses,' Thomas said, kicking the excavated earth away before starting another hole. All along the face of the hill archers were making similar small pits a score of paces in front of their positions. The enemy horsemen might charge at the full gallop, but the pits would check them. They could get through, but only slowly, and the impetus of their charge would be broken and while they tried to thread the treacherous holes they would be under attack from archers.

'There,' Eleanor said, pointing, and Thomas looked up to see a group of horsemen on the far hill crest. The first Frenchmen had arrived and were staring across the valley to where the English army slowly assembled under the banners.

'Be hours yet,' Thomas said. Those Frenchmen, he guessed, were the vanguard who had been sent ahead to find the enemy, while the main French army would still be marching from Abbeville. The crossbowmen, who would surely lead the attack, would all be on foot.

Off to Thomas's right, where the slope fell away to the river and the village, a makeshift fortress of empty wagons was being made. The carts were parked close together to form a barrier against horsemen and between them were guns. These were not the guns that had failed to break Caen Castle, but were much smaller.

'Ribalds,' Will Skeat said to Thomas.

'Ribalds?'

'That's what they're called, ribalds.' He led Thomas and Eleanor along the slope to look at the guns, which were strange bundles of iron tubes. Gunners were stirring the powder, while others were undoing bundles of garros, the long arrow-like iron missiles that were rammed into the tubes. Some of the ribalds had eight barrels, some seven and a few only four. 'Useless bloody things,' Skeat spat, 'but they might frighten the horses.' He nodded a greeting to the archers who were digging pits ahead of the ribalds. The guns were thick here – Thomas counted thirty-four and others were being dragged into place – but they still needed the protection of bowmen.

Skeat leaned on a wagon and stared at the far hill. It was not warm, but he was sweating. 'Are you ill?' Thomas asked.

'Guts are churning a bit,' Skeat admitted, 'but nothing to make a song and dance about.' There were about four hundred French horsemen on the far hill now, and others were appearing from the trees. 'It might not happen,' Skeat said quietly.

'The battle?'

'Philip of France is jumpy,' Skeat said. 'He's got a knack of marching up to battle, then deciding he'd rather be frolicking at home. That's what I hear. Nervous bastard.' He shrugged. 'But if he thinks he's got a chance today, Tom, it's going to be nasty.'

Thomas smiled. 'The pits? The archers?'

'Don't be a bloody fool, boy,' Skeat retorted. 'Not every pit breaks a leg and not every arrow strikes true. We might stop the first charge and maybe the second, but they'll still keep coming and in the end they'll get through. There's just too many of the bastards. They'll be on top of us, Tom, and it'll be up to the men-at-arms to give them a hammering. Just keep your head, boy, and remember it's the men-at-arms who do the close-quarter work. If the bastards get past the pits then take your bow back, wait for a target and stay alive. And if we lose?' He shrugged. 'Leg it for the forest and hide there.'

'What is he saying?' Eleanor asked.

'That it should be easy work today.'

'You are a bad liar, Thomas.'

'Just too many of them,' Skeat said, almost to himself. 'Tommy Dugdale faced worse odds down in Brittany, Tom, but he had plenty of arrows. We're short.'

'We're going to be all right, Will.'

'Aye, well. Maybe.' Skeat pushed himself off the wagon. 'You two go ahead. I need a quiet place for a second.'

Thomas and Eleanor walked back north. The English line was forming now, the scattered flags being swamped by men-at-arms who were forming into blocks. Archers stood ahead of each formation while marshals, armed with white staffs, made sure there were gaps in the line through which the archers could escape if the horsemen came too close. Bundles of lances had been fetched from the village and were being issued to the men-at-arms in the front rank for, if the French did get past the pits and the arrows, the lances would have to be used as pikes.

By mid-morning the whole army was assembled on the hill. It looked far bigger than it really was because so many women had stayed with their men and now sat on the grass or else lay and slept. A fitful sun came and went, racing shadows across the valley. The pits were dug and the guns loaded. Perhaps a thousand Frenchmen watched from the far hill, but none ventured down the slope. 'At least it's better than marching,' Jake said; 'gives us a chance for a rest, eh?'

'Be an easy day,' Sam reckoned. He nodded at the far hill. 'Not many of the bastards, eh?'

'That's only the vanguard, you daft bastard,' Jake said.

'There are more coming?' Sam sounded genuinely surprised.

'Every goddamn bastard in France is coming,' Jake said.

Thomas kept quiet. He was imagining the French army strung along the Abbeville road. They would all know the English had stopped running, that they were waiting, and doubtless the French were hurrying in case they missed the battle. They had to be confident. He made the sign of the cross and Eleanor, sensing his fear, touched his arm.

'You will be all right,' she said.

'You too, my love.'

'You remember your promise to my father?' she asked.

Thomas nodded, but he could not persuade himself

404

that he would see the lance of St George this day. This day was real, while the lance belonged to some mysterious world of which Thomas really wanted no part. Everyone else, he thought, cared passionately about the relic, and only he, who had as good a reason as any to discover the truth, was indifferent. He wished he had never seen the lance, he wished that the man who had called himself the Harlequin had never come to Hookton, but if the French had not landed, he thought, then he would not be carrying the black bow and would not be on this green hillside and would not have met Eleanor. You cannot turn your back on God, he told himself.

'If I see the lance,' he promised Eleanor, 'I shall fight for it.' That was his penance, though he still hoped he would not have to serve it.

They ate mouldy bread for their midday meal. The French were a dark mass on the far hill, too many to count now, and the first of their infantry had arrived. A spit of rain made those archers who had their strings dangling from a bowtip hurry to coil the cords and shelter them under helmets or hats, but the small rain passed. A wind stirred the grass.

And still the French came to the far hill. They were a horde, they had come to Crécy, and they had come for revenge.

The English waited. Two of Skeat's archers played straw flutes, while the hobelars, who were helping to protect the guns on the army's flanks, sang songs of green woods and running streams. Some men danced the steps they would have used on a village green back home, others slept, many played dice, and all but the sleepers continually looked across the valley to the far hill crest that was thickening with men.

Jake had a linen-wrapped lump of beeswax that he handed round the archers so they could coat their bows. It was not necessary, just something to do. 'Where did you get the wax?' Thomas asked him.

'Stole it, of course, off some daft man-at-arms. Saddle polish, I reckon.'

An argument developed over which wood made the best arrows. It was an old discussion, but it passed the time. Everyone knew ash made the best shafts, but some men liked to claim that birch or hornbeam, even oak, flew just as well. Alder, though heavy, was good for killing deer, but needed a heavy head and did not have the distance for battle.

Sam took one of his new arrows from his bag and showed everyone how warped the shaft was. 'Must be made of bloody blackthorn,' he complained bitterly. 'You could shoot that round a corner.'

'They don't make arrows like they used to,' Will Skeat said, and his archers jeered for it was an old complaint. 'It's true,' Skeat said. 'It's all hurry up and no craftsmanship these days. Who cares? The bastards get paid by the sheaf and the sheaves are sent to London and no one looks at them till they reach us, and what are we going to do? Just look at it!' He took the arrow from Sam and twisted it in his fingers. 'That's not a bloody goose feather! It's a goddamn sparrow feather. No bloody use for anything except scratching your arse.' He tossed the arrow back to Sam. 'No, a proper archer makes his own arrows.'

'I used to,' Thomas said.

'But you're a lazy bastard now, eh, Tom?' Skeat grinned, but the grin faded as he stared across the valley. 'Enough of the goddamn bastards,' he grumbled, looking at the gathering French, then he grimaced as a solitary raindrop splashed on his worn boots. 'I wish it would damn well rain and get it over with. It wants to. If it pisses on us when the bastards are attacking then we might as well run for home because the bows won't shoot.'

Eleanor sat beside Thomas and watched the far hill. There were at least as many men there as were in the English army now, and the French main battle was only just arriving. Mounted men-at-arms were spreading across the hill, organizing themselves into conrois. A conroi was the basic fighting unit for a knight or man-at-arms, and most had between a dozen and twenty men, but those who formed the bodyguards of the great lords were much larger. There were now so many horsemen on the far hilltop that some had to spill down the slope, which was turning into a spread of colour, for the men-at-arms were wearing surcoats embroidered with their lords' badges and the horses had gaudy trappers, while the French banners added more blue and red and yellow and green. Yet, despite the colours, the dull grey of steel and mail still predominated. In front of the horsemen were the first green and red jackets of the Genoese crossbowmen. There was only a handful of those bowmen, but more and more were streaming over the hill to join their comrades.

A cheer sounded from the English centre and Thomas leaned forward to see that archers were scrambling to their feet. His first thought was that the French must have attacked, but there were no enemy horsemen and no arrows flew.

'Up!' Will Skeat shouted suddenly. 'On your feet!'

'What is it?' Jake asked.

Thomas saw the horsemen then. Not Frenchmen, but a dozen Englishmen who rode along the face of the waiting battleline, carefully keeping their horses away from the archers' pits. Three of the horsemen were carrying banners, and one of those flags was a huge standard showing the lilies and the leopards framed in gold. 'It's the King,' a man said, and Skeat's archers began to cheer.

The King stopped and spoke with the men in the centre of the line, then trotted on towards the English right. His escort was mounted on big destriers, but the King rode a grey mare. He wore his bright surcoat, but had hung his crowned helmet from his saddle pommel and so was bare-headed. His royal standard, all red, gold and blue, led the flags, while behind it was the King's personal badge of the flaming sun rising, while the third, which provoked the loudest cheer, was an extravagantly long pennant which showed the fire-spewing dragon of Wessex. It was the flag of England, of the men who had fought the Conqueror, and the Conqueror's descendant now flew it to show that he was of England like the men who cheered him as he rode the grey horse.

He stopped close to Will Skeat's men and raised a white staff to silence the cheers. The archers had pulled off their helmets and some had gone on one knee. The King still looked young, and his hair and beard were as gold as the rising sun on his standard.

'I am grateful,' he began in a voice so hoarse that he paused and started again. 'I am grateful that you are here.' That started the cheering again and Thomas, who was cheering with the others, did not even reflect on what choice they had been given. The King raised the white staff for silence. 'The French, as you see, have decided to join us! Perhaps they are lonely.' It was not a great joke, but it prompted roars of laughter that turned to jeers for the enemy. The King smiled as he waited for the shouts to subside. 'We came here,' he then called, 'only to procure the rights and lands and privileges that are ours by the laws of man and of God. My cousin of France challenges us, and in so doing he defies God.' The men were silent now, listening carefully. The destriers of the King's escort were pawing the ground, but not a man moved. 'God will not endure Philip of France's impudence,' the King went on. 'He will punish France, and you,' he cast a hand to indicate the archers, 'will be His instrument. God is with you, and I promise you, I swear to you before God and on my own life, that I will not leave this field till the last man of my army has marched from here. We stay on this hill together and we fight here together and we shall win together for God, for St George and for England!'

The cheers began again and the King smiled and nodded, then turned as the Earl of Northampton strode from the line. The King leaned down in his saddle and listened to the Earl for a moment, then straightened and smiled again. 'Is there a Master Skeat here?'

Skeat immediately reddened, but did not confess his presence. The Earl was grinning, the King waited, then a score of archers pointed at their leader. 'He's here!'

'Come here!' the King commanded sternly.

Will Skeat looked embarrassed as he threaded through the bowmen and approached the King's horse where he went on one knee. The King drew his ruby-hilted sword and touched it on Skeat's shoulder. 'We are told you are one of our best soldiers, so from henceforth you will be Sir William Skeat.'

The archers shouted even louder. Will Skeat, Sir William now, stayed on his knees as the King spurred on to give the same speech to the last men in the line and to those who manned the guns in the circle of farm carts. The Earl of Northampton, who had plainly been responsible for Skeat's knighthood, raised him up and led him back to his cheering men, and Skeat was still blushing as his archers clapped him on the back.

'Bloody nonsense,' he said to Thomas.

'You deserve it, Will,' Thomas said, then grinned, 'Sir William.'

'Just have to pay more bloody tax, won't I?' Skeat

said, but he looked pleased anyway. Then he frowned as a drop of rain splashed on his bare forehead. 'Bow-strings!' he shouted.

Most of the men were still sheltering their strings, but a handful had to coil the cords as the rain began to fall more heavily. One of the Earl's men-at-arms came to the archers, shouting that the women were to go back beyond the crest. 'You heard him!' Will Skeat called. 'Women to the baggage!'

Some of the women wept, but Eleanor just clung to Thomas for a moment. 'Live,' she said simply, then walked away through the rain, passing the Prince of Wales who, with six other mounted men, was riding to his place among the men-at-arms behind Will Skeat's archers. The Prince had decided to fight on horseback so he could see over the heads of the dismounted men and, to mark his arrival, his banner which was bigger than any other on the right of the field was loosed to the heavy downpour.

Thomas could no longer see across the valley because wide curtains of heavy grey rain were sweeping from the north and obscuring the air. There was nothing to do but sit and wait while the leather backing of his mail became cold and clammy. He hunched miserably, staring into the greyness, knowing that no bow could draw properly till this downpour ended.

'What they should do,' said Father Hobbe, who sat beside Thomas, 'is charge now.'

'They couldn't find their way in this muck, father,' Thomas said. He saw the priest had a bow and an arrow bag, but no other battle equipment. 'You should get some mail,' he said, 'or at least a padded jacket.'

'I'm armoured by the faith, my son.'

411

'Where's your bowstrings?' Thomas asked, for the priest had neither helmet nor cap.

'I looped them round my . . . well, never mind. It has to be good for something other than pissing, eh? And it's dry down there.' Father Hobbe seemed indecently cheerful. 'I've been walking the lines, Tom, and looking for your lance. It's not here.'

'Hardly goddamn surprising,' Thomas said. 'I never thought it would be.'

Father Hobbe ignored the blasphemy. 'And I had a chat with Father Pryke. Do you know him?'

'No,' Thomas said curtly. The rain was pouring off the front of his helmet onto the broken bridge of his nose. 'How the hell would I know Father Pryke?'

Father Hobbe was not deterred by Thomas's surliness. 'He's confessor to the King and a great man. He'll be a bishop one day soon. I asked him about the Vexilles.' Father Hobbe paused, but Thomas said nothing. 'He remembers the family,' the priest went on. 'He says they had lands in Cheshire, but they supported the Mortimers at the beginning of the King's reign so they were outlawed. He said something else. They were always reckoned pious, but their bishop suspected they had strange ideas. A touch of gnosticism.'

'Cathars,' Thomas said.

'It seems likely, doesn't it?'

'And if it's a pious family,' Thomas said, 'then I probably don't belong. Isn't that good news?'

'You can't escape, Thomas,' Father Hobbe said softly. His usually wild hair was plastered close to his skull by the rain. 'You promised your father. You accepted the penance.'

Thomas shook his head angrily. 'There are a score of

bastards here, father,' he indicated the archers crouching under the rain's lash, 'who've murdered more men than I have. Go and harrow their souls and leave mine alone.'

Father Hobbe shook his head. 'You've been chosen, Thomas, and I'm your conscience. It occurs to me, see, that if the Vexilles supported Mortimer then they can't love our king. If they'll be anywhere today, it'll be over there.' He nodded towards the valley's far side, which was still blotted out by the pelting rain.

'Then they'll live for another day, won't they?' Thomas said.

Father Hobbe frowned. 'You think we're going to lose?' he asked sternly. 'No!'

Thomas shivered. 'It must be getting late in the afternoon, father. If they don't attack now they'll wait till morning. That'll give them a whole day to slaughter us.'

'Ah, Thomas! How God loves you.'

Thomas said nothing to that, but he was thinking that all he wanted was to be an archer, to become Sir Thomas of Hookton as Will had just become Sir William. He was happy serving the King and did not need a heavenly lord to take him into weird battles against dark lords. 'Let me give you some advice, father,' he said.

'It's always welcome, Tom.'

'First bastard that drops, get his helmet and mail. Look after yourself.'

Father Hobbe clapped Thomas's back. 'God is on our side. You heard the King say as much.' He stood and went to talk with other men, and Thomas sat by himself and saw that the rain was lessening at last. He could see the far trees again, see the colours of the French banners and surcoats, and now he could see a mass of red and green crossbowmen at the other side of the valley. They were going nowhere, he reckoned, for a crossbow string was as susceptible to the damp as any other. 'It'll be tomorrow,' he called down to Jake. 'We'll do it all again tomorrow.'

'Let's hope the sun shines,' Jake said.

The wind brought the last drops of rain from the north. It was late. Thomas stood, stretched and stamped his feet. A day wasted, he thought, and a hungry night ahead.

And tomorrow his first real battle.

An excited group of mounted men had gathered about the French King, who was still a half-mile from the hill where the largest part of his army had gathered. There were at least two thousand men-at-arms in the rear-guard who were still marching, but those who had reached the valley hugely outnumbered the waiting English.

'Two to one, sire!' Charles, the Count of Alençon and the King's younger brother, said vehemently. Like the rest of the horsemen his surcoat was soaking and the dye in its badge had run into the white linen. His helmet was beaded with water. 'We must kill them now!' the Count insisted.

But Philip of Valois's instinct was to wait. It would be wise, he thought, to let his whole army gather, to make a proper reconnaissance and then attack next morning, but he was also aware that his companions, especially his brother, thought him cautious. They even believed him to be timid for he had avoided battle with the English before, and even to propose waiting a mere day might make them think he had no stomach for the highest business of kings. He still ventured the proposal, suggesting that the victory would be all the more complete if it was just delayed by one day.

'And if you wait,' Alençon said scathingly, 'Edward will slip away in the night and tomorrow we'll face an empty hill.'

'They're cold, wet, hungry and ready to be slaughtered,' the Duke of Lorraine insisted.

'And if they don't leave, sire,' the Count of Flanders warned, 'they'll have more time to dig trenches and holes.'

'And the signs are good,' John of Hainault, a close companion of the King and the Lord of Beaumont, added.

'The signs?' the King asked.

John of Hainault gestured for a man in a black cloak to step forward. The man, who had a long white beard, bowed low. 'The sun, sire,' he said, 'is in conjunction with Mercury and opposite Saturn. Best of all, noble sire, Mars is in the house of Virgo. It spells victory, and could not be more propitious.'

And how much gold, Philip wondered, had been paid to the astrologer to come up with that prophecy, yet he was also tempted by it. He thought it unwise to do anything without a horoscope and wondered where his own astrologer was. Probably still on the Abbeville road.

'Go now!' Alençon urged his brother.

Guy Vexille, the Count of Astarac, pushed his horse into the throng surrounding the King. He saw a green-and-red-jacketed crossbowman, evidently the commander of the Genoese, and spoke to him in Italian. 'Has the rain affected the strings?'

'Badly,' Carlo Grimaldi, the Genoese leader, admitted. Crossbow strings could not be unstrung like the cords of ordinary bows for the tension in the cords was too great and so the men had simply tried to shelter their weapons under their inadequate coats. 'We should wait till tomorrow,' Grimaldi insisted, 'we can't advance without pavises.'

'What's he saying?' Alençon demanded.

The Count of Astarac translated for His Majesty's benefit, and the King, pale and long-faced, frowned when he heard that the crossbowmen's long shields that protected them from the enemy's arrows while they reloaded their cumbersome weapons had still not arrived. 'How long will they be?' he asked plaintively, but no one knew. 'Why didn't they travel with the bowmen?' he demanded, but again no one had an answer. 'Who are you?' the King finally asked the Count.

'Astarac, sire,' Guy Vexille said.

'Ah.' It was plain the King had no idea who or what Astarac was, nor did he recognize Vexille's shield that bore the simple symbol of the cross, but Vexille's horse and armour were both expensive and so the King did not dispute the man's right to offer advice. 'And you say the bows won't draw?'

'Of course they'll draw!' the Count of Alençon man interrupted. 'The damned Genoese don't want to fight. Bastard Genoese.' He spat. 'The English bows will be just as wet,' he added.

'The crossbows will be weakened, sire,' Vexille explained carefully, ignoring the hostility of the King's

416

younger brother. 'The bows will draw, but they won't have their full range or force.'

'It would be best to wait?' the King asked.

'It would be wise to wait, sire,' Vexille said, 'and it would be especially wise to wait for the pavises.'

'Tomorrow's horoscope?' John of Hainault asked the astrologer.

The man shook his head. 'Neptune approaches the bendings tomorrow, sire. It is not a hopeful conjunction.'

'Attack now! They're wet, tired and hungry,' Alençon urged. 'Attack now!'

The King still looked dubious, but most of the great lords were confident and they hammered him with their arguments. The English were trapped and a delay of even one day might give them a chance to escape. Perhaps their fleet would come to Le Crotoy? Go now, they insisted, even though it was late in the day. Go and kill. Go and win. Show Christendom that God is on the side of the French. Just go, go now. And the King, because he was weak and because he wanted to appear strong, surrendered to their wishes.

So the oriflamme was taken from its leather tube and carried to its place of honour at the front of the men-at-arms. No other flag would be allowed to go ahead of the long plain red banner that flew from its cross-staff and was guarded by thirty picked knights who wore scarlet ribbons on their right arms. The horsemen were given their long lances, then the conrois closed together so the knights and men-at-arms were knee to knee. Drummers took the rain covers from their instruments and Grimaldi, the Genoese commander, was peremptorily told to advance and kill the English archers. The King crossed himself while a score of priests fell to their knees in the wet grass and began to pray.

The lords of France rode to the hill crest where their mailed horsemen waited. By nightfall they would all have wet swords and prisoners enough to break England for ever.

For the oriflamme was going into battle.

'God's teeth!' Will Skeat sounded astonished as he scrambled to his feet. 'The bastards are coming!' His surprise was justified, for it was late in the afternoon, the time when labourers would think of going home from the fields.

The archers stood and stared. The enemy was not yet advancing, but a horde of crossbowmen were spreading across the valley bottom, while above them the French knights and men-at-arms were arming themselves with lances.

Thomas thought it had to be a feint. It would be dark in another three or four hours, yet perhaps the French were confident they could do the business quickly. The crossbowmen were at last starting forward. Thomas took off his helmet to find a bowstring, looped one end over a horn tip, then flexed the shaft to fix the other loop in its nock. He fumbled and had to make three attempts to string the long black weapon. Sweet Jesus, he thought, but they were really coming! Be calm, he told himself, be calm, but he felt as nervous as when he had stood on the slope above Hookton and dared himself to kill a man for the very first time. He pulled open the laces of the arrow bag.

The drums began to beat from the French side of the

valley and a great cheer sounded. There was nothing to explain the cheer; the men-at-arms were not moving and the crossbowmen were still a long way off. English trumpets responded, calling sweet and clear from the windmill where the King and a reserve of men-at-arms waited. Archers were stretching and stamping their feet all along the hill. Four thousand English bows were strung and ready, but there were half as many crossbowmen again coming towards them, and behind those six thousand Genoese were thousands of mailed horsemen.

'No pavises!' Will Skeat shouted. 'And their strings will be damp.'

'They won't have the reach for us.' Father Hobbe had appeared at Thomas's side again.

Thomas nodded, but was too dry-mouthed to answer. A crossbow in good hands, and there were none better than the Genoese, should outrange a straight bow, but not if it had a damp string. The extra range was no great advantage, for it took so long to rewind a bow that an archer could advance into range and loose six or seven arrows before the enemy was ready to send his second bolt, but even though Thomas understood that imbalance he was still nervous. The enemy looked so numerous and the French drums were great heavy kettles with thick skins that boomed like the devil's own heartbeat in the valley. The enemy horsemen were edging forward, eager to spur their mounts into an English line they expected to be deeply wounded by the crossbows' assault while the English men-at-arms were shuffling together, closing their line to make solid ranks of shields and steel. The mail clinked and jangled.

'God is with you!' a priest shouted.

'Don't waste your arrows,' Will Skeat called. 'Aim true, boys, aim true. They ain't going to stand long.' He repeated the message as he walked along his line. 'You look like you've seen a ghost, Tom.'

'Ten thousand ghosts,' Thomas said.

'There's more of the bastards than that,' Will Skeat said. He turned and gazed at the hill. 'Maybe twelve thousand horsemen?' He grinned. 'So that's twelve thousand arrows, lad.'

There were six thousand crossbowmen and twice as many men-at-arms, who were being reinforced by infantry that was appearing on both French flanks. Thomas doubted that those foot soldiers would take any part in the battle, not unless it turned into a rout, and he understood that the crossbowmen could probably be turned back because they were coming without pavises and would have rain-weakened weapons, but to turn the Genoese back would need arrows, a lot of arrows, and that would mean fewer for the mass of horsemen whose painted lances, held upright, made a thicket along the far hilltop. 'We need more arrows,' he said to Skeat.

'You'll make do with what you've got,' Skeat said, 'we all will. Can't wish for what you ain't got.'

The crossbowmen paused at the foot of the English slope and shook themselves into line before placing their bolts into their bows' troughs. Thomas took out his first arrow and superstitiously kissed its head, which was a wedge of slightly rusted steel with a wicked point and two steep barbs. He laid the arrow over his left hand and slotted its nocked butt onto the centre of the bowstring, which was protected from fraying with a whipping of hemp. He half tensed the bow, taking comfort from the yew's resistance. The arrow lay inside the shaft, to the left of the handgrip. He released the tension, gripped the arrow with his left thumb and flexed the fingers of his right hand.

A sudden blare of trumpets made him jump. Every French drummer and trumpeter was working now, making a cacophony of noise that started the Genoese forward again. They were climbing the English slope, their faces white blurs framed by the grey of their helmets. The French horsemen were coming down the slope, but slowly and in fits and starts, as though they were trying to anticipate the order to charge.

'God is with us!' Father Hobbe called. He was in his archer's stance, left foot far forward, and Thomas saw the priest had no shoes.

'What happened to your boots, father?'

'Some poor boy needed them more than I did. I'll get a French pair.'

Thomas smoothed the feathers of his first arrow.

'Wait!' Will Skeat shouted. 'Wait!' A dog ran out of the English battleline and its owner shouted for it to come back, and in a heartbeat half the archers were calling the dog's name. 'Biter! Biter! Come here, you bastard! Biter!'

'Quiet!' Will Skeat roared as the dog, utterly confused, ran towards the enemy.

Off to Thomas's right the gunners were crouched by the carts, linstocks smoking. Archers stood in the wagons, weapons half braced. The Earl of Northampton had come to stand among the archers.

'You shouldn't be here, my lord,' Will Skeat said.

'The King makes him a knight,' the Earl said, 'and he thinks he can give me orders!' The archers grinned.

'Don't kill all the men-at-arms, Will,' the Earl went on. 'Leave some for us poor swordsmen.'

'You'll get your chance,' Will Skeat said grimly. 'Wait!' he called to the archers. 'Wait!' The Genoese were shouting as they advanced, though their voices were almost drowned by the heavy drumming and the wild trumpet calls. Biter was running back to the English now and a cheer sounded when the dog at last found shelter in the battleline. 'Don't waste your god-damn arrows,' Will Skeat called. 'Take proper aim, like your mothers taught you.'

The Genoese were within bow range now, but not an arrow flew, and the red-and-green-coated cross-bowmen still came, bending forward slightly as they trudged up the hill. They were not coming straight at the English, but at a slight angle, which meant that the right of the English line, where Thomas was, would be struck first. It was also the place where the slope was most gradual and Thomas, with a sinking heart, under-stood he was likely to be in the heart of the fight. Then the Genoese stopped, shuffled into line and began to shout their war cry.

'Too soon,' the Earl muttered.

The crossbows went into the shooting position. They were angled steeply upwards as the Genoese hoped to drop a thick rain of death on the English line.

'Draw!' Skeat said, and Thomas could feel his heart thumping as he pulled the coarse string back to his right ear. He chose a man in the enemy line, placed the arrow tip directly between that man and his right eye, edged the bow to the right because that would compensate for the bias in the weapon's aim, then lifted his left hand and shifted it back to the left because the wind

422

was coming from that direction. Not much wind. He had not thought about aiming the arrow, it was all instinct, but he was still nervous and a muscle was twitching in his right leg. The English line was utterly silent, the crossbowmen were shouting and the French drums and trumpets deafening. The Genoese line looked like green and red statues.

'Let go, you bastards,' a man muttered and the Genoese obeyed him. Six thousand crossbow bolts arced into the sky.

'Now,' Will said, surprisingly softly.

And the arrows flew.

Eleanor crouched by the wagon that held the archers' baggage. Thirty or forty other women were there, many with children, and they all flinched as they heard the trumpets, the drums and the distant shouting. Nearly all the women were French or Breton, though not one was hoping for a French victory, for it was their men who stood on the green hill.

Eleanor prayed for Thomas, for Will Skeat and for her father. The baggage park was beneath the crest of the hill so she could not see what was happening, but she heard the deep, sharp note of the English bowstrings being released, and then the rush of air across feathers that was the sound of thousands of arrows in flight. She shuddered. A dog tethered to the cart, one of the many strays that had been adopted by the archers, whimpered. She patted it. 'There will be meat tonight,' she told the dog. The news had spread that the cattle captured in Le Crotoy would be reaching the army today. If there was an army left to eat them. The bows sounded again, more raggedly. The trumpets still screamed and the drumbeats were constant. She glanced up at the hill crest, half expecting to see arrows in the sky, but there was only grey cloud against which scores of horsemen were outlined. Those horsemen were part of the King's small reserve of troops and Eleanor knew that if she saw them spur forward then the main line would have been breached. The King's royal standard was flying from the topmost vane of the windmill where it stirred in the small breeze to show its gold, crimson and blue.

The vast baggage park was guarded by a mere score of sick or wounded soldiers who would not last a heartbeat if the French broke through the English line. The King's baggage, heaped on three white-painted wagons, had a dozen men-at-arms to guard the royal jewels, but otherwise there was only the host of women and children, and a handful of pageboys who were armed with short swords. The army's thousands of horses were also there, picketed close to the forest and watched by a few crippled men. Eleanor noted that most of the horses were saddled as though the men-at-arms and archers wanted the animals ready in case they had to flee.

A priest had been with the royal baggage, but when the bows sounded he had hurried to the crest and Eleanor was tempted to follow. Better to see what was going on, she thought, than wait here beside the forest and fear what might be happening. She patted the dog and stood, intending to walk to the crest, but just then she saw the woman who had come to Thomas in the damp night in the forest of Crécy. The Countess of Armorica, beautifully dressed in a red gown and with her hair netted in a silver mesh, was riding a small white mare up and down beside the prince's wagons. She paused every now and then to gaze at the crest and then she would stare towards the forest of Crécy-Grange that lay to the west.

A crash startled Eleanor and made her turn to the crest. Nothing explained the terrible noise that had sounded uncannily like a close clap of thunder, but there was no lightning and no rain and the mill stood unharmed. Then a seep of grey-white smoke showed above the mill's furled sails and Eleanor understood that the guns had fired. Ribalds, they were called, she remembered, and she imagined their rusting iron arrows slashing down the slope.

She looked back to the Countess, but Jeanette was gone. She had ridden to the forest, taking her jewels with her. Eleanor saw the red gown flash in the trees, then disappear. So the Countess had fled, fearing the consequences of defeat, and Eleanor, suspecting that the Prince's woman must know more of the English prospects than the archers' women, made the sign of the cross. Then, because she could not bear the waiting any longer, she walked to the crest. If her lover died, she thought, then she wanted to be near him.

Other women followed her. None spoke. They just stood on the hill and watched.

And prayed for their men.

Thomas's second arrow was in the air before his first had reached its greatest height and begun to fall. He reached for a third, then realized he had shot the second in panic and so he paused and stared at the clouded sky that was strangely thick with flickering black shafts that

425

were as dense as starlings and deadlier than hawks. He could see no crossbow bolts, then he laid the third arrow on his left hand and picked a man in the Genoese line. There was an odd pattering noise that startled him and he looked to see it was the hail of Genoese bolts striking the turf around the horse pits.

And a heartbeat later the first English arrow flight slammed home. Scores of crossbowmen were snatched backwards, including the one Thomas had picked out for his third arrow and so he changed his aim to another man, hauled the cord back to his ear and let the shaft fly.

'They're falling short!' the Earl of Northampton shouted exultantly, and some of the archers swore, thinking he spoke of their own arrows, but it was the Genoese bows that had been enfeebled by the rain and not one of their quarrels had reached the English archers who, seeing the chance for slaughter, gave a howling cheer and ran a few paces down the slope.

'Kill them!' Will Skeat shouted.

They killed them. The great bows were drawn again and again, and the white-feathered arrows slashed down the slope to pierce mail and cloth, and to turn the lower hill into a field of death. Some crossbowmen limped away, a few crawled, and the uninjured edged backwards rather than span their weapons.

'Aim well!' the Earl called.

'Don't waste arrows!' Will Skeat shouted.

Thomas shot again, plucked a new arrow from the bag and sought a new target as his previous arrow seared down to strike a man in the thigh. The grass about the Genoese line was thick with arrows that had missed, but more than enough were striking home. The

Genoese line was thinner, much thinner, and it was silent now except for the cries of men being struck and the moans of the wounded. The archers advanced again, right to the edge of their pits, and a new flight of steel poured down the slope.

And the crossbowmen fled.

One moment they had been a ragged line, still thick with men who stood behind the bodies of their comrades, and now they were a rabble who ran as hard as they could to escape the arrows.

'Stop shooting!' Will Skeat bellowed. 'Stop!'

'Hold!' John Armstrong, whose men were to the left of Skeat's band, shouted.

'Well done!' the Earl of Northampton called.

'Back, lads, back!' Will Skeat motioned the archers. 'Sam! David! Go and collect some arrows, quick,' he pointed down the slope to where, amidst the Genoese dying and dead, the white-tipped shafts were thickly stuck in the turf. 'Hurry, lads. John! Peter! Go and help them. Go!'

All along the line archers were running to salvage arrows from the grass, but then a shout of warning came from the men who had remained in their places.

'Get back! Get back!' Will Skeat shouted.

The horsemen were coming.

Sir Guillaume d'Evecque led a conroi of twelve men on the far left of the French second line of horsemen. Ahead of him was a mass of French cavalry belonging to the first battle, to his left was a scatter of infantrymen who sat on the grass, and beyond them the small river twisted through its water meadows beside the forest.

To his right was nothing but horsemen crammed together as they waited for the crossbowmen to weaken the enemy line.

That English line looked pitifully small, perhaps because its men-at-arms were on foot and so took up much less room than mounted knights, yet Sir Guillaume grudgingly acknowledged that the English King had chosen his position well. The French knights could not assault either flank for they were both protected by a village. They could not ride around the English right for that was guarded by the soft lands beside the river, while to circle about Edward's left would mean a long journey around Wadicourt and, by the time the French came in sight of the English again, the archers would surely have been redeployed to meet a French force made ragged by its long detour. Which meant that only a frontal assault could bring a swift victory, and that, in turn, meant riding into the arrows. 'Heads down, shields up and keep close,' he told his men, before clanging down the face-piece of his helmet. Then, knowing he would not charge for some time yet, he pushed the visor back up. His men-at-arms shuffled their horses till they were knee to knee. The wind, it was said, should not be able to blow between the lances of a charging conroi.

'Be a while yet,' Sir Guillaume warned them. The fleeing crossbowmen were running up the French-held hill. Sir Guillaume had watched them advance and mouthed a silent prayer that God would be on the shoulders of the Genoese. Kill some of those damned archers, he had prayed, but spare Thomas. The drummers had been hammering their great kettles, driving down the sticks as if they could defeat the English by noise alone and Sir Guillaume, elated by the moment, had put the butt of his lance on the ground and used it to raise himself in the stirrups so he could see over the heads of the men in front. He had watched the Genoese loose their quarrels, seen the bolts as a quick haze in the sky, and then the English had shot and their arrows were a dark smear against the green slope and grey clouds and Sir Guillaume had watched the Genoese stagger. He had looked to see the English archers falling, but they were coming forward instead, still loosing arrows, and then the two flanks of the small English line had billowed dirty white as the guns added their missiles to the hail of arrows that was whipping down the slope. His horse had twitched uneasily when the crack of the guns rolled over the valley and Sir Guillaume dropped into the saddle and clicked his tongue. He could not pat the horse for the lance was in his right hand and his left arm was strapped into its shield with the three yellow hawks on the blue ground.

The Genoese had broken. At first Sir Guillaume did not credit it, believing that perhaps their commander was trying to trick the English archers into an undisciplined pursuit that would strand them at the bottom of the slope where the crossbows could turn on them. But the English did not move and the fleeing Genoese had not stopped. They ran, leaving a thick line of dead and dying men, and now they climbed in panic towards the French horsemen.

A growl sounded from the French men-at-arms. It was anger, and the sound rose to a great jeer. 'Cowards!' a man near Sir Guillaume called.

The Count of Alençon felt a surge of pure rage. 'They've been paid!' he snarled at a companion. 'Bastards have taken a bribe!'

'Cut them down!' the King called from his place at the edge of the beech wood. 'Cut them down!'

His brother heard him and wanted nothing more than to obey. The Count was in the second line, not the first, but he spurred his horse into a gap between two of the leading conrois and shouted at his men to follow. 'Cut them down!' he called. 'Cut the bastards down!'

The Genoese were between the horsemen and the English line and now they were doomed, for all along the hill the French were spurring forward. Hot-blooded men from the second battle were tangling with the conrois of the first line to form an untidy mass of banners, lances and horses. They should have walked their horses down the hill so that they were still in close order when they reached the climb on the far side, but instead they raked back spurs and, driven by a hatred of their own allies, raced each other to the kill.

'We stay!' Guy Vexille, Count of Astarac, shouted at his men.

'Wait!' Sir Guillaume called. Better to let the first ragged charge spend itself, he reckoned, rather than join the madness.

Perhaps half the French horsemen stayed on the hill. The rest, led by the King's brother, rode down the Genoese. The crossbowmen tried to escape. They ran along the valley in an attempt to reach the northern and southern ends, but the mass of horsemen overlapped them and there was no way out. Some Genoese, sensibly, lay down and curled into balls, others crouched in the shallow ditches, but most were killed or wounded as the horsemen rode over them. The destriers were big beasts with hooves like hammers. They were trained to run men down and the Genoese screamed as they were trampled or slashed.

Some knights used their lances on the crossbowmen and the weight of a horse and armoured man easily drove the wooden spears clean through their victims, but those lances were all lost, left in the mangled torsos of the dead men, and the knights had to draw their swords. For a moment there was chaos in the valley bottom as the horsemen drove a thousand paths through the scattered crossbowmen. Then there were only the mangled remnants of the Genoese mercenaries, their red and green jackets soaked with blood and their weapons lying broken in the mud.

The horsemen, one easy victory under their belt, cheered themselves. '*Montjoie St Denis!*' they shouted. '*Montjoie St Denis!*' Hundreds of flags were being taken forward with the horsemen, threatening to overtake the oriflamme, but the red-ribboned knights guarding the sacred flag spurred ahead of the charge, shouting their challenge as they started up the slope towards the English, and so climbed from a valley floor that was now thick with charging horsemen. The remaining lances were lowered, the spurs went back, but some of the more sensible men, who had waited behind for the next assault, noted that there was no thunder of hoofs coming from the vast charge.

'It's turned to mud,' Sir Guillaume said to no one in particular.

Trappers and surcoats were spattered with the mud churned up by the hoofs from the low ground that had been softened by the rain. For a moment the charge seemed to flounder, then the leading horsemen broke out of the wet valley bottom to find better footing on the English hill. God was with them after all and they screamed their war cry. *'Montjoie St Denis!'* The drums were beating faster than ever and the trumpets screamed to the sky as the horses climbed towards the mill.

'Fools,' Guy Vexille said.

'Poor souls,' Sir Guillaume said.

'What's happening?' the King asked, wondering why his careful ordering of the battlelines had broken even before the fight proper had begun.

But no one answered him. They just watched.

'Jesus, Mary and Joseph,' Father Hobbe said, for it seemed as if half the horsemen of Christendom were coming up the hill.

'Into line!' Will Skeat shouted.

'God be with you!' the Earl of Northampton called, then went back to join his men-at-arms.

'Aim for the horses!' John Armstrong ordered his men.

'Bastards rode down their own bowmen!' Jake said in wonderment.

'So we'll kill the goddamn bastards,' Thomas said vengefully.

The charge was nearing the line of those Genoese who had died in the arrow storm. To Thomas, staring down the hill, the attack was a flurry of garish horse trappers and bright shields, of painted lances and streaming pennants, and now, because the horses had climbed out of the wet ground, every archer could hear the hooves that were louder even than the enemy's kettledrums. The ground was quivering so that Thomas could feel the vibration through the worn soles of his boots that had been a gift from Sir Guillaume. He looked for the three hawks, but could not see them, then forgot Sir Guillaume as his left leg went forward and his right arm hauled back. The arrow's feathers were beside his mouth and he kissed them, then fixed his gaze on a man who carried a black and yellow shield.

'Now!' Will Skeat shouted

The arrows climbed away, hissing as they went. Thomas put a second on the string, hauled and loosed. A third, this time picking out a man with a pig-snout helmet decorated with red ribbons. He was aiming at the horses each time, hoping to drive the wicked-edged blades through the padded trappers and deep into the animals' chests. A fourth arrow. He could see clods of grass and soil being thrown up behind the leading horses. The first arrow was still flying as he hauled back the fourth and looked for another target. He fixed on a man without a surcoat in polished plate armour. He loosed, and just then the man in the plate armour tumbled forward as his horse was struck by another arrow and all along the slope there were screaming horses, flailing hoofs and falling men as the English arrows drove home. A lance cartwheeled up the slope, a cry sounded above the beating hoofbeats, a horse ran into a dying animal and broke its leg and knights were thumping their knees against their horses to make them swerve about the stricken beasts. A fifth arrow, a sixth, and to the men-at-arms behind the line of archers it seemed as though the sky was filled with a never ending stream of arrows that were dark against the darkening clouds, white-tipped, and rising above the slope to plunge into the churning men-at-arms.

Scores of horses had fallen, their riders were trapped in their high saddles and ridden over as they lay helpless, yet still the horsemen came on and the men at the back could see far enough ahead to find gaps between the twitching piles of dead and dying. '*Montjoie St Denis! Montjoie St Denis!*' Spurs raked back to draw blood. To Thomas the slope looked a nightmare of heaving horses with yellow teeth and white eyes, of long lances and arrow-stuck shields, of flying mud, wild banners and grey helmets with slits for eyes and snouts for noses. The banners flew, led by a ribbon-like red streamer. He shot again and again, pouring arrows into the madness, yet for every horse that fell there was another to take its place and another beast behind that. Arrows protruded from trappers, from horses, from men, even from lances, the white feathers bobbing as the charge thundered close.

And then the French front rank was among the pits, and a stallion's leg bone cracked, and the beast's scream soared above the drums, trumpets, clang of mail and the beating of hoofs. Some men rode clean through the pits, but others fell and brought down the horses behind. The French tried to slow the horses and turn them aside, but the charge was committed now and the men behind pressed the ones in front onto the pits and arrows. The bow thumped in Thomas's hand and its arrow seared into a horseman's throat, slitting the mail like linen and hurling the man back so that his lance reared into the sky.

'Back!' Will Skeat was shouting. The charge was too close. Much too close. 'Back! Back! Back! Now! Go!'

The archers ran into the gaps between the men-at-arms, and the French, seeing their tormentors vanish, gave a great cheer. '*Montjoie St Denis*!'

'Shields!' the Earl of Northampton shouted and the English men-at-arms locked their shields together and raised their own lances to make a hedge of points.

'St George!' the Earl screamed. 'St George!'

'*Montjoie St Denis*!' Enough horsemen had got through the arrows and the pits, and still the men-at-arms streamed up the hill.

And now, at last, charged home.

If a plum was thrown at a conroi, the experts said, it should be impaled on a lance. That was how close the horsemen were supposed to be in a charge because that way they stood a chance of living, but if the conroi scattered then each man would end up surrounded by enemies. Your neighbour in a cavalry charge, the experienced men told the younger, should be closer to you than your wife. Closer even than your whore. But the first French charge was a crazed gallop and the men first became scattered when they slaughtered the Genoese and the disarray became worse as they raced uphill to close on the enemy.

The charge was not supposed to be a crazed gallop, but an ordered, dreadful and disciplined assault. The men, lined knee to knee, should have started slowly and stayed close until, and only at the very last minute, they spurred into a gallop to crash their tight-bunched lances home in unison. That was how the men were trained to charge, and their destriers were trained just as hard. A horse's instinct, on facing a packed line of men or cavalry, was to shy away, but the big stallions were ruthlessly schooled to keep running and so crash into the packed enemy and there to keep moving, stamping, biting and rearing. A charge of knights was supposed to be thundering death on hooves, a flail of metal driven by the ponderous weight of men, horses and armour, and properly done it was a mass maker of widows.

But the men of Philip's army who had dreamed of breaking the enemy into ribbons and slaughtering the dazed survivors had reckoned without archers and pits. By the time the undisciplined first French charge reached the English men-at-arms it had broken itself into scraps and then been slowed to a walk because the long, smooth and inviting slope turned out to be an obstacle course of dead horses, unsaddled knights, hissing arrows and leg-cracking pits concealed in the grass. Only a handful of men reached the enemy.

That handful spurred over the last few yards and aimed their lances at the dismounted English men-at-arms, but the horsemen were met by more lances that were braced against the ground and tilted up to pierce their horses' breasts. The stallions ran onto the lances, twisted away and the Frenchmen were falling. The English men-at-arms stepped forward with axes and swords to finish them off.

'Stay in line!' the Earl of Northampton shouted.

More horses were threading through the pits, and there were no archers in front to slow them now. These were the third and fourth ranks of the French charge. They had suffered less damage from arrows and they came to help the men hacking at the English line that still bristled with lances. Men roared their battle cries, hacked with swords and axes, and the dying horses dragged down the English lances so that the French could at last close on the men-at-arms. Steel rang on steel and thumped on wood, but each horseman was faced by two or three men-at-arms, and the French were being dragged from their saddles and butchered on the ground.

'No prisoners!' the Earl of Northampton shouted. 'No prisoners!' Those were the King's orders. To take a man prisoner meant possible wealth, but it also required a moment of courtesy to enquire whether an enemy truly yielded and the English had no time for such civility. They needed only to kill the horsemen who kept streaming up the hill.

The King, watching from beneath the mill's furled sails, which creaked as the wind twitched their tethers, saw that the French had broken through the archers only on the right, where his son fought and where the line lay closest to the French and the slope was gentlest. The great charge had been broken by arrows, but more than enough horsemen had survived and those men were spurring towards the place where the swords rang. When the French charge began it had been spread all across the battlefield, but now it shrank into a wedge shape as the men facing the English left swerved away from the archers there and added their weight to the knights and men-at-arms who hacked at the Prince of Wales's battle. Hundreds of horsemen were still milling about in the valley's muddy bottom, unwilling to face the arrow storm a second time, but French marshals were re-forming those men and sending them up the hill towards the growing mêlée that fought under the banners of Alençon and the Prince of Wales.

'Let me go down there, sire,' the Bishop of Durham, looking ungainly in his heavy mail and holding a massive spiked mace, appealed to the King.

'They're not breaking,' Edward said mildly. His line

of men-at-arms was four ranks deep and only the first two were fighting, and fighting well. A horseman's greatest advantage over infantry was speed, but the French charge had been sapped of all velocity. The horsemen were being forced into a walk to negotiate the corpses and pits, and there was no room beyond to spur into a trot before they were met by a vicious defence of axes, swords, maces and spears. Frenchmen hacked down, but the English held their shields high and stabbed their blades into the horses' guts or else sliced swords across hamstrings. The destriers fell, screaming and kicking, breaking men's legs with their wild thrashing, but every horse down was an added obstacle and, fierce as the French assault was, it was failing to break the line. No English banners had toppled yet, though the King feared for his son's bright flag that was closest to the most violent fighting.

'Have you seen the oriflamme?' he asked his entourage.

'It fell, sire,' a household knight answered. The man pointed down the slope to where a heap of dead horses and broken men were the remnants of the first French attack. 'Somewhere there, sir. Arrows.'

'God bless arrows,' the King said.

A conroi of fourteen Frenchmen managed to negotiate the pits without harm. *Montjoie St Denis!* they shouted, and couched their lances as they spurred into the mêlée, where they were met by the Earl of Northampton and a dozen of his men.

The Earl was using a broken lance as a pike and he rammed the splintered shaft into a horse's chest, felt the lance slide off the armour concealed by the trapper, and instinctively lifted his shield. A mace cracked on it, driving one spike clean through the leather and willow, but the Earl had his sword dangling by a strap and he dropped the lance, gripped the sword's hilt and stabbed it into the horse's fetlock, making the beast twist away. He dragged the shield clear of the mace's spikes, swung the sword at the knight, was parried, then a man-at-arms seized the Frenchman's weapon and tugged. The Frenchman pulled back, but the Earl helped and the Frenchman shouted as he was tumbled down to the English feet. A sword ran into the armour gap at his groin and he doubled over, then a mace crushed his helmet and he was left, twitching, as the Earl and his men climbed over his body and hacked at the next horse and man.

The Prince of Wales spurred into the mêlée, made conspicuous by a fillet of gold that circled his black helmet. He was only sixteen, well built, strong, tall and superbly trained. He fended an axe away with his shield and rammed his sword through another horseman's mail.

'Off the bloody horse!' the Earl of Northampton shouted at the Prince. 'Get off the bloody horse!' He ran to the Prince, seized the bridle and tugged the horse away from the fight. A Frenchman spurred in, trying to spear the Prince's back, but a man-at-arms in the Prince's green and white livery slammed his shield into the destrier's mouth and the animal twitched away.

The Earl dragged the Prince back. 'They see a man on horseback, sire,' he shouted up, 'and they think he's French.'

The Prince nodded. His own household knights had reached him now and they helped him down from the saddle. He said nothing. If he had been offended by the Earl, he hid it behind his face-piece as he went back to the mêlée. 'St George! St George!' The Prince's standard-bearer struggled to stay with his master, and the sight of the richly embroidered flag attracted still more screaming Frenchmen.

'In line!' the Earl shouted. 'In line!' but the dead horses and butchered men made obstacles that neither the French nor English could cross and so the men-at-arms, led by the Prince, were scrambling over the bodies to reach more enemies. A disembowelled horse trailed its guts towards the English, then sank onto its forelegs to pitch its rider towards the Prince, who rammed the sword into the man's helmet, mangling the visor and starting blood from the eyeholes. 'St George!' The Prince was exultant and his black armour was streaked with enemy blood. He was fighting with his visor raised, for else he could not see properly, and he was loving the moment. The hours and hours of weapons practice, the sweating days when sergeants had drilled him and beat at his shield and cursed him for not keeping his sword point high, were all proving their worth, and he could have asked for nothing more in this life: a woman in the camp and an enemy coming in their hundreds to be killed.

The French wedge was widening as more men climbed the hill. They had not broken through the line, but they had drawn the two front English ranks across the tideline of dead and wounded, and thus scattered them into groups of men who defended themselves against a welter of horsemen. The Prince was among them. Some Frenchmen, unhorsed but unwounded, were fighting on foot.

'Forward!' the Earl of Northampton shouted at the

third rank. It was no longer possible to hold the shield wall tight. Now he had to wade into the horror to protect the Prince, and his men followed him into the maelstrom of horses, blades and carnage. They scrambled over dead horses, tried to avoid the beating hooves of dying horses and drove their blades into living horses to bring the riders down to where they could be savaged.

Each Frenchman had two or three English footmen to contend against, and though the horses snapped their teeth, reared and lashed their hoofs, and though the riders beat left and right with their swords, the unmounted English invariably crippled the destriers in the end, and more French knights were pitched onto the hoof-scarred grass to be bludgeoned or stabbed to death. Some Frenchmen, recognizing the futility, spurred back across the pits to make new conrois among the survivors. Squires brought them spare lances, and the knights, rearmed and wanting revenge, came back to the fight, and always they rode towards the prince's bright flag.

The Earl of Northampton was close to the flag now. He hammered his shield into a horse's face, cut at its legs and stabbed at the rider's thigh. Another conroi came from the right, three of its men still holding lances and the others with swords held far forward. They slammed against the shields of the Prince's bodyguard, driving those men back, but other men in green and white came to their help and the Prince pushed two of them out of the way so he could hack at a destrier's neck. The conroi wheeled away, leaving two of its knights dead.

'Form line!' the Earl shouted. 'Form line!' There was

a lull in the fighting about the Prince's standard, for the French were regrouping.

And just then the second French battle, as large as the first, started down their hill. They came at a walk, knee to booted knee, lances held so close that a wind could not have passed between them.

They were showing how it should be done.

The ponderous drums drove them on. The trumpets seared the sky.

And the French were coming to finish the battle.

'Eight,' Jake said.

Three,' Sam told Will Skeat.

'Seven,' Thomas said. They were counting arrows. Not one archer had died yet, not from Will Skeat's band, but they were perilously low on arrows. Skeat kept looking over the heads of the men-at-arms, fearful that the French would break through, but the line was holding. Once in a while, when no English banner or head was in the way, an archer would loose one of the precious arrows at a horseman, but when a shaft wasted itself by glancing off a helmet Skeat told them to save their supply. A boy had brought a dozen skins of water from the baggage and the men passed the bags around.

Skeat lotted up the arrows and shook his head. No man had more than ten, while Father Hobbe, who admittedly had started with fewer than any of the men, had none.

'Go up the hill, father,' Skeat told the priest, 'and see if they're keeping any shafts back. The King's archers might spare some. Their captain's called Hal Crowley and he knows me. Ask him, anyway.' He did not sound hopeful. 'Right, lads, this way,' he said to the rest and led them towards the southern end of the English line where the French had not closed, then forward of the men-at-arms to reinforce the archers who, as low on arrows as the rest of the army, were keeping up a desultory harassment of any group of horsemen who threatened to approach their position. The guns were still firing intermittently, spewing a noisome stench of powder smoke on the battle's edge, but Thomas could see little evidence that the ribalds were killing any Frenchmen, though their noise, and the whistle of their iron missiles, was keeping the enemy horsemen well away from the flank. 'We'll wait here,' Skeat said, then swore for he had seen the French second line leave the far hill crest. They did not come like the first, in ragged chaos, but steadily and properly. Skeat made the sign of the cross. 'Pray for arrows,' he said.

The King watched his son fight. He had been worried when the Prince had advanced on horseback, but he nodded silent approval when he saw that the boy had possessed the good sense to dismount. The Bishop of Durham pressed to be allowed to go to Prince Edward's help, but the King shook his head. 'He has to learn to win fights.' He paused. 'I did.' The King had no intention of going down into the horror, not because he feared such a fight, but because once entangled with the French horsemen he would not be able to watch the rest of his line. His job was to stay by the mill and trickle reinforcements down to the most threatened parts of his army. Men of his reserve continually pleaded to be allowed into the mêlée, but the King obstinately refused them, even when they complained that their honour would be smirched if they missed the fight. The King dared not let men go, for he was watching the French second battle come down the hill and he knew he must hoard every man in case that great sweep of horsemen battered through his line.

That second French line, almost a mile across and three or four ranks deep, walked down the slope where its horses had to thread the bodies of the slaughtered Genoese. 'Form up!' the conroi leaders shouted when the crossbowmen's bodies were behind them, and the men obediently moved knee to knee again as they rode into the softer ground. The hooves made hardly any sound in the wet soil so the loudest noises of the charge were the clink of mail, the thump of scabbards and the swish of trappers on the long grass. The drummers were still beating on the hill behind, but no trumpets called.

'You see the Prince's banner?' Guy Vexille asked Sir Simon Jekyll, who rode beside him.

'There.' Jekyll pointed his lance tip to where the ragged fight was hottest. All Vexille's conroi had baffles on their lances, placed just back from the tip so that the wooden spears did not bury themselves in their victims' bodies. A lance with a baffle could be dragged free of a dying man and used again. 'The highest flag,' Sir Simon added.

'Follow me!' Vexille shouted, and signalled to Henry Colley, who had been given the job of standard-bearer. Colley was bitter at the assignment, reckoning he should have been allowed to fight with lance and sword, but Sir Simon had told him it was a privilege to carry the lance of St George and Colley was forced to accept the task. He planned to discard the useless lance with its red flag as soon as he entered the mêlée, but for now he carried it high as he wheeled away from the well organized line. Vexille's men followed their banner, and the departure of the conroi left a gap in the French formation and some men called out angrily, even accusing Vexille of cowardice, but the Count of Astarac ignored the jibes as he slanted across the rear of the line to where he judged his horsemen were precisely opposite the Prince's men and there he found a fortuitous gap, forced his horse into the space and let his men follow as best they could.

Thirty paces to Vexille's left a conroi with badges showing yellow hawks on a blue field trotted up the English hill. Vexille did not see Sir Guillaume's banner, nor did Sir Guillaume see his enemy's badge of the yale. Both men were watching the hill ahead, wondering when the archers would shoot and admiring the bravery of the first charge's survivors who repeatedly withdrew a few paces, re-formed and recharged the stubborn English line. Not one man threatened to break the enemy, but they still tried even when they were wounded and their destriers were limping. Then, as the second French charge neared the line of Genoese crossbowmen killed by the English archers, more trumpets sounded from the French hill and the horses pricked back their ears and tried to go into the canter. Men curbed the destriers and twisted awkwardly in their saddles to peer through visor slits to find what the trumpets meant and saw that the last of the French knights, the King and his household warriors, and the blind King of Bohemia and his companions, were trotting forward to add their weight and weapons to the slaughter. The King of France rode beneath his blue banner that was spattered with the golden fleur-de-lis, while the King of Bohemia's flag showed three white feathers on a dark red field. All the horsemen of France were committed now. The drummers sweated, the priests prayed and the royal trumpeters gave a great fanfare to presage the death of the English army.

The Count of Alençon, brother to the King, had begun the crazed charge that had left so many Frenchmen dead on the far slope, but the Count was also dead, his leg broken by his falling horse and his skull crushed by an English axe. The men he had led, those that still lived, were dazed, arrow stung, sweat-blinded and weary, but they fought on, turning their tired horses to thrash swords, maces and axes at men-at-arms, who fended the blows with shields and raked their swords across the horses' legs. Then a new trumpet called much closer to the mêlée. The notes fell in urgent triplets that followed one after the other, and some of the horsemen registered the call and understood they were being ordered to withdraw. Not to retreat, but to make way, for the biggest attack was yet to come.

'God save the King,' Will Skeat said dourly, for he had ten arrows left and half France was coming at him.

Thomas was noticing the strange rhythm of battle, the odd lulls in the violence and the sudden resurrection of horror. Men fought like demons and seemed invincible and then, when the horsemen withdrew to regroup, they would lean on their shields and swords and look like men close to death. The horses would stir again, English voices would shout warnings, and the men-at-arms would straighten and lift their dented blades. The noise on the hill was overwhelming: the occasional crack of the guns that did little except make

447

the battlefield reek with hell's dark stench, the screams of horses, the blacksmiths' clangour of weapons, men panting, shouting and moaning. Dying horses bared their teeth and thrashed the turf. Thomas blinked sweat from his eyes and stared at the long slope that was thick with dead horses, scores of them, hundreds maybe, and beyond them, approaching the bodies of the Genoese who had died under the arrows' lash, even more horsemen were coming beneath a new spread of bright flags. Sir Guillaume? Where was he? Did he live? Then Thomas realized that the terrible opening charge, when the arrows had felled so many horses and men, had been just that, an opening. The real battle was starting now.

'Will! Will!' Father Hobbe's voice called from somewhere behind the men-at-arms. 'Sir William!'

'Here, father!'

The men-at-arms made way for the priest, who was carrying an armload of arrow sheaves and leading a small-frightened boy who carried still more. 'A gift from the royal archers,' Father Hobbe said, and he spilled the sheaves onto the grass. Thomas saw the arrows had the red-dyed feathers of the King's own bowmen. He drew his knife, cut a binding lace, and stuffed the new arrows into his bag.

'Into line! Into line!' the Earl of Northampton shouted hoarsely. His helmet was deeply dented over his right temple and his surcoat was spotted with blood. The Prince of Wales was shouting insults at the French, who were wheeling their horses away, going back through the tangled sprawl of dead and wounded. 'Archers!' The Earl called, then pulled the Prince back into the men-at-arms who were slowly lining themselves into formation. Two men were picking up fallen enemy lances to re-arm the front rank. 'Archers!' the Earl called again.

Will Skeat took his men back into their old position in front of the Earl. 'We're here, my lord.'

'You have arrows?'

'Some.'

'Enough?'

'Some,' Skeat stubbornly answered.

Thomas kicked a broken sword from under his feet. Two or three paces in front of him was a dead horse with flies crawling on its wide white eyes and over the glistening blood on its black nose. Its trapper was white and yellow, and the knight who had ridden the horse was pinned under the body. The man's visor was lifted. Many of the French and nearly all of the English men-at-arms fought with open visors and this dead man's eyes stared straight at Thomas, then suddenly blinked.

'Sweet Jesus,' Thomas swore, as if he had seen a ghost.

'Have pity,' the man whispered in French. 'For Christ's sake, have pity.'

Thomas could not hear him, for the air was filled with the drumbeat of hooves and the bray of trumpets. 'Leave them! They're beat!' Will Skeat bawled, for some of his men were about to draw their bows against those horsemen who had survived the first charge and had withdrawn to realign their ranks well within bowshot range. 'Wait!' Skeat shouted. 'Wait!'

Thomas looked to his left. There were dead men and horses for a mile along the slope, but it seemed the French had only broken through to the English line where he stood. Now they came again and he blinked away sweat and watched the charge come up the slope. They came slowly this time, keeping their discipline. One knight in the French front rank was wearing extravagant white and yellow plumes on his helmet, just as if he were in a tournament. That was a dead man, Thomas thought, for no archer could resist such a flamboyant target.

Thomas looked back at the carnage in front. Were there any English among the dead? It seemed impossible that there should not be, but he could see none. A Frenchman, an arrow deep in his thigh, was staggering in a circle among the corpses, then slumped to his knees. His mail was torn at his waist and his helmet's visor was hanging by a single rivet. For a moment, with his hands clasped over his sword's pommel, he looked just like a man at prayer, then he slowly fell forward. A wounded horse whinnied. A man tried to rise and Thomas saw the red cross of St George on his arm, and the red and yellow quarters of the Earl of Oxford on his jupon. So there were English casualties after all.

'Wait!' Will Skeat shouted, and Thomas looked up to see that the horsemen were closer, much closer. He drew the black bow. He had shot so many arrows that the two calloused string fingers of his right hand were actually sore, while the edge of his left hand had been rubbed raw by the flick of the goose feathers whipping across its skin. The long muscles of his back and arms were sore. He was thirsty. 'Wait!' Skeat shouted again, and Thomas relaxed the string a few inches. The close order of the second charge had been broken by the bodies of the crossbowmen, but the horsemen were re-forming now and were well within bow range. But Will Skeat, knowing how few arrows he had, wanted them all to count. 'Aim true, boys,' he called. 'We've no steel to waste now, so aim true! Kill the damned horses.' The bows stretched to their full extent and the string bit like fire into Thomas's sore fingers.

'Now!' Skeat shouted and a new flight of arrows skimmed the slope, this time with red feathers among the white. Jake's bowstring snapped and he cursed as he fumbled for a replacement. A second flight whipped away, its feathers hissing in the air, and then the third arrows were on the string as the first flight struck. Horses screamed and reared. The riders flinched and then drove back spurs as if they understood that the quickest way to escape the arrows was to ride down the archers. Thomas shot again and again, not thinking now, just looking for a horse, leading it with the steel arrowhead, then releasing. He drew out a white-feathered arrow and saw blood on the quills and knew his bow fingers were bleeding for the first time since he had been a child. He shot again and again until his fingers were raw flesh and he was almost weeping from the pain, but the second charge had lost all its cohesion as the barbed points tortured the horses and the riders encountered the corpses left by the first attack. The French were stalled, unable to ride into the arrow flail, but unwilling to retreat. Horses and men fell, the drums beat on and the rearward horsemen were pushing the front ranks into the bloody ground where the pits waited and the arrows stung. Thomas shot another arrow, watched the red feathers whip into a horse's breast, then fumbled in the arrow bag to find just one shaft left. He swore.

'Arrows?' Sam called, but no one had any to spare.

Thomas shot his last, then turned to find a gap in the

451

men-at-arms that would let him escape the horsemen who would surely come now the arrows had run out, but there were no gaps.

He felt a heartbeat of pure terror. There was no escape and the French were coming. Then, almost without thinking, he put his right hand under the horn tip of the bow and launched it high over the English men-at-arms so it would fall behind them. The bow was an encumbrance now, so he would be rid of it, and he picked up a fallen shield, hoping to God it showed an English insignia, and pushed his left forearm into the tight loops. He drew his sword and stepped back between two of the lances held by the men-at-arms. Other archers were doing the same.

'Let the archers in!' the Earl of Northampton shouted. 'Let them in!' But the men-at-arms were too fearful of the rapidly approaching French to open their files.

'Ready!' a man shouted. 'Ready!' There was a note of hysteria in his voice. The French horsemen, now that the arrows were exhausted, were streaming up the slope between the corpses and the pits. Their lances were lowered and their spurs raked back as they demanded a last spurt from the horses before they struck the enemy. The trappers were flecked with mud and hung with arrows. Thomas watched a lance, held the unfamiliar shield high and thought how monstrous the enemy's steel faces looked.

'You'll be all right, lad.' A quiet voice spoke behind him. 'Hold the shield high and go for the horse.'

Thomas snatched a look and saw it was the grey-haired Reginald Cobham, the old champion himself, standing in the front rank.

'Brace yourselves!' Cobham shouted.

The horses were on top of them, vast and high, lances reaching, the noise of the hooves and the rattle of mail overwhelming. Frenchmen were shouting victory as they leaned into the lunge.

'Now kill them!' Cobham shouted.

The lances struck the shields and Thomas was hurled back and a hoof thumped his shoulder, but a man behind pushed him upright so he was forced hard against the enemy horse. He had no room to use the sword and the shield was crushed against his side. There was the stench of horse sweat and blood in his nostrils. Something struck his helmet, making his skull ring and vision darken, then miraculously the pressure was gone and he glimpsed a patch of daylight and staggered into it, swinging the sword to where he thought the enemy was. 'Shield up!' a voice screamed and he instinctively obeyed, only to have the shield battered down, but his dazed vision was sharpening and he could see a bright-coloured trapper and a mailed foot in a big leather stirrup close to his left. He rammed his sword through the trapper and into the horse's guts and the beast twisted away. Thomas was dragged along by the trapped blade, but managed to give it a violent tug that jerked it free so sharply that its recoil struck an English shield.

The charge had not broken the line, but had broken against it like a sea wave striking a cliff. The horses recoiled and the English men-at-arms advanced to hack at the horsemen who were relinquishing lances to draw their swords. Thomas was pushed aside by the men-at-arms. He was panting, dazed and sweat-blinded. His head was a blur of pain. An archer was lying dead in front of him, head crushed by a hoof. Why had the man no helmet? Then the men-at-arms were reeling back as more horsemen filed through the dead to thicken the fight, all of them pushing towards the Prince of Wales's high banner. Thomas banged his shield hard into a horse's face, felt a glancing blow on his sword and skewered the blade down the horse's flank. The rider was fighting a man on the other side of his horse and Thomas saw a small gap between the saddle's high pommel and the man's mail skirt, and he shoved the sword up into the Frenchman's belly, heard the man's angry roar turn into a shriek, then saw the horse was falling towards him. He scrambled clear, pushing a man out of his path before the horse collapsed in a crash of armour and beating hooves. English men-at-arms swarmed over the dying beast, going to meet the next enemy. A horse with an iron garro deep in its haunch was rearing and striking with its hooves. Another horse tried to bite Thomas and he struck it with the shield, then flailed at its rider with his sword, but the man wheeled away and Thomas looked desperately for the next enemy.

'No prisoners!' the Earl screamed, seeing a man trying to lead a Frenchman out of the mêlée. The Earl had discarded his shield and was wielding his sword with both hands, hacking it like a woodman's axe and daring any Frenchman to come and challenge him. They dared. More and more horsemen pushed into the horror; there seemed no end of them. The sky was bright with flags and streaked with steel, the grass was gouged by iron and slick with blood. A Frenchman rammed the bottom edge of his shield down onto an Englishman's helmet, wheeled the horse, lunged a sword into an archer's back, wheeled again and struck down at the man still dazed by the shield blow. *Montjoie St Denis!*' he shouted.

'St George!' The Earl of Northampton, visor up and

face streaked with blood, rammed his sword through a gap in a chanfron to take a horse's eye. The beast reared and its rider fell to be trampled by a horse behind. The Earl looked for the Prince and could not see him, then could not search more, for a fresh conroi with white crosses on black shields was forging through the mêlée, pushing friend and foe alike from their path as they carried their lances towards the Prince's standard.

Thomas saw a baffled lance coming at him and he threw himself to the ground where he curled into a ball and let the heavy horses crash by.

'*Montjoie St Denis!*' the voices yelled above him as the Count of Astarac's conroi struck home.

Sir Guillaume d'Evecque had seen nothing like it. He hoped he never saw it again. He saw a great army breaking itself against a line of men on foot.

It was true that the battle was not lost and Sir Guillaume had convinced himself it could yet be won, but he was also aware of an unnatural sluggishness in himself. He liked war. He loved the release of battle, he relished imposing his will on an enemy and he had ever profited from combat, yet he suddenly knew he did not want to charge up the hill. There was a doom in this place, and he pushed that thought away and kicked his spurs back. '*Montjoie St Denis!*' he shouted, but knew he was just pretending the enthusiasm. No one else in the charge seemed afflicted by doubts. The knights were beginning to jostle each other as they strove to aim their lances at the English line. Very few arrows were flying now, and none at all were coming from the chaos ahead where the Prince of Wales's banner flew so high.

Horsemen were now charging home all along the line, hacking at the English ranks with swords and axe, but more and more men were angling across the slope to join the fury on the English right. It was there, Sir Guillaume told himself, that the battle would be won and the English broken. It would be hard work, of course, and bloody work, hacking through the prince's troops, but once the French horsemen were in the rear of the English line it would collapse like rotted wood, and no amount of reinforcements from the top of the hill could stop that panicked rout. So fight, he told himself, fight, but there was still the nagging fear that he was riding into disaster. He had never felt anything like it and he hated it, cursing himself for being a coward!

A dismounted French knight, his helmet's face-piece torn away and blood dripping from a hand holding a broken sword, while his other hand gripped the remnants of a shield that had been split into two, staggered down the hill, then dropped to his knees and vomited. A riderless horse, stirrups flapping, galloped white-eyed across the line of the charge with its torn trapper trailing in the grass. The turf here was flecked by the white feathers of fallen arrows that looked like a field of flowers.

'Go! Go! Go!' Sir Guillaume shouted at his men, and knew he was shouting at himself. He would never tell men to go on a battlefield, but to come, to follow, and he cursed himself for using the word and stared ahead, looking for a victim for his lance, and he watched for the pits and tried to ignore the mêlée that was just to his right. He planned to widen the mêlée by boring into the English line where it was still lightly engaged. Die a hero, he told himself, carry the damned lance right up the hill and let no man ever say that Sir Guillaume d'Evecque was a coward.

Then a great cheer sounded from his right and he dared look there, away from the pits. He saw the Prince of Wales's great banner was toppling into the struggling men. The French were cheering and Sir Guillaume's gloom lifted magically for it was a French banner that pressed ahead, going over the place where the Prince's flag had flown, and then Sir Guillaume saw the banner. He saw it and stared at it. He saw a yale holding a cup and he pressed his knee to turn his horse and shouted at his men to follow him. 'To war!' he shouted. To kill. And there was no more sluggishness and no more doubts. For Sir Guillaume had found his enemy.

The King saw the enemy knights with the white-crossed shields pierce his son's battle and then he watched his son's banner fall. He could not see his son's black armour. Nothing showed on his face.

'Let me go!' the Bishop of Durham demanded.

The King brushed a horsefly from his horse's neck. 'Pray for him,' he instructed the bishop.

'What the hell use will prayer be?' the bishop demanded, and hefted his fearful mace. 'Let me go, sire!'

'I need you here,' the King said mildly, 'and the boy must learn as I did.' I have other sons, Edward of England told himself, though none like that one. That son will be a great king one day, a warrior king, a scourge of our enemies. If he lives. And he must learn to live in the chaos and terror of battle. 'You will stay,' he told the bishop firmly, then beckoned a herald. 'That badge,' he said, pointing to the red banner with the yale, 'whose is it?'

The herald stared at the banner for a long time, then frowned as if uncertain of his opinion.

'Well?' the King prompted him.

'I haven't seen it in sixteen years,' the herald said, sounding dubious of his own judgement, 'but I do believe it's the badge of the Vexille family, sire.'

'The Vexilles?' the King asked.

'Vexilles?' the bishop roared. 'Vexilles! Damned traitors. They fled from France in your great-grandfather's reign, sire, and he gave them land in Cheshire. Then they sided with Mortimer.'

'Ah,' the King said, half smiling. So the Vexilles had supported his mother and her lover, Mortimer, who together had tried to keep him from the throne. No wonder they fought well. They were trying to avenge the loss of their Cheshire estates.

'The eldest son never left England,' the bishop said, staring down at the widening struggle on the slope. He had to raise his voice to be heard above the din of steel. 'He was a strange fellow. Became a priest! Can you credit it? An eldest son! Didn't like his father, he claimed, but we locked him up all the same.'

'On my orders?' the King asked.

'You were very young, sire, so one of your council made sure the Vexille priest couldn't cause trouble. Sealed him up in a monastery, then beat and starved him till he was convinced he was holy. After that he was harmless so they put him into a country parish to rot. He must be dead by now.' The bishop frowned because the English line was bending backwards, pushed by the conroi of Vexille knights. 'Let me go down, sire,' he pleaded, 'I pray you, let me take my men down.'

'I asked you to pray to God rather than to me.'

'I have a score of priests praying,' the bishop said, 'and so do the French. We're deafening God with our prayers. Please, sire, I beg you!'

The King relented. 'Go on foot,' he told the bishop, 'and with only one conroi.'

The bishop howled in triumph, then slid awkwardly off his destrier's back. 'Barratt!' he shouted to one of his men-at-arms. 'Bring your fellows! Come on!' The bishop hefted his wickedly spiked mace, then ran down the hill, bellowing at the French that the time of their death had come.

The herald counted the conroi that followed the bishop down the slope. 'Can twenty men make a difference, sire?' he asked the King.

'It will make small difference to my son,' the King said, hoping his son yet lived, 'but a great difference to the bishop. I think I would have had an enemy in the Church for ever if I'd not released him to his passion.' He watched as the bishop thrust the rear English ranks aside and, still bellowing, waded into the mêlée. There was still no sign of the prince's black armour, nor of his standard.

The herald backed his palfrey away from the King, who made the sign of the cross, then twitched his ruby-hilted sword to make certain the day's earlier rain had not rusted the blade into the scabbard's metal throat. The weapon moved easily enough and he knew he might need it yet, but for now he crossed his mailed hands on his saddle's pommel and just watched the battle.

He would let his son win it, he decided. Or else lose his son.

The herald stole a look at his king and saw that Edward of England's eyes were closed. The King was at prayer.

The battle had spread along the hill. Every part of the English line was engaged now, though in most places the fighting was light. The arrows had taken their toll, but there was none left and so the French could ride right up to the dismounted men-at-arms. Some Frenchmen tried to break through, but most were content to shout insults in the hope of drawing a handful of the dismounted English out of the shield wall. But the English discipline held. They returned insult for insult, inviting the French to come and die on their blades.

Only where the Prince of Wales's banner had flown was the fighting ferocious, and there, and for a hundred paces on either side, the two armies had become inextricably tangled. The English line had been torn, but it had not been pierced. Its rear ranks still defended the hill while the front ranks had been scattered into the enemy where they fought against the surrounding horsemen. The Earls of Northampton and Warwick had tried to keep the line steady, but the Prince of Wales had broken the formation by his eagerness to carry the fight to the enemy and the Prince's bodyguards were now down the slope near to the pits where so many horses lay with broken legs. It was there that Guy Vexille had lanced the Prince's standard-bearer so that the great flag, with its lilies and leopards and gilded fringe, was being trampled by the iron-shod hoofs of his conroi.

Thomas was twenty yards away, curled into the bloody belly of a dead horse and flinching every time another destrier trod near him. Noise overwhelmed him, but through the shrieks and hammering he could hear English voices still shouting defiance and he lifted his head to see Will Skeat with Father Hobbe, a handful of archers and two men-at-arms defending themselves against French horsemen. Thomas was tempted to stay in his blood-reeking haven, but he forced himself to scramble over the horse's body and run to Skeat's side. A French sword glanced off his helmet, he bounced off the rump of a horse, then stumbled into the small group.

'Still alive, lad?' Skeat said.

'Jesus,' Thomas swore.

'He ain't interested. Come on, you bastard! Come on!' Skeat was calling to a Frenchman, but the enemy preferred to carry his unbroken lance towards the battle raging about the fallen standard. 'They're still coming,' Skeat said in tones of wonderment. 'No end to the goddamn bastards.'

An archer in the prince's green and white livery, without a helmet and bleeding from a deep shoulder wound, lurched towards Skeat's group. A Frenchman saw him, casually wheeled his horse and chopped down with a battle-axe.

'The bastard!' Sam said, and, before Skeat could stop him, he ran from the group and leaped up onto the back of the Frenchman's horse. He put an arm round the knight's neck then simply fell backwards, dragging the man from the high saddle. Two enemy men-at-arms tried to intervene, but the victim's horse was in their way.

'Protect him!' Skeat shouted, and led his group to

where Sam was beating fists at the Frenchman's armour. Skeat pushed Sam away, lifted the Frenchman's breastplate just enough to let a sword enter, then slid his blade into the man's chest. 'Bastard,' Skeat said. 'Got no right to kill archers. Bastard.' He twisted the sword, rammed it in further, then yanked it free.

Sam lifted the battle-axe and grinned. 'Proper weapon,' he said, then turned as the two would-be rescuers came riding in. 'Bastards, bastards,' Sam shouted as he chopped the axe at the nearer horse. Skeat and one of the men-at-arms were flailing swords at the other beast. Thomas tried to protect them with his shield as he stabbed up at the Frenchman and felt his sword deflected by shield or armour, then the two horses, both bleeding, wheeled away.

'Stay together,' Skeat said, 'stay together. Watch our backs, Tom.'

Thomas did not answer.

'Tom!' Skeat shouted.

But Thomas had seen the lance. There were thousands of lances on the field, but most of them were painted in spiralling colours, and this one was black, warped and feeble. It was the lance of St George that had hung in the cobwebs of his childhood nave and now it was being used as the pole of a standard and the flag that hung from the silver blade was red as blood and embroidered with a silver yale. His heart lurched. The lance was here! All the mysteries he had tried so hard to avoid were on this battlefield. The Vexilles were here. His father's killer was probably here.

'Tom!' Skeat shouted again.

Thomas just pointed at the flag. 'I have to kill them.'

'Don't be a fool, Tom,' Skeat said, then whipped back

as a horseman crashed in from the lower slope. The man tried to veer away from the group of infantry, but Father Hobbe, the only man still carrying a bow, thrust the weapon into the horse's front legs, tangling them and snapping the bow. The horse collapsed with a crash by their side and Sam whacked the axe into the screaming knight's spine.

'Vexille!' Thomas shouted as loud as he could. 'Vexille!'

'Lost his bloody head,' Skeat said to Father Hobbe.

'He hasn't,' the priest said. He was without a weapon now, but when Sam had finished chopping his new axe through mail and leather, the priest took the dead Frenchman's falchion that he hefted appreciatively.

'Vexille! Vexille!' Thomas screamed.

One of the knights about the yale standard heard the shout and turned his pig-snouted helmet. It seemed to Thomas that the man stared at him through the snout's eye-slits for a long time, though it could only have been for a heartbeat or two because the man was assailed by footmen. He was defending himself skilfully, his horse dancing the battle steps to keep itself from being hamstrung, but the rider beat down one Englishman's sword and slashed his left spur across the face of the other before turning the quick horse and killing the first man with a lunge of his sword. The second man reeled away and the pig-snouted knight turned and trotted straight at Thomas.

'Asking for bloody trouble,' Skeat growled, but went to Thomas's side. The knight swerved at the last moment and beat down with his sword. Thomas parried and was shocked by the force of the man's blow that stung his shield arm to his shoulder. The horse was gone, turned, came back and the knight beat at him again. Skeat lunged at the horse, but the destrier had a mail coat under its trapper and the sword slid away. Thomas parried again and was half beaten to his knees. Then the horseman was three paces away, the destrier was swivelling fast and the knight raised his sword hand and pushed up his pig-snout, and Thomas saw it was Sir Simon Jekyll.

Anger rose in Thomas like bile and, ignoring Skeat's warning shout, he ran forward, sword swinging. Sir Simon parried the blow with contemptuous ease, the trained horse sidestepped delicately and Sir Simon's blade was coming back fast. Thomas had to twist aside and even so, fast as he was, the blade clanged against his helmet with stunning force.

'This time you'll die,' Sir Simon said, and he lunged with the blade, thrusting with killing force on Thomas's mail-clad chest, but Thomas had tripped on a corpse and was already falling backwards. The lunge pushed him down faster and he sprawled on his back, his head spinning from the blow to his helmet. There was no one to help him any more, for he had dashed away from Skeat's group that was defending itself against a new rush of horsemen. Thomas tried to stand, but a pain ripped at his head and he was winded by the blow to his chest. Then Sir Simon was leaning down from his saddle and his long sword was seeking Thomas's unprotected face. 'Goddamn bastard,' Sir Simon said, then opened his mouth wide as though he was yawning. He stared at Thomas, then spewed a stream of blood that spattered Thomas's face. A lance had gone clean through Sir Simon's side and Thomas, shaking the blood from his eyes, saw that a Frenchman had thrust the blue and yellow lance. A horseman? Only the French were mounted, but Thomas had seen the horseman let go of the lance that was hanging from Sir Simon's side and now the Englishman, eyes rolling, was swaying in his saddle, choking and dying. Then Thomas saw the trappers of the horsemen who had swept past him. They showed yellow hawks on a blue field.

Thomas staggered to his feet. Sweet Christ, he thought, but he had to learn how to fight with a sword. A bow was not enough. Sir Guillaume's men were past him now, cutting into the Vexille conroi. Will Skeat shouted at Thomas to come back, but he stubbornly followed Sir Guillaume's men. Frenchman was fighting Frenchman! The Vexilles had almost broken the English line, but now they had to defend their backs while English men-at-arms tried to haul them from their saddles.

'Vexille! Vexille!' Sir Guillaume shouted, not knowing which visored man was his enemy. He beat again and again on a man's shield, bending him back in his saddle, then he chopped the sword down on the horse's neck and the beast dropped, and an Englishman, a priest, was slashing the fallen knight's head with a falchion.

A flash of rearing colour made Sir Guillaume look to his right. The Prince of Wales's banner had been rescued and raised. He looked back to find Vexille, but saw only a half-dozen horsemen with white crosses on their black shields. He spurred towards them, raised his own shield to fend off an axe blow and lunged his sword into a man's thigh, twisted it clear, felt a blow on his back, turned the horse with his knee and parried a high sword blow. Men were shouting at him, demanding to know why he fought his own side, then the Vexille's standard-bearer began to topple as his horse was hamstrung. Two archers were slashing at the beast's legs and the silver yale fell into the mêlée as Henry Colley let go of the old lance to draw his sword.

'Bastards!' he shouted at the men who had hamstrung his horse. 'Bastards!' He slashed the blade down, hacking into a man's mailed shoulder, then a great roar made him turn to see a heavy man in plate and mail and with a crucifix about his neck, wielding a mace. Colley, still on his collapsing horse, swung at the bishop, who hammered the sword away with his shield and then slammed the mace down onto Colley's helmet. 'In the name of God!' the bishop roared as he dragged the spikes free of the mangled helmet. Colley was dead, his skull crushed, and the bishop swung the bloody mace at a horse with a yellow and blue trapper, but the rider swerved at the last instant.

Sir Guillaume never saw the bishop with his mace. Instead he had seen that one of the Vexille conroi had finer armour than the others and he raked back his spurs to reach that man, but felt his own horse faltering and he looked behind to glimpse, through the constricting slits in his visor, that Englishmen were hacking at his horse's rear legs. He beat the swords back, but the animal was sinking down and a huge voice was shouting, 'Clear my way! I want to kill the bastard. In the name of Christ, out of the way!' Sir Guillaume did not understand the words, but suddenly an arm was around his neck and he was being hauled out of the saddle. He shouted in anger, then had the breath driven from him as he thumped onto the ground. A man was holding him down and Sir Guillaume tried to hit him with his sword, but his wounded horse was thrashing beside him, threatening to roll on him and Sir Guillaume's assailant dragged him free, then twisted the Frenchman's sword away. 'Just lie there!' A voice shouted at Sir Guillaume.

'Is the goddamned bastard dead?' the bishop roared.

'He's dead!' Thomas shouted.

'Praise God! On! On! Kill!'

'Thomas?' Sir Guillaume squirmed.

'Don't move!' Thomas said.

'I want Vexille!'

'They've gone!' Thomas shouted. 'They've gone! Lie still!'

Guy Vexille, assailed from two sides and with his red banner fallen, had pulled his three remaining men back, but only to join the last of the French horsemen. The King himself, with his friend the King of Bohemia, was entering the mêlée. Although John of Bohemia was blind, he had insisted on fighting and so his bodyguard had tied their horses' reins together and put the King's destrier in their centre so that he could not lose them. 'Prague!' They shouted their war cry. 'Prague!' The King's son, Prince Charles, was also tied into the group. 'Prague!' he shouted as the Bohemian knights led the last charge, except it was not a charge, but a blundering advance through a tangle of corpses and thrashing bodies and terrified horses.

The Prince of Wales still lived. The gold fillet had been half cut from his helmet and the top edge of his shield had been split in a half-dozen places, but now he led the countercharge and a hundred men went with him, snarling and screaming, wanting nothing else but to maul this last enemy who came in the dying light to the killing place where so many Frenchmen had died.

The Earl of Northampton, who had been mustering the rearward ranks of the prince's battle to keep them in line, sensed that the battle had turned. The vast pressure against the English men-at-arms had weakened and though the French were trying again their best men were bloodied or dead, and the new ones were coming too slowly and so he shouted at his footmen to follow him.

'Just kill them!' he shouted. 'Just kill them!'

Archers, men-at-arms, and even hobelars, who had come from their place inside the wagon circles that protected the guns on the flanks of the line, swarmed at the French. To Thomas, crouching beside Sir Guillaume, it was like the mindless rage at the bridge of Caen all over again. This was madness released, a blood-crazed madness, but the French would suffer for it. The English had endured deep into the long summer evening and they wanted revenge for the terror of watching the big horses come at them, and so they clawed and beat and slashed at the royal horsemen. The Prince of Wales led them, fighting beside archers and men-at-arms, hacking down horses and butchering their riders in a frenzy of blood. The King of Majorca died and the Count of St Pol and the Duke of Lorraine and the Count of Flanders. Then Bohemia's flag with its three white feathers fell, and the blind King was dragged down to be butchered by axes, maces and swords. A king's ransom died with the King, and his son bled to death on his father's body, as his bodyguard, hampered by the dead horses that were still tied to the living beasts, were slaughtered one after the other by Englishmen no longer shouting a war cry but screaming in a howling frenzy like lost souls. They were streaked with blood, stained and spattered and soaked in it, but the blood was French. The Prince of Wales cursed the dying Bohemians, blaming them for barring his approach to the French King, whose blue and gold banner still flew. Two English men-at-arms were hacking at the King's horse, the royal bodyguard was spurring to kill them, more men in English livery were running to bring Philip down and the Prince wanted to be there, to be the man who took the enemy King captive, but one of the Bohemian horses, dying, lurched on its side and the Prince was still wearing his spurs and one of them became caught in the dying horse's trapper. The Prince lurched, was trapped, and it was then that Guy Vexille saw the black armour and the royal surcoat and the broken fillet of gold and saw, too, that the Prince was unbalanced amidst the dying horses.

So Guy Vexille turned and charged.

Thomas saw Vexille turn. He could not reach the charging horseman with his sword, for that would mean clambering over the same horses where the Prince was trapped, but under his right hand was a black ash shaft tipped with silver, and he snatched up the lance and ran at the charging man. Skeat was there too, scrambling over the Bohemian horses with his old sword.

The lance of St George struck Guy Vexille on the chest. The silver blade crumpled and tangled with the crimson banner, but the old ash shaft had just enough strength to knock the horseman back and keep his sword from the Prince, who was being pulled free by two of his men-at-arms. Vexille hacked again, reaching far from his saddle and Will Skeat bellowed at him and thrust his sword hard up at Vexille's waist, but the black shield deflected the lunge and Vexille's trained horse instinctively turned into the attack and the rider slashed down hard.

'No!' Thomas shouted. He thrust the lance again, but it was a feeble weapon and the dry ash splintered against Vexille's shield. Will Skeat was sinking, blood showing at the ragged gash in his helmet. Vexille raised his sword to strike at Skeat a second time as Thomas stumbled forward. The sword fell, slicing into Skeat's head, then the blank mask of Vexille's dark visor swung towards Thomas. Will Skeat was on the ground, not moving. Vexille's horse turned to bring its master to where he could kill most efficiently and Thomas saw death in the Frenchman's bright sword, but then, in panicked desperation, he rammed the broken end of the black lance into the destrier's open mouth and gouged the ragged wood deep into the animal's tongue. The stallion sheered away, screaming and rearing and Vexille was thrown hard against his saddle's cantle.

The horse, eyes white behind its chanfron and mouth dripping blood, turned back to Thomas, but the Prince of Wales had been freed from the dying horse and he brought two men-at-arms to attack Vexille's other flank and the horseman parried the Prince's sword blow, then saw he must be overwhelmed and so drove back his spurs to take his horse through the mêlée and away from danger.

'Calix meus inebrians!' Thomas shouted. He did not know why. The words just came to him, his father's dying words, but they made Vexille look back. He stared through the eye slits, saw the dark-haired man who was holding his own banner, then a new surge of vengeful Englishmen spilled down the slope and he pricked his horse through the carnage and the dying men and the broken dreams of France.

A cheer sounded from the English hilltop. The King had ordered his mounted reserve of knights to charge the French and as those men lowered their lances still more horses were being hurried from the baggage park so that more men could mount and pursue the beaten enemy.

John of Hainault, Lord of Beaumont, took the French King's reins and dragged Philip away from the mêlée. The horse was a remount, for one royal horse had already been killed, while the King himself had taken a wound in the face because he had insisted on fighting with his visor up so that his men would know he was on the field.

'It is time go, sire,' the Lord of Beaumont said gently.

'Is it over?' Philip asked. There were tears in his eyes and incredulity in his voice.

'It's over, sire,' the Lord of Beaumont said. The English were howling like dogs and the chivalry of France was twitching and bleeding on a hillside. John of Hainault did not know how it had happened, only that the battle, the oriflamme and the pride of France were all lost. 'Come, sire,' he said, and dragged the King's horse away. Groups of French knights, their horses' trappers rattling with arrows, were crossing the valley to the far woods that were dark with the coming night.

'That astrologer, John,' the French King said.

'Sire?'

'Have him put to death. Bloodily. You hear me? Bloodily!' The King was weeping as, with the handful of his bodyguard that was left, he rode away.

More and more Frenchmen were fleeing to seek

safety in the gathering dark and their retreat turned into a gallop as the first English horsemen of the battle burst through the remnants of their battered line to begin the pursuit.

The English slope seemed to twitch as the men at arms wandered among the wounded and dead. The twitching was the jerking of the dying men and horses. The valley floor was scattered with the Genoese who had been killed by their own paymasters. It was suddenly very quiet. There was no clang of steel, no hoarse shouts and no drums. There were moans and weeping and sometimes a gasp, but it seemed quiet. The wind stirred the fallen banners and flickered the white feathers of the fallen arrows that had reminded Sir Guillaume of a spread of flowers.

And it was over.

Sir William Skeat lived. He could not speak, there was no life in his eyes and he seemed deaf. He could not walk, though he seemed to try when Thomas lifted him, but then his legs crumpled and he sagged to the bloody ground.

Father Hobbe lifted Skeat's helmet away, doing it with an extraordinary gentleness. Blood poured from Skeat's grey hair and Thomas gagged when he saw the sword cut in the scalp. There were scraps of skull, strands of hair and Skeat's brain all open to the air.

'Will?' Thomas knelt in front of him. 'Will?'

Skeat looked at him, but did not seem to see him. He had a half smile and empty eyes.

'Will!' Thomas said.

'He's going to die, Thomas,' Father Hobbe said softly.

'He is not! Goddamn it, he is not! You hear me? He will live. You bloody pray for him!'

'I will pray, God knows how I will pray,' Father Hobbe soothed Thomas, 'but first we must doctor him.'

Eleanor helped. She washed Will Skeat's scalp, then she and Father Hobbe laid scraps of broken skull like pieces of shattered tile. Afterwards Eleanor tore a strip of cloth from her blue dress and gently bound the strip about Will Skeat's skull, tying it beneath his chin so that when it was done he looked like an old woman in a scarf. He had said nothing as Eleanor and the priest bandaged him, and if he had felt any pain it did not show on his face.

'Drink, Will,' Thomas said, and held out a water bottle taken from a dead Frenchman, but Skeat ignored the offer. Eleanor took the bottle and held it to his mouth, but the water just spilled down his chin. It was dark by then. Sam and Jake had made a fire, using a battle-axe to chop French lances for fuel. Will Skeat just sat by the flames. He breathed, but nothing else.

'I have seen it before,' Sir Guillaume told Thomas. He had hardly spoken since the battle, but now sat beside Thomas. He had watched his daughter tend Skeat and he had accepted food and drink from her, but he had shrugged away her conversation.

'Will he recover?' Thomas asked.

Sir Guillaume shrugged. 'I saw a man cut through the skull. He lived another four years, but only because the sisters in the abbaye looked after him.'

'He will live!' Thomas said.

Sir Guillaume lifted one of Skeat's hands, held it for a few seconds, then let it drop. 'Maybe,' he sounded sceptical. 'You were fond of him?'

'He's like a father,' Thomas said.

'Fathers die,' Sir Guillaume said bleakly. He looked drained, like a man who had turned his sword against his own king and failed in his duty.

'He will live,' Thomas said stubbornly.

'Sleep,' Sir Guillaume said, 'I will watch him.'

Thomas slept among the dead, in the battle line where the wounded moaned and the night wind stirred the white feathers flecking the valley. Will Skeat was no different in the morning. He just sat, eyes vacant, gazing at nothing and stinking because he had fouled himself.

'I shall find the Earl,' Father Hobbe said, 'and have him send Will back to England.'

The army stirred itself sluggishly. Forty English men-at-arms and as many archers were buried in Crécy's church yard, but the hundreds of French corpses, all but for the great princes and noblest lords, were left on the hill. The folk of Crécy could bury them if they wished, Edward of England did not care.

Father Hobbe looked for the Earl of Northampton, but two thousand French infantry had arrived just after dawn, coming to reinforce an army that had already been broken, and in the misty light they had thought the mounted men who greeted them were friends and then the horsemen dropped their visors, couched their lances and put back their spurs. The Earl led them.

Most of the English knights had been denied a chance to fight on horseback in the previous day's battle, but now, this Sunday morning, they'd been given their moment and the great destriers had torn bloody gaps in the marching ranks, then wheeled to cut the survivors into ragged terror. The French had fled, pursued by the implacable horsemen, who had cut and thrust until their arms were weary with the killing.

Back on the hill between Crécy and Wadicourt a pile of enemy banners was gathered. The flags were torn and some were still damp with blood. The oriflamme was carried to Edward who folded it and ordered the priests to give thanks. His son lived, the battle was won and all Christendom would know how God favoured the English cause. He declared he would spend this one day on the field to mark the victory, then march on. His army was still tired, but it had boots now and it would be fed. Cattle were roaring as archers slaughtered them and more archers were bringing food from the hill where the French army had abandoned its supplies. Other men were plucking arrows from the field and tying them into sheaves while their women plundered the dead.

The Earl of Northampton came back to Crécy's hill roaring and grinning. 'Like slaughtering sheep!' he exulted, then roamed up and down the line trying to relive the excitements of the last two days. He stopped by Thomas and grinned at the archers and their women.

'You look different, young Thomas!' he said happily, but then looked down and saw Will Skeat sitting like a child with his head bound by the blue scarf. 'Will?' the Earl said in puzzlement. 'Sir William?'

Skeat just sat.

'He was cut through the skull, my lord,' Thomas said.

The Earl's bombast fled like air from a pricked bladder. He slumped in his saddle, shaking his head. 'No,' he protested, 'no. Not Will!' He still had a bloody sword in his hand, but now he wiped the blade through the mane of his horse and pushed it into the scabbard. 'I was going to send him back to Brittany,' he said. 'Will he live?'

No one answered.

'Will?' the Earl called, then clumsily dismounted from the clinging saddle. He crouched by the Yorkshireman. 'Will? Talk to me, Will!'

'He must go to England, my lord,' Father Hobbe said.

'Of course,' the Earl said.

'No,' Thomas said.

The Earl frowned at him. 'No?'

'There is a doctor in Caen, my lord,' Thomas spoke in French now, 'and I would take him there. This doctor works miracles, my lord.'

The Earl smiled sadly. 'Caen is in French hands again, Thomas,' he said, 'and I doubt they'll welcome you.'

'He will be welcome,' Sir Guillaume said, and the Earl noticed the Frenchman and his unfamiliar livery for the first time.

'He is a prisoner, my lord,' Thomas explained, 'but also a friend. We serve you, so his ransom is yours, but he alone can take Will to Caen.'

'Is it a large ransom?' the Earl asked.

'Vast,' Thomas said.

'Then your ransom, sir,' the Earl spoke to Sir Guillaume, 'is Will Skeat's life.' He stood and took his horse's reins from an archer, then turned back to Thomas. The boy looked different, he thought, looked like a man. He had cut his hair, that was it. Chopped it, anyway. And he looked like a soldier now, like a man who could lead archers into battle. 'I want you in the spring, Thomas,' he said. 'There'll be archers to lead, and if Will can't do it, then you must. Look after him now, but in the spring you'll serve me again, you hear?'

'Yes, my lord.'

'I hope your doctor can work miracles,' the Earl said, then he walked on.

Sir Guillaume had understood the things that had been said in French, but not the rest and now he looked at Thomas. 'We go to Caen?' he asked.

'We take Will to Doctor Mordecai,' Thomas said.

'And after that?'

'I go to the Earl,' Thomas said curtly.

Sir Guillaume flinched. 'And Vexille, what of him?'

'What of him?' Thomas asked brutally. 'He's lost his damned lance.' He looked at Father Hobbe and spoke in English. 'Is my penance done, father?'

Father Hobbe nodded. He had taken the broken lance from Thomas and entrusted it to the King's confessor who had promised that the relic would be taken to Westminster. 'You have done your penance,' the priest said.

Sir Guillaume spoke no English, but he must have understood Father Hobbe's tone for he gave Thomas a hurt look. 'Vexille still lives,' he said. 'He killed your father and my family. Even God wants him dead!' There were tears in Sir Guillaume's eye. 'Would you leave me as broken as the lance?' he asked Thomas.

'What would you have me do?' Thomas demanded.

'Find Vexille. Kill him.' He spoke fiercely, but Thomas said nothing. 'He has the Grail!' the Frenchman insisted.

'We don't know that,' Thomas said angrily. God and Christ, he thought, but spare me! I can be an archers' leader. I can go to Caen and let Mordecai work his miracle and then lead Skeat's men into battle. We can win for God, for Will, for the King and for England. He turned on the Frenchman. 'I am an English archer,' he said harshly, 'not a knight of the round table.'

Sir Guillaume smiled. 'Tell me, Thomas,' he said gently, 'was your father the eldest or a younger son?'

Thomas opened his mouth. He was about to say that of course Father Ralph had been a younger son, then realized he did not know. His father had never said, and that meant that perhaps his father had hidden the truth as he had hidden so many things.

'Think hard, my lord,' Sir Guillaume said pointedly, 'think hard. And remember, the Harlequin maimed your friend and the Harlequin lives.'

I am an English archer, Thomas thought, and I want nothing more.

But God wants more, he thought, but he did not want that burden.

It was enough that the sun shone on summer fields, on white feathers and dead men.

And that Hookton was avenged.

Historical Note

Only two actions in the book are pure invention: the initial attack on Hookton (though the French did make many such landings on the English coast) and the fight between Sir Simon Jekyll's knights and the men-at-arms under Sir Geoffrey de Pont Blanc outside La Roche-Derrien. Other than those all the sieges, battles and skirmishes are lifted from history, as was Sir Geoffrey's death in Lannion. La Roche-Derrien fell to escalade, rather than an attack from its riverside, but I wanted to give Thomas something to do, so took liberties with the Earl of Northampton's achievement. The Earl did all that he is credited with in the novel: the capture of La Roche-Derrien, the successful crossing of the Somme at Blanchetaque ford, as well as his exploits in the battle of Crécy. The capture and sack of Caen happened very much as described in the novel, as did the famous battle of Crécy. It was, in brief, an horrific and terrifying period of history which is now recognized as the beginning of the Hundred Years War.

I thought, when I began reading for and researching the novel, that I would be much concerned with chivalry, courtesy and knightly gallantry. Those things must have existed, but not on these battlefields, which were brutal, unforgiving and vicious. The book's epigraph, quoted from King Jean II of France, serves as a corrective; 'many deadly battles have been fought, people slaughtered, churches robbed, souls destroyed, young women and virgins deflowered, respectable wives and widows dishonoured; towns, manors and buildings burned, and robberies, cruelties and ambushes committed on the highways.' Those words, written some fourteen years after the battle of Crécy, justified the reasons why King Jean was surrendering almost a third of French territory to the English; the humiliation was preferable to a continuation of such ghastly and horrid warfare.

Set-piece battles like Crécy were comparatively rare in the long Anglo-French wars, perhaps because they were so utterly destructive, though the casualty figures for Crécy show that it was the French who suffered and not the English. Losses are hard to compute, but at a minimum the French lost two thousand men and the figure was probably nearer four thousand, most of them knights and men-at-arms. The Genoese losses were very high, and at least half of them were killed by their own side. The English losses were paltry, perhaps fewer than a hundred. Most of the credit must go to the English archers, but even when the French did break through the screen of arrows, they lost heavily. A horseman who had lost the momentum of the charge and was unsupported by other horsemen was easy prey to footmen, and so the cavalry of France was butchered in the mêlée. After the battle, when the French were seeking explanations for their loss, they blamed the Genoese, and there were massacres of Genoese mercenaries in many French towns, but the real French mistake was to attack in a hurry late on the Saturday afternoon instead of waiting until Sunday when they could have arranged their army more carefully. And, having made the decision to attack, they then lost discipline and so threw away their first wave of horsemen, and the remnants of that charge obstructed the better conducted second wave.

There has been a great deal of discussion about the English dispositions in the battle, most of it centring on where the archers were placed. Most historians place them on the English wings, but I have followed Robert Hardy's suggestion that they were arrayed all along the line, as well as on the wings. When it comes to matters about bows, archers and their exploits, Mr Hardy is a good man to heed.

Battles were rare, but the *chevauchée*, an expedition that set out deliberately to waste the enemy's territory, was common. It was, of course, economic warfare – the fourteenth-century equivalent of carpet bombing. Contemporaries, describing the French countryside after the passage of an English *chevauchée*, recorded that France was 'overwhelmed and trampled under foot', that it was on 'the verge of utter ruin' or 'tormented and war-ravaged'. No chivalry there, little gallantry and less courtesy. France would eventually recover and expel the English from France, but only after she had learned to cope with the *chevauchée* and, more importantly, the English (and Welsh) archers.

The word longbow does not appear in the novel, for that word was not used in the fourteenth century (it is for the same reason that Edward of Woodstock, the Prince of Wales, is not called the Black Prince – a later coinage). The bow was simply that, the bow, or perhaps the great bow or the war bow. Much ink has been wasted discussing the origins of the longbow, whether it is Welsh or English, a medieval invention or stretching back to the neolithic, but the salient fact is that it had emerged in the years leading up to the Hundred Years War as a battle-winning weapon. What made it so effective was the number of bowmen who could be assembled in an army. One or two longbows might do damage, but thousands would destroy an army and the English, alone in Europe, were capable of assembling those numbers. Why? The technology could not be simpler, yet still other countries did not produce archers. Part of the answer is surely in the great difficulty it took to become an expert archer. It needed hours and years of practice, and the habit of such practice took hold in only some English and Welsh regions. There had probably been such experts in Britain since the neolithic (yew bows as long as the ones used at Crécy have been found in neolithic graves), but equally probably there were only a few experts, but for some reason or another the Middle Ages saw a popular enthusiasm for the pursuit of archery in parts of England and Wales that led to the rise of the longbow as a mass weapon of war, and certainly once that enthusiasm waned then the bow quickly disappeared from the English arsenal. Common wisdom has it that the longbow was replaced by the gun, but it is more true to say that the longbow withered despite the gun. Benjamin Franklin, no fool, reckoned the American rebels would have won their war much more swiftly had they been practised longbowmen and it is quite certain that a battalion of archers could have outshot and beaten, easily, a battalion of Wellington's veterans armed with smoothbore muskets. But a gun (or crossbow) was much easier to master than a longbow. The longbow, in brief, was a phenomenon, probably fed by a popular craze for archery that translated into a battle-winning weapon for England's kings. It also raised the status of the infantryman, as even the dullest English nobleman came to realize that his life depended on archers, and it is no wonder that archers outnumbered men-at-arms in the English armies of the period.

I have to record an enormous debt to Jonathan Sumption, author of *Trial by Battle, the Hundred Years War, Volume 1*. It is a rank offence to full-time authors like myself that a man who successfully practices as a lawyer can write such superb books in what is, presumably, his 'spare' time, but I am grateful he did so and recommend his history to anyone who wishes to learn more of the period. Any mistakes that remain are entirely my own.